William J. Coughlin has combined a career as a United States administrative judge in Detroit with that of a bestselling novelist. His two previous highly acclaimed and successful novels were *The Twelve Apostles* and *Her Father's Daughter*.

Also available in Pan by the same author

Her Father's Daughter
The Twelve Apostles

William J. Coughlin

HER HONOR

Pan Books
in association with
Sidgwick & Jackson

First published in the USA 1987 by NAL Books
First published in Great Britain 1988 by Pan Books Ltd,
Cavaye Place, London SW10 9PG
in association with Sidgwick & Jackson
9 8 7 6 5 4 3 2
© 1987 by William J. Coughlin
ISBN 0 330 30278 7

Printed in Great Britain by
Richard Clay Ltd, Bungay, Suffolk

To Margaret Ann, William Jude,
Susan Marie, Dennis John,
Patrick Thomas, and Kathleen Mary

CHAPTER 1

THE RECEPTION ROOM for the prosecuting attorney faced the corridor, and Tina Welch's desk was placed so she would have a view of everyone who approached. Tina watched as her boss, Kathleen Talbot, strode along the long corridor toward the office. She was amused to see that the policeman assigned as Kathleen's bodyguard had to hustle to match the quick pace set by the young prosecuting attorney.

"Good morning, Tina." Kathleen nodded as she entered. "What's today's schedule look like?"

"Nothing unusual. Marty Kelly would like to discuss a murder case with you. He wants to accept a plea, but he's worried about political consequences." Tina handed her a batch of telephone messages. "Deputy Commissioner Sloan wants a meeting. He didn't like what you said the other night at that community dinner."

"He wasn't there."

"He doesn't like what he was told you said."

Kathleen's eyes narrowed. "You tell him that I'm not run by the police department. Tell him if he's so interested, he might do well to attend some of these meetings himself." She stopped. "Never mind. Get him on the phone. I'll tell him myself."

Men considered Kathleen Talbot stunningly beautiful and they were right. Her streaming, lush, jet-black hair caught and seemed to magnify light, like a dark mirror. Her smooth, perfect features were the classic sort sculptors dreamed of capturing. Tina's smile was wistful. The young woman, only a few years past thirty, could easily have been her own daughter. Things could have been so different for all of them. But all that was in the past now, reduced by the memory of what might have been. Big Mike Hunt lived in Florida. He had moved there with his latest wife after he retired.

Kathleen was different from her father in almost every way. Big Mike Hunt, a thick, sturdy man, always seemed like packaged thunder, a smoldering, powerful parcel of explosive that could erupt at any moment, always dangerous and often unpredictable.

Kathleen was tall, slim, and elegantly dressed. If Big Mike was fire, his daughter was ice.

To Tina it was the young woman's dark, beautiful eyes that provoked the sole echo of Kathleen's sometimes ruthless father. Dark blue, intelligent, quick—like her father's, her eyes seemed to miss nothing.

Kathleen had held the job of prosecutor for almost three years. She had succeeded Big Mike as the chief law-enforcement officer for the city. The election had been a mere formality once Big Mike gave her his support. Still, she's a smarter lawyer than her father ever was, Tina thought. He just played the game better.

"Are you going to the funeral home later?" Tina asked before Kathleen disappeared into her office.

"No. I'll go to Harry's funeral tomorrow, but I'm not going to waste my time today sitting around and gossiping with a lot of bloated politicians." Kathleen paused. "Will I have time to go home for dinner before that speech tonight?"

Tina consulted the appointment book. "Doesn't look like it, Mrs. Talbot. You're booked solid."

Kathleen nodded. "As soon as I'm finished with Sloan, send Kelly in." She paused again. "Did we send flowers?"

Tina nodded. "Oh yes. That's standard office policy, set up years ago by your father. We seem to be sending flowers more often lately. All the old tigers are dying off."

"Death is part of the law business. Surely my father told you that?"

Tina smiled. "Not quite in that way, Mrs. Talbot."

As Kathleen Talbot disappeared into her own office, Tina reflected for a moment before dialing Commissioner Sloan's number. Lately she found herself wondering if Kathleen was really always so in control, or if she simply had learned to convey that cool impression. She was still a puzzle. Big Mike had been all feeling and emotion. It seemed a shame that some of that throbbing human vitality hadn't been passed along to his beautiful and only daughter.

◄ ►

"Look at that."

"What?"

"The cops, out in front of the place."

Sullivan was busy watching oncoming traffic, looking for an opening to make a left turn, but he glanced at the funeral home. Four police officers stood guard at the front entrance of the large Georgian-style brick building, two on each side of the tall carved doors. Dressed in starched white hats, white silk scarves, and spotless white gloves, the officers stood at rigid attention, their polished drill rifles held at a precise angle on their shoulders, their dress-blue uniforms crisply pressed.

Sullivan chuckled. "They look like the Buckingham Palace guards, don't they?"

"More like some second-rate operetta company," Foley responded. "Absurd, if you ask me."

Traffic parted and Sullivan was able to turn into the arched vehicle entrance. A traffic policeman from the motorcycle division directed them toward the parking area in the back of the funeral home. The policeman, his helmet and boots polished to a high gloss, recognized them as they drove past and gave them a snappy military salute. He, too, wore spotless white gloves.

"Well, if you were going to stick up a gas station, this is the day to do it. All the cops are here," Sullivan observed.

Rows of concrete planters divided the parking lot into four long corridors. They rolled slowly past shiny luxury cars as they looked for an empty space. Another motorcycle officer standing near the end of the long row gestured to them.

"I wonder what the taxpayers would say if they knew their high-priced public-safety officers were being used as parking-lot attendants."

Sullivan had to maneuver the big Cadillac carefully to fit it in the empty space. The policeman was busy directing another car but he took time to salute them as the two men climbed out of their vehicle.

"I hate this goddamned place," Foley said.

They began to walk slowly toward the funeral home.

"That's because you know you'll end up here one of these days," Sullivan suggested.

"Not necessarily. There's other places, plenty of them."

He was answered by a chuckle. "None of them big enough. Besides, it's a tradition. If a public official dies, and he's an east-sider, it's here at Van Claiborne's. West-siders use Weber's. People expect it."

"And Appel's if they're Jewish."

"As I said, tradition."

"Look up there, at the back of the place."

The front entrance was mostly for show; the rear entrance facing the parking lot was the funeral home's main portal. Six officers, dressed identically to the ones in front, stood guard, facing each other, three to a side in front of the big glass doors.

"You'd think a pope died, from the looks of it. The mayor's responsible for this extravaganza. I wonder why?"

"The mayor remembers who saved his ass; it's that simple. Suppose Harry had assigned that grand-jury investigation to the wrong judge. The mayor and his staff would have been indicted, convicted, and doing time by now."

"He assigned that case to Francis Flanigan."

"Yeah. Francis the Thick, who has a hard time finding the courthouse, let alone a criminal conspiracy. Flanigan gave everyone a nice clean bill of health because he didn't understand the case in the first place. Giving Francis the case was an inspiration on Harry's part, and the mayor remembers. This is his way of saying thanks."

"I still think it's inappropriate."

"Look at it this way: the local pope has died. Harry Johnson probably had more power per square inch here than the pope does in Rome. His passing is a momentous occasion and it should be properly marked."

"This isn't Rome."

"No, but it's a huge, important Northern industrial city. We're bigger than Cleveland and damn near as important as Chicago. As far as the Midwest goes, this is Rome—we've got almost two million people here—and Harry Johnson was our pope, or at least close to it."

As they approached the files of policemen, Foley said: "Harry was a prick."

"I didn't say he wasn't."

"He did a lousy job."

"I agree."

"It *is* a lousy job."

"I agree again."

"But I want it."

"So do I."

"So does everybody. That's why we're all here."

The six policemen saluted as the two judges, Foley and Sullivan, walked between them to enter the funeral home. Inside, their arrival was noted by the cluster of men standing in the long hallway.

Judge Joseph Sadowski nodded toward them as they approached. "Well, it's official, the Irish Bobbsey Twins just arrived. I wonder if Foley and Sullivan have ever gone anywhere except together?" Sadowski smiled. He was tall, dignified, stern, and the smile seemed out of place. "Do you think they might be queer?"

Tim Quinlan, who had been a judge longer than anyone else there, shook his head. "Foley's got eight children, Sullivan ten." A gurgling sound, which was Quinlan's way of laughing, wheezed from his ancient throat. "I don't know how they managed that. I suppose one sits at the foot of the other's bed when they screw. They're both prudes, so I'm sure they'd keep their eyes closed." The gurgling wheeze sounded again. "Anyway, they're Irish and neither of them qualifies as an Irish queer."

"What's an Irish queer?" Sadowski asked, knowing he was acting as Quinlan's straight man.

"That's a mick who likes women better than he likes whis- key." Quinlan was the only one who laughed. "Both of them have demonstrated their fondness for the bottle, so they're okay."

Judge Jerome Foley was squat, and his square red face had the squinting look of a hostile bulldog. His companion, Judge Michael Sullivan, was a complete contrast, tall, painfully thin, and with the dreamy look of an ancient saint. Foley, despite his ferocious look, had the reputation among lawyers as being a soft touch, while Sullivan, the saintly, was said to delight in quiet viciousness. Both were in their late fifties, and both were circuit judges.

"Hello, Jerry. Hello, Mike," Sadowski greeted them. "A sad occasion."

Sullivan's smile conveyed the sweet sorrow of a professional mourner. "Depends upon your point of view, I suppose." He glanced in at the viewing room, which was packed. "Someone said Harry bit himself in his sleep."

Quinlan's wheeze caused several people in the viewing room to turn. He inhaled deeply, then nodded to those who seemed concerned as if to show he was fully recovered. "Our late leader," Quinlan said quietly, "according to the story being given out by the family, got pissed off at a neighbor's barking dog and was on his way over to brain the offending creature when he blew an infarct. Dead before he hit the ground, they say. Anyway, that's the official version."

Sadowski nodded as if about to impart a solemn judgment. "I knew that temper of his would get him one day. I told him so. Harry was always in a smoldering rage about something. It was bound to happen. Still, there are far worse ways to die."

"Of course, it didn't happen exactly like that," Quinlan said, his voice near a whisper. "He was over at Brenda's, so the cops tell me. Passion over the age of fifty can be dangerous. Brenda apparently got most of his clothes back on before she called."

They stood in embarrassed silence for a few minutes.

"Has the governor shown yet?" Foley asked, relieving the tension, as he studied the people crowding into the funeral home.

"No," Sadowski said. "I expect he'll pop in here a few minutes before the Masons begin their service. You know him, fast in, fast out. He has these things timed to the second."

"How's the family taking it?" Sullivan asked. "Given the circumstances . . ."

Everyone looked embarrassed.

"The widow's playing the usual role, looking properly solemn, if that's what you mean. The kids are pretty shook-up."

"The kids are pretty old by now," Foley said.

"The boy, the doctor, is about thirty. The daughter's a bit older."

"They know about Brenda?"

No one answered Foley's question.

Finally Quinlan said quietly, "Jerry, that's hardly the thing you go around asking the widow: did you know that your late husband was screwing a female judge, or did you just find out? Of course, she's in there, so if you want to ask, feel free."

"Brenda's in there?"

Quinlan scowled. "No. The widow."

"Anybody seen Brenda?" Foley persisted. "It must have been a hell of a shock for her."

Sadowski coughed decorously. "Brenda, I understand from the assignment clerk, has taken a few days' leave, canceled her docket, and gone to Philadelphia to visit her sister."

Foley nodded. "Strange, eh? A nice-looking girl like Brenda. Harry Johnson is . . . was, twenty years her senior, and looked like a dried-out old turkey. I could never understand the attraction."

"Power," Sadowski said, his tone implying there was no other answer possible. "Women are always attracted to power. It's that simple."

Sullivan's face showed the glimmer of a small smile. "Perhaps whoever gets Harry's job will get Brenda too. That's not a bad perk, all things considered."

"That brings up a nice little question," Quinlan said, this time quite serious. "Who's going to get the job?"

Another awkward silence ensued. Finally Quinlan's wheeze was heard again.

"I'm too old," he cackled. "I retire end of the year. So I suppose I'm the only non-candidate here." He looked in toward the flower-filled viewing room. "They hadn't got Harry's body out of Brenda's place before young Ted Sawchek threw his hat into the ring. But I understand organized labor wants Webster Broadbent to be named."

Sullivan sighed. "Well, there are thirty-eight circuit judges, and we do the electing. Now that Quinlan here has taken himself out, that leaves only thirty-seven candidates for the job."

Foley's expression became even more fierce. "Since it takes a majority vote of the judges sitting, nobody may ever get to perform Harry's job again."

Sadowski shook his head. "I've been a judge through two of these things. It's always the same—everybody scrambles at first, but eventually it comes down to two or three leaders. Then the bargaining gets serious and the political pressure groups put the real heat on. It gets ugly, but it gets done."

"What about the governor? He'll want a say in who we select," Foley said.

Sullivan looked down at his short friend. "He gets to appoint Harry's successor on the bench, but that's all. We still have full power to name the executive judge. The governor will have to wait outside on that, same as everyone else."

Quinlan's ancient face took on a look of grim concern. "There's talk he might appoint Kathleen Talbot to the bench."

Sullivan's benign serenity suddenly departed. His eyes narrowed as he looked at Quinlan. "That will never happen."

Quinlan shrugged. "I don't know what he will or won't do. I'm just telling what I've heard."

"She'd never take it," Foley said. "Hell, she scored a landslide running for prosecutor. She's got a good chance at the governor's chair. Good thing too. If she goes to the state capital she'll be out of our hair. Good-looking broad, but cold and vicious. I don't want her anywhere around me."

"Conjecture at this point is foolish," Sullivan said. "Come on, Jerry, let's sign the register, then pay our respects to the family. Besides, I want to see Harry."

"I didn't know you were so fond of him," Quinlan said.

"I wasn't," Sullivan replied. "The son-of-a-bitch stuck me with that Edison case, the one the Court of Appeals said I butchered. I want to look down and see Harry Johnson in his casket, just so that I'll know he's really dead."

Sullivan and Foley left the others and worked their way into the crowded viewing room.

"Do you think either of them might get Harry's job?" Quinlan asked.

Sadowski snorted. "Fat chance. They're both too lazy to put in the effort necessary to get it. They're great at mouth music but allergic to hard work."

"The man who gets that job will be more powerful than the governor," Quinlan said.

"Who says it will be a man?" Sadowski asked.

Quinlan stared at him, his expression shocked. "You couldn't possibly mean . . ."

"It's happening all over."

Quinlan shook his head as he looked up at Sadowski. "Not in this court, Joe. Never."

CHAPTER 2

Dennis Chesney made his way along the corridor, stepping around wheelchairs and cots, avoiding the patients who were aimless walkers as they shuffled past. Some were alert; he pitied them the most. The others were afflicted with varying degrees of senility, some babbling to images only they could see, some merely staring, no sign of intelligence showing in their dull eyes. The nursing home had the usual hospital odors—alcohol, disinfectant, medicines—but rising above them all was the pervasive stench of decay. Chesney hated the place.

He turned the corner, went past the nursing station, and entered a small room. Nothing had changed dramatically.

The man in the bed just seemed smaller, frailer. The monitors were alight as usual, little blips riding across green electronic screens. The respirator continued to breathe, its bellows rising and falling in the protection of the clear plastic cylinder.

A nurse's aide, a heavyset black woman, stuck her head in the door. "Whatcha doin' here? Only families allowed."

He nodded, took out his identification and flashed his gold badge.

She was unimpressed. "Police or no police, you're supposed to check in with the front desk."

"Is the doctor around?" he asked.

"He's here."

"Tell him Lieutenant Chesney of Homicide would like a word with him."

She scrutinized Chesney, her stern eyes suspicious. Chesney was not an imposing man. He was short and slight. His hair, once red, was now rusty gray and thinning. Rimless glasses hung halfway down on his long nose. The woman shook her head. "You don't look like no policeman."

"Can't argue that," he said quietly, his long face solemn, although his green eyes betrayed his amusement. "But that's what I am. And I need to talk to the doctor on police business."

She scowled. "He's a busy man, the doctor."

"I know that."

"I'll tell him, but that don't mean he'll have time to see you," she said as she left the room.

Chesney nodded and put the badge back in his coat pocket. He continued to study the form in the bed. He hadn't been here for three months. There was no point in it. Nothing changed. The man's arms were like sticks, his skin an ugly ominous gray. One eye stared from beneath a partially closed lid.

"You wished to see me?"

Chesney turned to face the doctor, a small Oriental man who blinked up at him, his face totally expressionless. "The aide said it was something to do with the police?"

Chesney nodded, again taking out and displaying his badge. "I'm Dennis Chesney. I'm a detective with the homicide division."

"Yes?" The doctor looked young, but his black hair was flaked with gray. And his eyes—the color of melted chocolate—seemed old and sad, as if having seen far to much human misery.

"This man, Paul Martin"—Chesney nodded at the form in the bed—"was assaulted a year ago and left for dead. He's been unconscious ever since. We have the man who did it."

The doctor continued to show no reaction. "So, what do you wish of me?"

"How's he doing?" Chesney looked at the man in the bed.

The question put the doctor on more familiar ground and he seemed to become less guarded. "Ah, not well, I'm afraid. It's a small miracle that he's lasted this long."

"He's going to die, then?"

A smile ghosted across the doctor's lips. "We all are, you

know, it's a question of when. This man"—he stepped by Chesney and picked up the thin wrist of the man in the bed—"has been brain dead, probably from the moment he was assaulted. The respirator is breathing for him, but even that will soon fail to meet the challenge." He had his fingers on the man's wrist, feeling for the pulse. "Very thready," he said. "It's hard to say, but he may last a week, give or take a few days."

"A burglar cracked his head," Chesney said, nodding toward the man in the bed. "This guy, Martin, is a well-known industrialist, lots of money. But despite that, he tried to keep the few bucks he had at his house. He put up a fight and got his head busted for it."

The doctor tenderly placed Martin's thin arm back on the bed. "I read about the case," he said. "And we've talked to the family, many times. A tragedy."

"Did they ever talk about taking him off the machines?"

The doctor slowly shook his head. "Even if such a thing were possible legally, it has never been discussed. The family has money, so there's no economic necessity to consider anything else, even though there is no hope of recovery." He sighed. "So he stays, as you see."

They both watched the inert form in silence for a moment; then Chesney spoke. "There's a legal problem."

"Oh?"

The detective nodded. "If he dies within a year and a day of the assault, we can bring a charge of murder. If he dies after that time, that's it, no murder charge."

"The murderer goes free?"

Chesney shrugged. "That's the point. You see, if he dies after the year and a day, it isn't considered murder. Of course, we nailed this guy on burglary, but the way the courts toss people out of jail nowadays, it's like a misdemeanor. He's a bad customer, too. If he gets out he'll kill again."

The doctor frowned. "This year-and-a-day business is an odd law. I've never heard of such a thing."

Chesney smiled. "It comes from the old English common law. I suppose you have to draw the line somewhere. Anyway, that was the law in old England, and whether we like it or not, that's the law in this state today."

"When is it up, this year and a day, for this man, I mean?"

"Tomorrow."

The doctor shook his head. "This is so foolish. There's no brain activity. The man is really dead now."

"Will you certify to that, doctor?"

"I can't, and you know it. Not until he stops breathing, of course. But you know the law here, probably better than I. Brain death is not the test in this state."

"Got about a week to live, you think?"

The doctor shrugged. "He could die tonight, or he could last another month. Not much beyond that, however."

"And if you took the respirator off?"

The doctor shook his head. "I can't. But if I did, it would be all over in a matter of ten minutes."

Chesney shook his head. "Well, I guess there's nothing more to be done then, is there?"

The doctor looked at the form on the bed. "Nothing." Then his sad eyes turned to study the detective's face. "I am sorry. I can understand your position."

Chesney chuckled. "Yeah. We got a pretty good case, too. I feel a little like the hunter when the fox escapes."

The doctor nodded. "Well, I have other patients. Will you excuse me?"

"Sure. Thanks for your time."

Dennis Chesney put a cigarette in his mouth, but didn't light it. He sat at the edge of the bed, amused at his own reluctance; the patient could feel no discomfort. Life, he mused, was a series of ironies. Paul Martin had had only a few hundred dollars of his extensive fortune in the house. Had he given it up, he might be alive, still running his manufacturing plants, but he was stubborn. Even now, he seemed to be clinging to existence the way he had clung to money. And it was ruining Dennis Chesney's plan to take a killer out of society. It wasn't fair.

Chesney got up and examined the monitors. His mother had been on similar equipment when she died. If the heart stopped, the monitors would sound an alarm. Unless, of course, they were turned off.

Chesney carefully flicked the switches, turning off each of

the machines, first the monitors, then the others. Then he walked to the other side of the bed and switched off the respirator.

He sat on the side of the bed and lit the cigarette.

The doctor had said ten minutes, but it went faster than that.

Dennis Chesney returned to police headquarters, got a warrant request, and walked it through the prosecutor's office and the court. The burglar, already in jail, would be brought back to be arraigned on the charge of murder.

When Paul Martin's family learned what had happened, they demanded that Lieutenant Dennis Chesney be arrested for murder.

To Dennis Chesney's shocked surprise, he was.

Governor Joshua Leonard looked just like his campaign pictures, a tall, stooped man with a long thin face. People said he resembled a beardless Abraham Lincoln, a comparison he encouraged. He was a lawyer by profession, but a politician by choice. At age sixty he had served in every level of state government. Elected to the state assembly, then the state senate, he had become minority leader, a powerful post that had brought him to the attention of the public.

Even so, he had won the gubernatorial race by a margin too close for comfort, and now he was determined to hold on to the job at any cost. He was in the midst of a fantasy, envisioning his reelection in a landslide, when his chief of staff, Bill Murray, walked in unannounced. Murray was the only staff member who had that privilege.

"How did it go?" Governor Leonard asked.

Murray grinned. He was a good twenty years younger than his boss, and not nearly as thin. His eyes danced nervously as he spoke. "It was a cross between a Roman circus and a Chinese fire drill. I've never seen anything like it. You should have been there."

The governor shook his head. "No. Too many job seekers for me. I would have been ravished like a naked virgin in a lumber camp. I trust they finally buried his honor?"

The younger man sat down, taking a chair across from the governor. "Amid pomp and splendor. The Masons were jockeying for position with the veteran groups, who were busy pushing and shoving among themselves. That, and all the hustling politicians, made it look as if a major riot was about to erupt. Too bad Harry Johnson was the guest of honor. He always loved to watch that sort of thing."

"Did you see Kathleen Talbot?"

Murray nodded. "Kathleen the Ice Queen was there with her retinue; a bunch of worn-out old hacks left over from her father's days."

"Did you talk to her?" The governor's tone reflected a hint of anxiety.

"Sure. As you know, we went to law school together. We exchanged pleasantries."

"Nothing more?"

"It wasn't the place. It was more like a mob scene than a funeral. Too many ears were listening, so I just said I'd call her for lunch."

"That might set a few tongues to wagging."

Murray smiled. "A romance? Don't I wish. God, we all wanted to hump her in law school. Did you ever take a close look? She's got a body that would make Marilyn Monroe look like a stick."

"You're free. Why don't you give her a whirl?"

"I would in a minute if I thought I even had a chance. But I'm running to fat, and balding. I'm no competition for the memory of Handsome Hank Talbot."

"Her husband? She's been a widow a long time, Bill. She must have adjusted by now?"

Murray looked past the governor, caught in some secret memory. "You didn't know Handsome Hank. He was in law school with us. No one ever called him anything but that. God, he looked like a movie star. Smart too, head of the law review. They made a hell of a fine-looking couple. Handsome Hank was a success right from the first. He could do everything well." Murray sighed. "Everything, of course, but fly."

"What?"

"That's how he died. He was taking flying lessons. Practicing takeoffs, I'm told. He didn't see another plane coming in for a landing and hit it. Quick end. Handsome Hank's first mistake, and his last."

"That's a shame."

"I'll say. Kathleen was pregnant at the time. The baby was born a month after his father's death. She's raising the kid by herself. Like I say, there was nobody like Handsome Hank."

"And she's still carrying the torch?"

Murray shrugged. "Why not? Who's going to replace someone like that? I suppose he's become even grander in her memory as the years pass."

"So after his death she threw herself into politics?"

Murray nodded. "That's one way of looking at it. Her father had been prosecuting attorney for over twenty years. He retired and she ran for the job."

"Do you think she might be interested in the vacant judgeship?"

"And not in the governorship?"

"Kathleen Talbot is the most powerful and visible woman politician in this state at the moment. If she runs, there's a damn good possibility she could beat me, you know that." The governor's solemn face became even more mournful. "I'm sure she knows it too."

"If she takes the judgeship, she can't run for any other office except judicial."

The governor nodded. "That's what the state constitution says. Maybe she's ready to retire to the bench. You never know."

Murray shook his head. "I wish she would, but she's only thirty-five. She's got a hell of a career ahead of her. If she becomes a judge, that ends any ambition she might have for being governor or senator. I'll make the offer, but I doubt she'll accept, to be frank."

"Don't make any offer, Bill. If you do, she'll know I'm scared and trying to take her out of the action. Bring up the subject of the judgeship, and let her ask, if she's interested. The other way is too dangerous."

"On the chance that she is interested, do you want any concessions?"

"Campaign contributions?"

"Whatever. It's expected."

The governor shook his head. "Not this time. We won't ask for any money. I would like her to vote for my candidate for executive judge, though."

"Who is that?" Murray sounded surprised.

"I don't know yet. But I'll have a horse running in that race. The wrong person as executive judge could ruin me."

"Or anybody else."

Governor Leonard nodded. "We need someone who has just the right touch. Harry Johnson may have become a dictator, but at least he was a reasonable tyrant. We need someone in that job who is politically aware, tactful, and who won't be tempted to turn the executive judge's chair into a throne."

"Any ideas?"

"A few. But let's wait until we see what Kathleen Talbot will do. What did you call her again?"

Murray laughed. "It's a nickname from law school. She's a beauty, but she has a regal air about her. We all called her Kathleen the Ice Queen."

Governor Leonard smiled. "You're right about the regal business, at that. She'd look real good up there on the bench." He chuckled. "Yeah. Kathleen the Ice Queen. It fits, you know?"

CHAPTER 3

KATHLEEEN TALBOT SAT behind her desk, a handsome walnut table. The large office had been redecorated after the election to reflect her own personality, not her father's. More like a throne room than a working office, its size, a political tradition, was meant to impress visitors with the importance of the prosecuting attorney. There was nothing she could do about the size but she had tossed out her father's worn leather furniture and replaced it with modern pieces, more in keeping with the new beige carpeting and the bright, cheerful paint she had demanded be applied to the walls.

The dozens of photographs that had covered her father's office walls had been removed and shipped down to his Florida home. She retained one nice color photograph of him, giving it a place of prominence on the far wall opposite her desk. He had used the photo for his last several campaigns; in it he looked serious, even grim. The wrinkles and gray hair had been air-brushed out, but it did capture the hard-eyed determination that had always been the dominant force in his life, a drive little diminished by retirement, just rechanneled.

A small photo of Kathleen's late husband, in which Henry Talbot's blond curls, gleaming teeth, and sparkling eyes were preserved for all time, also hung on the wall. She had displayed the photograph for two reasons: it was a nice political touch—people always warmed to the image of the brave but grieving young widow. The other reason was more personal. She wanted the picture of Handsome Hank as a reminder never to be tempted to marry again. Those smiling eyes, so attractive and hypnotic, had effectively masked the lying, conniving cheat who had lurked beneath them. She was determined never to expose herself again to such profound hurt and humiliation.

When she looked at the pictures of her father and her late husband, she felt conflicting emotions. She loved her father, although that love had never been returned. Her father had a way of inspiring fear rather than affection. And she had once loved Hank, but he had effectively ended that love long before his death. He had inspired no fear, or even respect.

The photograph that sat on her desk, however, produced no conflicting feelings. Little Mike, her son, grinned out at the world, his big blue eyes laughing, his blond hair combed to perfection. Although she often saw a trace of her husband in him, it never affected the overwhelming love she felt for the boy.

Mike's photograph reminded her. She picked up the phone and dialed her housekeeper.

"Marie, this is Mrs. Talbot. I won't be home for dinner tonight."

There was no reply, and Kathleen sensed the silent disapproval emanating from the other end.

"I have a meeting that I must attend. A political thing. I should be home about ten."

"Michael was asking about you again."

Kathleen looked at the picture on her desk. "Put him on, please."

"He's sleeping, Mrs. Talbot. Taking a nap."

She was disappointed. "Well, tell him I'll see him in the morning."

"Mrs. Talbot."

"Yes?"

Again there was a pause. "It's none of my business, of course, but I really think you should see more of your son."

Kathleen's first reaction was anger. The woman was almost twice her age, but that didn't give her the right to lecture. Kathleen also realized that the quick anger had been triggered by her own sense of guilt. Marie was right, and they both knew it.

"I'm doing my best, Marie," she said. "But I have to earn a living. He's young, he'll adjust."

"That's the problem, Mrs. Talbot. He isn't adjusting. He's too young. Except at breakfast, he hasn't seen you at all this week. It's not natural. He needs his mother."

Kathleen controlled herself. "I'm working on that, Marie. I'll be home at ten. Don't bother leaving anything out."

She hung up. She hadn't anticipated the problem when she had run for the job. She recalled that her father had been gone much of the time, but it hadn't really made an impression since she had always been away at school.

The job of prosecuting attorney had two sides. One was the work itself, running a large metropolitan law office devoted to law enforcement, protecting millions of people by bringing thousands of cases to trial, handling the constant and complicated challenges of the criminal justice system. The other, important to keeping that job, was the political obligations, also constant and complicated. She liked the meetings, the speeches, enjoying the applause and admiration, but it was taking all her time, even weekends. And Marie was right: her son did need her. And she needed him.

Tina Welch knocked, then entered. "Busy?" she asked.

"Not at all. What's up?"

"Two things. The jury just came back on the Helker case. They convicted on the nose—first-degree murder."

"That's good, but I would have been surprised if it had been anything else."

"The television crews are coming over. Arnie Nelson wants to know if you'd like to do the interview."

She laughed. Arnie Nelson, her deputy, was always trying to ingratiate himself. "No, have Tom Mease do it. He won the case, he deserves the glory."

"Okay. Now, what about the pornography investigation? The word is out that you're going to quietly quash it."

"So?"

Tina smiled. "I don't care, personally. But I hear some newspaper types are looking to harpoon you on that issue. Some women's groups are up in arms over it. I've had a couple of calls from the *Examiner* about it. Friendly, so far, but I think they're testing the water."

"Tell them, or anyone else, that the investigation is continuing. If the legislature had given us a better law to work with we wouldn't have all this trouble. If we don't present a good case, the law will be tossed out of court on constitutional grounds, and we'll be right back where we started."

"I just thought I'd alert you."

Kathleen nodded her appreciation. Tina had been her father's secretary. A plump woman, nearing retirement age, she had a warm personality and a sharp intellect. She actually ran the prosecutor's office, no matter what titles others had, and she did a splendid job of it. Kathleen had heard that in the distant past Tina also had been one of her father's many lovers. She seemed more like a pleasant grandmother than a femme fatale. But Kathleen knew looks could often be deceiving.

"Tina, who okayed that murder warrant against the policeman?"

"Arnie Nelson."

"Why wasn't I consulted?"

Tina shrugged. "You were away. It went through the usual channels. Arnie Nelson was here. He's the chief assistant prosecutor, so he signed it."

"He should know that all important cases go through me."

Tina nodded. "Arnie thought it was the right thing to do politically. He didn't want this office to look as if we favor the police. Other than that, I suppose he didn't think it was important."

Kathleen swore softly. "Not important, huh? The case may set *the* precedent for legally determining when death occurs. It's front-page news, that's all. Not to mention a certain amount of public outrage that the detective has been charged with murder, while the real killer may go free. Talk about a controversial issue. And if it isn't handled carefully, I could be defeated in the next election. Outside of that, I suppose Arnie saw nothing unusual."

Tina laughed despite Kathleen's obvious anger. "Arnie makes a nice appearance, though. Distinguished. He looks like a movie producer's idea of a prosecutor. He only gets in trouble when he tries to think."

Kathleen shook her head. "I guess it's hopeless, he'll never learn. Arnie's days around here are numbered, but I'll have a talk with him anyway."

Tina started to leave, then turned to remind her: "You know you're supposed to give a speech at that senior citizens' thing tonight?"

"Yes."

Kathleen stood up and walked to the window. There wasn't much of a view, just the bleak concrete walls of the court-complex buildings. And the jail, a dismal concrete high-rise with only long thin slits for windows.

She wondered how the policeman Chesney was doing in the jail. She presumed special precautions had been taken. If not, there wouldn't be a trial. He would be dead. Arnie Nelson had charged him with first-degree murder, and with that charge there could be no bail. She couldn't undo what Arnie had done, not now. An argument could be made whether Arnie's decision had been legally correct, but all that was in the past. The public debate was getting hotter, and she would look like a weak fool if she tried to reverse that decision. Still, she made a note to check and see if the policeman was adequately protected.

Kathleen went to her closet to take out the change of clothes she had brought from home. She had selected a form-fitting woolen outfit, since the morning had been chilly, but a warm breeze had blown all day and now it was almost balmy. The red-knit would be warm. Spring was so unpredictable. She wished she had picked something lighter.

As she dressed, she tried to concentrate on the speech she was to make, but her thoughts returned to her son. While Marie's disapproval irritated her, it also served to deepen the nagging sense of guilt she felt. She would have to make more time for Little Mike. She just didn't know how.

CHAPTER 4

THE JUDGE GLARED as he spoke between clenched teeth. "Mr. Mitchell, as reluctant as I am to grant your motion I find that I must."

Jeremiah Mitchell allowed himself a small smile. "We all have to follow the law, your honor."

"I have no doubt in my heart that justice has been twisted out of shape by you, but I am powerless to do anything but release your client."

Mitchell ignored the gasps of outrage from the spectators. "The presumption of innocence, judge, continues in a criminal charge until such time as guilt is found. My client is an innocent man.'"

"And I'm the Queen of Sheba!" the judge snapped.

Mitchell knew Judge Webster Broadbent was a man without a sense of humor, so he remained silent.

The short, stocky judge stood up. "The jury is dismissed, the bond is canceled, and the defendant is discharged!" He snapped out those words with obvious distaste, then stomped off the bench.

The court officers quickly began to disperse the angry spectators.

Jerry Mitchell, six-foot-three and a muscular two hundred pounds, towered above his short, paunchy client, Dr. Oliver Sampson. Sampson, bewildered, looked up at his lawyer. "What happens now?"

"The judge, as a matter of law, has determined the prosecution couldn't establish that your actions resulted in the death of that girl. No crime, no charge. You're free."

"Just like that?"

"Yes."

The little doctor slowly shook his head. "Jesus, that wasn't much, just a couple of witnesses. I expected this thing to go a couple of weeks."

"The result wasn't too bad."

Sampson's small eyes narrowed. "You didn't do much."

Mitchell's handsome features tightened slightly. "I got you off. The charge, doctor, was manslaughter. You performed an abortion while your license was suspended, and the girl died on the table. They were unable, legally, to show that your ministrations killed her. If the prosecutor could have shown your act was the cause of death, you would have ended up doing fifteen very long years. Since I'm the one who stopped them from proving your guilt, I think my services were of some value, don't you?"

Sampson sniffed. "Not fifty thousand dollars' worth. The whole thing didn't take over a day. I want half back."

Mitchell, who looked younger than his forty years, grinned. "My friend, when you came to me you said you'd heard I was the best criminal lawyer in this state. That, may I remind you, is why you retained me to defend your fat ass." He dropped his voice so that only Sampson could hear. "You are a disgusting little man and a disgrace to the medical profession. If there is any justice, the state board will jerk your license permanently for prescription abuse. Every time we've been together, you've been high on cocaine. Fortunately, doctor, I don't have to like my clients, only defend them. In this lovely old courthouse today I performed a miracle not unlike the parting of the Red Sea. And miracles don't come cheap."

"I should get some of that money back," he muttered.

"That would be even a greater miracle," Mitchell laughed. "Good-bye, doctor, and wipe your cocaine-damaged nose. May God have mercy on your patients."

Sampson colored, but he was too intimidated by Mitchell's size to do or say anything. He simply turned and walked away.

"Nice going, Jerry," one of the court officers said as he was leaving the courtroom. "But old Broadbent is really pissed."

Mitchell laughed. "Judge Webster Broadbent was born pissed."

"Are you going to celebrate?"

"There's no fun in winning unless you do, is there?"

As he left the Hall of Justice, Jerry Mitchell waved to the bored officer manning the court's metal detectors at the entrance. It was almost closing time for the court. The warm spring afternoon was surprisingly pleasant, so he walked the seven blocks to Brannigan's.

Mitchell ordered double Scotch, then made the phone call. She had been waiting, as he expected. "Hungry?"

"More or less."

"Any preferences?"

"Sexual or otherwise?"

Mitchell laughed. "Otherwise, to begin with. I could use a steak, Carol, but I'm open-minded."

"I'm off in half an hour, Jerry, and I make a hell of a steak. I could pick up a couple on my way home." She paused, then spoke with a mocking quality in her voice. "Unless you lust for the sociability of a restaurant?"

"Are you promising me a nice, juicy, warm—"

"Steak, honey," she laughed. "Just keep saying 'steak.' "

"See you in an hour?"

"Jerry?"

"Yes?"

"Did you sleep well last night?"

"What do you mean?"

"I hope you're rested, honey, because I'm horny, and you know what that means."

"Oh, Jesus, and here I'd hoped for a quiet evening watching television."

"One hour," she replied. "And you'd better be there, or I'll start without you."

Mitchell hung up and went back to the bar. The bartender was busy with the growing flood of after-work customers, but he nodded to Mitchell. "I saw you on television the other night, Jerry," he said. "You know, you look a bit like John Wayne."

"Or his horse."

The bartender pretended to squint. "By God, you're right!"

"Forget the comedy, Al, and give me a refill on the Scotch."

Soon Mitchell was surrounded by colleagues. The news of his victory had already gotten around the legal community, and everyone wanted the inside word on the case. He chatted with them, but kept an eye on the clock.

On his way to dinner, Mitchell stopped and bought wine to bring to Carol. That was expected. He also picked up some imported vodka and some caviar. He had no taste for either, but he remembered she did, and there were a number of uses for caviar besides spreading it on crackers.

Mitchell liked attractive women, and Carol filled the bill, with points to spare: she was tall and thick-boned, with pale blond hair and exotic blue eyes—gifts, no doubt, from distant Russian ancestors. She had been a cop, but was now a probation officer. They had been friends for years, and lovers when she was between husbands, which, given her roving ways, was often.

Jerry shifted his briefcase and the bag of goodies in order to push her apartment bell.

Carol answered, wearing a clinging crimson silk dressing gown. "You're almost late."

He handed her the gifts. " 'Almost' counts only in horseshoes and hand grenades."

Her lips brushed his. "Park your stuff, counselor," she said. "Something in a drink, perhaps?"

He slid his hand around her waist, and realized she was naked beneath the silk. "I could be persuaded. Look in the bag."

Her pale blue eyes sparkled. "Jesus, my favorites! If everyone drank expensive vodka and ate imported caviar, there'd be no poverty."

"I recall Marie Antoinette had a similar philosophy."

She laughed as she opened the bottle and poured. "Cake! Not booze. Not sex. No wonder they cut her silly head off." She handed him a glass of straight vodka that she had sprinkled with dark pepper. She raised her glass. "*Nostrovya!*"

Mitchell echoed the gesture, then sipped the clear liquid.

As Carol took a chair opposite him, she allowed her silk

gown to slide away from her thighs. "I hear you got that scumbag doctor off."

"An innocent man, caught in the web of the cruel criminal justice system," he said, admiring the display of flesh.

"God, don't you ever lose? You're becoming something of a legend, as I'm sure you know. I understand you have a regular fan club every time you try a case now."

"There's a bunch of retirees who haunt the criminal court. They like the drama. I have become one of their favorites." He shrugged.

Her pale eyes were half-hooded. "What's it like, being a legend?"

"A burden."

"Jerry"—she became serious—"we may not be seeing much of each other."

"Why?"

"I'm dating Sam Mossman."

"Captain Mossman, the Napoleon of the Tenth Precinct?"

"We were partners, years ago."

"Marriage?"

She shrugged. "You know me, Jerry, an incurable romantic. Sam's getting a divorce."

Mitchell sipped the vodka. "He's . . . well . . . kind of short, isn't he? They do call him Napoleon."

"He comes up to about my tits, if that's what you mean. But that's the only thing about him that's short."

"I thought the magazines said that didn't make any difference," he teased.

"Propaganda."

He grew serious. "You sure about this thing with Sam?"

"More or less. Everything is a crapshoot, right? You want another drink?"

"Sure."

She stood up and looked down at him. "God, you're something, you know that? I want to brag to my girlfriends that I'm balling you, the most famous lawyer in the state, but they wouldn't believe me."

"I'll give you references."

"I'll bet you would. Well," she said, slipping off the silk

gown, "you want to put that caviar to some good use? Or do you want a steak?"

"Fuck or die?"

"Something like that," she said, pulling him toward the bedroom.

They lay quietly together, both temporarily exhausted. Carol lit a cigarette.

"I'll miss all this, Jerry."

"You're serious about Sam Mossman?"

She inhaled, then let the smoke curl from her mouth and nostrils. "Yes."

"I'll miss you too."

It was true in a way. Carol was fun, and she fulfilled a sexual need without demanding anything in return. But recently Jerry had begun to feel the need for something more, something special, something lasting.

"This is going to be the last time," she whispered, reaching for him. She said that every time before she got married. She meant it, at least at that moment. Oddly, he decided it *would* be the last time, no matter what happened.

He didn't know what he wanted exactly, but it was something more than this.

"You're a great lawyer," she whispered, "but you're an even better lay."

CHAPTER 5

QUIETLY, KATHLEEN TALBOT let herself into her apartment. She felt a continuing sense of exhilaration. The dinner had been just another charity thing, with cardboard food and boring speeches, but she had been seated at the speakers' table and had been openly courted by all the prominent power brokers. She liked that. Her father had held the office of prosecutor for decades, and he was powerful, but he had made too many enemies too early in his career, and no other office was open to him. She knew he was bitter about that, and perhaps a touch envious that his daughter would have opportunities that had been denied to him.

She had only picked at the banquet food; now she was hungry and she headed for the kitchen. Marie had left some fried chicken in the refrigerator—Little Mike's favorite food, not counting ice cream.

Kathleen selected several pieces and sliced a tomato, then took her snack into the den and flipped on the television.

It was too late for the news. She kicked off her shoes and absently watched an old movie as she munched, her mind still on the charity dinner. She was the most powerful woman politician in the state, at least at the moment. And she was her father's daughter: she loved the accolades, the excitement of politics. Next, if she wanted it, was the governorship. After that the Senate. The United States would soon be ready for a woman president. Even that was within the realm of possibil-

37

ity. She was young; there was no telling just how far she might go.

She was startled as her maid walked into the den. Marie was wrapped in an old robe and wore worn leather slippers.

Kathleen used the remote control to turn off the television. "I hope I didn't waken you, Marie."

"I wasn't sleeping. Actually, I was waiting for you."

"Oh?"

Marie sat on the edge of a leather couch, her expression stern. "Mrs. Talbot, you know about Michael's friend Albert?"

Kathleen smiled. Little Mike could talk of little else lately. "Sure. His little friend."

Marie shook her head slowly. "I did a little checking, then I asked Michael about him."

"So?"

"There is no Albert. He isn't real."

Kathleen frowned. "Are you sure? He certainly sounds real, at least the way Michael talks about him."

"He doesn't exist. Michael says only he can see Albert."

Kathleen smiled. "Well, that's not too unusual, is it? Lots of children have imaginary friends."

Marie nodded. "Yes, that's true, but they usually have other friends too, flesh-and-blood ones. And they know their imaginary friend isn't real."

"I'm sure Michael does too."

"Mrs. Talbot, we had a long talk, Michael and me. He has no other playmates. There aren't any children his age in this apartment house. I honestly believe he thinks Albert is real and only he can see him." Marie frowned. "Michael has no father, and he doesn't have any uncles, and he never sees his grandfather except for a few minutes at Christmas or on special occasions." She looked directly at Kathleen. "And forgive me for saying this, but he has no mother either, not in the usual sense. You're just someone who sleeps here. Even on weekends you're gone. I try to fill in, but it just isn't the same."

Kathleen didn't feel angry. Marie's words worried her. "I'm going to try—"

"I'm going to quit, Mrs. Talbot. I love that little boy, and I think he's getting sick. He needs love, and he needs to know someone cares. All he has is a friend he's invented." She shook her head. "I've read a lot about children. What he's doing isn't healthy. I can't stand watching what's happening to him. I'll stay until you get someone else, but I have to leave."

Kathleen saw the woman's eyes were wet. "I don't know what to say, Marie. I have to make a living. We all have to adjust . . ."

Marie's features became stern again. "You're a brilliant woman, Mrs. Talbot, but you're putting yourself ahead of that wonderful little boy. You don't have to be in politics. You could make more money as a regular lawyer, and then you'd have time for your son." She stood up. "But you're a politician, Mrs. Talbot, and you like it. I doubt anything will ever change. God help your son. . . ." Marie stared at her. "Well, I'll stay until you get someone else," she said finally, then turned and left the den.

Kathleen sat quietly. Her exhilaration was suddenly gone and she felt cold and empty. She wished she could tell herself that Marie was wrong, but she knew she wasn't.

Big Mike was a drinker, and she disliked the effect it had on him, so she usually disdained alcohol. But now she needed something. Kathleen poured herself a brandy, then walked into the living room and turned off the lights. The city was lovely at night, glittering like diamonds, casting a soft glow into the dark sky above. She watched as she sipped the cognac.

Marie was right, she did love politics, it was a passion. She thought of little else, her mind alive with the thousand computations necessary for political existence and advancement. Just like her father.

Big Mike had neglected her, too, but she had had her mother, at least until her teens. She had known love and support, but not from her father. He was always caught up in the narcoticlike excitement of politics. And she had turned out to be just like him.

The thought was repugnant to her.

Kathleen got up and walked into her son's bedroom. Her eyes quickly adjusted to the dark. He lay so quietly, his little face cradled against one small arm. She reached down and smoothed out his soft blond hair. His skin was warm. He stirred in response to her gentle touch. Suddenly she felt herself close to tears.

Marie was right, Little Mike needed her, and he needed her now. But the idea of completely leaving public life seemed like a kind of death to her.

There had to be another way and she would have to find it quickly. Her son was the most important thing in her life and she could not risk him, no matter what.

Marty Kelly had been one of Big Mike Hunt's original crew. Kelly had come from Harvard Law and had done just about everything during his long legal career. He had clerked for several months with a Boston judge. He had gone to Washington and worked as a government lawyer for a few years. Admitted to the bar in a number of states, he had practiced in firms and individually in big cities and small towns. He had even served for a few months as a judge, appointed by a governor to an interim term, to fill in until a local election.

If he had been a racehorse, Marty Kelly would have been classified as a good starter but a poor finisher. He was still well regarded as a good lawyer, at least until noon. If the working day had officially stopped at noon, Martin Kelly might have ended up on the Supreme Court. But the day did not end at noon, at which time Marty Kelly unfortunately succumbed to a troublesome lifetime habit: he started drinking every day at lunch, and didn't stop until he went to bed or passed out, whichever happened first.

But Big Mike, the prosecuting attorney, had matched the job to the man. Marty Kelly, gray-haired and enormously experienced, was the assistant prosecutor in charge of the homicide division. He didn't have to try any cases, and all the effective work of evaluating warrants and passing out assignments was always done by lunchtime, so his brilliance was employed fully without being impaired by his problem.

There were a thousand hilarious Marty Kelly stories told whenever trial lawyers gathered, but they only concerned his antics after lunch, never before.

Now Kelly was worried that Big Mike's daughter might change his assignment, which would spell final disaster. He had known

Kathleen Talbot since she was a little girl and he hoped she would keep him on the homicide assignment, for old times' sake if nothing else. Still, he was concerned, and especially careful to discharge his duties in a way that wouldn't displease her.

He had occupied the same office for almost twenty years, a small cubicle near the stairs, well removed from the main traffic in the prosecutor's office. His furniture consisted of an old desk, some battered chairs and a cracked leather couch, patched and lumpy. He had spent many nights snoring drunkenly on that couch.

Kelly had been told he looked like the drawing of the dapper little man who had once been *Esquire* magazine's trademark. Like him, Kelly was short, round, and sported a small waxed mustache. And like that famous caricature, his eyes, which seemed a bit too big and bulgy for his round face, were accentuated even more by his florid complexion. Kelly also affected stylish dress. In the morning, he might indeed resemble the *Esquire* man, but by night no one would ever describe him as dapper.

"Marty, did you want to see me?" Thomas Mease stuck his head in the door. Mease was one of the young workhorses who were building reputations as good trial lawyers in the prosecutor's office.

"Sit down, Tom." Kelly indicated one of the battered wooden chairs. "You've been doing some rather good work lately. You're becoming the trial ace of the staff, according to the courthouse crowd."

Mease chuckled. "C'mon, Marty, can the bullshit. You only go in for that if you've something unpleasant to do. What's up?"

Kelly grinned. He liked Mease. In a way he reminded him of himself when he was young—fast mind, ambitious, short but muscular, a regular dynamo. But Mease could handle his liquor. "How's your schedule for September?"

Mease raised an inquisitive eyebrow. "You know the assignment docket better than anyone else. I have a gambling conspiracy starting in July. That should take all of August. With any luck, I'll be clear in September."

"Good." Kelly pulled out the file the police had given him. "I'd like you to try the Harold Malked case."

"The guy that shot his retarded daughter?"

Kelly nodded. "Shouldn't be much of a case. The doctors told him he's dying of heart disease and that he couldn't work anymore. He didn't want his daughter put into an institution after he croaked, so he killed her. He admits everything. He was going to plead guilty until the public defender got to him. It's open-and-shut."

Mease laughed. "Martin Kelly, you dirty old fuck, you know that's going to be front-page shit. Mercy killing, Marty, that's the issue! Jesus, I'd like to see the poor son-of-a-bitch go free myself. Even the newspapers say he's really dying."

Kelly shrugged. "I don't care what he's doing. If he's still alive in September and he hasn't offered a plea, he's going to trial. Somebody's got to try the thing."

Mease frowned. "I agree. But why me? I work my ass off around here and all I ever get is the tough cases. Why not Goldstein? He likes to see his name in the papers. Or Felker? Felker's good."

"Goldstein is trying a couple of big ones all during the summer. Felker I got assigned to the Chesney case, the cop who pulled the plug. You want that case? Maybe you'd like to switch with Felker?"

Mease shook his head but smiled. "No, the Malked case is a ball-buster, but I'd rather have that than the cop. If Felker wins that case, every policeman in the state will hate his guts."

"Both are front-page cases," Kelly said solemnly. "We need our best men to handle them. Even a minor fuck-up will draw headlines and editorials." Kelly shook his head. "The mercy-killing people will be all over your case, and the right-to-life people and their opponents will swarm all over Felker's case. Either trial could get blown up out of proportion. And if that happens, our lovely leader, Kathleen Talbot, is liable to get her cute little ass is very hot political water."

Mease nodded. "Any idea who will be named as executive judge? A lot will depend on which judge gets assigned to try these cases. A bad judge could hurt us."

Kelly shrugged. "Hey, you know those goddamned prima

donnas over there. They're clawing at each other now for the executive-judge job. I don't know which idiot will win. Anyway, no matter who does, we still have to do a good job."

Mease thought for a moment. "How much authority do I have on this case? Can I plea-bargain?"

"It's hot, so you better check with me. I suppose we could let Malked plead guilty to second-degree murder, but nothing less. We can't look like we took a dive. There'll be strong feelings each way." He handed the homicide file to Mease. "Do what you have to do, Tom, but give it your best shot."

"Somebody from the public defender's going to represent Malked?"

"They do now," Kelly replied. "But you know how these cases go—the ones that get all the publicity: some big trial man will step in at the last minute. It's a million bucks' worth of free publicity for somebody, and they'll make the most of it. You'll have your hands full."

Mease stood up. "Well, there goes September."

Kelly nodded. "And maybe even part of October. Just remember, this case could hurt the office, so be careful." Kelly glanced at his watch; it was almost noon, and he was grateful. "I hate these screwy killings, you know. Give me a nice ax maniac with a record, or a jealous husband, the good old routine nickel-and-dime shit." He shook his head. "Between mercy killings and overconscientious cops, they're taking the fun out of murder." He looked up at Mease. "I think I'll head out for lunch a bit early today. Want to come?"

"No thanks, Marty. I got things to do this afternoon. If I have to protect Kathleen the Ice Queen's ass, I better hop to it."

CHAPTER 6

"MRS. WHITEHALL?"

She looked up, squinting at him through the upper part of her new and annoying bifocals. "Yes?"

"I'm Chuck Jerome. Mr. Bennett, the managing editor, said I was to report to you." It was a statement, but his tone and inflection made it a question.

"The new intern?"

He nodded, relieved that she knew about him.

Jane Whitehall studied him for a moment. A bit on the short side but athletic-looking. Nice face, nice wavy blond hair. He was Jack Bennett's gift, a toy to play with so that she wouldn't bother him. The kid looked about twenty-two, and typically fresh and eager. She was thirty-eight, but she could still remember when she had been that age. That had been four newspapers, two husbands, and countless lovers ago.

"Sit down, Chuck."

He sat tentatively on the edge of the hard-backed chair next to her desk in the city room. She sensed that amused eyes were watching. Her sexual appetites were well known.

"Still in school?" she asked.

He nodded. "Yes, Mrs. Whitehall. Ohio State, with one semester to go."

"Call me Jane. Journalism major, I presume?"

"Yes."

"Ever work on a newspaper before, Chuck?" She leaned

45

back in her chair, allowing him a view of her thigh, if he cared
to look. She still had a good body and, she had been often told,
great legs.

"Just the university paper."

"As an intern," she said, "you'll be assigned to various duties.
As you know, there's no pay, but we figure the experience you
get will make the effort worthwhile."

He nodded. He had stolen a glance at her legs and was
trying to keep from looking again. She liked that. At least the
kid wasn't queer. Jack Bennett liked to play jokes now and
then, too.

"I'm the paper's political writer," she continued. "You'll be
assigned to me for a while. My job is to cover government at all
local levels. We have people assigned to the state capital and
Washington, but I take care of the locals. Understand?"

"Like the mayor's office, and things like that?"

She took the glasses off. She had had them only a week and
couldn't get used to them. She smiled. "That's part of it, the
city administration. Also I do the council and the courts."

"The courts too?"

He had good eyes and strong hands. She found that attractive. "For the time being. We had a court writer, a reporter who
was also a lawyer, but he left to become a flack with the gas
company."

"Flack?"

"Publicity man. He handles public relations. Until we find
someone else, I'll take care of the courts. In my own way, I
have a few qualifications." She didn't want to tell the kid that
her second husband was a lawyer, or that she had been the
lover of the chief judge of the intermediate appellate court,
Irving Kelman, at least until Mrs. Kelman found out. But by
that time she had become tired of Irving anyway.

"Right now there's a hell of a battle brewing among the
judges to see who will take over as executive judge of the
circuit court. Harry Johnson was executive judge for years, but
he just died."

She could see he didn't understand. "Chuck, our local circuit
court handles every case that comes up for trial in the city.
They have two main divisions: civil and criminal. The criminal

division hears every criminal case that happens in the city. The civil division takes care of everything else. In other words, they are the law, at least in these parts." He still wasn't showing any comprehension, only eagerness. He was inexperienced, but a good teacher could inspire him, she decided. "Are you married, Chuck?" she asked.

He grinned. She liked his smile. "No. I was engaged, but that fell through. Besides, I couldn't afford to get married, not until I graduate and get a job."

"Good healthy attitude," she replied. "Now, the executive judge is elected by the others. He, or she, although no woman has ever held the job, selects which case goes to which judge. That's why the job is so important."

He frowned. "I don't see . . ."

She smiled. "The executive judge can reward and punish. Look, if he doesn't like a judge, he can throw every shitty case his way. Or vice versa. The same goes for attorneys, other political leaders, and utility companies. Justice often depends on which judge hears a case. The Irish have a saying: it's better to know the judge than to know the law. Didn't they teach you that at Ohio State?"

"Well, not exactly that way."

"Right. That's why you're here, to learn the practical side of life. I'm going over to the court this afternoon to interview Judge Quinlan. He's the acting executive judge. Quinlin's retiring this year, so I suppose the others felt he was the least dangerous. Anyway, he has the job on a temporary basis. Would you like to come with me?"

The boy beamed as if she had just awarded him the Pulitzer Prize. "Sure!"

"Okay. So you'll understand what we'll be talking about, there are thirty-eight circuit judges. They are elected for eight-year terms and can run to succeed themselves. Fourteen of them are assigned to the criminal division. They can be shifted about, but only by the executive judge. He decides what cases they'll hear, both civil and criminal. Of the thirty-eight, only five are women. The damn court is like a mens' club in some ways, so it's unlikely any female judge will ever get the top job. I'll be asking Quinlan about that, by the way. I'll try to needle him into saying something that will give us a headline. But the old goat has been around a long time, so he probably won't rise to the bait. Watch what I do, maybe even learn something, okay?"

"You bet!"

"Let's have lunch first. Do you have any plans?"

He shook his head.

"Well, if you're going to be a newspaper person, you'd better start learning about cheap dives. We'll catch a sandwich and a quick beer at Max's Grill. You do drink?"

He nodded. "Beer mostly."

She stood up and held herself so that he could get a good view. "Let's go." Amused eyes followed their progress through the city room. He was a most attractive toy, and she appreciated it, but she hoped Jack Bennett wouldn't think the toy would be an acceptable substitute for the weekly column she had been asking to do.

-◀ ▶-

"Why not try it?" Jane whispered as they lay naked on her bed, her hand gently guiding his head downward.

"Ah . . . well, you know, it's just something that I haven't . . ."

Her voice was purring with encouragement. "If you're going to be a journalist, Chuck, you must learn to be investigative."

"But . . ."

She pushed with a bit more force. "And you might as well start now."

He tried to stop at her navel, but it was only a halfhearted attempt. She raised her hips.

"There," she whispered, "that's not so bad after all, is it?"

His virginlike reluctance and obvious inexperience were to her a powerful aphrodisiac, heightening her response.

"Oh, Chuck," she sighed encouragingly, "you're a natural. With a little practice and some good coaching, you could become a great investigator."

-◀ ▶-

Webster Broadbent drove his wife's car. His long Cadillac was too recognizable, and he wanted to avoid being seen driving into the parking lot of Gompers Hall. There was too much talk already about his connection with organized labor.

The Hall, as everyone called it, was an old square brick building housing a number of local unions, but its main importance was as the headquarters for the city's labor alliance, an informal council that represented all the unions and served as labor's political arm.

Judge Broadbent parked the old Ford and hurried in through the back door. It was early; only a few cars were in the paved adjoining lot. The halls were empty and his footsteps echoed as he hurried toward the familiar corner office.

The office was unlocked and the reception room empty. He looked into the inner office.

"Ah, come in, Webster, come in," Morton Penn said. "I hated to ask you to come out so early, but I go to Mass every morning, as you know. I have a quick breakfast here afterward and that's about my only leisure time for the entire day. I thought we could have a little talk over coffee. I made a fresh pot." He slid a chipped cup toward Broadbent, who took a seat at the desk opposite the union leader.

With shaking hands, Morton Penn carefully poured. He claimed to be only seventy, but rumor had it that he was somewhat older. His enormous head of white hair contrasted with the dark and weathered skin of his thin face. A local union leader and a hero of a number of organization wars, he now acted as a senior statesman, heading up labor's political arm. Some thought him a saint, while others believed he was evil and corrupt.

"I don't much hold with the new ways of the Catholic Church," Penn said, "but I've gone to Mass every morning since I was a little boy. It's an ingrained habit. I certainly hope that God exists—otherwise I've wasted an awful lot of mornings." He sipped from his cup. "Now, I understand you would like to become executive judge?"

Broadbent knew that was the reason for the invitation. "I think I could do a good job," he said. "I would seek and welcome labor's support."

Morton Penn laid the cup down on the stained wooden desk. "We have eight judges we know we can count on," he said quietly. "And three more who would probably go along with us. It's not a majority, but it's a substantial foundation."

"I would appreciate it very much if you could persuade them to support me," Broadbent said, sipping the coffee. It was strong and bitter.

Penn's eyes were striking, almost colorless. They resembled clouded agates. "We need certain concessions," he said.

"I've always been a friend of organized labor," Broadbent began. "Even as a young man—"

"As a young lawyer you represented a few locals and made a great deal of money. Let's not lose sight of reality, Webster. You've received more than you ever gave. When you ran, you needed money and support. Labor gave you that."

"And I've always appreciated it."

"Yes." Penn's smile was less than jovial. "Now, Webster, this executive-judge position is extremely powerful and we would like one of the judges friendly to us to get it."

"I've always been—"

Penn held up his hand. "We have other judges, as I said, also proven friends. But I think you may have the best chance of getting the job—that is, if we support you."

Broadbent sighed. "What are the concessions you want?"

"I like you, Webster, you get right to the point." Penn pulled out a worn pipe, filled it, and puffed up a cloud of aromatic smoke. "The attorney general is going to demand a grand jury to investigate the awarding of contracts for the Coleman Superdome. Several of our local unions will come under unwanted scrutiny if that happens."

"I've heard there have been some beatings to silence opposition," Broadbent interjected. "That plus rumors of alleged bribes and kickbacks—"

Penn removed his pipe and waved it to interrupt the judge. "We are trying to persuade the attorney general from taking such drastic action. Without a great deal of success, I'm afraid. Believe me, our people are all quite innocent, but these things have a way of making honest men appear crooked. If the grand jury is called, the judge who gets it should be a friend of ours, if you understand?"

Broadbent hoped the office wasn't wired. In any event, he

had to word his answer carefully. "Obviously, if I were to be the executive judge, I would pick someone who would do a good job but who wouldn't seek cheap publicity, someone with a good background and a proven record."

Penn chuckled. "We're not taping this, Webster, but I see you get the idea. Also, occasionally we would ask for certain cases to go to certain judges, perhaps even ask the executive judge to dismiss certain . . . well, foolish legal actions."

Broadbent was becoming increasingly uncomfortable. He would promise anything that wouldn't land him in jail. He presumed they knew that. But he considered it unfair that they ask him to say things that might incriminate him. "My record speaks for itself," he said. "I will do whatever is best for justice."

Penn shrugged. "I'll be talking to some other people too, Webster. This is a serious matter. Whoever gets that job will have it for years. It's terribly important to labor that he be a friend."

"I can understand that," Broadbent said. "I hope you decide on me."

"What about the grand jury? If it happens, we'd like George Hopkins to be assigned the case. If you get the job, do we have that assurance?"

Broadbent was sweating. He didn't want to answer.

"As I said, Webster, this is all off the record. We have no wires in here, and we make sure no one else does either. What's your answer? Will you assign the case to Hopkins?"

Broadbent nodded.

"C'mon, Webster, if you can't trust me, I can't trust you."

"Yes," he said reluctantly, "I'll see the matter goes to Judge Hopkins."

"And the other, ah, courtesies we ask?"

Broadbent sighed. "Of course."

Penn smiled. He stood up and offered his frail hand. "I'll talk to the others, Webster, and I'll be back to you soon. I appreciate your coming."

Eager to leave, Broadbent hurried from the office.

Penn's pipe went out and he scratched a match into life and again sent billows of clouds soaring up toward the ceiling.

A young man in shirtsleeves came up from the basement and walked into Penn's office. "Did you get all of that?" Penn asked.

The other man grinned. "Sure. Every word."

Penn nodded. "Good. That snake would sell out his own mother. Anyone else would have told me to go to hell, but he wants it so bad he'd do anything. If we do get the job for him, we'll let the honorable Webster Broadbent know we have preserved our little conversation, suitably edited. He's scared of his own shadow. He'll be ours forever."

"That business about you going to Mass every morning—is that true?"

Penn nodded thoughtfully. "Of course. You know, sticking your nose inside a church once in a while wouldn't do you any harm. It helps clear the conscience and the mind. I wouldn't think of starting a day without it."

CHAPTER 7

THE LUNCHEON WAS uncomfortable for both of them until Bill Murray began to regale Kathleen with insider stories of the state capital, the wilder members of the legislature, and even tales about his boss, Governor Joshua Leonard. Each seemed more hilarious than the last.

Kathleen recalled that Murray had been a wonderful raconteur when they were students in law school. The passing years seemed only to have sharpened his eye for the humor he found in life.

"Kathleen," he said, his manner suddenly serious, "I'm here on a fool's errand, but it's an errand nevertheless."

"You're Governor Leonard's chief of staff, Bill. I'm sure he doesn't send you out for coffee."

"Once in a while. I'm not proud. I already know your answer, but I must relay the governor's request."

"I'm intrigued. Go on."

He sipped at his coffee. "Look, I'm loyal to Josh Leonard, and he will have my complete support for reelection, but you stand a good chance of giving him a real run for his money in the next election if you challenge him."

"So I'm told."

"Even if you don't win, you'd cost him millions in campaign funds fighting you off."

"Oh?"

"Well, under the circumstances, it's silly to ask, but the

governor would like to appoint you to Harry Johnson's vacancy on the bench. He thinks you're perfect for the job, but since the state constitution would forbid you from running for anything but a judicial job if you accept the appointment, he's not sure you'd want it. That's why he's having me discuss the offer with you first."

"I think I can beat him, Bill."

He nodded slowly. "I told him it was useless to ask."

Kathleen smiled slowly. "You know I have a son."

"Yes."

"If I tell you something that won't compromise your loyalty, will you keep it confidential?"

He shrugged. "Yes, under those circumstances."

Her eyes met his. "I want to run for governor, but it would mean I'd never be home. A statewide campaign would demand every second of my time. And if I won, and I think I would, then I'd be twice as busy as I am now."

"Sure. That's the nature of the job."

She nodded. "I'm concerned about my son. I'm really all he has, Bill. And he's so little." She looked away. "If I were married it might be different. But I'm not, and I'm not planning to be. I owe him a life, Bill."

He frowned. "Are you kidding me?"

"No."

"Would you really be interested in the judge's job?"

"It's regular hours. I'd have time for my son."

She was surprised at his reaction. He seemed suddenly distressed.

"Hey, Kathleen, putting aside my loyalty to my boss for a moment, and speaking just as an old friend, have you gone nuts?"

"I don't think so."

"You'll never have a better shot, you must know that. The brass ring only comes by once, Kathleen. If you don't grab for it, it's gone. Usually for good. It seems like a hell of a sacrifice to make. There must be some other way."

"The governor would fire you if he heard you talking like that," she said, smiling.

"Probably. But I'm your friend too. This is pretty sudden. Why not take some time to think it over?"

She shook her head. "No. For me, it offers the best of both worlds. I can give my son the care and attention he needs, and I can still stay in public life. At this point in my life I find it's an acceptable compromise. If the governor will appoint me, Bill, I'll accept."

"You're absolutely sure?"

"I'll put it in writing if you like."

"I don't care, but I know he'll want that. Jesus, Kathleen, he'll go nuts with sheer joy. I shouldn't tell you, you might want to change your mind, but he'll regard this as being saved from certain electoral execution. And, frankly, I'll be regarded as a miracle worker."

She laughed. "I suppose I'll have to go through the usual bar-association committees?"

He grinned. "Are you kidding? If I know him, he'll make the announcement this afternoon. For all practical purposes, Kathleen, you're a judge as of this moment. Everything else is just follow-up ceremony."

"I suppose I should feel good. I don't, but maybe I will in time."

Leaning across the table, he kissed her cheek. "You will. And, let me predict, you'll get married again too."

"Always the romantic, aren't you? My husband was a louse. I'll never remarry, ever."

"Not everyone is a Handsome Hank. Some of the ugly guys, like me, for instance, have proven to be wonderful spouses."

"Is that a proposal, Bill?"

"Sure."

"If I ever change my mind, I'll let you know, okay?"

"It's a deal," he said. Then added, "Judge."

Dennis Chesney occupied one of the small apartments that had been constructed in the jail to house material witnesses. He had often visited them during his years with the police force. If there was a possibility that the life of a witness might be in danger, police officials used these secure and comfortable places to keep that person safely locked away from outside threats.

Chesney was a policeman, although officially suspended from duty, and a number of the prisoners occupying the city jail's cells were customers he had locked away. He wouldn't have lasted an hour if he had been put in with the jail's regular population.

The special-witness apartment wasn't bad. It was a small studio apartment with a galley kitchen, a tiny bathroom and a shower. The other homicide officers had brought him a small color television and kept him supplied with groceries.

The homicide officers had also hired Jeremiah Mitchell, the famous lawyer, to defend Chesney. Mitchell's first move was to try to get Chesney out on bail, but it was to no avail.

The guards ignored Chesney, not quite sure how he should be treated. He was a prisoner, charged with a major felony. But if he was acquitted he would resume his status as a policeman, assuming the police trial board reinstated him. Nothing was sure, except that Chesney's act had awakened warring elements—strident voices for and against so-called mercy killings. The newspapers were crammed with stories and opinions. His case would decide a number of complex legal issues.

Convicted, he would lose all special treatment. There were no "country-club" jails for convicted murderers. A conviction would place him in with the main population of the state's prison, and that, for him, would be the same as a death sentence.

Time passed with agonizing slowness for Chesney. He found little on television that he liked, and had never been much of a reader. He had no close family to visit him. Mitchell was arranging to have his trial advanced, and it couldn't come any too quickly for Dennis Chesney.

Even death seemed preferable to the tortuous waiting.

Marty Kelly was making his usual rounds, taking drinks at selected bars, exchanging talk and laughter with men and women he had known for years—bartenders, waitresses, hookers, and barflies like himself. He had a well-established route, and always ended up at a place near his apartment, where it wouldn't be too inconvenient for someone to help him home.

He lurched into the Money Bush, a small run-down bar not too far from the courts. It was still early in the evening, and a cluster of lawyers and policemen lingered to enjoy the hospitality of Mark Meehan, a sour little man whose mean mouth had earned him a local reputation as a nasty wit. That, plus the attraction of his waitress, Kitty, whose forty-two-inch bust lagged only slightly behind the measure of her IQ—a condition she often demonstrated with uproarious results—provided the place with a certain quirky uniqueness that appealed to the sometimes strange people who worked in and around the courts.

"You're late," Meehan said as Marty Kelly carefully mounted a bar stool. "If I lose your business, Kelly, I'll go broke. This dump has become known as the home of the world-champion lush."

"Curb your insolent tongue, innkeeper, or I shall have you thrashed." Kelly grinned at the other customers. "I'll have a glass of your best whiskey, poor as it is in this woebegone hole in the wall."

Meehan scowled and poured a double shot, then shoved the glass to the lawyer. "On your best day, Kelly, you wouldn't know good from bad."

Martin Kelly gulped down the drink and smiled. "There is no such thing as bad whiskey, Meehan. Another, if you please."

Kelly squinted at the mirror behind the bar, noting the arrival of Jeremiah Mitchell. The tall man waved to several lawyers sitting at one of the back tables.

"Well, now," Kelly proclaimed as he swiveled around. "We are honored by the presence of a legend, no less. The great and wonderful wizard of the courtroom himself, Jeremiah Mitchell."

Mitchell nodded and took a seat next to Kelly. "I should hire you as my publicist, Marty."

"What brings you to this foul den of iniquity, Jerry? You're more the uptown type."

"I was paying a small social visit to one of my customers at the jail, Martin, if you must know. As many times as I've been there, I still find it depressing. I felt the urgent need to see some happy people whose faces aren't shadowed by steel bars."

Kelly laughed. "That's a pretty sentiment, but all you'll find here, Jerry, are giggling alcoholics like myself. The joy you see is eighty proof and up."

"I'll buy you a jot of that joy, Martin."

"You're a mean man in a courtroom, Jerry, but I can't complain of your style here. I'll accept with alacrity."

A tall policeman in civilian clothes who served in the criminal court's lockup walked over. "How ya doin', Martin, Mr. Mitchell," he said in a soft hill-country drawl.

Kelly nodded. "Not bad, all things considered, Hoye. And you?"

"Two years, three months, and fourteen days away from retirement. I'll make it." The lanky policeman sipped at the glass of beer he held in his hand. "Marty, why do you think your boss did it? Hell, as Big Mike's daughter, she could have gone all the way."

Kelly turned and stared at Hoye to see if he was trying to make a joke. He appeared sincere. "Kathleen Talbot?" Kelly asked. "My lovely boss. Just what is it she's supposed to have done?"

The policeman shrugged. "I heard about it over to the court just before quitting time. The governor named her as a circuit judge."

The pleasant numbing effect of his alcoholic fog was suddenly blown away from Martin Kelly's consciousness. "What?"

"That doesn't sound right," Mitchell said.

"Don't know any more than that. True enough, I guess. They say it was on the radio. Of course, being a judge is a good job and all, but we kind of figured she'd shoot for the big time. I just wondered, Marty, if you knew why she did it, you being the chief of homicide over there, and all."

Kelly gripped the bar. If true, and he suspected it was, it was bad news. If he ever got into trouble, he figured he could always have Big Mike intercede with his daughter. Now, there was no telling who the new prosecutor would be. "I don't know why she did it," he said quietly. "Her father will be royally pissed, though. Big Mike gave up that office so she could run for it and get her start in politics. He thought that she would try for the big time too."

Jerry Mitchell shook his head. "Well, there are always surprises in life, aren't there? I wonder what her reason is? I don't know her well, but she seems like a sensible person. I think she would have defeated Josh Leonard."

Martin Kelly wondered if Kathleen Talbot had checked with her father about the judgeship. He hoped she had. Mike Hunt could be a maniac when he got mad. God pity her if she hadn't cleared it with him first. And, given all the circumstances, he thought, God pity poor old Martin Kelly too.

"Jeremiah Mitchell," Kelly said, forcing a smile, "living legend or not, I think I could do now with that drink you promised."

CHAPTER 8

KATHLEEN TALBOT FINALLY found a moment to be alone. The morning had been filled with a succession of reporters, camera crews, and a procession of well-wishers. She told Tina Welch to hold her telephone calls.

There had been no discussion of when the announcement of her appointment to the bench was to be made. She presumed that she would have to be interviewed by bar-association committees and other groups, a lengthy process that had become customary when filling judicial appointments. Kathleen was amused at Governor Leonard's speed in announcing his selection. Obviously, he didn't want to give her a chance for second thoughts.

But she had none. Taking the judicial robe was a compromise, a chance to continue in public life, but without the all-consuming duties of a politician. She had sacrificed political ambition to provide a more normal home life for Little Mike—a sacrifice she was now convinced was the right thing to do.

It was Big Mike that bothered her. She stared up at the picture of her father. His eyes seemed disapproving, although she knew that was only her imagination. She would have to tell him what she had done. He would soon find out—if he hadn't already—from the local newspapers he had mailed to his home in Florida, or from one of his cronies.

Kathleen dreaded making the call. The prospect of his awful temper still frightened her, just as it had when she was a child. Big Mike Hunt had that effect on most people, not just her.

She didn't like making calls to his Florida home even in the best of times. Her father subjected her to long political lectures. And she dreaded trying to make conversation with his present wife, Regina. The woman, who was only a few years older than Kathleen, seemed jealous of her, causing an unpleasant coolness to exist between them.

There had always been a procession of women in Big Mike's life. Kathleen's own mother, who had separated from him because of his flagrant infidelities, had died of cancer before her divorce had become final. Kathleen, whom Big Mike regarded as some kind of inconvenient cross to be borne, was sent off to schools and camps. He was far from ever being an ideal parent. Her father's two other marriages before the one to Regina had both ended in nasty divorces. Kathleen had liked Ruth, a happy, outgoing ex-policewoman, but Ruth didn't last more than two years. She was followed by Doreen, the heiress. For a while Big Mike seemed to enjoy mingling with Doreen's society friends, then that too ended when Doreen tried to match her husband's roving ways.

Regina, the latest, was a whining little blond who seemed perpetually sorry for herself, drank far too much and too often, but possessed the ultimate asset of being afraid of Big Mike, enduring his conduct without ever complaining to him. She complained to everyone else who would listen, but never him. Big Mike, apparently slowing sexually, had traded adultery for golf as his major sport, and used Regina more as a servant than a wife.

Kathleen looked over at the photograph of her late husband. Between Big Mike and the late Handsome Hank, she had little cause to respect men or marriage.

Reluctantly she picked up the telephone and dialed the Florida number.

When Regina answered, her speech was slurred, even at that early hour.

"How have you been?" Kathleen asked.

"This heat has been hell on my skin. I itch all the time and I must have been to every dermatologist in this damn state. Nothing helps. I'm up half the night. It's awful."

Kathleen had expected nothing less. There was always a

new ailment making Regina's life a living hell. "I'm sorry to hear that. I suppose the tropical sun doesn't help, either."

"Oh, I wouldn't think of sunning myself. I just sit under an awning near the pool. I don't even go in the water anymore. The chlorine seems to make things worse."

Kathleen knew anything she could say would just irritate the woman. "Is my father around?"

"Christ, he's been home all morning. It's been raining down here, so he hasn't been able to play golf. Sometimes I don't think I can stand much more."

"May I speak to him?"

Regina snorted. "If you want to. He's in the bedroom."

Kathleen heard Regina call out, her tone much sweeter when addressing her husband. "Your daughter's on the phone."

Big Mike sounded as if he had just awakened when he picked up the telephone in the bedroom. "What's up?" Kathleen noticed there was no click. Regina was listening in, as she often did.

"How are you, Dad?"

"How should I be? I'm down here in somebody's idea of heaven, stuck with a bunch of old people with bleeding hemorrhoids and bad hearts. That, plus my golf game sucks. Otherwise, I'm okay."

He tried to make it sound as if he were joking, but she knew that tone; something was irritating him and he was in the mood for a fight. She regretted calling.

"There's been quite a political development up here," she said.

"What?"

"Ah, you know Harry Johnson died, of course?"

He grunted. "That damned old fraud. None too soon, from my point of view. He was always trying to nail my ass. The other judges must be fighting like cats over a fish, trying to get the executive appointment, right?"

"Yes. Nothing's been decided yet. Judge Quinlan is acting executive judge."

"Tim's not too bad. A toothless tiger," her father said.

"The governor just filled Johnson's vacancy on the bench."

Another grunt. "You can bet it was a black or a woman,

probably a black woman. He doesn't have any balls, but he knows who votes. Who did he pick?"

She took a deep breath. "Me."

He laughed. "Oh sure! He'd love to do that. He knows you can beat him in the next election. He'd do cartwheels if that were true."

"It is true," she said evenly.

"Kathleen, I hope to Christ you're kidding?"

"No, I'm not. The prosecutor's job has been too demanding. I haven't had any time for Little Mike. He hardly sees me. So I—"

"Listen to me." The words came out in a snarl. "I stepped aside so you could become prosecuting attorney. I gave up that for you! I owned that office. It was mine. You have no right to give it away!" The snarl had risen to an angry shout.

"The only one I owe anything to is my son."

"Like hell! You owe me, and you owe the staff I built, the staff who supported your election. I can't believe this."

Kathleen was frightened. It was a learned response, but she refused to give in to it. "You had better believe it, Dad. It's in all the newspapers. I wanted you to hear it from me first."

"Oh, isn't that sweet, isn't that touching? You goddamned little bitch"—his voice was now low and raspy—"you could have been governor, even senator. Have you lost your fucking mind?" He seldom used coarse language when he talked to her; it was one measure of just how angry he had become.

"What good would that do me, if Little Mike—?"

"Fuck that kid! Don't hide behind him. He'd do okay no matter what you did. You're just a lazy, ungrateful—"

"I'm going to hang up if you continue." Her heart was beating rapidly, and she tried to keep the terror out of her voice.

He didn't reply immediately. When he did speak, his tone was unemotional but stern. "You haven't been sworn in, have you?"

"No. But the announcement's been made."

"Announcements are just pieces of paper. Everybody has the right to change his mind. We can think of something."

"But I'm not changing my mind."

"Kathleen"—now the tone was commanding—"you've been under a lot of stress, obviously. I'll drive up there. Regina and I will be there in two days. You go home and don't talk to anyone. I'll handle everything as soon as I get there."

"Dad, I am accepting the judgeship."

Again he paused before speaking. "Look, you owe me a great deal. I raised you, I put you through the best schools. I even gave you my job, the only thing in the world I really loved, so you could use it as a stepping-stone to greater things. You owe me."

"Dad, I—"

"I'm not asking much." He snapped the words. "All you have to do is sit tight until I get there. No interviews, nothing, until you talk to me."

"I—"

"You're making the greatest mistake of your life, throwing your future away. I'm not going to let you do that. I'll be there in two days. And I'm not asking anymore, Kathleen, I'm telling."

He slammed down the receiver. She heard the soft click as Regina also hung up.

Kathleen realized she was trembling. It was so foolish; she was a grown woman, and yet she was still so afraid of him. She tried to force herself to remain calm, keeping her eyes averted from the now threatening image of her father's picture.

CHAPTER 9

NELSON BRAGG CAREFULLY followed all the requirements set up in his order of probation. He actively looked for work. He reported monthly to his probation officer, and he attended the mental-health clinic every Wednesday, going to group-therapy sessions, and faithfully accepting the medicine given him.

Bragg wasn't a criminal in the usual sense. The ever-present voices, audible only to him, had ordered him to disrupt the pro-abortion rally. In the resulting shoving, shouting melee, Bragg grabbed a hand-held sign away from a large noisy woman and hit her with it. Her dignity was the only casualty. Originally, he had been charged with a felony. But an overburdened criminal justice system had no meaningful way of dealing with people like Nelson Bragg. There was just no time to deal effectively with minor mental cases. Bragg pled guilty to a misdemeanor, subjecting himself to supervision and agreeing to seek work.

No one hired Nelson Bragg. He was obviously mentally ill; his gaunt face, slow speech, and staring eyes sounded alarms in all prospective employers. They took his application politely, expressed hope that something would soon open up, then quickly ushered him out.

The probation officer assigned Bragg was swamped with work. He had only a few brief moments each month to spare him. A quick review of Bragg's file, a few questions about employment and continued mental treatment, then Bragg was moved along to make room for the next man, the next file.

Social Services provided rent, a small amount of cash, and food stamps. Bragg had a room in a dingy neighborhood. It was above a boarded-up store, and he shared a bathroom with three other men who also had rooms. Like himself, the other roomers were regulars at the nearby mental-health clinic.

. Although Bragg accepted the medicine from the clinic, he never consumed it, carefully keeping the bottles in neat rows in a small chest near his cot. The medicine made him drowsy, interfering with his mental processes, making even reading the newspaper a chore.

Without the medicine Bragg once again heard the voices, but that didn't bother him—they had become like old friends.

He had saved up his money, often eating just one bowl of oatmeal a day, until he had sufficient funds to buy a gun. Stolen guns were plentiful and cheap. He kept his carefully hidden. Possession of a firearm was a violation of his probation. The small .22-caliber revolver was old, but it still worked. Just owning it made him feel strangely secure.

Nelson Bragg read about the appointment of the woman prosecutor to the bench. He recalled her name, recognizing it as the same name printed on the court forms showing he had been charged with a crime. He studied her picture. In his opinion she was just a whore, but then most women were. The story and picture produced an undefined anger in him. His voices became strident and he felt uncomfortable.

Women, they ruined everything. He threw the newspaper into a corner, then went for a long walk until he grew calmer. When he returned, he clipped the picture and the story, neatly tucking them away in the drawer that held his unused medicine.

CHAPTER 10

REGINA CAREFULLY HID her anger from her husband. She hated long drives. It would have made more sense to fly, since he was in such a big hurry. But no, Big Mike had to be behind the wheel of his beloved old Cadillac, the last truly big model made by General Motors. He loved the luxury, the room, the power, so he kept the car in top condition. And he enjoyed driving it, especially on long trips. Although from the taut expression on his face, he didn't seem to be enjoying this trip at all.

They had come up to Tampa and picked up the interstate highway from there. Now he was roaring along at over ninety miles an hour, passing trucks and cars as if they were standing still, confident that his radar detector would warn him of any unseen police attention.

Regina's head was pounding. After the telephone call from his daughter he had been like a madman, screaming and cursing. Frightened, she had drunk her way into a foggy state, and now, as the alcohol wore off, she was suffering and desperately needed a drink. She asked him to stop at a bar or restaurant, but he said they had to keep going. She had packed a bottle of brandy in her bag, but it was in the Cadillac's trunk, and he would have disapproved of her drinking even if she could have gotten the bottle.

She tactfully tried to find out what he planned to do, but he was grimly uncommunicative, his nostrils wide in supressed anger, a blood vessel dilating his right temple. Regina decided she would wait for a better time to make any more inquiries. His daughter, Kathleen, had accepted a judgeship, and that had caused him to become almost insane. She remembered that much, but she couldn't really remember why.

They stopped for dinner outside of Atlanta. He was still in a hurry, eating fast and irritated by the slow service, but she managed to get down three double vodkas before they got back on the road.

Regina was dozing off when the car became erratic, swinging wildly as it zigzagged on and off the shoulder. She looked over at her husband.

His eyes were wide, his face contorted. He was twisting frantically in the seat, his right arm dangling uselessly. He was steering with his left hand and managed to hit the brake with his left foot. The big car slowed as he brought it under control, steering it with difficulty onto the shoulder. He stopped, reached awkwardly across the steering column and with his left hand put the automatic shift into neutral.

"Hop ma! Hop ma!" His face became even more contorted. She couldn't understand what he was saying at first. Then she realized he was trying to say "Help me."

"Jesus, Mike, what can I do!"

Again he spoke a kind of gibberish, his eyes fearful. It was the first time she had ever seen him afraid, and that unnerved her more than anything else.

Spittle flew from his mouth as he tried to talk. She finally understood that he wanted her to drive, and she thought he said the word "hospital."

Regina was terrified. She lifted her armrest and tried to pull his heavy body to her side of the car. He struggled to help her, but was unable to move effectively. She got out, ran to the driver's side, and heaved against him, rolling him so that his knees were on the car's floor, but clear of the pedals, and his head was resting on the passenger side of the front seat.

She had never liked driving the Cadillac; it was such an unwieldy monster to her. She shifted into gear and headed the car back on the highway. An enormous truck sounded a frightening horn blast as it shot around her. She started to cry.

Big Mike was trying to talk, but she couldn't understand a word. She pulled off at the next exit and a man at a gas station gave her directions to a hospital. She thought she was lost and was about to turn back on the paved country road when she saw the sign. . . .

It was a small one-story hospital with several brick wings. Signs pointed the way to the emergency room.

She rushed through the sliding glass doors, tears streaming down her face. "My husband," she gasped to a startled nurse. "My husband is . . ." She couldn't think of the right words, so she pointed out at the car.

The nurse, a husky young woman, walked purposefully to the car, took one look at Big Mike, who was still trying to talk, then ran back into the hospital, passing by Regina and disappearing through a door.

Regina wondered if she might be experiencing some kind of alcoholic hallucination. It had happened once before, years ago. To her great relief, the nurse reappeared, still running, this time followed by a doctor and a stocky young orderly.

Through the glass doors Regina could see they were having difficulty getting Big Mike onto a rolling stretcher. Soon they were rushing by Regina again, rolling Big Mike through two large metal doors which closed behind them.

Regina sat down on a metal folding chair near the sliding glass doors. She sat quietly for a moment, then remembered the car. Both car doors were still open, and the motor was running. She went out to the car and turned off the engine. No one had returned to the reception area. Regina flipped the inner trunk release, got out, and quickly located the bottle of brandy. She unscrewed the cap and took a big gulp.

The area was a pleasant one. The hospital was set in a glen, with a spacious, well-lit parking lot. An early-evening breeze stirred the trees. The brandy made her feel better. She laid the bottle on top of the luggage and closed the trunk.

She returned to her seat in the reception area. Everything was tile and metal, designed for efficiency and not for looks. The acid smell of disinfectant seemed particularly strong. A chill went through her.

She was about to make another trip to the Cadillac's trunk

when the white-coated doctor came through the metal doors. He was tall, thin, young, and very serious.

"I'm Dr. Grapentine," he said. "Are you his daughter?"

She was flattered, although Big Mike actually was old enough to be her father. "I'm his wife," she said. "What's happened?"

"He's had a stroke. In fact, two of them. The first is the one that brought him here. It didn't look too bad. However, just as we were hooking him up to the machines, he had a second one, apparently worse. We won't know the extent until we run tests."

"Is he going to . . . ?"

"I'd like to reassure you," he replied quietly, "but I can't. Some people snap right back, some are crippled, some die. We can't predict, at least not this soon. He's listed as critical, and we will transfer him into our intensive-care unit as soon as we feel he's stabilized."

Regina felt as though it were all a bad dream—nothing seemed real.

"My nurse will get all the necessary information—health background, insurance, that sort of thing."

"We're from Florida. We were heading north when this happened. How long do you think he'll be here?"

The doctor's eyebrows raised slightly. He wondered if the woman fully understood him. It was always difficult. "If he makes it, he won't be in any condition to be transferred to another hospital for days, perhaps even weeks."

"If he makes it?"

He never knew exactly what to say, especially with strangers. "It's quite serious, as I said. Do you have any relatives around here?"

"No."

"Well, there are several excellent motels in town. You might wish to make arrangements to stay there, at least for a few days until we see how this will turn out."

She nodded. "May I see him?"

He shrugged. "All right, come with me." He held open the metal doors and she stepped into a long white room filled with empty carts and glittering medical apparatus. He led the way to a bed at the rear.

Big Mike lay still. Tubes ran into both arms, carrying liquid from plastic bags hung on metal stands. Part of his face was obscured by piping from a wheezing machine. Monitors resembling small televisions had various little squiggly lines endlessly passing over their screens.

He looked like someone she had never seen before. She found the sight repelling.

"He looks dead," she whispered.

"He's not," the doctor said. "He's holding on."

She stepped back and averted her eyes. The doctor nodded to the young nurse who stood nearby.

"C'mon, honey," the girl said, her voice thick with a soft Southern accent, "you come with me, and we'll get you all settled down nice and comfy."

Regina allowed the nurse to lead her back through the metal doors. She felt a bitter, rising anger at Big Mike. It was just like him, she thought, to leave her all alone, surrounded by a bunch of ignorant hillbillies. It was so typical, she fumed silently, never thinking of anyone but himself.

The nurse took down the information, taking the medical-insurance card and making a copy for the hospital records. Regina's sense of abandonment grew and she began to cry softly.

"Does your husband have any other family?" the nurse asked.

Regina nodded. "A grown daughter."

The nurse pursed her lips, trying to find an easy way of saying what was so obviously necessary. "Perhaps you better give her a call? You know, let her know what's happened to her daddy?"

Regina shook her head. Big Mike was her husband, it was none of Kathleen Talbot's damn business. Besides, Regina didn't like talking to her icy stepdaughter. "I wouldn't know what to say," she replied to the nurse.

"Would you like me to call her?"

Regina forced a smile. "If it's not too much trouble." She took out her small address book. "This is her home number."

"I'll take care of it."

"Is it all right if I go sit in our car for a while? I think I'd like to be alone for a bit."

The nurse smiled. "Of course, honey. You do whatever makes you feel comfortable."

Regina walked slowly to the car, again opening the trunk. She took the bottle back with her into the front seat.

He looked dead, she thought. She wondered what she would get if he did die. Big Mike, a clever, vengeful man, was just the kind who would try to keep her from living comfortably. She feared him and had often wished him dead, but now she was afraid of being left alone. Her fear of the unknown was even greater than her fear of Big Mike.

--◄ ►--

Kathleen flew into the small airport aboard the propeller-driven plane belonging to the rural feeder airline. The rental car was waiting. This was her third trip since her father's stroke.

The people at the motel greeted her as though she were family. She had stayed with them for a week the first time, immediately after her father's stroke. Then, after Regina drank herself into alcoholic collapse, Kathleen had come down again, this time staying only a few days to arrange for Regina's stay in the alcoholic rehabilitation unit at the hospital and to get an order as temporary guardian of both her comatose father and Regina, who was violently opposing hospitalization.

They even gave her the same room. The walls were painted cinder block and the ceiling tiles were stained, but the bed was comfortable and it was clean. Kathleen planned to drive to the hospital after she washed up. She tried not to think about what she had to do.

She called Marie to let her know she had arrived safely. Marie was in a far better temper now that her employer would be spending more time with her son.

The swearing-in ceremony was set for Thursday in the city council's auditorium. It was attracting far more attention than she had expected. She knew it was partly because of her father and the power and influence he once commanded. She was convinced the fact that Big Mike's daughter was being sworn in as a judge was what was causing most of the attention.

It was best to get everything over as quickly as possible, Kathleen thought as she drove to the hospital.

Dr. Grapentine was waiting for her. He escorted her to Big Mike's room. He had been removed from intensive care and placed in a small room near the entrance to the hospital. The machines and monitors caused an eerie humming sound.

"Brain death occurred four days ago," the doctor said quietly. "We believe he suffered a third cerebral vascular accident. Whatever the cause, the machines are breathing for him and feeding him."

Kathleen nodded. "I appreciate the time you've spent talking to me on the phone. You've explained all this very well." She paused, looking down at her father. "It makes this easier."

His face was solemn. "Not much easier, I'll wager."

She tried to smile. "No. I hope you'll be patient with me. Again, what would happen if we just left him like he is?"

The doctor leaned against the bed. "Oh, nothing would improve, he's far beyond that. I suppose the machines could keep him going for a few months, maybe more, maybe less. But it would be the machines only, I'm afraid." He looked down at the figure on the bed. "Medical technology has made rather a mess of things for the survivors in cases like this. One day, I hope, we'll catch up with the marvels of engineering. But, as of the moment, we don't really prolong life, we merely give the appearance of it."

"Do you have many cases like this?"

He shrugged. "Some. Each is different, of course. Sometimes I think the worst ones are those who aren't brain dead but who will never have a chance, no matter what. Eventually, infection or something of the sort finishes the job, but until then the patient and the family are in a kind of hellish limbo."

She looked down at her father. He looked so small, so helpless, not at all like the muscular, quick-tempered man he had once been. He was so thin, so white.

"What has to be done?"

The doctor stroked his chin. "We need a signed release."

She opened her purse. "You might want to put these in your file. They show I have the authority to sign. They are court orders making me guardian of both my father and his wife."

He nodded. "She's doing well, by the way. Physically she's in good shape. Still addicted, although we hope she may gain a bit of insight before we release her from the program."

"Does she know I'm here?" Kathleen asked.

He shook his head. "No. I thought it better to let you make that decision."

"Where's the form?"

The doctor held out the clipboard. The legal release was on top. Kathleen took a few minutes to read it. It was simple, well drawn, but she was having a hard time reading. Despite all her resolve, her eyes filled with tears. She signed and dated it, then handed the clipboard back to the doctor.

"Would you like a moment alone?"

She shook her head. She gently stroked Big Mike's large hand, then bent over and kissed her father's forehead. He seemed warm. She had not expected that.

"What now?"

The doctor took her by the arm and led her out of the room. "There's a small lounge down at the end of the hall. Perhaps if you waited there."

"I'll just stand here in the hall."

"Will you be all right?"

She nodded.

He hesitated, then went back into her father's room. She fought against an impulse to run after him, to tell him to stop. She felt faint and leaned against the wall.

A doctor was being paged by an impersonal voice over a muted loudspeaker. A young nurse's aide walked down the hall delivering flowers. She smiled at Kathleen as she passed. Everything seemed so alive, so normal.

She began to tremble. It was taking so long.

Finally Dr. Grapentine came out of the room. He forced a smile, then put an arm around her. "It's all over," he said gently.

"Oh my God." The words came out as a soft moan.

The doctor squeezed her tightly. "It was all over last week. That's when he died. You have to remember that, Mrs. Talbot. I just shut off the machines—I didn't do anything else. He was already dead."

Tears came involuntarily. She put her hands over her face.

"Anything I can do?" he asked quietly.

She shook her head. "No, thank you. I suppose I should tell Regina."

He patted her shoulder as he released his grip. "Oh, I don't know. I don't think you're quite up to it. I'll tell her if you like."

"No. She is . . . was . . . his wife. The funeral will be at home in three days. Can she be released to come?"

He nodded. "Sure. I suppose we can send someone along with her."

"I'll pay for it."

"Well, we'll work it out. Don't you worry. Your dad was a big shot back home, wasn't he?"

"Yes. He was very well-known. He was the prosecuting attorney."

"The job you have now?"

"Until the day after the funeral. That's the day I'm being sworn in as judge."

He seemed lost in thought for a moment. "Are you sure you're not biting off a bit too much? I mean, everything will be happening at once. This rather shaking experience, the funeral, the new job. Don't you think you should take some time off? You've just had some of the most stressful things that can happen to a person all coming at you within a week." He smiled, but his eyes were serious. "We all have a cracking point, Mrs. Talbot, no matter how tough we might think we are."

She wiped away the last trace of tears. "Thanks for your concern, but I can handle it. Taking the new job is really the start of a new life for me, in a way. A lot of stress is being eliminated." She took his hand for a moment. "I can't tell you how much I've appreciated your kindness these past weeks."

He shrugged. "It's my job. Are you sure you feel up to seeing your stepmother?"

"Might as well get it all over at once. Will Regina be able to take the shock?"

He nodded. "Physically, sure. If we had a bar here, she'd sure have one hell of an excuse to tie one on. If it gets too bad, we can sedate her to help get her over the hard part."

He guided Kathleen toward another wing of the hospital. Her arrival was greeted with mild curiosity. The patients here were all in regular street dress. The doctor led the way to a small lounge. Regina was sitting at a table playing solitaire.

"Hello, Regina."

Regina turned, at first confused. When she recognized Kathleen, she forced an obviously phony smile. "Kathleen, what a pleasant surprise. I didn't know you were coming." She frowned at the doctor. "No one told me."

"Don't get up, Regina." Kathleen had thought she knew what to say. Now she suddenly wasn't so confident. "I have bad news. Dad is dead."

Regina registered real surprise. Her face jerked for a moment. "Oh, my dear God." Tears formed, then rolled down her cheeks. "Oh, I just knew something bad was going to happen."

Kathleen awkwardly rubbed Regina's back as she cried. "It was for the best," she said, her words sounding somehow trite and insincere. "We wouldn't have wanted him to continue to suffer."

Regina nodded as she sobbed. The other patients in the lounge tactfully left. Regina looked up. "When did it happen?"

"Just a while ago," Kathleen said.

"He had another stroke a few days ago," the doctor said. "There was no saving him, I'm afraid."

Regina looked from Kathleen to the doctor and then back. "A little while ago?" she asked.

Kathleen nodded.

"Then how did you manage to make the trip down here so fast? It takes hours." She paused, her eyes widening. "Unless . . ."

"Your husband suffered brain death a few days ago. There was no point in telling you at that time," the doctor said in his professional voice.

"Did you have them turn off the machines?" Regina's question came out as a hissing accusation.

The doctor spoke quickly. "There was no hope—"

"I asked you," she spoke sharply to Kathleen as she stood up, "did you have them turn off the machines?"

"He was dead, Regina. There was no point—"

"Bitch!" Regina hit her, smashing an open hand across the side of Kathleen's face. The doctor quickly restrained her. Regina's eyes became narrow slits. "You goddamned murdering bitch!" she screamed. "You killed Big Mike! You killed your own father!"

"Regina, he was already dead."

An orderly came quickly into the room and helped the doctor restrain Regina. Although she was small, she was thrashing about with surprising strength. "Murderer! That's all you are."

"I think you had better leave, Mrs. Talbot," the doctor said, trying to keep his voice calm.

Kathleen nodded and walked from the lounge. But Regina's shrill voice echoed down the hospital corridor. "Some judge you're gonna be," she screamed. "You're a killer, you don't know the meaning of justice. One day they'll get you, you bitch, one day somebody will judge you!"

Regina's scream sounded more like a wailing dirge, a howling curse. Her words had a haunting resonance all their own, and they followed Kathleen as she made her way past the staring patients.

Kathleen kept her composure until she got into the rented car. Her hands were shaking as she worked the unfamiliar gearshift.

Everything was done. Big Mike's funeral would be held, a suitable sendoff to a dead chieftain. Then she would take the robe. Everything was done.

In planning, it had all seemed so right, so intellectually and morally correct. But Regina's hurt and angry scream of murder echoed endlessly in her mind. Kathleen had expected grief, but not so much; nor had she expected to feel the wrenching agony of guilt.

Tears streamed down her face as she drove away from the hospital's parking lot.

CHAPTER 11

JEREMIAH MITCHELL GOT to the ceremony late. The executive judge's courtroom was packed. He managed to find a place to stand just inside the door.

"Hey, Jerry, how are you?" George Stendall, a short, rotund criminal lawyer grinned up at him.

"I'm good, George. Have I missed much?"

Stendall shook his head. "Naw, just the usual bullshit. The governor just finished speaking. He looks as happy as if he'd just laid her."

Mitchell looked up at the bench. Governor Leonard, whose expression usually resembled that of a bloodhound, was beaming.

"He's going to swear her in now," Stendall said.

Kathleen Talbot was a beauty, there was no denying that. As she raised her hand and repeated the short oath given by the governor, her face shone. Then two officials of the police union presented her with a black robe and helped her put it on. The crowd applauded and she smiled in response.

When she began her acceptance speech, Mitchell turned to leave. "I'll see you, George," he whispered.

"Not going to stick around for the reception?"

Mitchell shook his head. "No. Pete Norbanski can represent me. Take it easy."

Mitchell, as usual, took the back booth in Columbo's. The restaurant was far enough from the courts to ensure that his lunch would not be spoiled by unwanted intrusions of court personnel with their never-ending gossip about judges, cops, and lawyers. When he had the chance, he liked to eat in peace. Columbo's catered to the financial-district trade, people who had no interest whatsoever in the city's number-one criminal defense lawyer. The anonymity, plus an excellent steak sandwich, made Columbo's his favorite midday oasis.

He had just finished eating when Pete Norbanski walked in. Mitchell watched, amused, as Norbanski swaggered through the tables of conservatively dressed men and women. Norbanski was known as Polish Pete by the criminal-court crowd. He wore an iridescent green suit of a shiny material that picked up light like a metal reflector. His silk shirt was deep green, fixed at the collar with a large gold clasp that shoved the knot of his white silk tie up almost into his jutting chin. Norbanski, only twenty-six, was thin and short but he walked with the arrogance of a giant. Fresh out of city law school, he had been working for Mitchell six months now. Mitchell had recognized the potential in the inexperienced young man, potential that was quick to bloom in the hectic pace of the criminal court. Norbanski was making great progress, but despite everything, Mitchell had been unsuccessful in changing Polish Pete's taste in clothes.

Mitchell nodded to his young assistant as he slid into the booth. "How did it go, Pete? I stopped by and saw her honor sworn in, but I ducked out before it was over."

Norbanski's thin face projected a foxlike quality when he smiled. "Hey, terminal fuckin' boredom, that's how it went. You didn't miss a thing."

"They're all pretty much the same."

"That broad must have ice water for blood. Her old man isn't in his grave a day and she's making an acceptance speech like nothing ever happened. Did you hear it?"

"No."

"She's a good speaker, but it was the usual drivel about the importance of the courts, justice, and the American way." Norbanski ordered a double vodka, then looked at Mitchell.

"Hey, don't worry, I'm not drinking on duty. They closed all the courts today in honor of her majesty being sworn in. Yesterday they closed 'em because her old man was getting planted. If this keeps up, we may all be out of business."

"Did you see my old partner?"

Norbanski snorted. "You were lucky you missed him. Jesus, Sawchek goddamn near took over the ceremony. I said hello, but he was so busy campaigning for executive judge he had no time for me. He did send along his regards to you, though. Also, he asked if you might be able to help him line up some votes."

Mitchell laughed. "No one ever said Ted Sawchek doesn't have balls. He tried to screw my wife when I was married, stole me blind, and damn near ruined my practice. If he got in as executive judge, he'd run an auction or a raffle for every case. Harry Johnson was onto him—that's the only reason Sawchek's stayed honest. Now, with Harry gone, my old pal Ted is probably preparing a price list to be posted in his courtroom."

"Every one of those judges was trying to line up votes. From start to finish, it looked more like a political convention than a swearing-in ceremony. But it got done, and we now have Kathleen the Ice Queen as our newest judicial officer." Norbanski accepted the drink from the waitress and sipped with obvious pleasure. "She had her kid there, did you see him?"

"No. I was in the back."

"Cute little guy. I wonder if she got him through artificial insemination. She doesn't look the type that would lower herself to employ the usual method."

"I knew her husband slightly," Mitchell said. "Good-looking guy, and he knew it. He was with one of those blue-chip firms. Got killed flying a small plane."

"I heard she's still pining away."

Mitchell shrugged. "Who knows? Death has a funny way of affecting survivors. I heard that he was a skirt-chaser. Maybe she loved him, maybe not."

"What about her old man? She didn't look all broken up about burying him just yesterday." He took another sip of his drink.

"She looked shaken at the funeral."

Norbanski shook his head. "Not to me. She's a cool one."

Mitchell signaled for a refill of his coffee. "I talked with Harold Malked this morning at the jail."

"The guy that shot his retarded kid?"

Mitchell nodded. "The public defender is getting a little shaky about trying the case. It's going to be a front-page tearjerker. They're worried that bad publicity might hurt their funding. There's strong feeling on both sides about mercy killing. They're afraid pressure groups might go after their source of public money, no matter which way it goes."

Norbanski ordered a sandwich, then turned to Mitchell. "So?"

"They want me to take the case."

"There's no money in it," Norbanski said. "The guy's just an unemployed waiter. He probably doesn't have a nickel."

"He doesn't."

"Then why take it, Jerry?" Norbanski had started calling his employer by his first name about five minutes after being hired. "I thought you said we don't do that *pro bono* crap?"

"I would if I had the time, but I don't. I leave that up to the young men in the big firms."

"So they'll have to get someone else for Malked then?"

"No."

"You said . . ."

Mitchell chuckled. "This isn't for the public good, Pete. It's for mine—and yours too."

"Me?"

"The Malked case will be front-page news for weeks. We'll do the usual thing—the sanity hearings, the motions for dismissal. It's a hot case, the newspapers will love it. You couldn't buy that kind of publicity, even if you could afford it."

"It might be good for you, maybe, but I'm just your errand boy, Jerry. I run around and adjourn things, make the two-bit motion now and then. How's this going to be any good for me?"

"I'm going to try the Chesney case, right?"

"That's an important case, and that's for money. So?"

Mitchell sipped his fresh coffee. "Both cases will probably

come up for trial about the same time. I'll work something out with the new executive judge, whoever he may be. I believe I'll be able to try each, one after the other. But in the meantime, you'll have to cover for me on some of the Malked casework."

Norbanski seemed to lose some of his usual assurance. "Like you say, it's front-page. I'm pretty new to this business, Jerry. Maybe you should bring in someone a little more experienced."

"You won't have to try it. All you'll have to do is make a motion or two. Anyway, it may never come to trial."

"You think they'll go for a plea? Jesus, not with all those right-to-life people looking over the prosecutor's shoulder, they won't."

Mitchell nodded. "You're absolutely right, but Harold Malked, poor devil, is sick, really sick. He has cancer. They have him in the infirmary over at the jail. He shot his daughter, all right, but only because she was retarded and he's a widower. He didn't know who would care for her and he couldn't bear putting her in an institution. Well, he may not even live until the trial."

Norbanski shook his head. "It sounds awful risky to me, and you know I usually like to play fast and loose, Jerry. Suppose you can't work something out? Suppose both trials come on at the same time? Then what?"

Mitchell's smile broadened. "Then, Pete, you're going to become famous, or infamous. You'll have to try the Malked case."

Norbanski said nothing, but his eyes widened in unaccustomed anxiety.

"Don't worry, Pete. Everything will work out. We all have to balance several balls in the air at the same time. It's part of practicing criminal law. It's what makes our business so exciting, or a pain in the ass, depending on your viewpoint."

Norbanski ordered another vodka.

"Relax, I'll walk you through everything." Mitchell sat back. "By the way, Pete, did you pick up any word over at the ceremony as to who might have the inside track for the executive judge job?"

"Rumors, apparently nothing more," Norbanski replied. "All the judges are in heat to get it, even the criminal-division judges. Old tight-ass Broadbent looks like he might have the best chance, but nothing is settled."

"And the newest member of the bench, any indication as to what she'll be doing?"

Norbanski laughed. "Yeah. I heard that Quinlan, as acting executive judge, has assigned her to the criminal division."

"Makes sense. She was the prosecutor—not for long maybe, only three years—but she should know criminal law pretty well."

"Jerry, you know how it is with the courts, the goddamn place has more going on than an Istanbul café, more rumors, more deals, more everything. I hear she is royally pissed."

"Oh?"

"Yeah, they say Talbot didn't want to go into the criminal division. And to top things off, Quinlan has assigned her to the misdemeanor court to start, just like she was brand-ass new."

"She is," Mitchell said.

"Sure, as a judge. But, like you say, she was the prosecuting attorney, and to put her to listening to the morning lineup of drunks and bums is pretty insulting. At least to her. Anyway, that's the word."

Mitchell nodded. "Well, it looks like I'll be one of the first to test out Judge Kathleen Talbot. I have a misdemeanor case up tomorrow morning. It was scheduled for today, but the court was closed."

Norbanski looked hurt. "I thought you hired me to do that minor shit."

Mitchell laughed. "That, and to train you to become a master lawyer. However, in this case, although the charge is only a misdemeanor, our client has a great deal at stake."

"Oh?"

"He's an engineer, and a highly paid one. Comes from Hungary, and is a naturalized citizen. He's charged with exposing himself to a waitress in an all-night hamburger joint. He's been convicted of indecent exposure once before. If he's convicted again, that's two crimes of moral turpitude, and he could lose his citizenship. Then it would be back to Hungary, and a very chancy future."

"Damn. That should be one hell of a fee."

"It is," Mitchell replied. "And, given his record, it's going to be one hell of a problem too. Anyway, it will come before the Honorable Kathleen M. Talbot tomorrow. We'll see just what kind of a judge she is."

"Don't look for mercy," Norbanski said. "She looks cold as ice."

"My ex-wife looked cold as ice," Mitchell replied. "So I've had experience."

"Was she?"

"What?" Mitchell asked as he signaled for the check.

"Your ex-wife, was she as cold as ice?"

Jerry Mitchell half-grinned. "Ice could never get that cold. That's why I'll never marry again, Pete. I'm like one of those guys in the old horror movies, I've been frozen clean through." Mitchell eased his long body from the confines of the booth. "Go easy on the vodka, we still have work to do today. I'll see you back at the office."

Arnie Nelson called a meeting of all division chiefs. Marty Kelly, despite the awareness of beginning tremors, put off lunch until after the conference. Nelson was the acting prosecuting attorney, and temporarily the boss. Kelly no longer had the protection of Big Mike or his daughter. He was worried, and he desperately needed a drink.

Tina Welch smiled at him as he walked with the others into the prosecutor's office. He managed to smile back.

Arnie Nelson sat on the edge of the large desk that had belonged to Kathleen Talbot. Even Marty Kelly had to admit he looked impressive. A cross between a movie star and an evangelist, Nelson would inspire confidence in anyone who didn't know him. But to men like Kelly, and the others, they knew he was extremely limited, despite appearances. Nelson had already announced that he was a candidate for the job, and was openly campaigning for the position. No one would have taken him seriously, except that the judges who were going to make the appointment were all jockeying themselves, and the prosecutor job could well become a bargaining chip in the frantic trading going on. It was conceivable that Arnie Nelson might end up the one to be picked.

Big Mike had set up divisions within the office, with chiefs of appellate, homicide, traffic, felony, and misdemeanor, all with well-defined responsibilities, all accountable to the prosecutor. During her three years as prosecutor, Kathleen Talbot had kept the office exactly as her father had organized it.

"Gentlemen, I want each of you to know that I will be making no changes as far as chiefs of divisions are concerned," Arnie said, "so no one need worry about his job."

Marty Kelly settled into his chair, slightly less apprehensive than when he entered.

"However," Nelson continued, "I will be making some changes in how this office is managed. I fully realize I'm just interim head, but these are changes I think long overdue."

Marty Kelly's anxiety returned in full force. He listened carefully as Nelson outlined meaningless and make-work proposals. The changes he wanted were all cosmetic, and none of them concerned the homicide division.

Nelson finished with a boring speech about the sanctity and importance of good law enforcement, then thanked them for their cooperation. Everyone was glad to be excused.

"Oh, Martin, can you spare a moment?" Arnie Nelson called just as Marty was about to make his escape.

"Yeah," he replied, turning.

Arnie Nelson wrapped one large arm around Martin's shoulders and beamed down at him. "Martin, we are in a bit of a bind on the Chesney matter."

"Oh?"

"I've been rather vigorously criticized for signing a murder warrant charging that officer," he said. "Of course, it's clearly first-degree murder, but that doesn't silence the critics. Obviously, it's a case that must be won."

"Felker is assigned to try it. He always does a good job."

Nelson sighed. "They tell me the entire state law as to the definition of death will be established in the Chesney case. That's important, Martin. We must make sure the office looks good."

We must make sure *you* look good, Martin thought, but said nothing.

"Anyway, young Felker is excellent, but I think this calls for a more experienced hand."

"Who?"

Arnie Nelson flashed his famous broad smile. "You, Martin. You're the most experienced trial man we have. You're head of homicide and have been for years. No one can say we didn't give it our best shot if you try the case."

"I haven't tried a case in years, Arnie."

Nelson chuckled. "Come now, Martin, it's like riding a bicycle, it's something you never forget. You'll do splendidly."

Marty Kelly's heart was beating at an enormous rate. His very existence was suddenly at risk. "I haven't been too well lately, Arnie."

"Nonsense. You look in the peak." He squeezed Marty's shoulders. "Do this as a personal favor to me, Martin. I need this office to look good, very good." He released Kelly and winked. "I'm sure you know I'm trying for the job on a permanent basis. This is important to me, Martin, very important."

Kelly always knew Arnie Nelson wasn't smart, but he was stunned that Nelson was so thick that he didn't know about Kelly's problem, the worst-kept secret in town.

But before he could find the words to protest, Kelly found himself outside the office with the door shut behind him.

"Anything wrong, Marty?" Tina Welch asked.

Marty slowly shook his head. "That man doesn't have a brain in his head."

Tina laughed quietly. "But for the moment he's our boss."

"He wants me to try that cop that turned off the machines."

Tina's eyes widened in shock. "But . . ."

Kelly nodded. "That's right, Tina. It's the same as a death sentence for me."

"I can talk to him, Marty, let him know . . ."

"That I'm a drunk? He's too wound up in himself to even consider anything but firing me. No, don't say a word."

"What will you do?"

Kelly laughed. "I know I can't stop drinking. I've tried often enough. I'll just have to think of something else. I have a while to go before I qualify for retirement, Tina, so I'll think of something."

"Good luck, Marty," she said quietly.

"I'll need it," he replied as he walked out of her office.

"Well," he said softly to himself as he walked down the empty corridor, "at least today I have a real excuse for getting plastered."

CHAPTER 12

SUMMER HAD ARRIVED, if not by calendar, then certainly by thermometer on a day that saw it shoot up to almost ninety, although the warm air was beginning to cool as evening approached.

The day had been a jumble of impressions for Kathleen, a collage of many faces and speeches. Beginning with the wake for her father, his funeral, her own robing ceremony and reception, the whole week had created a peculiar dreamlike feeling, not quite a nightmare, but close.

Kathleen was surprised she wasn't exhausted. If anything, she felt an almost manic energy. Little Mike had patiently endured the boredom of watching his mother take the judicial robe, conducting himself with almost adult reserve.

Partly as a reward, but also to have some time alone with her son, Kathleen took him for a walk in the park, something she knew he loved. They stopped for a cone, and his shirtfront was soon covered with chocolate and his little hands sticky, but he looked happily contented.

She led him to a vacant bench. Some older boys were playing a noisy scrub game of soccer. The sun was beginning to set. Soon Kathleen would have to take her son home, because the park could be dangerous at night, but for now it was a pleasant haven.

"Those boys are playing soccer," she said.

"I know."

"Oh?"

He always seemed so much older than just four. "Marie takes me here a lot. We watch them when the weather's nice."

"Would you like to learn to play?"

He shook his head. "No."

"Why?"

"There's a lot of kicking. Sometimes they kick each other."

"But they have fun."

He shrugged. "Getting hurt isn't fun."

Although he was little more than a baby, she couldn't argue with such a sensible answer.

They watched a small bird as it flew to the concrete and began to peck at crumbs. "What happened to Grandpa?" he asked.

She had taken him to the funeral home for a few minutes, but not the funeral. Death was a difficult thing to explain to a child. "He's gone to heaven," she said. "I told you that."

He nodded slowly. "Will he come back?"

He had asked the same question before.

"No. He's with God."

"Is he happy?"

"I think so."

Her son nodded as if she had supplied the definitive answer. The bird flew away. Little Mike jumped down from the bench. "Can we go home now?"

"If you want to."

"I want to play with Alfred."

Alfred was the imaginary playmate, the cause of Marie's major worry. Kathleen had made an appointment with a child psychologist, although she didn't share Marie's depth of concern. Many children had imaginary playmates. Still, Little Mike seemed to be more withdrawn lately, and that worried her.

"Won't Alfred wait?" she asked.

He nodded solemnly. "Yes, but I don't want him to get lonesome."

She stood up and took his sticky little hand. "Okay, let's go."

They walked slowly. Kathleen enjoyed the park's tranquillity. It was the first time in days that she felt relaxed.

"Alfred hates grandfather," her son said quietly.

The statement startled her. "Why?"

"Because he left."

"And why would that bother Alfred?"

"He hates anyone who leaves."

"Michael," she said, looking down at him, "Alfred is a made-up person, he doesn't exist, not really."

His small eyes seemed for a moment to become fearful. "He is real."

"I can't see him."

"He doesn't let you see him," he replied evenly.

"I can't hear him."

"I can," he said. "Sometimes I hear him when he's not there."

Her sense of relaxation was suddenly gone.

The parking attendant smiled at her as she drove into the garage. "Good morning, your honor." He raised the mechanical gate, allowing her to pass. "The judges all park on the first floor, over there at the north end."

"Thank you." Carefully, Kathleen navigated the narrow lane between rows of parked cars. It felt strange, driving herself to work. As prosecuting attorney she had always had a government car and a police chauffeur, one of the perks of that office. But that was in the past, and she wondered what other subtle changes might await her.

As she had kissed Little Mike good-bye after breakfast, she was full of confidence about her new job and duties, but now, as she parked her car, her confidence begin to ebb.

She entered the criminal-court building through a basement door from the parking garage. A policeman stood guard in the hall.

"Good morning, your honor." He grinned. "You can use the last elevator. It's called the judges' elevator, and only you folks can use it. You're assigned to courtroom number five. That's on the third floor."

"Thank you."

"Good luck," he called after her.

Kathleen pushed the button and went up to the third floor.

The elevator was located in a private hall near the courtrooms. She was disoriented for a moment.

"This way, your honor," a middle-aged man said, smiling at her. "I'm Matt Linden. I'll be your clerk today. I'm the clerk assigned to the misdemeanor court." He led the way into the courtroom and pointed. "Those are your chambers."

She entered the sterile office. The furniture was of good quality, but there was no hint of the personality of the previous occupant. Kathleen knew that the courtrooms were allocated on a seniority basis. The courtroom and chambers had belonged to Judge Ted Sawchek, who obviously had moved to a better spot. She took her new robe—a gift given her at the ceremony—out of the garment bag and hung it on the coat rack.

Linden poked his balding head in the door. "It's about average today, your honor," he said. "We have about one hundred and fifteen cases to hear."

At first she thought he was joking; then she realized he was completely serious. She felt a rising sense of panic.

"And Judge Williams is out here. He'd like to see you."

"Send him in."

Jesse Williams had once been on her father's staff. In recognition of his reputation as a gifted trial lawyer, he was eventually given a judicial appointment, one of the first black lawyers to be named to the circuit bench. She remembered him well.

"Good morning, Kathleen." Jesse Williams was tall and gangly, and an expression of mild amusement seemed a permanent fixture on his ebony features. His hair had turned pearl gray, and the reading glasses perched near the tip of his nose gave him a scholarly appearance. He had greeted her at the swearing-in ceremony, but they hadn't had time to talk. He glanced over at the robe. "All ready for work, I see."

"As ready as I'll ever be, Judge Williams."

He chuckled. "You used to call me Mr. Williams when you were little. We're both judges now, and even though I have several decades on you, I'd feel embarrassed if you didn't start calling me Jesse." He sat down on the long leather sofa. "Usually a new judge isn't thrown into the fray without some training. Apparently Judge Quinlan decided that you didn't need any preparation."

"Nothing was said to me about training."

He nodded. "Well, Kathleen, to be frank, some of the judges are a half-century behind society. Some resent women on the bench." He shrugged. "As a black man, I had a few of those problems myself when I was appointed. It's like anything else in life, I suppose—you have to establish yourself. I don't think you'll have much trouble, not in the long run."

"Thank you."

"Ever work in misdemeanor court when you were practicing?"

"No."

He looked a little less amused. "Hmm, I was afraid of that. As prosecuting attorney, the boss, no one would ever expect you to show up for this little stuff." He took off his reading glasses and twirled them slowly. "Would you be offended if I gave you a short course in how to be a judge?"

She sat behind her desk. "I'd be grateful. I don't want to look a fool."

He laughed. "You wouldn't. You might be a bit embarrassed, but nothing more. Kathleen, you are about to sit in judgment on your fellow humans. As prosecutor you probably rarely saw the flesh-and-blood people, just made policy decisions, signed warrant requests, and the like. Even experience as a practicing trial lawyer won't help much. Here, in this job, it's different, and you have to prepare yourself for the shock."

"Shock?"

He nodded. "In a few minutes you'll step out there and look down into the worried face of some poor miserable member of the human race whose future is in your hands alone. You'll listen to testimony from both sides, then you'll decide, in all fairness, that guilt has been established. Then comes the hard part. You'll gaze down into two big pleading eyes staring up at you, and you will realize that you will have to send that person to jail, big tearful eyes or not. He or she could be penned away for months, families will be affected, marriages, dreams, futures of all kinds, but if it's the right thing to do, you will have to do it, despite all that."

"I don't think that will give me any problem."

He arched one eyebrow. "Not in here, it won't, but out there, in the courtroom, it'll be quite a different story. You're human. You'll feel terrible, at least at first. We all do, but you should be aware those feelings aren't unique to you. It's a tough thing being a judge."

She hadn't really considered the emotional side of the job.

"You'll find out shortly what I'm talking about," he said. "We only have a few minutes, so let me give you a brief rundown of your duties this morning.

"Kathleen, I'm told you have roughly one hundred and fifteen cases to hear. When you get a busy morning, and that's a morning docket of over one hundred and fifty cases, the executive judge ordinarily will assign another judge to help out. But an experienced judge should be able to dispose of a hundred or so of these cases by lunchtime."

"That doesn't seem possible."

"This is misdemeanor court. The most you can give is ninety days and a fine not to exceed five hundred dollars." He tapped his glasses on his knee. "You'll start with the drunks, who'll make up about half of the total cases. Most of them will plead guilty. If you have a contest, it's usually just the word of the arresting officer against the defendant. It's a question of which one's telling the truth, or lying the least. Some who can manage it will have attorneys, or some will be represented by Legal Aid. Usually, nothing's complicated. You make your decision, and if it's guilty, a probation officer—he'll be standing next to the bench—will give you the defendant's record. Usually he'll make a recommendation for sentence, if you're unsure."

"That doesn't sound legal."

"Oh, he isn't being the judge, not by any means. But he's interviewed everyone who will be coming before you. He starts work at five in the morning. He'll know everyone's background pretty well. Today old Benny Majorski is the probation officer assigned. He knows most of the regular customers on a first-name basis. Much of your docket will be repeaters. Benny is a good man, trustworthy."

"I presume I don't have to follow his recommendations?"

Judge Williams chuckled. "Of course not. But you'll find him a help. After the drunks, you'll have a parade of prostitutes.

The rule of thumb around here is that if a girl has been found guilty during the same month, she goes to jail. Same rule for the men, although we get few of them in proportion to the women. If anyone has a social disease, hold them for the board of health—you have that power under statue. For the drunks, the usual sentence is twenty-five dollars or thirty days. For the prostitutes, unless they're really bad news, it's a hundred dollars or ninety days. The pimps usually pay the fines."

"It sounds like a licensing arrangement."

He chuckled. "That's what it is, after a fashion. We keep the street trade from getting out of hand, and the government gets a cut of the pimps' profits."

"What about putting the prostitutes on probation?"

He shook his head. "Don't put any of the girls on probation unless you have a very special reason and you feel it will actually help them. If you put a girl on probation, the vice cops will go looking for her, and if they arrest her, probation violation is a two-year felony."

"Maybe that's what should happen."

He shrugged. "Kathleen, I'm just telling you what usually occurs here, not what you should do. You make up your own mind. But remember, you are now dealing with human beings, not statistics. These girls, most of them, are, for a number of reasons, incapable of being anything but prostitutes. The legislature made prostitution a misdemeanor, and it's up to the legislature to change the law, if it needs changing, not you. Judges don't make the law, they just ensure it's justly enforced. Some of our brethren forget that, but it's well to keep it in mind."

"Does this probation officer help out with the prostitutes too?"

"Yes. And after those charming people, you'll have the simple assault cases, the fistfights in bars, the husbands and wives who have knocked each other about. Usually those people have no records. For them, if you think they're guilty, probation is a pretty good sentence. I usually give a stiff fine to the bar fighters. A little pain in their pocketbooks helps to curb their aggressive tendencies the next time they're tempted."

"The whole process sounds like a factory."

He nodded slowly. "In a way, it is. It moves along like an assembly line. In spite of it all, it's your job to see that justice is done. Kathleen, you'll see a whole new side of life here, until you're assigned to felony trials. You'll deal with petty thieves, pickpockets, small-scale con artists, everything under the sun. I kind of enjoy the assignment. We all take turns about once a year. It's quite a show."

"What about jury trials?"

He placed his glasses back on his nose and looked at her from over the rim. "Everyone is entitled to a jury trial if they demand it. Here, few do, even the people who have lawyers. It's just more practical for everyone to get things done quickly. They generally know what they can expect from a judge. And a jury will make little difference in most of these cases, so why bother? However"—he smiled—"occasionally someone will request a jury trial. This is misdemeanor court, so the law only requires a six-person jury. The cases are usually simple and fast, so we wait until all the other cases are disposed of, and then we pick a jury."

"But what if the jury trial goes on into the next day?"

"No problem. You just wait until you've finished your regular daily docket, then you resume. The attorneys know they can be tied up for days on a two-bit case, so they don't ask for juries unless they have a good reason, usually. There's a lot of practical checks and balances in all courts that aren't apparent to the casual observer."

His expression suddenly became serious. "Oh, one other thing, perhaps most important. Don't allow your own morality or prejudices to interfere in your decisions. You may not like prostitution, but that doesn't matter, you must administer the law as the legislature intended. Also, you may have your own weaknesses, and see those same traits in the people who come before you. If, for instance, you had a problem with alcohol, you shouldn't go easy on the drunks because of that, or harder. In this job you have to rise above yourself. Everyone stands up when you come into the courtroom, everyone calls you 'your honor,' and that's what you have to be, honorable, no matter what the cost."

Suddenly he laughed. "I hope I'm not scaring you. I suppose somewhere inside me there's a preacher crying to get out."

"Preacher or not, I greatly appreciate your help."

He grinned as he stood up. "Well, Kathleen, I have my own work to do this morning. I'm in the middle of an armed-robbery jury trial. It's dull, very routine, and both lawyers lack fire. My main problem is trying to stay awake." He stopped at the door. "If you get in a bind and need a little advice, just call."

"You may regret that," she called after him as he left.

She sat quietly for a moment, digesting what he had said.

The clerk looked in. "Everything's all ready to go, judge, whenever you are."

Kathleen stood up. "I'll be right there." She slipped on the black robe and pulled up the zipper. She inspected herself in a small mirror near the door, adjusting the shoulders of the robe. Despite her determination to remain calm, her pulse was racing.

She left her office, walked through a reception area, then stepped out into the courtroom.

"All rise," someone called, accompanied by the crack of a gavel. She was startled by the numbers; the courtroom was packed. Everyone stood, and all eyes were on her as she mounted the few steps to the bench.

"The circuit court, criminal division, is now in session," the clerk called. "The Honorable Kathleen M. Talbot presiding."

As Jesse Williams had predicted, the drunks were first. A line of defendants stretched across the courtroom and into the private hallway.

"*People versus Walters*," the clerk called. The man first in line stepped up in front of the bench, turned, and faced Kathleen.

A uniformed policeman walked up and stood beside the man.

"You're charged with being drunk and disorderly. How do you plead, guilty or not guilty?" the clerk asked in a loud voice.

The man called Walters was almost sixty, stooped, and very thin. His clothes were wrinkled and old. His suit jacket didn't match his trousers, and neither garment fit. When he spoke he exhibited several missing teeth. "Guilty," he said softly.

Kathleen looked down at the policeman, a balding man with a thickening stomach and expressionless eyes. "What did he do, officer?" she asked.

"Your honor, while on patrol duty last night"—he referred to a notebook—"at ten-forty-five I observed the defendant standing between parked cars, shouting at the passing traffic. I got out of the patrol car and asked him what he was doing. He replied he was trying to find a friend who would lend him some money. His speech was slurred, he could hardly stand up, and I detected a strong odor of alcohol on his breath. I advised him to go home, but he refused. He was staggering. I advised him of his rights, then I placed him under arrest for being drunk. When I got him to the station he blew a point-twenty-two on the breathalyzer."

Kathleen noticed the man standing next to her in the witness box. He was white-haired, and his weathered face showed no emotion. She presumed he was the probation officer.

He leaned over and spoke in a quiet, firm voice. "Walters is one of our occasional customers. He has a job as a dishwasher. Every so often he goes on a bender. He looks in pretty good shape. If your honor wants, a fine of twenty-five dollars would probably do the trick. At least that would dry up some of his drinking money for a while." He paused, looking at her, then spoke in a near-whisper. "The usual thing to do is to give a jail sentence with the alternative of a fine, usually twenty-five dollars or thirty days in a case like this."

She looked down at the defendant. His eyes seemed wider, fearful. He bit nervously at his lower lip.

"Don't worry," the probation officer whispered, as if reading her mind, "he has the money."

"I find you guilty as charged," she said, her voice sounding a bit too loud to her own ear. "Twenty-five dollars or thirty days."

Walters nodded, the fear suddenly gone from his eyes. A uniformed court officer led him away.

The next man shuffled forward, and another officer stepped from a knot of uniformed policemen standing near the spectator rail.

"*People versus Brookline*," the clerk called. "The charge is being drunk. How do you plead?"

"Not guilty." The man was even older than the first defendant, and much thinner. His eyes, like emerging pods, protruded from his yellowing face. His frail body shook with continuing tremors.

The clerk went through a short singsong routine, obviously perfected after years of practice, putting in all the legal steps required, as he asked if Brookline wanted to decline a jury trial and be tried by the judge.

The old man, his eyes staring straight up at Kathleen, spoke in a surprisingly firm voice. "I wish to waive trial by jury."

A young prosecutor stepped forward. He had worked for her, but she had never gotten to know the young man. He looked now as if he wanted to show off his skill. He quickly put in the people's case, which consisted only of the officer's testimony that Brookline had been discovered lying drunk in an alley.

The prosecutor paused for a moment, apparently to determine if she wished to ask questions, and when Kathleen remained silent he started questioning Brookline, who denied he was drunk, saying that he was merely asleep and that the alley was his home. His tremors increased as he talked, forcing him to grab the rail in front of the bench to keep his balance. His large staring eyes never left her face.

"I find you guilty as charged," she said.

Brookline half-slumped, his eyes suddenly tearing. "Don't send me back, for God's sake. I'm too old, and I can't protect myself. You don't know what they do there. Please, I'm sorry. I won't drink anymore, but please don't send me back." His face was contorted as if in real pain.

Kathleen, shocked, felt a rush of pity for the old man.

"Brookline is a regular," the probation officer said quietly. "He's done more time on the farm for drinking than most men do for murder—he just does it thirty days at a time. It's not going back that bothers him so much, he just doesn't want to be separated from cheap wine."

The probation officer handed her a computer printout. "This is his record," he said. "I talked to him this morning. He's in bad shape physically. If he isn't taken off the streets, he'll drink himself to death in a couple of weeks. He will anyway, eventually. But I'd recommend giving him ninety days straight time.

They'll dry him out, feed him regular, and he'll snap right back; he always does."

"But what about his age?" she whispered.

The probation officer's stern features exhibited the ghost of a wry smile. "I was a drunk for years," he said. "I've been up there as a customer. Believe me, it's no picnic, but a lot less will happen to him up there than out on the streets."

Kathleen looked again at Brookline. His big eyes were silently pleading, as if in frantic prayer.

"Ninety days," she said, feeling her stomach turn as she said the words.

"Oh, my God," Brookline cried, slumping almost to the floor. He was grabbed and quickly led away by the burly court officer.

"People versus Sullivan," the clerk intoned, and the dismal parade continued.

Kathleen desperately wanted the quiet of her office, but she knew that was impossible. There were still over a hundred cases to be tried, and she had to hear them all. Who is the prisoner here, she wondered.

CHAPTER 13

NELSON BRAGG SAT in the last row in the crowded court-room jammed with families and friends of persons await-ing trial. He didn't understand why he had come. He knew only that it was in response to the voices, but he couldn't remember why it was important. Sensing the danger all around him made him feel more and more defenseless. Today he had left his revolver back in his room, since he knew he would have to pass through the court's metal detectors. Possession of a gun would cause them to revoke his probation and send him to jail.

He glared up at the judge. She looked evil, her manner cold and icy. Nelson Bragg was being troubled more than usual by the voices; they made it difficult for him to hear what was being said in the court. He tried to concentrate, but that only seemed to make it worse.

When he tried to answer the voices, people told him to be quiet. He was afraid he might attract the unwanted attention of one of the court officers, so he forced himself to remain silent.

The woman judge—he remembered her name, Kathleen M. Talbot—seemed like a black-clothed robot on the bench, her eyes steely, her stern expression fixed. Bragg felt he had seen her before, though he had no recollection of the press clipping with her photograph tucked away in his drawer. He wondered if she was connected with the murderous abortion clinics he hated so much. The voices grew louder as he tried to remember.

The line of drunks was finally processed, and the policemen began to line up the prostitutes. Nelson Bragg stared at the women, cesspools of sin and disease. His mother had taught him that women and lust were the messengers of the devil. His father, who had deserted the family, was often used as a prime example of carnate evil. It was all in the Bible, quoted chapter and verse by his mother. His own two sisters had inspired him to sinful thoughts, parading around as they did, displaying their wantonness. His mother knew his evil thoughts. She always knew. His two sisters thought the beatings he received somehow amusing. They seemed to delight in torturing him. They were no better than the whores being paraded up to the bench. His loathing of the whores was matched by an unknown dread, as if somehow the prostitutes might infect him or hurt him, even at a distance.

When the first case began, the voices—all mixed together and unintelligible—rose to such a level that he couldn't hear the testimony. He whispered a protest.

Someone close by told him to be quiet. He turned but could not identify the source. He was aware one of the court officers was now watching him.

He knew he had to escape. Nelson Bragg got up and quickly pushed his way out of the spectator row. As he reached the courtroom doors, he turned. The prostitutes were all clustered up in the front of the courtroom near the judge. In his mind, the woman judge was no different from any of those loathsome women—evil, stinking with sin, threatening creatures, all of them. Nelson Bragg hated sin, and now he hated the black-robed woman who, in his tortured mind, embodied everything he despised.

The voices were screaming, and he was frightened. He raced out of the courthouse, but he couldn't escape the unintelligible screeching.

CHAPTER 14

KATHLEEN FELT FAR beyond mere exhaustion. She had allowed only a thirty-minute break for lunch at noon, and other than that they had worked steadily. Now it was almost four o'clock.

Her mind was numb. Case after case had rolled past her like a human assembly line. There was no room for indecision or second thoughts. Surviving to the end with some measure of dignity had become her primary concern.

The courtroom was almost empty, with just a few officers, lawyers, and spectators remaining.

"People versus Miklos," the clerk intoned in that singsong nasal quality, a monotonous tone that was becoming increasingly irritating.

She was surprised to see Jeremiah Mitchell step forward to take his place next to a small, nervous man who was smartly dressed. The young prosecutor, no longer quite so eager and fresh, also stepped up to the front of the bench.

The clerk continued in the same annoying tone. "You're charged with indecent exposure, how do you plead?"

Mitchell smiled up at Kathleen. "We stand mute, we're ready for trial, and we request trial by jury."

Kathleen was shocked. She knew a jury trial, even for a simple misdemeanor charge, could take hours, perhaps days. What could Mitchell be planning? He was an experienced criminal lawyer, and his plea of standing mute had preserved his right to appeal any errors committed prior to trial. The judge would have to enter the plea, and the defendant's rights were thus preserved. But calling for a trial seemed risky.

"Enter a plea of not guilty," she said. Kathleen hoped the prosecutor might ask for an adjournment. It would be an easy way out. "Are the people ready?"

The prosecutor nodded. "The people are ready for trial," he said, but with a notable lack of enthusiasm.

"Mr. Mitchell, the hour is late. Do you wish to proceed now? We may have to try this piecemeal if it goes beyond today."

Mitchell, aware of her implied threat to pen him up for several days, spoke almost gently. "I know this is your honor's first day, and I imagine you're tired, but this shouldn't take long. I understand the prosecution has two witnesses, the complainant and the arresting officer. We have just one witness." He paused for a moment. "There are certain circumstances in this case that require my request for a jury."

"There's no need to apologize, Mr. Mitchell. Your client has a right to a trial by jury." She regretted that her words sounded so harsh. She continued in a softer voice. "Are there any other cases to be tried?" she asked the clerk.

He turned and looked up at her. "This is the last one."

She nodded and stood up. Her legs felt cramped. "All right, we'll take a short break, then we'll select the jury."

The clerk rapped the gavel as she walked off the bench.

She sat quietly in her office for a moment, then dialed Judge Williams and explained her problem. He said he would come right down. Then she called Marie and told her she would be late. She wondered why she felt she had to explain herself, but she knew she felt guilty about Little Mike. She talked for a few minutes to her son, then Judge Williams came in.

He carried a steaming cup and a loose-leaf binder. "These are two things you'll need," he said, setting the cup in front of her. "Hot tea—I took the liberty of liberally lacing it with sugar. It will help pick you up a bit." He grinned and handed her the binder. "And these are the standard jury instructions. I marked the ones you must use with a red check. At the end of the trial, you have to instruct the jury as to the law involved. We all use these standard instructions. Most of us read them verbatim."

He laughed. "Of course, the trick is to look as if you aren't reading. Look up and make eye contact regularly. The jury will think you're the greatest legal scholar that ever lived. Obviously, you have to alter some of them to suit the circumstances, but you don't have to worry about looking like an idiot on appeal. The Supreme Court has approved every word."

She sipped the tea. "This is good. I appreciate it."

He shrugged. "I would have put a little brandy in it, but I didn't think it wise, at least not on your first day." He chuckled. "This may be a bit rough, but you're getting a rounded education rather quickly. This jury demand may be someone's idea of testing you out, just to see what you're made of."

"Jeremiah Mitchell is the lawyer."

Williams nodded slowly. "Jerry Mitchell is one of the best. He wouldn't be wasting his time doing anything silly. And he's a good workman, fast and competent. At least that's a plus. You may finish this case tonight. Don't worry about staying late, the officers will make sure everything is all right." He stood up. "Good luck. Look at it this way, Kathleen. When they give you your first paycheck, you'll feel you really earned it."

She laughed. "Thinks for the tea. It's helping already."

After Judge Williams left, she finished the tea, then once again went out into the courtroom.

The panel of jurors—she guessed about fifty of them—sat in the spectator rows.

The clerk turned and whispered, "They were almost on their way home, but I stopped them in time. These are all one-day people—if they don't get picked for a case today, they don't have to come back. But none of them seemed miffed about staying. I think they're happy for the chance to maybe finally hear a case, even if it's only a misdemeanor case."

As Judge Williams predicted, Mitchell was a quick workman. The jury was selected in minutes. The prosecutor didn't challenge anyone, and Mitchell excused only two—both rather severe-looking older women. Three men and three women took their places in the jury box and were sworn in by the clerk. The remainder of the jury panel filed out, leaving the courtroom again almost deserted.

The prosecutor made a brief opening statement, then called

a thin woman, who appeared to be in her early forties, to the stand. She was sworn.

"What is your name, please?" the prosecutor asked.

"Martha Taylor."

"You're a waitress, employed at the Café Diner, located at Third and Lennox in this city?"

Kathleen looked over at Mitchell, but he made no objection to the leading question.

"Yes." The witness's voice reflected her nervousness.

"And you were working there Wednesday, June fourteenth, of this year?"

"Yes."

"Did you see the defendant at your place of work on that day?"

"Yes."

"Tell us what happened."

Again, Mitchell made no objection.

The woman's thin cheeks flushed in embarrassment. "I work afternoons, from four to midnight. About seven o'clock that night he came in."

"Who?"

She pointed at the defendant. "Him."

"Let the record indicate that the witness has identified Zolton Miklos, the defendant," the prosecutor said. "Go on, please."

"It was a slow night. We have a long counter, with three tables at the back of the place. He came in and sat down at the counter, on a stool."

"Were there any other customers in your diner at that time?"

"One other man, he was at the other end of the counter. He was having some pie and reading a newspaper."

"You were the lone employee in the diner?"

"No. But I was out front. The cook was back in the kitchen."

The prosecutor walked to the far end of the jury box, putting distance between himself and the witness, forcing her to keep her voice up so that the jury could hear. "Go on."

"He came in and ordered coffee and a roll. I got the coffee and the roll and when I placed them down in front of him, I could see . . . ." She faltered, her cheeks suddenly flushed.

"What did you see, Mrs. Taylor," the prosecutor asked. "I know this is embarrassing, but you must tell us."

"He had his thing out of his pants." She stared at her hands clasped tightly in her lap.

"You mean his penis?"

Mitchell stood quickly. "Objection. I'd prefer if Mrs. Taylor testified and not the prosecutor."

"Sustained." Kathleen was surprised at how easily she had said the word.

"What did you see, if anything?" the prosecutor asked, irritation in his tone.

"His . . . penis," she said.

"Did he say anything?"

She shook her head. "He just stared at me, no words, nothing. I was shocked. I went in and told the cook. He called the cops, then came back out with me, but by that time the man was gone. They arrested him a block away."

"And you're sure this is the man who exposed himself to you?" The prosecutor pointed at Miklos, who, Kathleen noticed, had not once looked at the witness.

"Yes."

"Your witness," the prosecutor said, sitting down.

Mitchell stood up and walked to a point directly in front of the witness and the jury. "Mrs. Taylor, you are a married woman?"

"Divorced."

"How long ago?"

"Objection," the prosecutor snapped. "That's hardly relevant."

Mitchell turned and looked up at Kathleen. "I think it may become relevant, your honor," he said.

"I'll take the answer," Kathleen said.

"How long?" Mitchell repeated.

The witness paused, as if silently counting. "Almost twelve years."

"Prior to the day in question, did you ever see my client, Zolton Miklos, before?"

"No."

Mitchell's manner was polite, even friendly. "When he came into your diner, did he have anything with him?"

"A bag."

"A grocery bag, perhaps?"

"Yes."

"Were there groceries in it?"

"I don't know, I didn't look."

Mitchell nodded. "Where did he put the bag, on the counter?"

"No. I think he put it on the floor next to him."

"You think?"

"I'm not sure."

"Could it have been between his legs?"

"I suppose. As I say, I didn't look."

Mitchell seemed to consider her statement as he walked to the far end of the jury box. "I don't wish to embarrass you, Mrs. Taylor, I know how difficult all this must be, but when you say you saw my client's 'thing,' was it erect?"

"Pardon me?" Her shaking response showed she had understood the question.

"Again, not to cause you any undue problems, Mrs. Taylor, but was he erect? In other words, was he sexually aroused? If you don't understand the question, just say so."

"I understand. I don't think he was . . . aroused."

"You're not sure?"

She shook her head. "No."

Mitchell paused for a moment. "I have no more questions. Thank you, Mrs. Taylor."

The woman hurried from the witness stand and took a seat in the first row of benches.

The prosecutor called the arresting officer and quickly put in the policeman's testimony.

Mitchell questioned the officer carefully, leaving no room for a damaging answer.

"He had a bag of groceries when you arrested him?"

"Yes."

"Did you look in the bag?"

"Yes. That's standard procedure, to make sure the accused isn't armed."

"And what did you find in the bag?"

The big policeman shrugged. "A package of pasta, a couple cans of tomato sauce, and some sausage."

"What kind of sausage?"

The policeman smiled. "I don't know, all sausage looks alike to me."

"Was it packaged, wrapped in plastic?"

The policeman shook his head. "No. It was the fresh kind, like you buy in a butcher shop. As I recall, it was loosely wrapped in white butcher's paper."

"Did you that night determine if Mr. Miklos was employed?"

"Yeah. After we took him to the station, and after the lady identified him. He's an electrical engineer and he works for Brooks Manufacturing."

"Did you find out how long he has worked for Brooks?"

"He said nine years, but I didn't check on that."

"That's all I have," Mitchell said.

The prosecutor stood up. "The people rest."

Kathleen expected Mitchell to make a motion to dismiss. It was customary, although she had already decided that the people had established a sufficient case to proceed. But he surprised her by calling a witness.

A large man in an ill-fitting suit walked up to the stand. The clerk swore him in. The man smiled at Kathleen, then the jury, and sat down in the witness chair.

"You are Casmir Kultuncheck, and you own and operate a butcher shop at Third and Slocum?"

"Yes."

Kathleen saw the prosecutor start to rise, then change his mind.

"Have you ever seen my client, Zolton Miklos, before?"

The butcher nodded. "He's a regular customer, comes in two, maybe three times a month. I never knew his name before this, but that's him."

"Was he in your shop last Wednesday?"

The man shrugged. "Could be. He was in a couple of days ago. I'm not absolutely sure it was Wednesday, could be though."

"On the day you saw him, did he buy anything?"

"Oh, sure. Usually he buys the same thing, our fresh sausage. It's good stuff." He looked at the jury, who returned his smile. "A lot of people from the old country come by, just for that sausage."

Mitchell walked back to the counsel table and opened his briefcase. "Did I buy some of that sausage from you today?"

"Yes, you did."

Mitchell took out a greasy parcel of white paper. The end of a pale white sausage dangled from one end. "Does this look like the sausage?"

"Objection," the prosecutor snapped. "He hasn't offered that as an exhibit. And if he does, I'll object. It's not relevant, it's not the sausage the defendant is alleged to have had with him, it's not the—"

Mitchell stood in front of the jury, the sausage dangling from the white paper. "If the prosecutor doesn't want the jury to see this, I can understand, but—"

Kathleen sat up straight. "There's been an objection, well taken," she said. "Sustained."

Mitchell nodded, looked woefully at the dangling end of sausage, then at the jury, shrugged, and returned the package to his briefcase. "As your honor wishes," he said. "You may take the witness."

"No questions," the prosecutor said quickly.

"I think the case is clear enough," Mitchell said. "The defense rests."

Kathleen looked up at the courtroom clock. It was six-thirty. "Do you gentlemen wish to argue now, or wait until tomorrow afternoon?"

"I'm ready," the prosecutor said.

Mitchell stood up. "I don't think this will take long," he said. "I would beg the court's indulgence, and the jury's. We are prepared to argue now."

The prosecutor, showing fatigue, made a brief, standard argument, emphasizing the word "perversion," using it in almost every other sentence. Without saying so exactly, he intimated that Mrs. Taylor had probably saved herself from hideous rape by her quick, intelligent actions. He asked for a verdict of guilty.

Mitchell, who seemed as fresh as when he started, walked to a place directly in front of the jury. He smiled and waited until most of them smiled back.

"Ladies and gentlemen," he began in a pleasant voice, "what

we have here, in very elemental terms, is a case of mistaken identity, pure and simple." He waited as the jurors frowned, then looked at each other. "Oh, no, I don't mean that Mrs. Taylor was confused as to her identification of my client, Zolton Miklos. She was mistaken, however, when she identified his 'thing,' as she so quaintly called it, because what she really saw was a sausage."

One of the male jurors laughed. Mitchell continued, but his tone was now more serious. "Mrs. Taylor is a nice woman, and truthful. She served my client his coffee, glanced down, and saw the sausage. But she honestly mistook it for something else. Obviously she isn't the kind of woman who would stare or be titillated. It was only a glance. Remember, she wasn't sure about very much, groceries, sexual arousal, or much else. She was frightened, and I don't blame her. But she was mistaken. She ran to the cook, in turn frightening my client, obviously, who left. Moments later the arresting officer found what she had seen—a link of sausage."

Mitchell paused. "Her honor will instruct you as to the law when we attorneys are through speaking. I will ask you to pay special attention to her instructions on reasonable doubt. No one can be convicted on mere suspicion in this country. I know you will be fair. My client, as you heard, is an engineer, gainfully employed. He did not expose himself to Mrs. Taylor or anyone else that night. This is not a case where anyone is lying, ladies and gentlemen. It is a case, as I say, of mistaken identity. It would be a miscarriage of justice if my client was put in prison because a very nice woman didn't take the time to tell a penis from a link sausage. I ask for a verdict of not guilty. Thank you."

The prosecutor, having the greater burden of proof, had the opportunity to rebut Mitchell's statements. He made much of the fact that Miklos had fled the restaurant without finishing his coffee and roll, and again made repeated references to perversion and its dire consequences.

Kathleen's fatigue vanished as she prepared to read the instructions to the jury. Judge Williams had marked most of the passages she had to use, and she found the paragraph stating a defendant's failure to take the stand could not be used against him.

She read carefully but slowly, noting that the six jurors hung intently on every word she uttered. She managed to make eye contact and speak with some animation so they wouldn't be bored by the dry language of the law.

When she finished, one of the court officers led the six to the jury room on the far side of the bench. He closed the door after them, then turned and stood, crossing his arms at the chest like a guard at a harem.

She was startled by the crack of the gavel as she moved off the bench and toward her chambers—a sound, she suddenly realized, that would always accompany her comings and goings from now on.

Kathleen took off her robe and hung it up. It was almost eight o'clock. She had been in the court for over twelve hours, but it seemed more like a week, a very long week. She sat behind her desk, her mind blank, absently grateful for the chance to relax. And for the first time she realized just how hungry she had become.

"May I come in?"

Jeremiah Mitchell seemed to fill the office doorway.

She wished he would go away. "What can I do for you, Mr. Mitchell?"

He laughed, and without invitation walked in and sat down on the office couch. "You did very well today."

"What is it you want?"

He sighed. "Nothing really. Except I thought I had better explain why I asked for a jury."

"You don't have to."

He nodded. "I know, but I didn't want you to think I don't have confidence in your fairness or competency."

"Oh?"

Mitchell's rugged face became nearly solemn. "Zolton Miklos has a problem. He's well-educated, married, has a couple of kids, but every so often, usually under prolonged stress, he has the compulsion to wave his penis at women." Mitchell sighed. "He's been arrested a couple of times. Some of the ladies declined to prosecute, and a kind judge let him off once on the promise that he'd seek psychiatric care. Then, about a year ago, he wasn't so lucky and got himself convicted. He only received a small fine as punishment, but the conviction—the immigration people call it a crime of moral turpitude—is on his record for good."

"I don't think we should be discussing the case, Mr. Mitchell. It's not over yet. And if he's convicted I'll have to sentence him."

Mitchell shrugged. "If he's convicted, the probation department will report to you everything I'm saying—it's all part of Zolton's history."

"Still . . ."

He leaned forward. "If I hadn't asked for a jury, you would probably have convicted him. I would, given the circumstances. That's why I had to go to a jury. The business about the sausage was real, he did buy it and have it with him. But as lawyers you and I would probably have believed the woman, given our legal sophistication. The jury, however, may give Zolton the benefit of the doubt. That's why I made the request. He stands to lose his citizenship if he's convicted."

She nodded. "I understand."

Mitchell started to get up, then stopped. "Men like Zolton are sick, but usually not dangerous. I'll make a plea in open court if he's convicted. Perhaps probation on the condition that he get help, and that it be monitored this time? That would seem reasonable, judge."

She still wasn't accustomed to being called judge. "You can make your request in open court, Mr. Mitchell. I've always hated judges who have made back-room deals. I wouldn't want to become one."

He stood up and looked down at her, then smiled. "You won't. And this isn't a 'deal.' If Zolton gets convicted I'll have to fight with immigration. I'll probably lose, but I can assure him of a few more years in this country. I would hope, given the background, that you might temper any punishment, if you have to, that is."

"Do you think he'll be convicted?"

Mitchell shrugged. "I hope not, but I have never yet felt

confident about predicting what a jury might do. My guess is conviction. What do you think?"

"I'd think they'll acquit."

"Want to bet?"

"That's hardly the thing for a lawyer and a judge to do about a case, is it?"

"Just dinner? We both have to eat."

She laughed, wondering if her fatigue was affecting her judgment. "That's innocent enough. All right, you're on."

The clerk looked in from the doorway. "They've got a verdict," he said.

She stood up. "I guess we'll find out who won now."

Mitchell looked at his watch. "They weren't out long enough to even have a cigarette. I always worry if they come in too fast."

He left and she once again donned the robe and took her place on the bench.

The court officer led the jurors from the jury room. They formed a line in front of the bench.

"Have you reached a verdict," the clerk asked, "and if so, who will speak for you?"

"We have," one of the men said, "and I shall."

"How do you find the defendant, Zolton Miklos, guilty or not guilty?" asked the clerk.

Miklos, who stood in the prisoner's box, was visibly shaking. Mitchell, who stood near him, reached over and gripped the small man's arm as a gesture of support.

"We find the defendant not guilty." The man's voice seemed to echo in the nearly empty courtroom.

Miklos started to collapse, but Mitchell caught him.

"So say you Mr. Foreman, and so say you all, members of the jury?" The clerk asked the standard question in a form that had been asked for hundreds of years in both English and American courts.

The jurors nodded.

"The defendant is discharged," Kathleen said.

The clerk rapped the gavel as she walked off the bench. "This honorable court stands adjourned," he sang in his usual nasal tone.

She was hanging up her robe when Mitchell came in. "You won the bet," he said. "Where would you like to have dinner?"

Kathleen was about to refuse, but then she realized her son would already be in bed. And she did have to eat, and although she was tired, she knew she wouldn't be able to go to bed without first unwinding. "I'll meet you at Giovanni's."

"Whatever you say. Need a ride?"

"I have my car."

Mitchell grinned. "I have to take a few minutes to persuade Zolton that even a miracle won't save him next time. I've already arranged for treatment. I think he'll follow through, given the possible alternative. So I may be a few minutes late. Don't wait for me. Go ahead and order—I'll catch up."

Mitchell left, and the clerk looked in again. "I'm taking off now, judge, okay?"

She nodded.

He made a timid little smile. "You did real good, judge, real good. Good night."

Kathleen didn't know whether she had done well or not, but she had survived, and that seemed like the real accomplishment.

-◄ ►-

Regina sat in the dayroom, staring out at the trees and watching the branches perform a vigorous ballet in the freshening wind.

"Got a minute, Regina?"

She turned and looked up at Russ Lafferty, a psychologist who was one of her counselors in the hospital's drug-and-alcohol-abuse unit.

"That's all I have is time, isn't it? What do you want?"

He pulled up a chair and sat down. "I hear you raised a fuss at lunch. I thought you were all over that."

She smirked. "They tell you everything, don't they? God, I'll be glad to get out of here—it's worse than prison."

He merely smiled. "Having a few problems since the funeral?"

"Problems, me? Why? My colossal bitch of a stepdaughter murdered my husband with the help of this praiseworthy organization—why would that give me any problems? I'm certainly all for progress."

Lafferty sighed. "It would have helped if you had gone north for the funeral. Funerals aren't really events of choice, you know, but they do allow people to vent their grief. You haven't, and because of that, you're building this into outlandish proportions, Regina."

"I don't consider murder anything trivial."

"It wasn't murder, and you know it. Your husband was brain dead from a series of strokes. The machines merely made his lungs and heart work artificially. He was dead, and for your own mental health, you must accept that as a fact."

She snorted. "I was his wife. If anyone had the right to make any decision to turn off the machines, it was me. And I personally wouldn't have done it. You people here are just as guilty as that bitch daughter of his."

Lafferty pursed his lips before speaking. "Look, in twelve days we have to let you go. That's the law in this state. If you keep everything bottled up and boiling, Regina, you won't make it on the outside. You'll have no emotional control, and you'll hit the first bar you see when you get out."

"Don't be so sure," she snapped.

"Are you telling me you're through with drinking?"

She shook her head. "I'm not an alcoholic—I've told you people that from the beginning. His daughter signed me in here, against my will. I take a few drinks, sometimes too many, but I'm not a drunk."

"What are you going to do when you get out of here? You can't hide from the world like you did from your husband's funeral."

"I have plans."

"Like what?"

She looked away from him. "That's my business." She became uneasy under his silent stare and continued to avoid eye contact. "My husband left me some money, not much, but enough to get by. And I have my home in Florida."

"You're telling me what you have, but not what you plan to do."

She looked back at the trees. A storm was building, the sky

was darkening, the wind becoming even more violent. "I'm getting out of here, that's my plan."

"Nothing more than that?"

She shook her head.

He looked at his watch. "It's getting late, but I think we should talk. I'll see you tomorrow." He patted her on the shoulder as he left.

Regina watched the approaching storm. She had plans, lots of them. They had all humiliated her, and they had robbed her of Big Mike. And they all seemed so damned sure that they would get away with it, especially Big Mike's vicious daughter. She had disliked Kathleen Talbot all along, but now she hated her with an all-consuming passion. It was murder, legal or not, and Regina was determined that Kathleen Talbot would pay for what she had done.

CHAPTER 15

KATHLEEN REGRETTED HER decision to have dinner with Jerry Mitchell. Socializing with a lawyer who had just won a case before her could cause tongues to wag. It wasn't prohibited ethically, but some, she knew, would consider such conduct a breach of judicial propriety. Appearances were as important as facts in public life. She resolved to be more circumspect in the future. But right now there was no way to reach Mitchell to tell him she had changed her mind. So she ignored the twinges of guilt, got into her car, and headed for Giovanni's.

It was late, and only a few tables were occupied at the famous Italian restaurant. Just inhaling the delicious aromas coming from the kitchen turned her hunger into something approaching lust. Despite that, Kathleen restrained herself, ordering only a dry white wine and an appetizer of prosciutto and melon. She felt it would be impolite to order anything more before Mitchell arrived.

She was surprised when he walked in only a few minutes later.

"That didn't take long," she said.

He laughed. "I'm sure you observed my client's near-collapse when the jury found him not guilty. You'd have thought he'd just been saved from the hangman."

"It looked genuine."

He ordered a Scotch and water. "Oh, it was, at that moment.

But in just the few minutes I spent talking to you, arrogance had replaced apprehension in full measure. By the time I got back out in the courtroom, Miklos was surprised I felt a need to lecture an innocent man."

"Didn't he understand that without you . . ."

"They never do; it's part of the business." Mitchell loosened his tie and sat back. "If I wanted gratitude, I would have picked another type of practice or gone into medicine. Oh, once in a while someone will actually thank me. But that's rare. I'm more accustomed to people like Miklos."

"What did you say to him?"

The waitress brought Mitchell his drink. He raised it in salute, then drank. "He's my client. Part of the fee for my services was for advice, which I then proceeded to give him. I told him he had better follow up on the therapy I arranged, because if he didn't, even having a handy sausage around wouldn't save him the next time."

"Will he go through with the therapy?"

Mitchell shrugged. "I hope so, for his sake." He took up the menu. "Hungry?"

She had finished the prosciutto and was onto the bread-sticks. "I'm starved."

"May I order? They serve a nine-course meal here that is unbelievable. It starts as an adventure but ends up as an endurance contest. Are you game?"

She laughed. "Sure."

Mitchell ordered a good wine to go with the feast. Almost immediately, plates of rich and exotic food began to appear from the kitchen. Kathleen ate ravenously.

Mitchell paused, taking a moment to let the food settle. "I didn't realize how hungry I was." He refilled her wineglass. "By the way, you did very well today."

She, too, paused. She knew she was eating too fast, although the food was helping dispel the crush of fatigue. "Considering my training and background, did that come as a surprise?"

He smiled easily. "The courts are my home and family," he said. "My life, really. I've seen a lot of lawyers become judges. I don't think anything really prepares them for the job. I've never been a judge, but it's obvious to me that it's entirely different from being a trial lawyer. I've seen men and women I've admired as seasoned trial attorneys take the robe and freeze, barely able to carry out their duties. Most of them come to terms with the new challenges eventually. Some don't. But you had no problems today. You looked as though you had been a judge for years."

"You're not above a bit of flattery now and then, are you, Mr. Mitchell?"

He didn't laugh. "No, I'm not. But I'm being quite sincere. You did well." He smiled slightly. "I admit I probably wouldn't have told you if you hadn't done well—but what I said isn't idle flattery, just the judgment of a courthouse creature who's been around awhile."

"I appreciate it, flattery or not." The waiter brought some hot cheese rolls smothered in tomato sauce. She thought she would take just a taste, but ended up finishing them. "I may burst," she said, washing the food down with wine. "You said some people can't handle being a judge. I don't recall anyone quitting for that reason."

"I think John Gregory was before your time. He was appointed as a circuit judge."

She nodded. "I remember that he was a friend of my father's. He died after being named to the bench, didn't he?"

Mitchell sat back in his chair. "I was a year out of law school at the time. John Gregory was a hell of a good lawyer, a negligence man, primarily, and he knew his way around a courtroom. He'd made a fortune and wanted to retire to the bench. The governor was persuaded to appoint him. It was the worst thing that could have happened to him."

"Why?"

"He couldn't bring himself to make a decision. He took every case he heard under advisement, and never issued a judgment or order. He even ducked doing anything about injunctions. Everything started piling up. The executive judge got after him, even offered to assign someone to help him, but Gregory declined. One night, after everyone went home, he took a handful of pills—he knew a lot about medicine because of the type of cases he had handled as a lawyer—and drifted off into that last, long sleep. It was hushed up, everyone liked him. But the cases had to be retried. He was an excellent lawyer, but he couldn't hack it as a judge."

"Are you trying to frighten me by any chance? That sounds like the kind of story they tell around the fire at summer camp."

Mitchell's deep laugh echoed through the restaurant. "It does at that. No, I wasn't trying to scare you. I wouldn't have said anything if you hadn't demonstrated you were born to the job. You won't have any problems making decisions."

"You think not?"

The waiter brought another steaming course of food. She shook her head. "I can't. There isn't room."

"Take a bite, just a sample," Mitchell said. "Otherwise, they'll be hurt."

Kathleen took a forkful. Each course seemed more splendid than the last. "I don't think I'll be able to sleep tonight. I won't be able to lie down without rolling off the bed like an over-stuffed ball."

"You have no worries in that department. Most women would kill to look like you."

She pretended to ignore the compliment. "Did you ever think about becoming a judge?" she asked.

Mitchell shook his head. "Never, and that's an honest answer. I like what I do; in a way, it's something like a game to me—every case is a contest, every case is different." He grinned. "Don't get me wrong—I realize it's no game to my clients. I do my very best for them, but I also enjoy myself doing it."

"I understand you do only criminal work."

He nodded. "I've always been a trial lawyer. Years ago I suppose I handled just about every kind of case, but now I limit myself to criminal law. I don't know why exactly, but I find it fascinating, always have. Not only the cases, but the people. Clients, witnesses, cops, even judges, all seem larger than life in the criminal courts."

Kathleen declined the last course offered. She looked up at the waitress. "If I even take one more bite, I will die, happy maybe, but dead nevertheless." She took a sip of wine, then looked again at Mitchell. "Wouldn't you do better financially in some other kind of trial practice?"

He shrugged. "Perhaps, but I do pretty well now."

"I didn't mean to—"

Mitchell laughed. "Whoa, judge. My life is an open book. I don't have to chase clients anymore. In the beginning I did. But now the big silk-stocking firms refer all their criminal work to me. That's how I came to defend Zolton Miklos. His company called their corporate law firm, who were wise enough to contact me. It's a good arrangement. They don't want any referral fee, just a good job done, so they look good. I get the money up front, and while I may not enjoy the income of some of our brethren in the posh partnerships, I do all right."

Kathleen was beginning to feel relaxed, and she now knew sleep would be no problem. But she didn't want to go home quite yet. He was an interesting man, and her curiosity was aroused.

"I know the reputation of Jeremiah Mitchell, and I've just watched a demonstration of how that reputation was acquired. What about the man himself—that fellow behind the reputation—what's he like?"

He shrugged. "Nothing complicated, nor very interesting, I'm afraid. I started at Yale, but changed over after military service. I'm a home-state product, both undergraduate and law school. I was married for a couple of years, but that didn't work out."

"Any children?"

He laughed. "No, thank God."

"Why do you say that?"

He became serious. "My divorce wasn't very friendly. If we had had children, they would have become pawns, I'm afraid. Anyway, I wouldn't make much of a father."

"Oh?"

He half-smiled. "I work very hard. These trials take up a lot of time. Despite appearances, I do my homework. I run a one-man office, or I did until recently. I employ a young lawyer now to do some of the scut work, but I handle almost everything else myself. I'd have no time for a family, and that wouldn't be fair to them."

She nodded. "I know."

"That's really why you took the judgeship, isn't it? Because of your son?"

Kathleen instinctively kept such matters to herself, but somehow she felt she could talk to him. "My son is four years old.
His father died before he was born. I'm afraid I've neglected
him in the last few years. Regular hours should free me to give
him the attention he needs."

"He's pretty young. Did your father's death have an effect?"

For a moment she found herself surprisingly near tears, but
she quickly regained her composure. "He hardly knew my
father. Big Mike was just a big gruff man who was around
once in a while for holidays. Dad wasn't the kind of man who
paid much attention to children."

"That's a shame. My grandfather practically raised me. And
that was important. I needed someone, and he was there."

"Were your parents dead?"

Mitchell laughed. "No, just drunk most of the time. They
weren't bad people, really. Life, for them, was just one long
party. My brother and I were bothersome extra baggage, so
they checked us, like coats, with my grandfather."

"Your parents, are they . . . ?"

He shook his head. "My father died of a heart attack, and my
mother kicked off from liver complications." He sipped his
wine slowly. "My grandfather outlived them, but he died last
year." He grinned. "My brother is an engineer in California. I
think he's on his third or fourth marriage. So there you have it,
judge, the history and progress of the Mitchell family right up
to the moment. As I said, not very exciting."

She knew he was concealing his own feelings, treating everything as though he were describing strangers.

"And what about your hopes and dreams and aspirations, as
they say?" she asked.

He sighed. "None, I guess. I'm doing what I want to do, and I
like it. I have no other ambitions." He looked at her. "How
about you?"

She thought for a moment before answering. It had been a
long time since she had lowered her defenses to anyone. "Well,
I have a new job, more complicated than I thought. I want to
master it. That, and raise my son."

"Boyfriends?"

She chuckled. "Who would want an old widow with a child?

What about you, or did you take a vow somewhere along the way?"

He grinned. "I am, as they say in show business, between engagements. Besides, my work pace leaves little time for developing what's termed these days as lasting relationships." He laughed quietly. "I do have lady friends. But sex is a little like my golf game. I like it, too, but I just don't seem to find the time to play anymore."

"Do you expect me to believe that?"

"In the same way I believe you have no gentleman friends."

They both laughed.

Kathleen glanced at her watch. It was almost midnight. Time had passed too quickly. "I have to go," she said. "I have to be ready for tomorrow, whether I want to or not. How shall we settle the check?"

Mitchell frowned. "I presume you're worried about appearances? That someone might think I was buying influence along with dinner?"

"These are modern times, Mr. Mitchell. Men and women can split checks without embarrassment."

"How about this: how about if I get the check? Would that arouse any feminist sense of outrage?"

She laughed. "Not at all."

"Good." He got up. "But as with almost everything in life, judge, there is a condition."

She looked up at him, surprised again at how tall he was. "And that is?"

"That you take me to dinner, say, next week. Then it will be your turn to pay. That seems only fair, doesn't it?"

Kathleen had intended to decline gracefully, but she enjoyed his company, and she found she could relax with him without any fear that it might be construed as some kind of invitation. "Okay, Jerry, you have a deal."

—◄ ►—

Judge Webster Broadbent disliked Judge Timothy Quinlan. He considered Quinlan crude, intellectually limited, and a buffoon. Fortunately, Broadbent generally kept his opinions about

Quinlan to himself, sharing them only with a handful of attorneys he felt he could trust.

Broadbent made the trip from the old Hall of Justice to the civil-court building to keep an after-hours meeting he had requested with Quinlan.

Quinlan had taken over the late Harry Johnson's courtroom as soon as the judges had named him as Johnson's temporary replacement. Only a few months from mandatory retirement, Quinlan was enjoying exercising the power of executive judge, making full use of every privilege associated with the title.

Quinlan's secretary escorted Broadbent into Quinlan's chambers. Webster Broadbent had long admired, and secretly coveted, the huge office and palatial courtroom, both designed to serve as physical symbols of the regal authority of the court's executive judge.

Quinlan, in his shirtsleeves, sat dwarfed behind Johnson's enormous mahogany desk.

"Sit down, Webster," Quinlan said. "Use the big couch, if you like. Maybe we should designate that thing as a historic monument. I'd like to have a dollar for every time Harry screwed our Brenda on that baby."

Broadbent primly took one of the leather-covered chairs.

"Want a drink?" Quinlan produced a bottle of brandy and two glasses. "Helps pick you up after a tough day."

"No, thanks," Broadbent said. "But you go ahead."

Quinlan shrugged and poured a healthy amount into one of the water glasses. He drank, then smacked his lips. "Well, that's better." He grinned at Broadbent. "What can I do for you, Webster?"

"As you know, I'm in the running for the job of executive judge."

"So's everybody else. What else is new?" Quinlan drank again.

Broadbent forced a smile. He wanted an important favor, and there was no point in irritating this foolish old man. "You're quite right, of course, Tim." He tried to make it sound as if he considered Quinlan one of his oldest and dearest friends. "But I'm led to believe I may have a better chance than some of the others."

"Labor may get behind you, that's what I hear."

Broadbent smiled. "It's a possibility. But as we both know, that in itself is no guarantee that I'd get the job."

Quinlan sat back in Johnson's chair, looking like a wizened king perched upon a giant leather throne. "You'd have to have more than labor, that's true. But it's not a bad start." He sipped at the brandy. "I'd like to pledge my vote to you, Webster, but I really have to be impartial in this job, even if I am a short-termer. But when the time comes, we'll talk."

"I couldn't ask for more," Broadbent said, annoyed that Quinlan chose to sit on the fence. The old man would wait until the very last, then throw his vote to the obvious winner. Many of the judges would probably do the same. The winner might have a long memory, and no rational person would wish to make a needless enemy.

"I'm not here to solicit your vote, Tim. I'm here to ask a rather special favor."

Quinlan's small eyes narrowed with interest.

"As you know, I'm assigned to the criminal division. I've always liked it there."

"I heard you asked Johnson for a transfer to civil and that he turned you down." Quinlan finished the brandy and poured more.

"Ah, that was some time ago. But I changed my mind. You know how it is."

Quinlan's peculiar wheezing laugh always sounded as if he were strangling. "Sure."

"Anyway, Tim, there are a couple of rather delicate cases coming up for assignment in the criminal division, cases that'll produce a great deal of publicity for someone, but which are also rather controversial."

"So? That's what we're here for, isn't it, to hear and decide cases?"

Broadbent found it difficult to maintain his smile. He wondered if Quinlan was playing with him. "Of course. But given all the circumstances, I would like to avoid any kind of controversy at this time."

"You think trying either one of those cases might hurt your chance to become executive judge?"

Broadbent nodded. "It's possible. Extremely vocal pressure groups will be monitoring both cases. They could pose a serious problem. As we both know, you can't please all sides. The losing side could mount a very nasty campaign against a judge who displeased them."

Quinlan sat forward and placed the brandy glass down on the desk before him. "Are we talking about the same two cases? Chesney, that cop, and Malked, the guy who shot his daughter?"

Broadbent nodded. "Both are potentially dynamite."

Quinlan shrugged. "I wouldn't want to play favorites, Webster. Some of the other guys over in the criminal division have a chance at this job too."

"Not only the guys," Broadbent said.

"Oh?"

Broadbent knew Quinlan's opinion of women, and he felt he could now use that prejudice to his advantage. "I've heard talk that Kathleen Talbot might try for executive judge."

Quinlan's face reflected his surprise and revulsion. "Christ! She's brand-new. How the hell would they expect that she could even do the job, let alone get it?"

It was a rumor invented by Broadbent and designed especially for Quinlan. "I'm just telling you what I've heard, Tim."

Quinlan bolted down the remaining brandy in his glass. "Jesus, they're everywhere, you know. Doctors, lawyers, I've even seen women out on roadwork crews. Fuck, what is this country coming to? It's just political, it's got nothing to do with merit."

"That's why Talbot may have a chance." Broadbent was delighted at Quinlan's expected response. "Of course, if she had to try one of those touchy cases, her chances might be considerably slimmer."

Quinlan nodded. "She's inexperienced. She might really screw up." He grinned suddenly. "And wouldn't that be too damn bad."

Broadbent remained silent.

"Malked, the widower, dying of cancer, who shot his retarded kid—that's the one where all hell is going to break loose. Shit, mercy killing or not, a jury's going to have to convict that guy. And the judge that salts him away won't be very popular doing it."

Again Broadbent was silent.

Quinlan's face creased into a mischievous leer. "Okay, I've just decided. Talbot gets the Malked case. That suit you?"

"Good choice," Broadbent replied. "What about the other?"

Quinlan rocked back in the chair. "You know, Webster, the executive judge has the power to call a retired judge back to sit on a case now and then."

"That's true."

"If I do you a favor now, will you consider me for assignment after I retire?"

Broadbent solemnly nodded. "If that's what you want, of course."

"Do I have your word on it, Webster?"

Broadbent managed a smile. He would never call old Quinlan back to serve—the man was incompetent. And, more important, the old fool was holding back his vote. He felt no obligation. "You have my word, Tim."

Quinlan nodded. "Okay. I do you a favor, you do me a favor. That young prick Sawchek is in the running too, right?"

"So I've heard."

Quinlan's rasp seemed to echo in the large office. "Well, I think I'll assign him the cop's case. I never much liked Sawchek anyway."

Broadbent carefully concealed his exultation. It had worked out much better than he had hoped. He stood up and extended his hand. "I deeply appreciate this, Tim. And I promise I won't forget it."

"I'll remind you, you can be sure of that, Webster."

Broadbent quickly left the office.

Alone, Quinlan poured some more brandy. Webster Broadbent was an ass, he thought, but the pompous idiot did have a good chance of the top job. He didn't trust Broadbent's promise, not at all. But it was a beginning. Sticking it to the Talbot woman would be gratifying. And Ted Sawchek, in times past, had often made fun of Quinlan in front of people. It was time to even a few scores.

Quinlan sipped the brandy. He didn't care if he got a little stiff; one of the perks of being executive judge was a car and driver. He looked around at the huge office. It would be difficult giving all of it up, but he'd find a way to make it pay off before they put him out to pasture. And Webster Broadbent might prove to be just the right ticket if everything was handled skillfully.

The world belonged to a clever man.

--◄ ►--

Jane Whitehall had taught her young apprentice well, and while it was questionable that Chuck Jerome had learned much about journalism that summer, there was no doubt that he became an enthusiastic student of the flesh. But his eager-beaverness got to be a bit much, even for Jane.

At first, it had been fun for her, teaching him every sexual nuance she knew or could imagine. But then her pupil began to get possessive, something Jane Whitehall had never tolerated in any of her husbands or former lovers. The "toy" given her to play with for the summer by her managing editor was fast becoming a nuisance and a bore.

She had made the mistake of allowing the young man to move in with her; and soon he was tagging after her like a lovesick puppy, never giving her the chance to be alone. On the rare occasion when she did manage to slip away, she returned to find him brooding with jealousy. She could hardly wait for September to come around, when he would be going back to college.

And it wouldn't be long now, the calendar on her desk informed her, giving her something to be cheerful about for a change.

"Chuck, here are my notes on the council session this morning. You were there. Take them and try to work up a short account of what happened. Emphasize the growing tension between the mayor and the council over who will pick the developer for the proposed addition to the municipal building."

He grinned, grateful for the assignment. She had already written the story in her mind, so she wasn't really relying on his efforts. Besides, it wasn't much of a story, but it would serve to keep him busy. It would also give her a chance to get out of the office and tap a few sources. Some interesting political maneuvers were taking place on the courthouse scene, and Jane could smell an opportunity for advancing her own career.

She had found over the years that reporting meant much more than merely observing and interviewing. She had successfully built up a network of people, officials and civil servants, who required only the satisfaction of her attention—and an occasional favorable mention in the paper—to keep her up-to-date on the hidden workings of local politics. But it was a network that needed tending, and she had been neglecting it lately.

The Learned Hand, a small dimly lit bar named after a famous jurist, was conveniently located just behind the soon-to-be-demolished Hall of Justice. Lawyers, clerks, and other personnel of the criminal courts had made it a second home.

Jane walked the few steps down into the bar. She recognized several lawyers, a few detectives, and a handful of court clerks. The clerks, all middle-aged men, were sitting around a table, drinking and playing "liar's poker" with dollar bills.

"Hey, Jane!"

Marty Kelly waved to her. He was sitting at a back table with a young man who looked vaguely familiar.

"How are you, Marty?" she said, pulling out a chair and joining them.

"I am remarkably well," he said, a bit too loudly. His face was flushed, his collar open, tie askew. He was a bit stiffer than usual, given the hour, she thought.

"And this rising star of the courts you may already know—if not, allow me to present the honorable Thomas Mease, demon prosecutor."

Mease was not drunk. He was good-looking in a rough and knowing way, short and muscular. His crooked grin was appealing.

"Prosecute any demons lately?" she asked. "By the way, Marty has forgotten his manners. I'm Jane Whitehall."

Mease had already made a bold appraisal with a quick appreciative glance. "I know. We've met before. How're things at the newspaper?"

She ordered a gin and tonic from the bored waiter. "Everything is slow during the summer. We have to really hump to dig up an interesting article."

"Aha!" Kelly said. "Suspicions confirmed! That's how you people gather the news, you hump!"

"Only for the really good stories, Marty," she replied.

"Damn, and me without a good story," he mumbled with a grin. "Say, what's the word on the race for executive judge? Any inside information?"

She shrugged. "I know what you know. The judges have met, but no one has enough votes as yet. Broadbent is pushing hard; so is Sawchek, plus a couple others."

"I'm interested because my own future may depend on who gets it and how," Marty Kelly said.

"Oh? How can that be?"

Martin finished his drink, then called for another. She noticed that Mease was nursing his drink.

"They are using the prosecutor's job as a bargaining chip," he said.

"How so?"

Kelly sighed. "Well, a couple of judges are interested in Arnie Nelson getting the job permanently—old pals of his, you know—and they are promising their votes for executive judge in return for a commitment from others to vote for Nelson as the prosecutor. Labor wants Jake Gittle, and they are pushing both Broadbent for executive and Gittle as prosecutor—sort of a package deal."

"And how does that affect you? Other than that the new prosecutor will be your boss?"

Kelly shrugged. "Janey, you may have noticed over the years that I have a tendency to drink a bit."

She laughed.

"Well," he continued, "Big Mike and his daughter didn't care as long as I did my job. But someone new might find it annoying that I work only half a day."

"Arnie Nelson has assigned Marty to try the Chesney case," Mease said quietly.

She liked Mease's eyes; they conveyed intelligence and sensitivity.

"That case is scheduled for late September. By that time, Arnie Nelson may be history," she said.

Mease shook his head. "Could be, but the betting is against it. The judges are in no hurry to fill either job. It could be quite some time before they agree."

"You're going to try the Malked case, aren't you?" she asked Mease.

"Yes."

"How do you feel about that? I think the poor bastard should go free. He's dying according to what we hear at the paper. Why not let him plead to something and let him die in peace?"

Mease smiled. "The prosecutor's office is nonjudicial. We have to charge and prosecute if the law has been broken. If a judge wants to let Malked go free, that's a different matter. But we can't, not on the facts. He planned to shoot his retarded kid, and he did. He wasn't insane at the time, and there's no legal reason that would allow a lesser charge."

"Mercy killing—what's your position on that?" she asked.

He laughed. "Hey, I just try the cases they assign me. I'm a worker, like a house painter or a plumber. I have a job to do, and I do it."

"You still haven't answered. What's your position on mercy killing?"

His expression became serious. "It's murder. I may empathize with Malked; I might even do the same thing in his shoes, but that doesn't change things. Killing people has a price tag attached. If you want to do it, be prepared to pay the price; it's as simple as that."

"Is that what you're going to tell the jury?"

She found his laughter charming. "Hell, no," he said. "I'll throw everything I can at Malked. I'm not going to discuss philosophy with the jury. They'd acquit if they thought I didn't have confidence in our case. A jury trial is a primitive thing. Twelve intelligent people become one big ball of primal emotion. The defense will try to make the man look like a tortured saint. I'll try to convince them he is a scheming devil. And in an adversary proceeding, that's the job of the lawyers—to beat the crap out of the other side and win."

She shook her head. "What about justice, doesn't that come in somewhere?"

Mease grinned. "Maybe. That's up to the jury."

Kelly hiccuped. "Jane, that reminds me of the old joke. This law firm sends this kid upstate to try a losing case. He does, but he wins. He's proud and excited, so he telegraphs the firm with the words 'Justice has triumphed.' They immediately wire back: 'Appeal at once!' "

She had heard the same story in a number of versions, but she laughed to be polite.

"What about you," she said to Mease, "wouldn't you like to be prosecuting attorney?"

"Sure," he replied. "But I'm too young, and I don't have any political connections."

"No friends in high places? How about your old boss, Kathleen Talbot—wouldn't she go to bat for you?"

Mease shrugged. "Like I said, I'm a working lawyer, not a politician. Maybe Judge Talbot would vote for me, maybe not. Anyway, I'm not going to ask."

"Why?"

"Because I don't have a chance."

She liked him. He was young, vigorous, and obviously intelligent. He would make a very good prosecutor, she decided.

"Who knows," she said. "Maybe you have a fairy godmother you don't even know about." She sipped her gin and tonic. A speculation piece about the candidates for prosecutor might make a good Sunday feature. And, if handled right, perhaps she might be able to become this promising young man's sponsor. He looked the type who might show some appropriate gratitude.

"Tell me a little more about the other people vying for the prosecutor's job," she said.

CHAPTER 16

"YOU SEEM TO be angry," the doctor said quietly.

"I'm not, at least not at you," Kathleen replied, surprised that her feelings were so transparent. Dr. Jeffrey Goodman was a child psychologist, highly recommended, and she had brought Little Mike to him.

He showed no emotion himself; she presumed this was part of his professional attitude. Dr. Goodman, who looked about forty, was lean, tan, and exuded an almost detached calmness.

"I'm asking not out of curiosity, judge, but we find that we must look at the family as a total unit in order to treat a child. I presume you are angry at someone; is this a frequent occurrence?"

Kathleen smiled. "No. It has to do with a matter connected with my work."

Goodman's office resembled a playroom, containing only a few pieces of formal furniture, and most of those designed to be unbreakable. He sat in a low-slung chair behind a transparent plastic table. Kathleen sat primly on a stuffed chair that suggested the contours of a stuffed animal.

"Your son, by the way, is being tested by a clinical psychologist at the moment. At age four we do the testing in the form of play. Right now your Michael is having a very good time, and we'll have a reasonably complete personality profile when he's done."

She had described the phantom playmate and given the

doctor other examples of Little Mike's behavior that had alarmed
Marie and prompted Kathleen to seek a professional assessment.

"You've talked with Little Mike—what do you think at this
point?" she asked.

"Do you always call him Little Mike?"

She nodded. "He's named after his grandfather."

"The one who just died?"

"Yes."

The doctor's eyes seemed almost uncomfortably steady as he
gazed at her. "What was your late husband's name?"

"Henry."

He nodded. "He died, you said, before the boy was born?"

"Yes."

He leaned back in the chair and casually put his hands
behind his head. "What were the conditions of your marriage
when the child was conceived? Did you both want a child
then?"

She felt a flush of embarrassment, then anger. "I don't see
what that has to do—"

His smile was coldly polite. "I'll be blunt. If the child wasn't
wanted at the time of conception, there's a possibility he's been
paying for that parental attitude since his birth. I must know
everything that has touched the life of that boy if I'm to make
any kind of informed judgment. Now, what was the situation?"

She was shaken, finding the memory painful, but she decided to answer. "We were both young lawyers, just starting
out. He didn't want to start a family until we were established,
but I wanted children."

"So?"

"I had been on the pill, but I stopped."

"Did you tell your husband?"

Kathleen nodded. "Of course. I wasn't playing a trick, if
that's what you mean."

His steely eyes remained enigmatic. "What was his attitude
when he found you were pregnant? Did he wish it terminated?"

"We talked about it, yes. But I wouldn't agree. He was angry,
but then he seemed to accept things."

"And your marriage? How were you getting along?"

She wished he would stop asking such questions, and she

was tempted to lie, but it was Little Mike's future that was at stake, not hers. "Look, I'll be frank. My husband was cheating on me. I found out about it while I was pregnant. He had never been faithful, as it turned out. I demanded a divorce, to be started as soon as the baby was born."

"Did he agree?"

Kathleen suddenly felt herself crumbling inside and came close to tears. "Yes. He was delighted. We lived in the same house, but no longer as man and wife."

"And then he was killed in the flying accident, only weeks before your son's birth?"

"Yes."

Dr. Goodman lowered his arms and sat forward. "Did you feel guilt at the time? That maybe your pregnancy might have been the indirect cause of his death?"

"Jesus! What a question! No. I felt badly, of course. To be frank, I'm ashamed to say that I actually experienced a sense of relief."

"And that's all?"

She glared at him, surprised at her rising anger. "What else should I have felt?"

He made no immediate reply, then spoke softly. "What you've described are conditions normally causing an emotional hurricane, repressed in your case, but a hurricane nevertheless. I imagine some of it washed back on the newborn baby."

"Like hell! My son means everything to me; I'd never do anything like that."

He seemed entirely unmoved by her outburst. "But you have worked very hard since, haven't you? I don't think you paid very much attention to your son, not from the sound of it."

She was shaking, and she found it difficult to keep from screaming at him. "I had to work to support the two of us! I just gave up a golden political future in order to take care of my son; does that sound as if I've neglected him?"

He sighed. "Do you resent doing that?"

She was about to deny it strongly, but stopped. She fought to keep her composure. "I hadn't thought about it, but I suppose I do." She looked away from him. "You'd make a very successful prosecutor."

He chuckled. "I doubt it. You're easy."

"What do you mean?"

Once again he leaned back, but this time he crossed his arms over his chest. To her surprise, he grinned. "We're all afraid, down deep, that somehow we've caused all the problems of the world, but it's only a human condition."

"Do you think I'm responsible for Little Mike's problems?"

He shrugged. "Well, we don't know if he has a serious problem. He may, he may not. We'll know more from the tests. He's been in a terrible bind for a kid, no fault of his or yours or anyone's, but a bind, nevertheless."

He got up and walked to the window. "Michael's only four, but he's going through the so-called Oedipal phase. It's a rite of passage, the burning desire for the complete attention of the parent of the opposite sex. He may be misinterpreting your attitudes, your anger. He may believe that he's the cause. It can get complicated." He turned. "By the way, why were you so angry when you came in here today?"

"It has nothing to do with Little Mike . . . Michael."

"You don't have to tell me if you don't want to."

Kathleen glared up at him. "I'm a new judge. I was assigned to the criminal division—I wanted civil, but because I had been the prosecuting attorney, I was told criminal court was the more logical spot. Then, I think as an insult, they put me to hearing misdemeanor cases. Hardly an enormous challenge. Usually a judge is assigned only for one month to that duty. Today I was told by the acting executive judge that I had to put in another month; then he assigned me to a very controversial mercy-killing case to be tried in September, a case all of the other judges were trying to duck."

"Did you protest?"

"You're damn right I did!"

He seemed to look at her with almost clinical detachment, as if she were some kind of bug. "And what do you intend to do about it?"

"There isn't much I can do, at least immediately. But I have several things in mind."

"Like what?"

"Like running for the executive-judge job myself." She regretted she had told him. She had spoken to no one else, and it was unlikely she would even have a chance.

"Feisty little broad, aren't you?"

Her mouth dropped open. "Broad? Listen, you—"

He laughed. "Judge, your reactions are very predictable, did you know that?"

"That's news to me. Usually I'm told it's quite the opposite."

He nodded. "I suspect that might be true, especially to your young son. He'd recognize the anger, but not the source. That may be the root of the whole problem, if there is one."

"So, where do we go from here?"

The doctor smiled, and for the first time it looked genuine. "Michael may be exhibiting the signs of a beginning schizoid personality—isolated and preoccupied with a rich fantasy life— but I rather doubt it. We'll see. He might need some therapy, probably in conjunction with you."

"Me?"

"When we treat a child that young, we often treat the entire family unit. We have to."

"I'll do what is necessary, of course, but . . ."

His eyes seemed to be gentler suddenly. "You might benefit from some therapy yourself. I rather doubt you've resolved the emotional conflicts connected with your husband's death—and with the birth of your son. That may be interfering in your own personal development and enjoyment. And you seem to be treating very lightly—too lightly perhaps—the death of your father and the sudden change in your career."

"Do you think me emotionally ill?"

He shook his head. "No. Not at all. But considering the stresses, past and present, I'd liken you to a person sitting on a keg of dynamite while smoking a cigarette. You may get away with it, or there may be one hell of an explosion. I don't think you really appreciate the danger. Perhaps we can help you as well as your son."

At that moment the office door opened and Little Mike came running in, followed by a young woman. He seemed so happy, so glad to see her. So normal.

He ran to her and threw his small arms around her legs. He looked up at her and smiled. "I've been playing."

"Have you?"

"We played lots of games." He looked up shyly at the young woman. "Blocks and balls, and lots of things."

Kathleen stroked his hair. "Did you have fun?"

He nodded.

"Do you like it here?"

He returned his gaze to her. "Yes."

"Would you like to come again?"

He squeezed her legs. "Would you come too?"

"Yes."

"Okay," he said. "I like games. Maybe next time they'll let you play too." His eyes seemed to sparkle.

"Yes, honey, maybe they'll let me play too," she replied, struggling to hold back the tears.

-◀ ▶-

"They tell me you're not eating." Jerry Mitchell sat across a table from his client. Since Dennis Chesney was being held in the special-witness section of the jail, Mitchell did not have to speak to him through the protective glass cubicles used for conferences with other prisoners.

"There's not much opportunity for exercise in here," Chesney said, trying to smile, "so I don't work up much of an appetite."

Chesney seemed to be aging visibly, his skin now stretched tightly against his facial bones. His clothes hung on him.

"Dennis, from what the staff tells me, you don't do much of anything. They say you don't even look at the newspapers anymore, you don't watch television, you don't read. According to them, you just lie in your bunk most of the day. They think you may be coming apart, to be frank."

Chesney looked away from him. "I've been in here a long time. It's beginning to get to me, I admit it. I suppose if I were a run-of-the-mill prisoner I'd have others like myself to talk to."

"Your friends in homicide still visit, don't they?"

He nodded. "Yeah, but what do we have to talk about? They have lives, interests, things to do. I just sit here." He sighed. "I almost wish they wouldn't come. It's like talking to strangers."

"We can't risk putting you in with the other prisoners, you

know that. You're a detective lieutenant. They'd skin you alive in five minutes."

Chesney showed no reaction. "At this point, I really don't give a shit."

"Ever see this kind of reaction, what's happening to you, before?"

Chesney ran his hand through what was left of his rusty gray hair. "Sure, we've both seen it. It's the old jailhouse rot. I've agreed to lesser pleas in murder cases just to get some poor declining son-of-a-bitch out of this holding tank and up to the prison. At least there prisoners can be given jobs, make friends, do something about what's left of their lives. Here, you just sit."

"I think I'll ask Dr. Miller to stop by and see you."

"I don't need a shrink," Chesney said. "At least, not yet."

Mitchell studied his client. "It sounds to me as if you're seriously depressed. Miller's good, we both know that. Maybe he can give you something to perk you up a bit."

"There is one thing he can give me that will help," Chesney said.

"What's that?"

Chesney looked at Mitchell over the glasses perched on his nose. "A key."

Mitchell laughed, but he noticed that Chesney didn't even smile. "Well, we'll get you a key eventually, Dennis," he said. "It won't be long now until your trial."

Chesney showed no emotion, but spoke in a low voice. "You know, I've put thousands of people in jail as a cop, thousands. I never knew what it was really like." He looked directly at Mitchell. "Even if I get out, and they don't fire me, I don't think I could ever be a policeman again. I could never again lock anyone up, not after this."

"They've assigned the judge who will hear your case," Mitchell said, changing the subject, alarmed at the depth of his client's emotional agony.

Chesney said nothing.

"It will be before Judge Sawchek, scheduled for the second week in September."

"That figures." Chesney slowly shook his head. "I get a young hustler who doesn't know his ass from third base." He looked at Mitchell. "Didn't he used to be your partner?"

"Yes."

"Think that will help?"

Mitchell laughed, despite himself. "No."

"Do you think he'll be hostile toward you?"

"No. We get along. I understand Ted, and that will help."

"Who's going to prosecute?"

"Martin Kelly."

For the first time Chesney reacted seriously. "Marty doesn't try cases, he can't."

"Arnie Nelson is the acting prosecuting attorney. He assigned Marty."

"Jesus," Chesney said. "Marty will never make it, not with his problem."

"Maybe that's a break for us," Mitchell replied.

Chesney sighed. "Don't count on it. I know Martin and I like him. He's as good as there is—until noon. You watch, they'll pull him off and assign one of their really top guys. Nothing's going to be easy."

Mitchell stood up. "Anything you need?"

Chesney shook his head.

"I'll send Dr. Miller over, and I'll get back to you next week. Cheer up, Dennis. It won't be long now."

Chesney just shrugged.

Jerry Mitchell was glad to leave the jail. No matter how often he went there to see clients he never got used to it. It was depressing under any circumstances, but particularly now. Dennis Chesney looked bad, deteriorating both physically and emotionally. Mitchell knew that if he didn't do something quickly to help the policeman, there might never be a trial.

Judge Jesse Williams had read the pre-sentence report that morning. The probation department had prepared the usual synopsis of the crime, and the consequences to the victim. A psychological profile of the defendant was included, together with his history and family background. Lately, every report looked alike to Williams, only the names and a few of the facts changed. The probation department, under pressure of an ever-increasing flood of cases and an inadequate staff to handle them, was reducing everything to convenient forms requiring as little work and thought as possible.

Williams looked down at Donald Reese, the defendant, as his attorney made a lukewarm plea for leniency. The lawyer, assigned as defense counsel, had done a workmanlike job at the trial, but the evidence was overwhelming and the jury had quickly found Donald Reese guilty of assault with intent to rob. Williams had then set the sentencing for two weeks, the usual period given to allow the probation department to do its job. Now it was over, and Donald Reese was about to learn his fate.

The sentence of Donald Reese was Williams' last formal work of the day. The judge planned to use the newly found time to do some legal research he had put off far too long.

Reese stood next to his counsel. He was a young black man, just twenty-two, small and thin, with an apathetic expression. He glanced up only once at Williams when his attorney asked that the judge give his client one more chance.

Reese didn't look threatening, in demeanor or appearance, but he had been convicted of a string of violent crimes, starting with assault upon an elderly man and a stabbing that had been reduced to a lesser charge but had led to a short jail term. He was already on probation, resulting from an attempted robbery charge that had reduced to aggravated assault.

Reese had used a knife to rob a man making a withdrawal at an automatic teller machine and had been caught in the act by police. There wasn't the slightest doubt of his guilt. Reese had been a problem to the police beginning in grade school. His father had served time in prison and had abused his children, including his son, Donald. His mother had once been arrested for stabbing her husband during an argument, and she had been put on probation after assaulting a neighbor woman. The psychologist reported that Reese was a passive-aggressive personality, but that had become the usual diagnosis given for almost everyone convicted of a crime.

Social help from family guidance centers, the juvenile court, or the probation counselors had done nothing to change Reese or his family. Judge Williams had listened to the lawyer but heard nothing to cause him to reconsider his planned sentence.

He looked down at the young man, who now lifted his eyes up to stare at him. There were so many defendants who had committed such horror that Reese's transgression tended to look mild in comparison, but Williams knew that was an attitude criminal judges had to guard against. Prison was the only answer, although Williams knew Reese wouldn't do well there; he was too small, and not quite vicious enough, or sufficiently intelligent to fend off the human sharks who would prey upon him.

Reese's eyes were wet. He wasn't crying, but tears had formed.

"Mr. Reese," Williams said quietly, "you have been convicted of assault with intent to rob, a serious felony. You heard what your lawyer said. Is there anything more you wish to tell me before I pass sentence?"

Reese dropped his eyes and silently shook his head.

"You were on probation when you committed this crime. And you have been convicted of other crimes of violence. There is no excuse or extenuating circumstance for your actions. You have made yourself a danger to society, and you will have to be removed from it."

Williams looked at his note. "It is the sentence of this court that you be confined at the state prison for a period of not more than ten years and not less than five."

Reese showed no reaction. The court officer led him away as the clerk cracked the gavel and announced to the few people who remained that the court was adjourned.

Jesse Williams was surprised to find Webster Broadbent sitting in his chamber. Williams took off his robe and threw it over the back of a chair. "Well, Webster, to what do I owe this honor?"

Broadbent sat ramrod straight on the edge of Williams' leather couch. "I think you can guess. I'm here to solicit your support and vote for my candidacy for executive judge."

"I understand the unions are backing you." Williams sat behind his desk and filled one of his battered pipes with tobacco.

Broadbent nodded. "It's informal, of course, but I'm told they're approaching judges on my behalf."

Williams lit the pipe and sat back almost hidden in the billowing white smoke. "Morton Penn called me."

"So I understand. He said you were noncommittal."

Jesse Williams grinned. "I told him I hadn't made up my mind."

"It's coming down to the wire, Jesse. This has been going on for a couple of months now. It's a long, hot summer and the judges are all anxious to get this settled. I'm sure you don't wish to be left behind. It's always nice to be with a winner."

"That's precisely why I haven't committed, Webster. I'm not sure who's best qualified, or who has the best chance, to be blunt about it."

Webster Broadbent frowned. "You know me, we've served together in the criminal division. And you know who's behind me. Labor has always been friendly to you, Jesse. They always endorse you."

"I was under the impression that they thought I was qualified."

Broadbent, who Williams knew was without a sense of humor, scowled. "Of course, but it's customary to show some gratitude."

"Depends. I hear Ted Sawchek is considered a serious candidate by a number of our brethren."

"Sawchek you know as well as I do. He's strong-armed some business people—some quite questionable—to back him. They are contacting friends on the bench. And I understand he's promising plums to a number of judges in exchange for their votes."

Williams puffed on his pipe. Sawchek had already offered him a transfer to the civil appeal section and a coveted trip to the National Judicial College in Reno. "And what about Irving Solomon? He's being backed by some of the civil-division judges. They outnumber us. He's a good man. I would think he'd be a threat."

Broadbent quickly shook his head. "Nice man, I agree, but too scholarly. And too slow. The executive judge has to be a good administrator and make quick decisions. Irving would make a wonderful law professor, but he could never run a court this size."

"So, how many votes have you lined up, Webster?"

Broadbent's smile seemed a bit forced. "Enough to win."

Williams chuckled softly. "Webster, if that were true, you wouldn't be here now. We've both spent years in politics. Don't indulge yourself in any games, not if you're serious about getting the job."

"I'm close," he said, the smile gone. "If you minority people will come in with me, I will have enough to win."

"By 'minority,' I presume you mean blacks?"

"Yes. Counting yourself, there are eight black judges. Labor has already lined up four. If you and the rest come in, I have more than enough. As I say, I'm that close."

"What about Judge Moy?"

"Pardon me?"

Williams kept his expression serious. "Chester Moy, over in the civil division. Are you counting him as a minority?"

"He's Chinese."

Williams couldn't suppress the grin. "Some might think this city less than half Chinese; thus, Chester would be in a minority."

Broadbent frowned again, exhibiting his failure to understand. "Orientals make up a small fraction of the population. Anyway, Moy is voting for Solomon."

"How about Hernandez and Lopez?"

"Hernandez is for me. Lopez is uncommitted."

"And what about the ladies of the court?"

"Stewart is for me. Morton Penn talked to her. The rest are uncommitted."

Williams blew out the match. "Who are you considering for prosecutor? I'm sure you've had to make some promises."

Broadbent shook his head. "A number of candidates have been proposed. Foley and Sullivan are moving heaven and earth to try to get Foley's nephew the job. Do you have someone in mind?"

"There are several qualified attorneys who come to mind."

"Black?"

Williams chewed on the pipe for a moment. "Some, not all."

"I'm not opposed to a black getting the job, provided, of course, you people support me."

"You didn't hear a name. It might be someone unqualified."

Broadbent smiled. "Not if you recommended him, Jesse. I know you."

"So you'd be willing to bargain? A black prosecutor in exchange for the votes of the remaining black judges?"

"You make it sound unethical. It isn't, we both know that. As you say, we've both been in politics a long time."

Williams tapped out his pipe. "I promise you that I'll think about it, maybe even talk to some of the other judges. That's not a commitment, Webster, just an assurance that I'll consider your offer."

Broadbent stood up quickly. "You and the others won't regret it, Jesse. I always remember who my friends are. Let me know your decision." He paused at the door. "But be quick, this is moving along very fast. If you people are going to do any bargaining, now is the time."

After Broadbent had departed, Jesse Williams leaned back contemplatively. Webster Broadbent both amused and irritated him. He had known hundreds of Webster Broadbents in his life, all just as transparent. Broadbent would be completely unsuitable. He would be a nasty, vindictive executive, completely in the pocket of Morton Penn. Williams knew and liked Morton Penn, but the court was too important to fall under the control of any particular group, good or bad, of any kind.

Sawchek, who was showing surprising strength, was untrustworthy. If he were named executive judge, it wouldn't be long before justice would carry a price tag.

And in Williams' opinion, Broadbent had been right about Irving Solomon. Solomon was a delightful man and an excellent judge, but he was so painstaking about details that the machinery of the court would soon grind to a halt. Legal excellence didn't guarantee management ability.

Some wild-eyed judge who could put a few votes together might end up deciding the contest.

Something had to be done. Jesse Williams himself didn't want the job of executive judge. He was content, and with age, his once fierce ambition had ebbed. But he was proud of the circuit court; he considered it outstanding. And if it were to remain that way, someone obviously had to propose a new candidate.

Whoever it might be would have to be qualified, and attractive to the uncommitted judges. The men and women who served on the circuit bench represented all sectors of community thought, all races and ethnic groups. The judges had a personal stake; they had to feel that the executive judge, whoever it might be, would be fair with them, as well as evenhanded in dealing with controversial legal issues.

But it would boil down in the end to a political solution.

Jesse Williams smiled to himself. He had been in politics all his adult life, and now was the time to put all that experience and knowledge to work.

He had the ideal candidate in mind.

CHAPTER 17

KATHLEEN'S THURSDAY-NIGHT dinners with Jerry Mitchell had become a fixed ritual for them both. She looked forward to them, finding her friendship with the tall trial lawyer pleasant and surprisingly comforting. Not only was he someone she could talk to, confide in, but he was an endless font of amusing courtroom stories. There was nothing romantic or sexual in their relationship; they were just two people who had come to like each other.

At first, inviting Jerry Mitchell to her apartment for the weekly dinner seemed like a good idea, but now she wondered about her motivation. She wanted him to meet Michael after having told him so much about her son. And, for some inexplicable reason, she also wanted him to see where she lived, to know a little more about her.

Marie protested being given the night off, although she seemed privately pleased that Kathleen was finally beginning a social life not connected with politics. Kathleen had never considered herself much of a cook, but she felt she did several simple things well. And tonight's dinner provided an opportunity to show off her limited skills. She had prepared a salad and had two steaks ready to be cooked. Mike had already eaten, since dinner would now be after his bedtime.

Although Kathleen saw little change in her son, Marie claimed the boy had definitely improved since she was able to spend more time with him. In conjunction with her son's treatment,

151

Kathleen was also seeing a therapist every Tuesday afternoon, and reluctantly she had to admit to herself that she was beginning to feel more relaxed and contented.

When the doorbell rang, Kathleen quickly took off her apron and did a fast check of the new dress she was wearing. Mike trailed behind her as she went to answer the door.

Jerry Mitchell, towering above her, grinned and handed her a bottle of wine.

"Thank you. You didn't have to."

"It's the custom, Kathleen. Somehow a six-pack wouldn't quite live up to accepted practice."

"Come in."

Mitchell stepped through the door. Mike stood before him looking up.

"Are you a giant?"

Mitchell looked down, his features suddenly solemn. "Yes, I am. Are you Michael?"

Kathleen was about to reassure her son that Mitchell was joking, but he held out his little hand. "I never met a giant before," her son said, showing a surprising confidence.

Mitchell bent down and shook hands. "I have met many Michaels," he said, "but none quite as fine as you. How are you?"

"This is Mr. Mitchell," Kathleen said.

"We giants prefer to be called by our first names. Mine is Jerry." He smiled slowly as he handed a package to her son. "I found this. It's too small for me, maybe you could use it?"

Mike tore open the package and whooped as he discovered a toy car.

"It runs on batteries," Mitchell said, reaching over and flipping the switch. The toy made a loud buzzing sound as its wheels churned. "It's guaranteed to drive parents nuts before the batteries wear down."

Her son ran off to play with his new toy.

"Come and sit down." She wondered why she suddenly felt so nervous.

He looked around at the apartment. "Nice."

"Would you like some of this wine?"

He grinned. "Wine, as John Wayne used to say, is for wimps and women. Got any Scotch?"

He followed her to the kitchen. "I never quite pictured you as a practitioner of the pot and pan."

She laughed as she prepared his drink. "I'm not. I can make a salad and fry a steak. That, and coffee, mark the outer limits of my expertise."

Kathleen handed him the wine bottle and corkscrew. "Will you do the honors?"

Mitchell expertly opened the wine and poured the pale red liquid into the glass she held.

She led the way into the living room and sat on her favorite chair. Mitchell sprawled out, taking up most of her large sofa. "This is very comfortable."

"I like it."

"We're almost neighbors."

"Oh?"

He looked out the window. "I have an apartment just across the park, in the Whitney. Do you know the building?"

She laughed. "Who doesn't? No offense, Jerry, but the Whitney looks like the background in a Charles Addams cartoon. I'm surprised you'd live in anything so grim and Victorian."

Mitchell loosened his tie. "It's something of a relic, I'll admit, but it has its own archaic charm. The tenants are a mixed bunch of individualists, with the exception of me, of course, but I like them." He sipped his drink. "We have a few artists, a couple of musicians, a collection of local professors, and a number of other interesting people. There's a spirit of live-and-let-live at the Whitney that you won't find everywhere."

Mike came running in, waving his new toy before him and making motor noises to accompany the whine of the battery-driven engine. He scrambled up on the couch and bounced to a stop next to Mitchell.

"This is neat," he said.

"It's a model of a Porsche," Mitchell said. "When you get a little older, your mother can buy you a real one."

"He can get a job and buy his own," she said, noticing the easy rapport her son seemed to have with Jerry Mitchell. "Anyway, it's your bedtime, Michael. So you'll have to put this Porsche away for the night."

Mike climbed down from the couch and looked up at his new benefactor. "Are you really a giant?"

"Do you like giants?"

Her son smiled shyly. "Yes."

"Then, Michael, that's what I am. You go along with your mother, and I'll see you again soon. Okay?"

When they reached his bedroom her son put on his pajamas without the usual protest. "I like him," he said quietly to his mother. "Will he come over again?"

"We'll see," she said, tucking him in. "Probably."

Mitchell had taken off his suit coat when she returned. He stood at the window looking down at the park below. "Nice view, Kathleen. Very pastoral. You wouldn't think we were in the middle of a big city."

She sat down and sipped the wine. "You know I've been assigned the Malked case, don't you?"

He returned to the couch. "And you know I'm his lawyer."

"Do you think I should excuse myself?"

"Take yourself off the case? Why? Because we're friends?"

"Something like that."

He stretched out his long legs. "There's nothing unethical about you hearing that case, Kathleen. I have a number of friends who sit on the court. If everyone decided friendship barred participation, I'm afraid I'd be out of business, as would most lawyers. There's nothing wrong with it."

"Someone might think there was."

"May I help myself?" He got up and walked toward the kitchen. "Would our friendship mean you'd give me an unfair advantage?" he called from the kitchen.

"No."

His big voice seemed to rumble through the apartment. "Would it force you to lean the other way—to favor the other side?"

"Of course not."

He returned with his freshened drink and took up his seat on the couch. "Is it because you're a woman and I'm a man?"

"The code of judicial ethics forbids judges from even giving the impression of impropriety."

He grinned and sipped at the Scotch. "I'd agree if you and I were lovers, Kathleen. But we aren't. Tom Mease is assigned as the prosecutor. He used to work for you. Wouldn't that be equally questionable, given your premise?"

"That's different."

"Why? We merely have dinner together on Thursday evenings. If I were a woman lawyer, would you have any reservations? I think not. Appearances are important, I agree. And perhaps years ago, given different standards, you might be right; but not now."

"Suppose I rule against you on some substantial point—wouldn't that affect our friendship?"

He shook his head. "No. We might even end up shouting at each other—it's been known to happen in the heat of trial—but that's part of the business, and it's all put aside when the day ends." He sipped his drink. "It's almost a traditional thing, friendship between trial lawyers and the judges they appear before. When Abe Lincoln was a circuit-riding lawyer, he traveled on horseback along with the judge and the other lawyers. They stayed in the same boardinghouses and inns, took their meals together, drank and joked together. It didn't affect their performance the next day when they had to try a case. It's a natural thing, friendship between the trial bench and the bar. If it's abused, that's different, but we all live in the same tight little world of the law, Kathleen, so it's only normal that we should tend to hang together after hours."

"Suppose we end up really angry with each other. I might end up sending you to jail—then what?"

He grinned. "Well, if you do, and it's for thirty days, it means we'll miss four Thursday dinners." He laughed. "Anyway, that won't happen. I've gone to jail for contempt a couple of times, but I was young and inexperienced. Now I'm so smooth I'm almost unbearable." Mitchell laughed again. "Once, when I was starting out, I was before old Judge Dowd. I was yelling and jumping around. He asked me to step up to the bench to have a little sidebar conference." Mitchell smiled at the memory. "Anyway, the old man, who was the personification of dignity, whispered: 'Son, if someone has to go to jail, make sure it's your client and not you.' It's a lesson I took to heart. Anyway, the case may never be tried."

"Why?"

He became serious. "I won't discuss the facts—that would be unethical—but Harold Malked is a very sick man. He may not live to trial. So this discussion may be just wasted speculation."

"But you can understand my concern?"

Mitchell nodded. "Yes, I can. It's one of the reasons I never wanted to become a judge. The job demands more than I would care to give."

"What do you mean?"

"Being expected to be completely impartial. A judge can't allow normal prejudice, attitudes, or background to influence judgment. A Catholic judge may have strong religious opinions about abortion, but those beliefs must be subjugated to an evenhanded application of the existing law in such cases, beliefs or no. A judge in a death-penalty state may abhor imposing such a sentence, but it has to be done if the law requires it. It's all a matter of honor."

"Some judges are notorious for exercising prejudice," Kathleen said.

"And often being reversed, too, just for that reason. I'm not saying all you black robes are saints, far from it. But I've seen many judges rise above themselves, many times to their detriment, both personal and political. Sooner or later, Kathleen, win or lose, all judges are forced to the ultimate test of their integrity." He sipped again at his drink. "I suppose that's why they preface the judge's name with the title 'the honorable.' That honor gets tested often enough."

She smiled. "I feel like I should take notes."

Mitchell laughed. "Pontification is one of my more appealing qualities. I hate to do it, but I force myself. My ex-wife, for some strange reason, found it less than enthralling. I have often suspected it was one of the major causes for our divorce."

Kathleen was surprised. Jerry Mitchell seldom talked about his personal life. "How is it that you've never remarried? I would think you'd have discovered an adoring follower by now, one who would hang on every golden word." Despite her intentions, the observation ended with a giggle.

He pretended to frown. "You'd be surprised how difficult it is to find a good disciple these days. You women all seem to have developed minds of your own. It's a sinister trend."

"Suppose I ask the same question seriously?"

Mitchell shrugged. "I married rather early. I was just out of law school. I'm afraid I really didn't appreciate the sacrifices required, nor did my wife. Now that I do, I'm not prepared to make them, frankly. When I'm old, gray and tottering, I'll marry some young nurse and let her take care of me in my declining years."

"I hate myself for asking, Jerry, but curiosity is killing me: what about girlfriends?"

A slow smile ghosted across his features. "Would you want me to lie?"

"No. You don't have to answer at all. It's none of my business anyway."

He shrugged. "I lead a life that's comfortable for me. I work very long hours, but I don't have to account to anyone but myself. I never have to worry about anyone else, or how they might feel. It may be selfish, I suppose, but I'm happier that way." He looked at his drink as if studying the ice cubes. "I have dated some very terrific women, and I know this sounds presumptuous, but I've always made it clear to each lady that I never intend marriage, ever. And usually, at first, that's acceptable, but then things always seem to change." He grinned as he looked up at her. "Kathleen, there are patterns in all things. From painful experience I can tell when that change takes place, despite assurances. I start getting invited to family functions, and soon thereafter the lady starts planning the redecoration of my apartment. Then I know it's time to break off."

"Cruel man."

"Smart man," he laughed. "Anyway, lately I've been too busy for anybody but my clients."

She stood up. "Well, those steaks won't cook themselves."

"Can I watch?"

She nodded, then laughed. "Oh, Jerry, my aunt is planning a nice little family dinner next Saturday, and I wondered . . ."

"You can go to hell, your honor. I don't even know yet if you can cook."

-◀ ▶-

Ted Sawchek was late as usual, but he didn't care. He was the judge, and they couldn't start without him. He had spent a long night seeing people, seeking out power brokers who might have enough clout to get to any of the uncommitted judges. He entered his new courtroom, the one he had claimed on the basis of seniority after Harry Johnson's death. Sawchek nodded to his court clerk. "What's up?"

The clerk, a stout, balding man with a feisty manner, looked up at him. "We have to finish that burglary case we started yesterday. I called the executive judge's clerk and told him we were still booked. He said it looked like a light day, so we may not get another case."

"Good. We should finish with the burglar and get out of here by noon."

"Jeremiah Mitchell is out in the courtroom, along with young Tom Mease. Mitchell's bringing a motion to reduce the charge in that cop case, the one who turned off the machines. He wants you to reduce it to second degree, so that bail can be granted."

"Oh yeah? That should be interesting." Sawchek took off his jacket and hung it on the rack. He slipped into his black robe and zipped it up. "But I don't want to spend too much time on it. Better send them in here. We'll talk it over."

The clerk got up and walked to the courtroom door. "Mr. Mitchell, Mr. Mease, the judge would like to see you in chambers."

Mitchell towered over the shorter prosecutor as the clerk ushered them into Sawchek's inner office.

"Good morning, your honor," Mitchell said.

"How you doing, Jerry? Why don't you boys sit down. Coffee?"

"No, thanks," Mitchell said. Mease shook his head.

"Okay. Now, before you guys go out there and bore me silly, what's this shit all about?"

"Dennis Chesney," Mitchell said.

"Hey, I know all about that case. I even know Chesney.

Good cop, too. But it's going to be a ball-buster of a case."
Sawchek paused, then raised his voice. "Henry," he called to
his clerk, "get a large coffee, black, and put a little sugar in it."

They heard an answering grumble from the outer office.

"You want me to drop the first-degree charge down to second, right?" he said, leaning back in his chair and putting his
feet up on his desk.

Mitchell nodded. "I made a similar motion before Judge
Quinlan, before you were assigned the case; also a motion to
dismiss. He turned both down."

Sawchek looked over at Mease. "What's your position, Tom?"

Mease shrugged. "This is Felker's case. I'm just pinch-hitting
for him on this motion. Personally, I have no problems with it,
but I have to officially oppose the reduction. Arnie Nelson's
given orders to take a hard line on this case all the way."

"So, out in open court, you'll raise hell about dropping the
charge, right?"

"That's right, judge. I have no other choice, unless I want to
start looking for another job."

Sawchek frowned. "Tom, would you mind if I talked with
Jerry here privately for a minute?"

"About this case?"

Sawchek smiled. "Of course not."

"No problem." Mease got up. "Give a call if you need me,
judge." He walked out of the office.

Sawchek waited until he was gone. "What's the real purpose
in asking for a lesser charge?"

Mitchell smiled. "I thought you weren't going to talk about
the case?"

"Shit, I don't want that kid posturing all over the place.
We're old business associates. We can talk turkey. Now, why
do you want this, Jerry?"

"Chesney isn't taking confinement very well. He's coming
apart in that jail. I want to get him out on bond. That's the
reason."

"That's all? Hell, Jerry, the trial's scheduled to begin in a
month. Can't Chesney stick it out until then?"

"I doubt it."

Sawchek yawned. "Fuck, this is a dangerous case. Every

loony in town is watching what happens. Besides, you're raising a hell of a legal question, too. I have to be careful. Those
idiots on the Supreme Court will be nit-picking every goddamn
thing I do."

"It really isn't first-degree murder," Mitchell said. "He never
should have been charged with that."

"That's your opinion. There's a strong argument the other
way."

Mitchell noticed Sawchek's eyes had narrowed slightly, a
sure sign that his former law partner was busy calculating the
possibilities of personal gain.

"I take it, then, that you'll rule against the motion?" Mitchell
asked.

"Did I say that?" Sawchek grinned. "I hear, by way of the
grapevine, that the cops and their union are paying Chesney's
legal fees."

"That's true."

"They must feel very strongly about Chesney."

Mitchell nodded. "So it seems."

"Maybe if they feel strongly enough, they might consider
backing me for executive judge."

"It's a possibility."

Sawchek took his feet off the desk and sat forward. "That cop
union has a couple of judges who are beholden to them. I
know those judges—both are uncommitted."

"So?"

"Look, I like Chesney. And I want to do you a favor too, but I
have to be practical. If I reduce the charge, the crazies and the
newspapers will howl like maddened wolves, and I can't afford
that without getting something in return to make it worth the
trouble."

"Like what?"

Sawchek's eyes were now almost gleaming slits. "If the
police union can get those two judges to commit themselves to
vote for me, I'll knock the charge against Chesney all the way
down to manslaughter. Hey, you can't beat that deal."

"How about dismissing the charges?"

"Never. Too much heat on this one. But you talk to the

union guys. As soon as I hear from those two judges, I'll knock the charge down and grant bail."

"No other way?"

Sawchek grinned. "Nope, that's it, take it or leave it. You can speak your piece out there. I'll say I'm taking it under advisement."

"What about Mease, shouldn't he know about this?"

"Are you nuts? Anyway, Mease doesn't give a shit. You heard him, it isn't his case. He'll oppose it formally; otherwise he doesn't care. Anyway, he doesn't want to make an enemy of me. They say he's in the running for the prosecutor's job. He won't want to piss off any judges, not now."

"Will you back him?" Mitchell asked out of pure curiosity.

"Naw. He's good, but I already traded my vote to old Foley. He wants his nephew in there. I pick up Sullivan's vote too. I'm close, Jerry. If I make it, the sky's the fucking limit, you know?"

Mitchell nodded. "It's a powerful job."

"I'll be running the whole goddamned show. You talk to your people. If they agree we can do business."

His clerk brought in a large plastic cup filled to the top with steaming coffee. "Have a seat out there, Jerry. As soon as I finish this I'll be out. And keep it short, will you? I have to get out of here early today."

"I certainly wouldn't want to interfere with the administration of justice," Mitchell said.

"Hey, I knew you'd understand."

CHAPTER 18

"COAT-HANGER KILLERS!" The seedy preacher shouted the words into a hand-held remote microphone as he paced the stage of the converted former theater.

Nelson Bragg nodded as a murmur of amens rippled from the sparse congregation.

"Oh, they got fancy medical degrees, but they still use little things that look like coat hangers. They kill without mercy, brothers and sisters. And with no risk—protected by an evil law which is carried out by corrupt judges!"

Bragg liked coming to the church. Like the run-down neighborhood and its ragged people, the building had seen better days, but Bragg felt comfortable there. People stared at him in other public places, but no one noticed him in the dimly lit auditorium. And the voices seemed less strident when the preacher talked. Then came the hymn-singing, which seemed to muffle his own voices altogether, leaving Bragg momentarily feeling pacified and safe.

Now the preacher was screaming about doctors. "Mercy killing and abortion—they call it scientific," the preacher cried. "But it is murder, no matter what name the courts give to it."

The amens rose in a disjointed chorus.

"And having a judge make murder legal is nothing new! Why, my friends, when they killed Jesus, they too had a judge— old Pontius Pilate himself. They had a trial and everything, nice and legal, but it was still murder, right?"

The people around Bragg responded with vigor, the noise intruding on Bragg's precarious sense of peace.

"Only God can decide to take human life," the preacher snarled. "No one else. Abortion, no matter how scientific, no matter what the situation, is murder."

Bragg felt a rising sense of discomfort. The congregation was getting too loud. And abortion always provoked memories in him. He had heard the word when they had brought him home from the hospital after his first stay there. His mother and sisters acted oddly, whispering often, constantly watching him. He had been only fifteen, but he still remembered.

His mother had whispered the word to one of his sisters. He had wondered what it meant. Whatever it was, his mother said she should have had it done before his birth.

He heard it often when she didn't think he was listening.

Finally he asked his youngest sister what "abortion" meant.

To his horror, still vivid in his mind, he realized his mother wanted him dead. She wished she'd had him killed.

His sister thought it was amusing; he remembered that too.

Women were killers, he had decided. They had wanted him dead. Even his own mother.

He hated abortion. It was evil. It had to be stopped.

Sometimes, especially at night, he worried that somehow, retroactively, they would still manage to take his life. The revolver made him feel safer.

"We must stop them!" the preacher shouted, his voice coming again into Bragg's consciousness.

"Yes!" Bragg heard his own voice scream in answer. He realized he was standing, his arms raised above him, his fists clenched. Even the preacher stared.

He tried to smile, making things worse. He quickly made his way out of the church, aware that all eyes were on him.

Out on the street, his own inner voices seemed to come together, speaking in the words of the preacher, telling him what he had to do.

CHAPTER 19

TRYING TO PARK anywhere near the city bar-association headquarters was too much of a hassle, so Judge Jesse Williams took a cab from the Hall of Justice. He was a bit late, but he found Brenda Hastings patiently waiting for him in the association's elegant lounge.

She looked up from the newspaper she was reading. "I thought you had forgotten about me."

He grinned and sat down on a large leather chair, separated from her by a small table. "You people sitting over on the civil division don't have to put up with the last-minute stuff we criminal judges have to handle," he said with a laugh. "I had to dispose of a request for a writ of habeas corpus brought in by a young lawyer just before I left. His client had bashed in his dear mother's head this afternoon with a claw hammer, and the lawyer wanted me to decide the legality of detention, since his client had not yet been formally charged. The prosecutor said homicide charges would be brought in the morning, so I listened to the young man's impassioned speech, adjourned it to tomorrow, then hurried over here. I'm sorry to be late."

Brenda Hastings was an attractive woman in her forties, who had a reputation as a good judge, one who was prepared and diligent. That reputation had been lessened in the eyes of some of the legal community when it became known that she was the lover of the feared executive judge Harry Johnson.

"We get our share of the last-minute stuff, Jesse, so don't

feel you people in the Hall of Justice are the only judges put upon by young lawyers with half-baked theories." She smiled as she spoke. "Anyway, I was enjoying the few minutes of peace and quiet. Now, what's this all about? You sounded so mysterious on the phone."

He stretched out his long legs. "I haven't seen you since Harry's death," he said.

She nodded. "Yes. You know, you were the only judge to send me a note. All the rest treated me as some kind of updated version of Hester Prynne."

"Well, some of the brethren weren't too wild about Harry. Some of that probably got directed toward you."

"He was going to leave his wife," she said quietly.

Jesse Williams said nothing. He had known Harry Johnson too well to believe that, but perhaps Brenda did.

Her smile became a bit stiff. "We would have been married, eventually."

He reached across and patted her hand. "I'm sure you would have, Brenda. Life is odd sometimes. What we really want is so often snatched away just as we're about to grasp it."

She nodded; then, as if dimissing the past, she grinned. "Okay, Jesse, enough of this, what's the mystery?"

He shrugged. "Nothing sinister, Brenda, nothing at all. I merely wanted to talk to you about the race to replace Harry."

She laughed. "You mean as executive judge?"

He felt a rush of embarrassment. "Yes."

"Don't look so astonished, Jesse. Half the men on the bench have made guarded propositions, as if I were some hot young thing back on the market. If they weren't so damned insulting, it would be funny. Anyway, go on, what about the election?"

Williams looked around. They were seated well away from anyone else so that whatever was said couldn't be overheard. "So far, there are three major candidates remaining. Sawchek, Solomon, and Broadbent. Have you committed your vote to any of them?"

"I know two of them are your colleagues over at the Hall, Jesse, but they're both horses' asses, as far as I'm concerned. I love old Irving Solomon—he's a darling—but if he gets in, nothing will ever get done."

"Webster Broadbent asked for my support as a 'minority.' I got the impression that he might work for the abolition of slavery. I didn't have the heart to tell him about Lincoln."

Brenda laughed. "It will come as a shock."

"Ted Sawchek promised me everything except the rights to distribution of drugs on the west side."

She nodded. "Me too. He's one of the wonderful gentlemen who made a pass. I think he believes I go with the job."

"Not much of a choice, over all," Williams said.

"I don't think Irving really wants the job. He's being pushed into it by some of the judges in our building."

"So, Brenda, what do we do about the situation?"

She had clear, very light blue eyes. She looked at him. "Are you a candidate?"

"No. I wouldn't want the headaches that go with being executive judge."

"Then, Jesse, why did you ask to meet me here?"

He grinned. "To make a pass?"

She smiled. "No, you're not the type. I know you, my friend; behind that quiet, pleasant exterior something is going on at a furious clip in your clever brain."

Jesse Williams sat forward, his voice barely audible. "This is a nation of minorities, one way or another, Brenda. The bench reflects that. We have blacks, like myself, Hispanics, Jews, every kind and type of minority, even women."

She laughed. "Even, eh? And here I thought you were a modern man."

"Some of us are committed to one of the candidates because of political ties, but many are not. I suspect that almost everyone feels just as we do about the present group of candidates. If we come up with the right person, we can overcome even the organized strength of some of the pressure groups who have such a driving interest in naming someone to that job."

"Who?" she asked.

"A woman."

She looked surprised. "Not me. After the business with Harry, I couldn't get my mother to vote for me. Besides, there are so many male chauvinists on the bench, a woman wouldn't stand a chance."

"I think you're wrong about that, Brenda."

"Okay, Jesse, whom do you have in mind?"

"Kathleen Talbot."

"Too new. She's only been a judge for a few months."

Williams shrugged. "It's a two-edged sword. She hasn't had time to make any enemies or to inflame any jealousies. That's a plus that could offset inexperience."

"But she has practically no judicial background."

"True, but she's been an administrator. The executive judgeship is mostly an administrative job. Kathleen ran the prosecutor's office for three years, and ran it well. That's a big job, with lots of employees, problems, and decisions. She's probably better fitted for running the court than anyone else on it."

Brenda nodded slowly. "And she has political experience—she knows the game, so to speak."

Williams smiled. "She could have been governor. The court would be in good hands if we elected her."

"Does she want the job?"

"I haven't asked her."

"You're kidding."

Williams shook his head. "No. I don't think she'd try unless a group of us expressed support. I wanted to talk to you and some others. If it sounded like a good idea, then we could ask her to become a candidate."

Brenda frowned. "I still don't think a woman can pull it off."

"We'll never know unless someone tries, will we?"

She shrugged. "You have a point, judge. Okay, I'll back her if she wants the job." Then she laughed.

"What's so funny?"

"Harry would spin in his grave if he knew a woman might end up taking his place."

Kathleen was glad to be free of the oppressive burden of misdemeanor court. The parade of human sadness every morning took an emotional, at times even a physical, toll. Two months of hearing drunks, petty thieves, prostitutes, and battered spouses had become an endurance contest. Each morning she had looked out at the line and wondered if she could possibly survive the task. But she had, and even Timothy Quinlan had admitted, albeit grudgingly, that she had done a good job. Quinlan's hostility toward her was obvious despite his attempts to conceal it. As acting executive judge, he would have kept her confined to presiding over the dreadful daily parade if he could, but once he had assigned her the controversial Malked case, he was forced to pass the misdemeanor assignment on to another judge for the month of September and give her felony trials until the much publicized murder case began.

She was listening to testimony in a narcotics case. The defendant, arrested in a public restaurant as the result of an undercover police operation, was charged with possession of cocaine valued at several thousand dollars.

The defense counsel had waived trial by jury, so Kathleen's job, as trial judge, was to decide both the facts as well as the law. The non-jury, or so-called "waiver" trial before a judge was sometimes wryly referred to as a "slow plea of guilty" by defense lawyers—judges being considered somewhat less gullible than jurors and more inclined to convict. However, it was also the standard method of trial when, as in this case, the defense consisted of a legal technicality. Jurors failed to appreciate delicate legal nuances, and judges, whether they believed the defendant guilty or not, were bound to follow the law and acquit if the technicality applied.

Everything in the case before Kathleen turned on the legal status of an ordinary restaurant napkin-dispenser.

The prosecutor had introduced the small metal dispenser as an exhibit.

"Officer, you seized that dispenser at the time of arrest, did you not?" Roscoe Kiska, the defense attorney, looked more like a bank president than the prime defender of persons accused in the narcotics trade. He dressed conservatively, wore old-fashioned steel-rimmed glasses, and his gray hair was worn short and parted in the middle. Despite appearances, Kiska was considered the legal frontman for most of the city's powerful narcotic dealers. He was experienced, knew the law, and was famous for his successful search and seizure defenses.

"I took it from the restaurant, yes." The witness was a

narcotics squad officer who worked undercover. He wore a grimy buckskin outfit, scuffed cowboy boots, and hair that cascaded down over his thin shoulders.

"Did you have a warrant to take that dispenser"—Kiska pointed at the box on the table—"or to search it?"

"No."

"Had you, or any member of your squad, tried to get a lawful search warrant, prior to arresting my client?"

"No."

Kiska nodded, took off his glasses and polished them with a large white handkerchief. He looked up at Kathleen. "If the court please, I would like to move to dismiss this case. Obviously, the officers seized the dispenser without legal authority, in violation of my client's constitutional rights."

Kathleen kept her features purposely emotionless. "Did you make a motion to suppress that evidence prior to this trial, Mr. Kiska?"

He nodded. "I did, before the executive judge. He declined to rule, saying it was a matter to be considered at trial."

"On what do you base this motion, counsel?"

Kiska half smiled. "The exclusionary rule, if the court please. Whatever the officers may have found in that dispenser is tainted beyond repair by their illegal seizure and must be excluded from consideration in this trial."

Kathleen had been thinking about Jerry Mitchell and her surprising feelings about the tall lawyer. It was almost a relief to be forced to other considerations.

"So far, the testimony puts your client at a booth in a restaurant. According to the officers, he spends most of the day in that restaurant and at that table."

"Which, as the court knows, is no crime."

She nodded. "However, they saw him taking small packets from that napkin dispenser and giving the packets to a variety of people, who, in turn, gave him money. And, after the arrest, the napkin dispenser was found to contain not only paper napkins but also a number of packets of cocaine valued at over several thousand dollars. Is that not correct?"

Kiska nodded. "We agree, but we deny the packets belonged to, or were in the control of, my client. He has a constitutional right of privacy, and that was breached when the officers seized the napkin dispenser. What they found, whether cocaine or candy, can't be introduced as evidence, since it was obtained in the process of an illegal search." Kiska then read a list of court cases which he said supported his theory.

"The restaurant is a public place, is it not?" Kathleen asked, before the prosecutor had even the chance to reply to Kiska.

"Yes, but the booth . . ."

"When he was arrested, did your client own that restaurant?"

Kiska postured, putting one hand on his hip and gesturing with his glasses. "No, but he still had rights."

"The supreme court has made several exceptions to the so-called exclusionary rule," Kathleen said. "Public places, under circumstances similar to these, are one of the exceptions. The police didn't need a search warrant, not under these facts, Mr. Kiska."

Kiska knew she was about to rule against him, a ruling that would lead to the conviction of his client, a wolfish-looking man who glowered at the world from half closed eyes. The attorney began a theatrical speech full of legal history and case law. Once Kathleen realized he was doing it for the client's benefit, not hers, she let him make his statement without interruption. The prosecutor—who also realized which way the wind was blowing—then made a short formal reply.

"The motion to dismiss is denied," she said, when both lawyers were through. "Please proceed, gentlemen."

Both lawyers recognized that the key issue in the case had been decided, and Kiska apparently knew he hadn't a chance of bargaining with the prosecutor for a reduced plea, so the trial continued, but without any sense of contest or drama, just the routine performance of a necessary ritual.

Once again Kathleen's thoughts returned to Jerry Mitchell. She was wary of allowing herself to even fantasize about making love with him. Her dinners with Mitchell had become an important part of her life, and recently he had taken to dropping in at her apartment. Ordinarily, such an intrusion would have been unwelcome, but more and more she found herself hoping that he would come by. And her son seemed enthralled with the man he fondly described as a giant. There was no place in her life for any kind of relationship—she wanted no more Handsome Hanks. Of course, Jerry Mitchell had made no advances, they were just friends—but she was becoming aware of a nagging desire within herself for something more. That mere thought, she found, was both appealing and frightening.

When the prosecutor rested his case, Kathleen was once again brought back to the courtroom as Kiska made another half-hearted motion for dismissal. She denied his motion, and Kiska also rested. Both men made very brief closing statements.

"I find the defendant guilty as charged," she said. The defendant looked unmoved by her decision. "He will be referred to the probation department for a pre-sentence investigation and report."

"I would ask that bail be set," Kiska said quickly.

"If the court please," the prosecutor said, "the defendant has been convicted twice before of narcotic-related offenses. He is a known dealer and a danger to the community. Given the sentence that he might receive in this case, it is probable that he might find it convenient to disappear, rather than face the consequences of his act. We oppose bail."

Kiska snorted. "My client has a constitutional right to bail, as the court knows. This isn't a first-degree murder case. And, I might point out, every time he has been given bail he has always appeared. There is absolutely no foundation to the statement made by the prosecutor, and he knows it."

Kathleen raised her hand to restrain the prosecutor. "That well may be, Mr. Kiska. But the prosecutor raises some valid points to be considered. The court, unless under certain narrow statutory provisions, must grant bail. I will set bond at five hundred thousand dollars."

"That's a very stiff bond, your honor," Kiska said.

"I think it's justified," she replied. "You can always appeal if you think otherwise."

Kiska shrugged. He knew he wouldn't have a chance of getting it reduced on appeal, not in a narcotics case.

"Anything else?" Kathleen asked.

The clerk didn't even wait for a reply. He cracked the gavel. "This court stands adjourned," he said loudly.

Kathleen stood up, and discovered her legs felt slightly cramped. She hadn't realized just how long she had been sitting. She moved down the few steps from the bench, then went into her chambers.

"Well, was justice done, or done in?" Jesse Williams grinned at Kathleen. He sat on her couch alongside Brenda Hastings. "I presume you know Brenda?"

Kathleen nodded. "We've met. How are you, judge?" Kathleen slipped out of her robe and hung it up. "To what do I owe the honor of your honors," she said.

"May I close the door, Kathleen?" Williams stood up.

"Sure." She took a seat behind her desk.

"We have a proposition to make to you," he said, taking his seat again.

"Oh?"

"Brenda and I have been hatching a small plot," he said, grinning. "And we've discussed it with a number of the judges. Since it concerns you we thought it only fair that we let you know about it."

Kathleen looked at Brenda Hastings. She had always admired Brenda, both personally and as a judge—despite the affair with Harry Johnson. Brenda looked tired. Kathleen wondered if perhaps mourning might be more intense for a mistress than a wife. Even if the deceased didn't merit it, it might be more heartbreaking, since grief had to be concealed and unshared.

"Jesse makes this sound as if we're about to introduce you into some secret and forbidden order," Brenda said. "But it's not quite that sinister."

"We want you to run for the job of executive judge," Williams said, this time not smiling.

Kathleen laughed. "You're not serious?"

He nodded. "Very serious, Kathleen. It's come down to a contest between Broadbent, Sawchek, and Solomon. Each has a following, but not enough to win. Most of the judges don't like the choice they're being offered. We think you could win."

Kathleen shook her head. "I don't think so. I'm too inexperienced. Also, I wouldn't want the job. True, it offers power, we all know that. But also it means facing some very difficult challenges. There's nothing honorary about that job. And for every friend you might win, you make ten enemies. I appreciate the thought, but I really wouldn't want the job. Besides, I find I rather like being a trial judge. As executive judge I would run the court, but I'd never hear any cases."

Williams nodded. "Everything you say is true, except the inexperienced part. As prosecutor you administered a large office with hundreds of employees; that's the kind of experience needed. How well you do as a trial judge has practically no relationship to what would be required of you."

She laughed. "Even if I wanted the job, what makes 'you think I could possibly win?"

"We've been counting noses," Brenda said. "We have ten judges, counting ourselves, who would vote for you."

"That's hardly enough."

Brenda nodded. "True, but we've only talked to judges who we felt could keep their mouths shut. There are still a number of uncommitted ones whom we haven't approached. And those judges pledged to Broadbent might be persuaded to switch—it would depend on labor. We wouldn't want to kid you, Kathleen. It would be tough, but it could be done."

"You sure you're not just looking for a token woman?"

Brenda smiled. "Not a token, you can be sure of that. However, this court has a history of being sexist, as you know." She paused, coloring slightly. "Even under Harry."

Williams nodded. "And if a judge is anything but a WASP, he or she can expect to get short shrift. Community values may be changing, but it has never been reflected in this court. I think change at the top is the only way to get change all down the line." His smile seemed almost wistful. "I'm not proposing special privilege, Kathleen, just essential fairness. We need a candidate who can pull that off. We think you can."

"There must be others."

Williams chuckled. "Oh, yeah. Dozens. But none of them can muster enough votes to even be considered seriously. If you don't run, Kathleen, we may end up with Ted Sawchek."

"That's impossible."

Williams shook his head. "He doesn't have enough to win, but he is leading at this point. Regrettably, there are several judges on the bench who possess ... well ... instincts not unlike Judge Sawchek's. If he should get in, I think we all know what will happen. Eventually we'll have our own Graylord scandal."

"You mean when all those Chicago judges were sent to jail?" Kathleen asked.

"It could happen here. I hate to think of the consequences if the executive-judge position was occupied by someone who was ... well, less than honest."

Kathleen sighed. "It's no secret, but people say I would have had a pretty good chance at the governor's chair if I had waited and run next year."

Williams nodded. "Better than good, I hear."

"I took this job because I have a small son who needs me. As prosecutor I never had the time, and I'm sorry to say that I neglected him. I will never do that again. So you see, I couldn't even consider becoming executive judge. It would be too demanding, too time-consuming."

Brenda looked away, directing her gaze at the windows. "Harry Johnson kept regular hours, even less, and he did a good job. As executive judge people come to you, Kathleen. You set your own hours. It's demanding only in having to make hard decisions. Frankly, you'd probably have more time for your son than you do now." Her voice wavered slightly. "Harry always had plenty of time."

"Kathleen, if Broadbent gets in, Morton Penn will be running the show. I like Morton, and he's always supported me, but the people didn't elect him. Justice has to be equal. Any case where labor's interest was involved would get special handling. I don't think any of us want that."

"Irving Solomon is a wonderful man, Kathleen, as I'm sure you know. But"—Brenda spread her hands in a gesture of doubt—"the court would be in chaos within weeks. Irving can't keep a checkbook. If he had to run a court with hundreds of employees and thousands of cases, it could be ruinous."

Kathleen laughed. "You make this sound like a patriotic duty."

Williams shrugged. "That's close. Also, we're realists. We need a new candidate. No one else is acceptable, or has a chance. So you're really our only chance."

Kathleen frowned. It seemed an imposition. She was just getting used to her new duties, even beginning to feel comfortable as a judge.

"Really, I appreciate the compliment, but I just—"

Williams interrupted her. "This has come out of the blue. Suppose you give it some thought before you make up your mind?"

"You know my answer."

He shook his head. "I know how you feel now, but maybe if you reconsider, it might be different. Why not take a few days to think about it? We obviously can't wait too long, but nothing's going to happen right away. How about it, Kathleen? Just consider it for a while? That's not too much to ask, is it?" His smile had become a grin.

She sighed. "Okay. I'll mull it over, but I'm not promising anything."

Jesse Williams stood up. "That's fair. Well, I have a jury sitting upstairs waiting for my wise words."

Brenda Hastings hesitated. "I have to get back too." She looked almost shyly at Kathleen. "Could we get together for lunch, maybe dinner? Just to talk? It has nothing to do with being executive judge."

"Sure. Anytime, Brenda. Just give me a call."

Jesse Williams opened the door. "Remember, Kathleen, if you decide to run, and you win, you'll have a lot more power than the governor, at least in these parts. That might ease any second thoughts you have about your decision to become a judge."

"I never had any reservations."

He laughed. "On your honor?"

She nodded. "On my honor."

Roscoe Kiska felt no sense of defeat in losing the narcotics case. His client had already paid his fee. Kiska was a workman, and win or lose, he treated each case and client with professional detachment. He used his skills in the courtroom with no more emotional commitment than a bricklayer putting up a wall. It was a job, nothing more, and he did it very well, which, in addition to being well paid, was all the satisfaction he required.

Kiska walked into Ted Sawchek's courtroom. He nodded to the clerk. "The judge busy?"

The clerk, who knew Kiska and Sawchek were friends, shook his head. "Not as far as I know. He's in his office."

Kiska walked in without knocking. Sawchek sat with his feet up on his desk reading a magazine. "Hey, Roscoe, how you doing?"

Kiska sat down and lit one of his imported cigars, using the flat solid gold lighter given to him by one of his clients. "Not bad, Ted." He puffed the cigar into life. "Just lost one in front of Talbot, but other than that, okay."

"How is she? Legally, I mean." Sawchek grinned.

"Not bad. Knows her stuff. Does a creditable job. Completely different from her old man, but competent. You still assigned to the Chesney case?"

Sawchek nodded. "I called up old Quinlan and raised hell, but I don't think he likes me very much. I asked to be taken off that case, but he wouldn't go for it."

Kiska's eyes, two icy blue agates, unblinkingly regarded Sawchek from behind steel-rimmed glasses. "You're going to have to figure some way to get out of it."

"Hey, it's just a case, hot maybe, but just another murder trial. I've tried more than my share."

Kiska nodded. "Yes, you have, but you haven't been a candidate for executive judge before."

Sawchek took his feet off the desk and sat forward. "So?"

"Certain people have been talking to me, the ones who have gone to bat with some of the judges for you. You understand?"

Kiska's narcotics dealers had hidden but strong connections with some of the circuit judges. The dealers could provide unlimited campaign funds, and had. Now they were calling in some of their markers on Sawchek's behalf. He needed their support, and he knew what Kiska's people would expect of him if he got the job. He also knew they were dangerous, volatile people who had to be handled very carefully.

"So, what do they say?"

"They think Quinlan is screwing you with the Chesney case.

The trial is going to be the biggest show in town—even bigger than the Malked case; lots of press and lots of heated opinion both ways. They think Quinlan's put you into a no-win situation just to fuck up your chances to become executive judge."

"I can handle it, they shouldn't worry."

Kiska tapped the cigar on the side of Sawchek's large ashtray. "It's more than worry. If you end up trying that case, they are going to tell their people not to vote for you."

"Jesus Christ!"

Kiska nodded. "They'll look around for someone else to support. This is strictly business, Ted. They want to have an executive judge who owes them a favor or two. They figure, and I agree, that if you try the Chesney case, you'll end up looking like an asshole. Those judges who are fence-sitting now wouldn't touch you with a ten-foot pole if that happened. You'd wind up a loser."

Sawchek's face reflected the sudden fear he felt. "I'm an experienced trial judge, for Christ sake. I won't drop the ball, they should know that. If there's one thing I am, it's smooth."

Kiska half-smiled. "It isn't a question of smooth. I don't think you really appreciate the significance of that case. It's the biggest thing around. You'll have all kinds of nuts crawling out of the woodwork—the right-to-lifers and their opponents, cop-lovers, cop-haters, everyone. No matter which way you go, you'll offend someone. You have to find a way to duck the damn thing."

Sawchek sat back. "What do you suggest? Given what's up for grabs, I just can't call in sick for a few days. Everyone would know I was ducking. Besides, old Quinlan wouldn't assign it to anyone else. As soon as I came back, I'd still have to try it."

"Not if you were in the hospital."

Sawchek laughed. "What hospital? The booby hatch? Jesus, Roscoe, that sure wouldn't help my chances, would it?"

Kiska slowly shook his head. "No, it wouldn't. I don't have any other solution for you, Ted. But you have to figure a way out, or my people will have to look elsewhere."

Sawchek's forehead was glistening with small beads of perspiration. "That trial is set for next week."

Kiska stood up, again tapping the ash off his cigar. "There's not much time, Ted. I wish I could help, but I can't. I'm just the messenger boy. Maybe you can make it on your own, without my people."

Sawchek looked miserable. "You know I can't. They've lined up three judges. If I lose those three, I won't find enough votes to replace them. No matter what happens, I need those judges."

Kiska nodded in agreement. "I hope you think of something."

Sawchek sat motionless after he left. Then he stood up to look out the window as he tried to muster his thoughts. His right knee made the usual small protest of pain. It never bothered him unless he had been sitting for a while, and then only for a few seconds until he worked the joint free. It didn't interfere with his golf game or racketball, or anything else of significance.

He stood at the window and exercised the knee for a moment; then he suddenly grinned at his own reflection in the glass. He dashed to his desk and dialed on his private phone.

"Orthopedic Consultants," the girl answered.

"This is Judge Sawchek. I'd like to talk to Dr. Lindell."

"What kind of medical insurance do you have?" the girl asked mechanically.

"It's a personal matter."

"Just a minute."

He waited, his mind racing like a computerized printer.

"Dr. Lindell's office." This woman sounded older.

"This is Judge Sawchek. I'd like to talk to Dr. Lindell."

"What kind of medical insurance do you have?"

"It's a personal matter."

"We still need to know your coverage." Her tone was authoritative and unyielding.

"Blue Cross, dammit."

"That's Sawchek?" She spelled out his last name.

He was becoming angry. "Yes, and I'm not a patient, I'm a goddamned personal friend of the doctor's. But I won't be for long unless I talk to him, understand?"

"I'm just doing my job."

"I'm sure you are."

"Just a minute."

Again he waited, this time in frustration.

"Hey, Teddy, how the fuck are you?"

Sawchek's anger vanished. Chuck Lindell was an old friend and a longtime golfing companion.

"You know my trick knee?"

"Fuck your trick knee. It hasn't hurt your golf game."

Sawchek chuckled. Lindell was an easy mark, an unskilled golfer who made sucker bets. "Well, maybe not, but I need an operation on it."

"C'mon, Teddy. I looked at that knee. You won't need anything done on it for years, maybe never."

"Chuck, I don't want to explain, but I need a real good excuse to be off the bench for about a month. Foolproof. If I have the operation, will you certify that I have to have bed rest for at least a month?"

"That's no problem. But I wouldn't suggest surgery. You don't really need it."

"I need it, believe me. Could you do it quickly, like tomorrow?"

There was a pause. "Sure, I guess so, if I had to."

"If I come in, can you admit me through the emergency room?"

"You mean make it look like a medical emergency?"

"Exactly. Look, I'm asking a favor here."

Again there was a pause. "Well, I'm sure you have a good reason. Okay, drop by McManus Hospital tonight. Meet me there about eight o'clock, okay?"

Sawchek was grinning. "And you'll give me a letter that I can't get out of bed for a month?"

"Sure. But I'll have to repair the knee first."

"I'll see you at the hospital, and I won't forget this, Chuck."

"That's okay." He paused. "Say, Ted?"

"Yes?"

"What kind of medical insurance do you have?"

Martin Kelly had vowed that, no matter what, he would never begin drinking before noon. Like every vow he had ever made in his life—religious, marital, or medical—he finally broke this one too.

The tremors had begun shortly after Arnie Nelson assigned him to try the Chesney case. Mornings had always been bad, but now they were becoming unbearable. He drank a few shots of vodka to steady himself. That, orange juice, and breath mints had become his breakfast.

Tom Mease stuck his head in Kelly's office door. "Did you hear about Judge Sawchek?"

"The less I hear about him, the better."

"He's in the hospital."

"Nothing minor, I hope."

Mease grinned and came in. "It's his leg; he hurt it or something. Anyway, they had to do some surgical repair."

Kelly's apathy vanished instantly. "Then he won't be able to try the Chesney case, maybe for a long time?" He wondered if he would be allowed one more escape.

Mease shrugged. "He won't be able to try it at all, I understand. I just came back from court. They say Quinlan will have to assign it to another judge."

"If that happens, they may want to adjourn it for a while, don't you think?"

Mease felt sorry for Marty. The Chesney case was far too hot to be adjourned. It had attracted even national press. But Marty needed a little respite from worry. "It's possible," Mease said.

"I wish you could try it," Kelly continued. "God, I'm not only rusty, I don't think I've worked in the afternoon in twenty years. It's just not my style, you know?"

"I now," Mease said. "I'd like to help you out, Marty, but Arnie views me as a rival for the prosecutor's job and he wants me to risk my career as much as possible. That Malked case will be a ball-buster. Arnie hopes my political balls will get busted as well."

"Has he said anything to you?"

Mease grinned. "No. You know him. He's all smiles and handshakes when I see him, but I hear he's saying some pretty rough things about me on the outside. He must be really worried."

Kelly had been too preoccupied with his own problems to think much about Tom Mease's situation, although Kelly had been the one who had started the ball rolling in his behalf. "Anything new on that?"

"On my great chance at the age of twenty-nine to become the head of this throbbing collection of political and legal power? A couple of the judges have said they might think about supporting me. Kathleen Talbot said she would. But a great tide of support is not building for my candidacy, although Arnie Nelson thinks it is."

"You never know, Tom. Things over in the court are pretty volatile. No one can come up with enough votes to become executive judge. Miracles have been known to happen in such circumstances."

Mease laughed. "Yeah, particularly if you're old Jerry Foley's nephew. If anyone knocks Arnie off, he might be the one to do it. Foley and Sullivan can be effective when they want to."

Kelly nodded. "Well, let's hope something good happens, eh?" He was dying for a drink. "Life's not much without hope, is it?"

--◄ ►--

Jerry Mitchell had just turned out the light when the telephone rang. Late calls usually meant someone was in trouble. He rolled over, switched the light back on, and picked up the phone. "Yes?"

"Mr. Mitchell, this is Deputy Dinkins over at the jail. I hate to call you at home like this."

"That's all right. What's up?"

"Harold Malked is your client, the guy that shot his retarded daughter, right?"

"Yes."

"Well, he just died."

Mitchell sat up. "What happened?"

"Nothing. The orderly in the infirmary went to check him and he was stone dead. He had a bad heart, but I guess you knew that. Nice guy, Malked, no trouble or anything like that. We checked his file. There's no family listed. Just you. That's why I'm calling."

"He had no family," Mitchell said, remembering that was the

reason the terminally ill man had shot his retarded daughter: there would be no one to take care of her when he died. "I'll make the necessary arrangements."

"Thanks, Mr. Mitchell. There has to be an autopsy. That's the rule when somebody dies in the jail. But I suppose you knew that already. There's no question about the cause. We all thought Harold would croak before he came to trial. He was really sick. After the autopsy, the body's yours."

"Okay."

"Sorry to be the one to break the bad news, Mr. Mitchell," the deputy said.

Mitchell sighed. "Well, it was for the best. The man was dying. At least he's troubled no longer."

"Yeah," the deputy agreed. "We all liked him here."

Mitchell hung up the telephone and lay back on the bed. The deputy's words weren't much of an epitaph, but they were all Harold Malked was likely to receive.

He stared up at the ceiling. The trial would have been a heartbreaking affair. Even if he had won, the victory would have meant nothing, at least to the ill Harold Malked, whose days were numbered no matter what the jury verdict might have been.

The end of the Malked matter perhaps would ease the strain between himself and Kathleen Talbot. There was nothing improper in their relationship, and they both knew that. But she was uncomfortable knowing she would hear a major murder case in which he was the defense attorney. It was the appearance of impropriety that concerned her. But now she wouldn't be sitting as the judge in the Malked trial, and he had nothing else scheduled before her.

He felt a bit guilty thinking such thoughts. He took no gratification from Malked's sad death, but he found it a touch ironic that it served other purposes.

Malked's death changed a lot of things. Tim Quinlan, a woman-hater, had assigned the controversial Malked trial to Kathleen out of spite, hoping to embarrass her. Now death had thwarted that plan. Quinlan was a mean one. Mitchell wondered what he would do now.

CHAPTER 20

"GOOD AFTERNOON, Judge Talbot." The clerk spoke but made no effort to stop Kathleen as she stormed through the empty courtroom toward Judge Timothy Quinlan's office. The clerk was a senior civil servant, assigned the sensitive job of court clerk to the executive judge, and his many years of experience had taught him never to get between warring judges; or to be a witness. He jumped up and scurried for the hallway door and safety.

Kathleen walked through the open door and found Quinlan, in his shirtsleeves, lying on the large leather couch and reading a newspaper.

Quinlan lifted his head and peered through the top part of his thick bifocals. "It's customary to knock," he snapped in his rasping high-pitched voice.

"I have just been informed that I've been assigned to try the Chesney case."

He put the newspaper on the floor and showed his age as he struggled awkwardly to a sitting position. "According to the governor, you're a judge." He was slightly flushed from his exertions. "And unless I'm greatly mistaken, a judge's job is to try cases."

"I don't think this is fair."

His high, wheezing laugh contained a note of disdain. "You don't, eh?" He stood up and walked to the oversize desk, as if sitting behind it would give him a sense of strength and power.

186 ♦ WILLIAM J. COUGHLIN

He buttoned the collar of his shirt but forgot to adjust his tie. "Judge Sawchek is in the hospital, recovering from surgery. He can't hear the damn case. You were assigned the Malked murder case, but Malked died, so you're open, right?"

"But—"

His cackle cut her off. "Look, toots, you're the new kid on the block, right? You have to earn your spurs around here. Jesus, what kind of a court would we have if every judge got to pick what he wanted? Chaos, that's what we'd have. You bitched when you were assigned to the criminal division. You bitched about hearing misdemeanor cases. Now you're handling felonies, and you apparently want your pick of the cases. I'm afraid it just doesn't work that way around here."

"I don't want to try the Chesney case," Kathleen insisted.

"Why?"

"It's personal."

"Aw, that's too bad. I'm sure it's a good reason, too. Now, you being a judge, you can recuse yourself. You don't even have to ask me, just put the reason on the record, and you're off the case, it's as simple as that. Of course, the reason has to conform to the code of judicial ethics, but I'm sure it does. So, why don't you do that?"

Kathleen knew she could never tell him her real reason. Quinlan would find a way to use it against her. She was being asked to sit on a case in which the defendant was accused of doing just what she herself had done—shutting off life-sustaining machines. Her actions, in the state where her father had died, were perfectly legal. But Dennis Chesney, because of differing state laws and differing relationships, now stood in jeopardy of losing his freedom forever.

"What do you have against me?" she asked, still standing. "Is it because of my father?"

He smirked. "I don't have a thing against you, and I liked your father. You have nothing to complain about."

"Why was I assigned to the criminal division? I told you I didn't want to go there."

He nodded. "Because you had been the prosecutor? Hey, that was no reason. Who would know criminal law better than a prosecuting attorney? I explained that at the time."

"If I'm such an authority, why did you stick me with misdemeanors, and for two months?"

"You're a new judge. It's like any job. Most people start at the bottom, doing the simple things. You wanted special treatment, but you needed the experience."

She sat down. Her anger was beginning to focus. She wondered if he really thought her such a gullible fool. "And then you assigned Malked to me? If I was so inexperienced, I would think you'd have wanted a more seasoned judge to handle such an explosive case."

Without blinking, he replied evenly, "You did a good job on misdemeanors. On that basis I believed you could handle a difficult case. That's the same reason I just assigned the Chesney case to you." His cackle sounded like a rusting gate slowly swinging. "See, I have confidence in you. Now, come on, what's the reason you don't want that case? You can tell me."

He was playing with her, which made her even more angry. "As I said, it's personal."

He shrugged. "If I don't know, I can't help you, can I?"

She had faced prejudice before, and often. Her father had been a chauvinist of the first magnitude when it came to questions of women's equality. Quinlan obviously was of the same school.

"I understand if one judge asks a favor of another, and it's possible, there's an unwritten rule that says it will be granted if it's not unreasonable."

He grinned. "Sure, if it's reasonable. So far you haven't given me any reason at all."

"I have personal reservations about the charge."

He sneered. "You do? Strange, you didn't when it first came up. Hell, your office is the one that brought the charge of first-degree murder against the man. Where were your reservations then?"

Her father had been alive then. But in a way, Quinlan was right. She couldn't say she had moral strictures now, not when she had been prosecuting attorney when Chesney had been arrested. It didn't matter that Arnie Nelson had acted in her absence. It had been her responsibility.

"I know why you don't want to try it." Quinlan's raspy voice took on a sharp, hostile edge.

"Oh?"

His face wrinkled into a leer. "Hey, I never bother judges about their private lives."

"What do you mean?"

The irritating cackle sounded again. "Look, kid, we're all a small community here, the judges and the court personnel. It's like being in a fish bowl sometimes. I don't think it's any reason to try to get out of the case, though."

"I don't understand what you mean."

His eyes, slightly magnified by his thick lenses, reflected his distaste. "Okay, don't think you're fooling anyone. It's your business. But everyone knows you're sleeping with Jerry Mitchell."

"What?"

His eyes narrowed. "Hey, I'm not throwing any stones here. You sleep with the guy, that's your business. Hell, your old man used to boff anything in skirts. But don't come around here looking to get out of work because you can't control yourself."

"You son-of-a-bitch!"

He cackled even louder. "You even sound like your old man. Like I say, what you do in private is your business. You aren't the first judge to jump in the sack with a lawyer. But if you think I'm going to let you out of the Chesney case on that basis, you're full of shit."

Kathleen stood up. She wanted to hit him, to really unleash the rage she felt. She took a breath to control herself. "This may come as a shock to someone of your delicate sensibilities," she said slowly, "but Mr. Mitchell and I have absolutely no sexual relationship. We are friends, that's all."

He smirked. "Oh sure. Then why do you want off the Chesney case?"

She knew if she spoke one more word, she would give vent to the mounting anger. She turned on her heel.

"Hey, your old man would have been proud of you," he called after her. "The guy was a real sack athlete. It must run in the family."

His cackle seemed to follow her as she rushed through the deserted courtroom to the hall.

Quinlan's clerk was in the hall, nervously puffing a cigarette. He merely nodded at her as she stalked by him.

"Where are the public phones?" she demanded.

"They're in the lobby," he called after her. Then, in a very tentative voice he added: "Have a nice day."

Anger turned into resolute determination. She felt as if she had just been raped. The lobby of the new court building contained clusters of telephones set in open pods. She didn't care if anyone heard her or not.

Digging in her purse, she finally found a coin. She had to work her way through a court officer and the clerk before she got Judge Jesse Williams on the line.

"Well, Kathleen, how are you?"

"Does that offer to back me for executive judge still stand?" There was a pause. "Yes."

"Good." Her hand was trembling as she gripped the receiver. "Then I'm a candidate."

"You sound angry, Kathleen. Are you all right?"

"I am both angry and all right. And I mean to shake this damn court up, win or lose."

He chuckled. "I don't know what happened, and I'm not sure I want to, but I'm glad you changed your mind."

"I want to kick some ass!"

He laughed heartily. "Kathleen, if you can just hold on to that evenhanded attitude, you will make a splendid executive judge."

"The usual, Mrs. Hunt?"

Regina nodded as she climbed up on the stool at the far end of the long bar. It had become her accustomed place.

"Hot outside, huh?" The bartender made the vodka martini with a practiced flourish.

"It's boiling out there," Regina replied. "Even in September, Florida's like an oven. I thought I was gonna die from suffocation just coming from the car in here, the air's so hot."

"You drove?"

"Too hot to walk today. The sun would bake your brains. The

Cadillac's air conditioner doesn't help, not in such a short distance, but at least I'm out of the sun." She took the martini from him and sipped. "Don't worry, Harold. If I get a snootful, I'll walk home, sun or no sun. It's only a couple of blocks anyway."

"Just looking out for one of my best customers," he said smiling.

She wondered whether he was gay. He never showed anything but a polite interest. She still had her looks, she knew that, and men seemed to like small blonds. Big Mike was dead and buried, but she still felt peculiar about bringing men back to the house. It was as if he were still alive and might walk in any minute. She felt like she was cheating on him. Regina had decided to sell the house anyway, as soon as the sun-followers from up north started coming down at the first breath of winter and the real-estate market improved.

"I'm going to be gone for a couple of days," she said to the bartender.

"Oh? Where you going, Mrs. Hunt?"

He had time to talk; there was only one other customer at the bar, a man she hadn't seen before.

Regina set the martini glass down on the bar. "Up north—to square up some accounts."

"Yeah, lots of things to do when somebody dies," he said.

She snorted. "Not that kind of business. I'm gonna get even."

He glanced at her to see if she were already drunk.

Regina noticed that the man at the bar was smiling at her in the mirror. She didn't smile back, but she didn't look away either. "My husband was killed by his black-hearted daughter—I thought I told you that."

He smiled. "Several times."

"Well, it's important. The bitch killed him and got away with it. She's a judge now too. Anyway, I'm going to square accounts with her, but good."

The bartender shrugged. "Revenge usually isn't very satisfying."

She laughed. "This time it will be. This bitch is about to try a case—just read about it in those newspapers—some cop who did exactly what she did, killed a guy in the hospital by pulling the plug. They got him charged with murder, and that's just what they should have done to her." She sipped again at the martini, this time giving the man in the mirror a small, tentative smile. He had nice eyes. "By the time I'm through, she'll get hers."

The bartender found this turn of conversation uncomfortable. "You may regret something like that. After all, she's your stepdaughter."

Regina shook her head. "She's not much younger than me, so I don't count her as any kind of daughter. If she were mine, I would have drowned her at birth. Anyway, I'm going up and telling the fucking world about her. She'll be goddamned sorry, I promise you."

He shrugged. "Well, I suppose you know what you're doing."

She lowered her voice. "Harold, who is that guy at the bar? I've never seen him before."

The bartender was relieved to change the subject. "He's staying down at the hotel. A salesman, he says."

"Looks like a nice guy. He reminds me of my deceased husband. You know—big, muscular."

Harold nodded.

"If he wants to buy me a drink, it's okay. You get my meaning?"

Jane Whitehall felt a glorious sense of freedom as she drove away from the busy airport. Getting rid of Chuck Jerome was like having a boil lanced. She felt absolutely wonderful.

As she wheeled into the fast-moving traffic on the interstate heading back into the city she turned her thoughts to the interview she had scheduled.

Summer had been slow for political news; it always was. But September had come and governments were shaking themselves awake, gearing up after the hot-weather doldrums. It would be exciting again, a feast for a political writer like her.

Even something as dreary as the fight for the vacant executive-judge spot was turning newsworthy. Few readers knew of the enormous power and importance of the court's top job. To the public, whoever had the title was just another judge, but the city's power structure knew better, and a bitter battle loomed over who would end up controlling the judicial machinery. Personalities—that's what people loved to read about. The nice and not-so-nice background pieces about men and women in power—that was how to keep the reading public informed—and titillated.

Kathleen Talbot had announced she was a candidate for the court's top job. Now, that was something Jane Whitehall could dig her teeth into. A woman fighting to make her way in a male-dominated world—and the courts were nothing if not that—was always a strong, hot angle. The Talbot woman, although Jane thought her icy and aloof, took a good picture. And Talbot was assigned to try the Chesney case, a real sizzling potato with lots of front-page potential. Medicine, machines, death—the Chesney case was a treasure trove of explosive possibilities.

Jane Whitehall knew she needed controversy. Nothing sold more newspapers than a good old-fashioned controversy.

She turned off the interstate and moved with traffic, heading toward the Hall of Justice. Jane had a late-afternoon interview with Judge Talbot. If she were lucky, Jane hoped to scratch up something that would make a juicy story, maybe even ignite a blistering public debate. And if she could find the right angle, the story just might find its way onto the front page.

A couple of big front-page stories, hot and readable—with Jane Whitehall's byline in ten-point bold caps—could prove to be just the ticket to get her the regular column she lusted for. And Judge Kathleen Talbot looked like a very promising prospect in deed.

--◄| |►--

"Sit down, Martin." Arnie Nelson's apparent nervousness only caused Marty Kelly to become even more anxious. Kelly was so close to retirement, only a few short years away. If they kept him on, he could live out his remaining years in comfort. If not, Marty Kelly feared his ultimate fate would be that he'd end up on skid row, cadging drinks along with the other growling half-human denizens, fighting out the last drops of cheap wine.

"What's up?" Kelly controlled his voice to conceal his fear.

"This can be an unpleasant job at times, Martin." Nelson looked away from Kelly. "Nevertheless, I have the duty, unpleasant or not."

Kelly was afraid to breathe.

"You must understand, Martin, I am acting only for the good of the office."

Kelly's mind raced, conjuring up a thousand arguments against being fired. He quickly reviewed his legal remedies, finding little solace in the prospect.

"I want you to know there's nothing personal in this."

"I think I have been doing a good job, Arnie," Kelly said, choosing his words carefully.

Nelson finally looked at him. "Of course, that's one of the reasons I'm taking you off the Chesney case."

"Pardon me?"

Nelson's expression was pompous, defensive. "I realize you're prepared to try it, and it is a big case, Martin. But you're head of our homicide department, and that's quite a heavy responsibility all by itself. I really wasn't thinking too clearly, I suppose, when I assigned you to the trial. Your true value is back here in the office. Anyone can do the trial work. We need your good judgment and experience to decide policy matters." Nelson's smile was sudden and forced.

Kelly felt as if he had just been saved from the hangman. Nelson was actually apologizing for taking him from a job that would have been Kelly's ruination. There was no chorus of angels or triumphant trumpets, but Kelly's imagination filled in very nicely. "This comes as quite a disappointment," Kelly said, again controlling his tone to hide his relief and exaltation.

Nelson's features turned solemn, nearly mournful. "As I said, Martin, it's for the good of the office. I hope you understand that."

Kelly had been around too long not to know something else had dictated Nelson's decision. Arnie Nelson wasn't smart enough to be devious. A few questions would unearth the real reason. "Well, if I can't do it, I'll have to assign someone. Felker seems the most logical man."

194 ◇ WILLIAM J. COUGHLIN

"Oh, nothing wrong with him, of course. But I think we must put our best foot forward on this one." Nelson pretended to consider the possibilities. "Say, Tom Mease is available, now that Malked is dead. Let's assign him."

Kelly tried to keep from smiling. Nelson was so transparent. Mease was a rival for the prosecutor's job, and Arnie was handing him the Chesney case in the hope the young man would be damaged politically. "Mease is good, but he isn't as experienced as Felker." Kelly, despite his relief at being rescued, couldn't pass up the chance to goad Nelson a bit.

Arnie Nelson frowned. "I think the young man has shown real ability, and he's not new to homicide. Of course, this case could backfire on the man trying it; there are so many divergent interests involved. Still, Mease can do it. It'll be a learning experience for him." Then Nelson smiled. "Say, I have a great idea, Martin. You've prepared the case, you can supervise him."

"Well, I . . ."

"Oh, you don't have to try it, but you can help him along, you know, provide wise counsel and advice."

Marty Kelly knew Mease would be enraged by Nelson's crude political ploy. It was insultingly obvious. "Mease may not like that."

"It will be good for him. But keep your role unofficial, Martin. The responsibility for the trial will be his alone, at least as far as the public is concerned."

"When are you going to break the news to him?"

Nelson's face became solemn. "Well, I'm not, actually. I have so much to do, Martin. Since you know all about the case, and you are the head of homicide, I think you're the one to tell him."

Kelly nodded, then stood up. He turned at the door and spoke to Nelson. "Oh, Arnie, how's your campaign to get this job on a permanent basis coming along?"

Nelson beamed. "Oh, better, much better now."

Kelly glanced at Tina Welch as he closed Nelson's door. He saw the concern in her eyes.

He chuckled. "Don't worry, I haven't been fired. God looks out for fools and drunks. But I'm heartbroken to report that I'm not being allowed to try the Chesney case."

She laughed. "You certainly look heartbroken."

"Don't I, though?"

Kelly whistled without realizing it as he walked through the hallway. Tom Mease glanced up as Kelly entered his small cubicle, more suitable for a closet than a trial lawyer's office. "You sound happy." Mease glanced at his watch. "Sort of early in the day, isn't it?"

Martin Kelly sat down in the only other chair, an ancient hard-backed relic. Prosecutors never believed in wasting good money on outfitting the meager working spaces of low-ranking employees. "You know the old saw, one man's prosperity is another's poverty."

"No, but I do now." Mease cocked an eyebrow. "Go on."

"I have just seen our interim leader and he has taken me off the Chesney murder case."

Mease grinned. "Now I know why you're so damned happy."

Kelly nodded. "That's the good news. The bad news is that you've been assigned to try it."

"What!"

"Arnie figures you're free, since poor Harold Malked went to his final reward. I suggested Felker, but he designated you. I think you know why."

"That pompous, posturing prick!"

Kelly beamed. "Oh, I like that. I'll use that, it has a nice ring to it."

Mease's face was coloring. "He knows the cops will hate my guts if Chesney's convicted. They'll make sure I'll never become prosecutor. Nelson may not be too smart, but even he knows that."

"Oh, I agree." Kelly pretended to a sudden interest in the inspection of his fingernails. "Of course, a bright young man could always find a way to lose gracefully."

Mease snorted. "I wouldn't do that, and you know it."

Kelly looked up at him. "It's been done before—by a number of very successful people. Taking a dive isn't unknown in the boxing ring or in the courtroom."

"Did you ever do it, Martin?"

Kelly shrugged. "On occasion, but never in an important case."

"Why not?"

Kelly laughed. "Oh, I wouldn't pretend to be so honorable that I couldn't do it. I suppose a perverted sense of pride prevented it, or I had nothing of significance to gain or lose."

Mease's eyes narrowed. "Don't bullshit me, Marty. Only part of it's pride."

"Oh? And what's the other?"

"Honor."

Kelly chuckled. "Pride or honor? Frankly, I never saw much difference between the two. We all tend to kid ourselves a bit now and then. I can't see any real distinction."

"We act out of pride when everyone else is looking. Honor dictates our actions when we are accountable only to ourselves."

Kelly squinted at Mease. "The Jesuits got hold of your young mind at some point, didn't they?"

"I did my undergraduate work at a Jesuit school, but they had no influence over me. Hell, I'm not even Catholic."

Kelly slowly shook his head. "Oh, they had input, Tom, more than you even suspect."

"What if I see Nelson and refuse to try the case?"

"He won't let you off. You might consider quitting. I know you've had some good offers. No one would blame you."

Mease shook his head. "If I can't get out of it, I won't quit. Maybe afterward, but not now. I don't care if it stops my chance for prosecuting attorney—I never had much hope there anyway. I'll try the shit out of that case, win or lose."

"It might result in drying up those offers you've had. The case raises emotional issues, and the media will have a field day. If you win, they'll call you vicious. If you lose, they'll say you're incompetent or a wimp. You could come out of it looking very bad."

"Piss on it. The case is a ball-buster, and Mitchell is about the best there is. I might end up looking like an asshole. But I don't run from anything, or anyone."

Kelly laughed gently. "Pride?"

"No." Mease's eyes flashed. "Honor."

CHAPTER 21

NELSON BRAGG HAD wandered down to the courthouse. He wanted to go in, but stopped when he got to the top of the long marble stairs. He had forgotten about the metal-detector device inside the door that everyone had to pass through. He seemed to be forgetting so much lately. He turned and hurried back down the steps, acutely conscious of the small revolver in his coat pocket.

They would have caught him. His heart beat faster as he realized the full extent of that implication. The voices seemed to be howling all around him, as if they had picked up his fear and excitement. If he was caught with the gun, his probation would be canceled and they would lock him away. That would ruin the plan. Bragg didn't know what the plan was, except that something was expected of him, and he couldn't carry it out if he were locked up.

He had no destination in mind, so he strolled around the old criminal-court building aimlessly. He stopped behind two uniformed policemen who paused to allow a large car to come out of a garage exit.

The man driving the car looked angry, his mouth a thin line set above a jutting jaw. Bragg wondered who he was.

"There goes the prize jackass of the world," one policeman said to the other as the car pulled past them and out into the street.

"That old fucker thinks he owns the universe. All those bastards have a God complex."

The word "God" attracted Bragg's interest. He quietly followed behind the two patrolmen as they walked toward the police headquarters.

"Didja see the way he swung that Cadillac out? Jesus, no one would have had a chance to jump out of the way."

The other officer laughed. "Hey, what do you expect from a judge? Suppose everyone stood up when you came into a room, or if everybody was always busy kissing your ass? It would do something to you. Even the good ones get affected by that sort of thing sooner or later."

"Do all those assholes park in there?" The policeman jerked a thumb back toward the garage exit. "They get free parking, in addition to everything else?"

The other officer laughed. "The criminal-division judges park in there—free. Everybody else—the court workers, if they're lucky enough to get a spot—has to pay. I read about it when the public employees' union was bitching about it."

Nelson Bragg stopped. The officers walked away without noticing him. Bragg turned back to the garage. A striped wooden beam barred the entrance. A bored attendant sat in a small booth just inside the exit. The man was reading a newspaper.

Bragg stood there. Another car rolled up to the attendant's booth. The attendant looked in at the driver, then did something that made the wooden arm go up. The driver waved to the attendant as the car rolled through the exit.

The voices were becoming excited again. Bragg couldn't make out what they were saying. Sometimes it was like a telephone line with a number of faraway voices all talking at once.

The attendant noticed him.

As the barrier was lifted, another car rolled through. Bragg immediately recognized the woman. He didn't remember her name, but the sight of her instilled an excited anger. She was evil, he knew that much.

"Good night, judge," the attendant called to the driver. Then he stepped out of the booth. "Hey!"

Bragg looked around. There was no one there but him.

"Hey," the man repeated. "You want something?"

Bragg shook his head.

"Then move along," the attendant said. "This isn't a public garage."

Bragg slowly walked on. The judges parked their cars there. She parked there. That was important. The voices were now almost unbearable in their agitation. He fingered the revolver in his coat pocket, finding some peace and assurance in the touch of the cold metal.

CHAPTER 22

KATHLEEN WATCHED Jerry Mitchell with her son. Michael—she never called him Little Mike anymore—skipped ahead of Mitchell as they moved toward the zebras. The two of them had seemed unaware of her presence almost from the minute they first entered the zoo. She was dismayed at the petty jealousy she was feeling. Even if they ignored her, it was nice to see her son enjoying himself so openly and without restraint. The two of them seemed so natural together.

They had a good day for their outing. It had rained most of the week, but the sun had come out for Saturday. Jerry had suggested the trip to the zoo. She strolled, tagging along behind them, relaxing. Autumn would be early. Some of the trees had begun to show the change of color, and there was an unseasonal nip in the air.

After visiting the zebras, they proceeded to the lion house. The stench bothered her, so she stepped back out into the open, leaving the two to marvel over the big cats, whose roars were amplified by the closed space.

A young man, his track suit wet with perspiration, trotted by her, his face a picture of intensity. Small children ran in the other direction, followed by two harried young parents who looked completely exhausted. In the far distance, white clouds billowed up like snow mountains against a slate-blue sky.

Everything was so tranquil.

When they came out of the lion house, Jerry was holding

Michael, who looked comfortably dwarfed in the tall man's arms.

"Somebody's getting pooped," Jerry said, grinning.

Her son looked up at Kathleen and tried to keep his eyes from closing.

"I think the troops need to get back to camp," she said.

By the time they reached the car, Michael was fast asleep. Jerry placed him gently in the back seat, then propped his coat around the boy so he couldn't fall.

Jerry drove out of the zoo's parking lot and merged into the heavy weekend traffic.

"How about dinner? We can drop Michael off and try the new Greek place everyone's talking about."

She shook her head. "Dinner? Not me, Jerry. I'm near bursting. You've already fed us enough hot dogs to supply an army. If Michael doesn't get sick, it'll be a minor miracle. I've never seen him eat so much."

Jerry grinned. "Hey, he's really loosening up. Let him be a kid, Kathleen. God knows, it doesn't last very long, so it should be enjoyed. Anyway, I'm having more fun than he is. If I went to the zoo by myself, I'd look out of place—this way I can be a kid too, without having any eyebrows raised. Maybe next weekend we could drive out and hit one of those county fairs?"

The day had been perfect. She didn't want to ruin it by mentioning her growing reservations about being with him until after the Chesney trial. "If you're really hungry, Jerry, I can whip you up something at my place. Marie is visiting relatives so I'm chief cook this week."

"Ordinarily I want the first team or nothing, but this time I'll make an exception."

-◄ ►-

Mike woke for only a moment, but he was so exhausted he didn't protest being put to bed. He was asleep before Kathleen turned out the light.

Jerry had his shoes off when she returned. He saluted her with his raised glass. "I made a pitcher of martinis," he said, smiling. "I can't boil water, but I am a respectable hand at mixing a drink."

He poured a drink for her as she sat next to him. "Is he asleep?"

"From the look of him, he may sleep for the next three days. You've worn him out, but he's happy."

"And his mother?"

Kathleen sipped her drink, finding the tang of the gin pleasantly relaxing. "Yes, I'm quite contented, now that you mention it, counselor. Thanks to you."

"I'm not responsible, Kathleen. We all make our own happiness."

She nestled down into the softness of the sofa, accidentally touching his leg with her knee. "Do you really believe that?"

He grinned. "More or less. Life is what we make of it."

Her drapes were open, and they watched the early-evening purples as they developed in the soft late-summer sky. "Well, even if you chose to deny it, Mr. Mitchell, I find you guilty of making me very happy indeed."

She moved to him, kissing him softly on the lips. It was the first time they had kissed.

For a moment they didn't move, their eyes the only communication between them; then he kissed her back, gently but with firmness, his lips sweet to her taste.

"Jerry, I . . ." But her protest was lost in her own erupting desire, and she tasted him with longing and passion, experiencing feelings she thought she had forgotten.

Time was lost for both of them.

--◄ ►--

She lay snuggled against him, her nakedness feeling natural and good against his skin.

"You're quite the lover," she whispered, kissing him just below the ear.

He smiled slowly. "I'd usually make a joke, Kathleen, but this has been just too beautiful to treat flippantly."

The sky was now dark, and wispy clouds scudded by a hazy moon.

She sat up and looked at him. She had been surprised; he was tall and lanky but much more muscular than she had imagined. "God, as the girls say, you're a hunk."

This time he laughed. "You're still a girl, Kathleen, a very lovely, supple girl."

She shivered a bit and covered her shoulders with her discarded blouse. "I've a few miles on me, Jerry."

He leaned forward and touched her back, gently rubbing the area between her shoulder blades. "I have never seen a woman quite so lovely," he said quietly.

Kathleen enjoyed the sensation of his firm strong hand. "Well, this certainly came as a surprise."

"Did it?"

She looked around at him. "Didn't it? Or did you have this carefully planned out? Maybe you take all your dates to the zoo first."

He laughed. "Well, I never did before. But if something works . . ."

"Nasty man!"

He chuckled. "Not really. And you're right, this was a complete surprise, a delightful one, but I assure you I never plan anything quite this well."

"Nor do I," she said, leaning back and taking his hand. "In fact, this makes what I want to talk about all the more difficult."

"What do you mean?"

"I planned to tell you that we shouldn't see each other for a while, at least not until after the Chesney trial."

"Seriously?"

"Yes."

"Well, I'm glad this happened—for a number of reasons, but especially if it changed your mind on that point."

She continued to hold his hand, reluctant to let it go. "It didn't, it just made my decision more firm."

He didn't reply at once. "You really mean we shouldn't see each other until the Chesney trial is over?"

"Yes."

"Isn't that overreacting a little?"

She shook her head. "No, I don't think so. The media pressure will be intense—even the national press is interested. We'll both be living in a fishbowl until it's over, Jerry. We know everything is on the up-and-up, but I'd hate to think of the public reaction if during the trial we were shown on the eleven-o'clock news coming out of a restaurant together."

He spoke quietly. "I think you're being too sensitive."

"It's the Caesar's-wife rule, Jerry. Even the appearance of evil has to be avoided. The code of judicial ethics says the same thing, basically."

He was quiet. She looked at him; his expression had suddenly turned grim. "It won't be too long," she said. "We start the Chesney case next week."

Mitchell again shook his head. "The jury selection may take a week or better, Kathleen. And the trial, depending on a number of things, could run several more weeks. That's a long time. You really can't mean this."

"You know I'm right," she said quietly.

"I can understand what you're thinking, but . . ."

"Especially now, Jerry."

"I don't think things have changed."

She smiled and kissed the top of his hand. "You don't?"

"Oh, Christ!" he muttered softly in protest.

"Our lives will be too public for a while. There's no other way."

"I have a few ethics too, believe it or not."

She touched his arm, then drew her hand away. "I know you do, Jerry."

"Does this include Michael too?"

She nodded. "I'm afraid so." In a way, she knew that would be the worst part. Michael would be the most affected. Jerry Mitchell had become a major part of his world, and her son was too young to understand the fine points of legal ethics "He'll miss you greatly, but it's not forever."

He frowned. "I think this is a mistake, Kathleen."

"How many trial judges do you know who sleep with attorneys who appear before them?"

He shrugged. "It's happened before, to be frank."

"And what did you think of them? Did you think them ethical?"

He grinned, but without real humor. "Sure."

"Answer me honestly, Jerry."

The grin faded. "Well, that was different."

"It won't be long, not really."

He sat up and took a sip of his drink. "Maybe I could wear a disguise and sneak over once in a while."

She laughed. "A mystery man? I don't think you'd look so good in a cloak and floppy hat. Anyway, you wouldn't want to get caught and end up as a feature on a CBS special. We'd both have to leave town."

"How about telephone contact, or is that out too? There are laws against wire-tapping, you know."

It had all seemed so logical before. Now Kathleen found herself close to tears. "We can always talk on the phone."

"Kathleen, I think we had better reassess our positions."

"What do you mean?"

"You know what I mean, our relationship, to use a very weak word. Things have changed. We need to talk."

"This isn't the time, Jerry."

"When? After the trial?"

"Perhaps. We should move slowly."

He drew her to him. "Why?"

She looked up at him. "I don't want to make another mistake."

"You won't be making a mistake. Kathleen, I'm in—"

She kissed him suddenly, cutting off the words. "Now isn't the time, Jerry," she whispered, her lips caressing his cheek.

"Oh, God . . ."

She held him tightly, fighting against tears. She knew she would see him every day in the courtroom and that would only make it even more painful. But it had to be done. They kissed again. "Jerry, I'll miss you so."

--◄ ►--

Jane Whitehall rolled over, half-awake, and reached out. For a moment she was surprised that she couldn't locate the warm body of her college-boy lover; then, as she became more alert, she recalled that she had put him on a plane. He was history.

She stretched and luxuriated in the memory that it was Sunday and she didn't have to get up if she didn't want to.

The early edition of the Sunday paper she had picked up the night before lay at the foot of the bed and she reached for it. Although she had worked as a newspaper writer for years, she still got a thrill out of seeing her words in print, even if they had been butchered by some idiot editor. They had given her the full front page of the paper's comment section, one of the most popular segments of the big Sunday edition.

There was plenty of light streaming in from the noon sun. She propped herself up and again reviewed her work. The artwork was eye-catching, with photographs of the main players in the court drama arranged like playing cards above the banner headline.

Dominating the middle was the hard-eyed photo of the wealthy industrialist whose death had caused it all. After the machines supporting Paul Martin were shut off, he achieved in death a degree of fame denied him in life despite his business success. His features were set in a defiant challenge, probably reflecting the same attitude he had taken with the burglar, also pictured, who cracked his head. Martin's wife's photograph showed a woman who had lived under those challenging eyes, and looked it. But she, more than anyone else, was pressing for a murder conviction.

Jeremiah Mitchell, the big defense lawyer, looked out at the readers, his expression serious and grim. Thomas Mease, whom Jane fancied, had photographed poorly, a boyish grin on his face that looked more appropriate for a high-school yearbook.

Dennis Chesney, the guest of honor at the murder trial, had refused to let anyone take his picture, but Jane had obtained his official identification photograph from a pal in the police public-relations section. Chesney didn't take a good picture, and looked more like a criminal than a cop

But the main photo was of Judge Kathleen Talbot. Jane envied her; the woman was truly beautiful, with a face that easily could have earned her a place among high-fashion models. The judge's attempt to look severe somehow hadn't come off, and she looked more like a gorgeous young woman in a black choir robe. Jane recognized that Kathleen Talbot would be getting a lot of attention, so she had played that angle as much as she could.

The newspaper's chief artist had done a spectacular haunting drawing of the courtroom, catching the sense of ominous drama about to unfold. The editor had wisely used it as a background for the photographs.

All in all, a nice piece of work, and she loved seeing her by-line displayed in nice dark lettering: BY JANE WHITEHALL. She would drop a note to the managing editor, pointing out just how nice that byline would look atop a regular column in the paper. But she doubted it would do any real good. She needed something more than just good, competent reporting. She needed a real zinger—something that sold papers and that she could use as a surefire bargaining chip. And if her own newspaper wouldn't give her what she wanted, there was always the possibility of negotiating with the opposition.

She got out of bed, taking the section with her. Jane was naked. Nightgowns were boring, and she was proud of her body. As she padded into her small kitchen and began making coffee, she thought about how much she liked living alone. Once in a while she missed a regular mate, but that was a passing thing. She had done all that, blessed and unblessed. It was nothing but a burden and a bore.

As the coffeemaker gurgled into life, she reread her own piece. It was good, but mostly an overview of the coming trial and the legal issues. The woman judge eventually would be the main focus—it was bound to happen. Jane wished she had something more, anything, she could use to exploit that angle. The almost too-pretty woman and the power of that black robe she wore—that's where the story would be.

Jane poured the steaming coffee into a large mug. If there was something there, she would find it; it was just a matter of digging. Like a famous Hollywood gossip columnist had once said: "The deeper you dig, the dirtier it gets."

--◄ ►--

"Marty, you worry too much. I'm ready." Mease grinned as he lounged on Martin Kelly's battered couch. "As I've heard you say time and again, murder is just a fatal assault and battery. This will be easy."

Kelly smiled without enthusiasm. It was Monday morning, and Mondays were always the worst. A weekend of nonstop drinking had left his body and mind a mass of ill-defined pain. "If this were the usual run-of-the-mill saloon cutting, I'd agree. But you've got a legal tiger by the tail in this case. Even if you prove every fact you allege against Dennis Chesney, you still have to show what he did was murder. That's going to be the tricky part."

"Marty, you did a good job of preparing," Mease replied. "The law's clear in this state. Until the heart stops pumping, you're alive. If somebody comes along and stops the old pump, then it's a killing. And that's what Dennis Chesney did."

"Did you look up any law yourself?" Kelly asked. "It always pays to do your own homework. I make it a rule never to rely absolutely on anyone else's research. You're stepping into this thing at the last minute. If I were you, I wouldn't start getting cocky."

Tom Mease stretched. "Hey, I'm always cocky, that's part of my charm. Besides looking at those photocopies you made of most of the cases on point, I did a little independent reading. I'm ready, Marty."

Kelly sighed. "That's what Napoleon said at Waterloo, and all he had to face was Wellington. You're looking into the guns of Jeremiah Mitchell."

"So what? I'm not underestimating him, Marty, but what can he do? The facts will be fairly easy to establish. Mitchell will bring in a parade of doctors to claim death occurs when the brain stops functioning. I've always done well cross-examining doctors, you know that. And the law is still the law, no matter what his witnesses say. Kathleen the Ice Queen will have to follow the law, and she'll have to give the jury instructions conforming to that law. Unless they go hog-ass nuts—which I'll admit is always a possibility—they'll come in with a guilty verdict, probably less than first-degree, a compromise, but murder, or manslaughter at the very least."

"I wish I had your confidence." Kelly knew that Mease, like any good trial lawyer, was psyching himself up. "I asked Dr. Farrell to drop by this morning. You got a minute?"

Mease shrugged. "I talked to him on the telephone. I don't see what you expect to accomplish, but I've got nothing better to do."

"It can't hurt. By the way, what do you hear on your quest to become boss of this zoo?"

Mease grinned. "Not much. Nothing's happening. The judges are deadlocked over who will become executive judge. Now that Kathleen Talbot has thrown her hat in the ring, they're all excited, like a bunch of coiling rattlesnakes, hissing and biting at each other. I imagine her candidacy may be the catalyst to break everything loose. None of them seem to be wild about supporting me for prosecutor. Arnie's scared shitless, but for no reason. I don't stand a chance. So if you're thinking of buttering me up as the new boss, you can relax."

Kelly smiled. "Life's like a roulette wheel, Tom. You never know when the little ball may land on your number. This trial may be the vehicle that will break you out. You'll never get publicity like this again."

"Publicity or not, I wouldn't bet on me, Marty."

Dr. Farrell stepped in before Kelly had a chance to reply. "You wanted to see me, Martin?" he said, looking at Mease as if the young prosecutor were trespassing.

"Come in, doctor. You've worked with Tom Mease, I believe?"

Farrell, a short thin man, seemed perpetually nervous. He nodded. "On several cases. How are you?"

"Sit down, doctor," Kelly said. "Tom and I would like to run over some of the aspects of the Chesney trial with you."

"I don't have much time, Martin. The citizens were up to their usual little hobbies over the weekend. I have to get back."

"What was the body count?" Kelly asked.

Farrell sat on the edge of the couch. "Five dead by gunshot wounds, four stabbings, two bludgeoned to death, and one possible poisoning. All that, plus the usual run of suicides, auto accidents, and unexplained deaths. We're going to have to work around the clock to handle all the bodies. I hate weekends."

"We won't keep you long," Kelly said. "We've both read your autopsy report. It's pretty complete."

Farrell almost sneered. "It's perfect."

"Jeremiah Mitchell might not share your opinion," Mease said.

"He never does," Farrell snapped.

"Are you prepared for what he might ask?" Kelly rubbed his aching temples.

"Certainly."

Kelly smiled. "Suppose we play a little game, doctor? I'll pretend to be Mitchell and ask you a few questions."

"I hate games. Tell me what you want me to say, and I'll say it."

Kelly shook his head. "I'm afraid it doesn't work like that, doctor. That would violate a number of rules, both legal and ethical. You're the person testifying, not me. I might suggest emphasizing something, if it should come up, but I can't tell you what to say."

Farrell smirked. "But you will. And you'll use this foolish little game to do it. Then you'll tell me to say, if I'm asked, that we merely discussed the case and that I wasn't instructed on what to say. I've been around. You lawyers and your games. It's all so silly."

Kelly noticed Mease's annoyed expression. Farrell was good in the lab, but on the stand he made a bad impression. But he was the medical examiner, a doctor with a list of impressive credits, and whether they liked it or not, he had done the autopsy and he was the witness who had to establish the death and the circumstances that had caused it.

"We'll abbreviate this game a bit," Kelly said. "Assume you're on the witness stand, and you've already testified to your report. Tom Mease will sit down and turn you over to Mr. Mitchell for cross-examination."

"Go on."

Kelly hoped Farrell wouldn't appear quite so arrogant in the courtroom. "Based upon your examination of the deceased, you testified that he died after the life-support machines were turned off, is that correct?"

Farrell's fingers drummed impatiently on the couch's arm. "Yes."

"Now, doctor, if the machines had not been turned off, the deceased would have gone right on living, isn't that correct?"

Farrell raised one eyebrow. "Living?"

"Yes."

He shrugged. "I hate these games. He wasn't living when the machines were turned off, at least not in a true scientific sense."

Mease sat up straight.

"What do you mean, doctor?" Kelly suddenly forgot all about his aches and pains.

Farrell grimaced. "See, that's the problem with undefined terms. His brain wasn't functioning. If you perceive life and living as dependent upon self-sustained body systems, then he was dead."

"Jesus!" Mease said.

Farrell turned to look at him, a self-satisfied smirk on his features. "See! Now you'll want to tell me what to say."

"If you testify to that on the stand, that's the end of our case, doctor," Kelly said quietly.

Farrell chuckled smugly. "You're not the only ones who can play games, gentlemen. I will testify that he was alive, based upon the action of his heart and lungs at the time the machines were turned off. You see, I do know what to say, even without your help."

Kelly slowly shook his head. "Your perception of what prosecuting attorneys do is a bit flawed. Prosecutors may get carried away sometimes—these are adversary proceedings—but we are supposed to see that justice is done. So if it's your honest medical opinion that he was not living when the machines were turned off, you must say so."

Farrell beamed triumphantly. "But it's not. Oh, there's a raging controversy in medical circles about when death really occurs. I was just giving the answer of someone who might believe that brain function is the test."

"And you don't?"

He shrugged. "I really don't care; I'm a pathologist. In the privacy of this office, I might admit I think the brain-death people have a good argument. But the other side does too. Dr. Franklin Armory, a Catholic, I believe, lectured on the subject last spring at the state medical convention. He opposed the brain-death people. I found him very persuasive."

"I don't believe I know this Dr. Armory." Kelly exchanged glances with Mease.

"Oh, a very good man indeed. Not a pathologist, but I don't hold that against him. An internist, he's a professor at some Chicago medical school."

"Do you remember which one?"

"I have my notes. I can look it up."

Kelly smiled. "Would you give me a call?"

Farrell's features seemed almost sly. "No more games?"

Kelly shook his head. "No. I think you'll do fine, doctor. Just tell the truth as you know it, and let the chips fall where they may."

Farrell stood up. "That's a nice thought, although I know you don't mean it."

Farrell nodded to Mease, then left. They could hear the receding sound of his heels clicking along the tiled hallway as he made his way back to the elevators.

"Still think it will be an easy case?" Kelly asked.

Mease shook his head. "Mitchell will have him for breakfast. Do you think we should follow up on this Dr. Armory he mentioned?"

"I'll get the phone number, but we won't have to call him. I don't like using experts I don't know. Whatever Farrell lacks, we'll make up with Dr. Bertram Shaheen. He's nationally known, good on the stand, and we know what he'll say. Mitchell won't have such an easy time with him. Shaheen is just what we need, a strong knowledgeable medical authority, one who knows what he's talking about, and someone who won't look like a horse's ass."

Mease was no longer smiling. "The trial starts tomorrow, Marty. We don't have much time. Maybe we should contact this Armory now?"

Kelly grinned. "There's no need. Bertram Shaheen will be

there with bells on. For all his dignity, he's a fanatic. This trial will again provide the good doctor with a national audience for his point of view. You read his deposition. Shaheen will make a very convincing witness. I'll get Armory's number just in case, but given the exposure, you couldn't keep Shaheen off the stand even if you wanted to." Kelly became suddenly serious. "And you'll need someone to offset Farrell. What Mitchell will do to him won't be pretty."

Mease stood up. "Damn you, Marty. I was so relaxed, so ready. Now you've gone and scared the shit out of me."

Kelly looked up at him. "That was exactly my purpose, Tom. At least now you know it isn't going to be easy."

Regina Hunt knew she had to get something in her queasy stomach or she would be sick. She showered in the unfamiliar hotel bathroom, dressed quickly, surprised to find that she had hung up her things. She didn't remember much about the plane flight from Florida, or the hotel, though she remembered landing and taking a cab. She fuzzily recalled registering, and finding the hotel cocktail lounge. After that only brief flashes of faces and conversation seemed to bubble up from her headache-tortured mind.

In the hotel lobby, Regina bought a Sunday paper at the newsstand, selecting the one that Big Mike had favored. She tried to walk a poise she didn't feel as she ventured outside. She found a small bar open, went in and took a stool. The bartender, who looked incapable of smiling, nodded at her. She was his only customer.

"Bloody Mary," she said.

He nodded again and slowly set about making the drink.

She opened the paper, flipping through the numerous sections. She almost dropped it all when she saw the picture of Kathleen.

Regina read the article with a sense of rekindled anger. She gulped down the drink as she read and signaled for another. Her rage drove out any residuals of her hangover.

She finished the second drink, folded the newspaper, and flipped a bill to the bartender.

Then she hurried back to her room, found the number in the telephone book, and dialed.

She finally got through to someone in the newspaper's city room. He didn't sound happy about being called to the phone.

"I want to speak to . . ." She looked again at the byline. ". . . Jane Whitehall."

"She isn't here, can I help you?" The offer was made with a decided lack of enthusiasm.

"Can you give me her home telephone number?"

"I'm sorry, lady, we have rules against that. Would you like to leave a message?"

Regina thought for a moment. She decided against it. "Is she working tomorrow?"

There was a pause. "I suppose so. You could try her then."

"I will," Regina said, hanging up.

She looked again at Kathleen's picture, then ripped the page to shreds.

"I'll get you, you goddamned murdering bitch!"

CHAPTER 23

"I'M GLAD YOU could meet me for lunch," Brenda Hastings said as Kathleen joined her.

"Today is my last really free day. Tomorrow I start the Chesney case. And it's drawing almost frantic attention. My clerk tells me the national television people asked Tim Quinlan for an office in the Hall of Justice to use as headquarters."

"He turned them down, of course."

Kathleen shook her head. "No. As a matter of fact, he set up a special press room on the first floor. He's even made arrangements for the installation of special electrical outlets for cameras, computers, and telephones. I've been besieged by people from every network and news service, even some foreign journalists. This thing is being turned into a circus."

"Quinlan can't do that, not in this state. The court rules forbid it," Brenda said.

"Oh, he won't let them actually film in the courtroom. But he's made sure they can set up in the halls and every other public place. He's making sure that if I make a mistake it won't be missed. I think he should have gone into public relations rather than law. He's good at it. The media folks love him."

"Damn him," Brenda snapped. "Damn this whole court."

"It's not the entire court, Brenda. Quinlan just hates women."

Brenda smiled sardonically. "He's not alone. Most of the male judges are sexist. And those that aren't don't give a damn anyway. No one ever wants to rock the judicial boat." She paused. "Not even my beloved Harry, God rest him."

Kathleen said nothing.

"Oh, don't be embarrassed, Kathleen. Everyone in town knows the story, or thinks they do." She looked directly into Kathleen's eyes. "Would you be offended if I talked about it . . . him?"

"Of course not."

"I really don't have anyone to talk to," Brenda said. "Being a judge, as I'm sure you'll find out, can be a very lonely business. Everyone has an angle, either present or future. Everyone wants to be your pal. You have to pick your friends carefully."

They gave the waiter their orders.

Kathleen ordered only coffee, but Brenda asked for a vodka martini. "I'm through with my court work for the day," she explained. "Several of our brethren have a bottle problem, but I'm not one of them, or at least I hope I'm not. But I've been drinking more since Harry's death." She tried to smile. "It's been difficult."

Kathleen nodded. "I'm sure it has."

"You'd know better than anyone else about that. Your husband died while you were pregnant. That had to have been just awful." Brenda paused. "But at least you had the support of your family and friends after he died. God, even my own sister refused to discuss my situation." She smiled wistfully. "It's not easy being a fallen woman, especially under these circumstances."

The waiter brought Kathleen's coffee and set the drink in front of Brenda, who waited until he left, then quickly gulped half of it down.

Brenda studied her glass. "Of course, it was worse for you."

"Why?"

She looked at Kathleen. "Your husband was so young. You were expecting. It must have been hell."

"Did my husband ever sleep with you?" Kathleen asked.

Brenda's shock was genuine. "No! Of course not!"

Kathleen smiled wryly. "I don't know how he missed you. You're certainly pretty enough. Maybe it was your intelligence. Handsome Hank preferred them a little less than bright."

"I don't understand."

"Brenda, my husband was a lying, cheating son-of-a-bitch.

We had agreed on a divorce. Then I found out I was pregnant. I decided to wait until the baby was born before making it legal. He didn't care either way. When he was killed I felt guilt, pity, and a number of other painful feelings, but lost love sure wasn't one of them. So, you see, I think your situation was much more difficult than mine. You loved Harry Johnson."

Brenda finished the rest of her drink. "Well, Kathleen, you can't be accused of beating around the bush. You certainly believe in telling it like it is."

"Sometimes. It depends on whom I'm talking to. Anyway, I'm truly sorry about Harry, and although our positions are different, I think I know how you must feel."

"Thanks. I'm finding it hard to adjust. It's as if I have no future."

Kathleen smiled. "That feeling I do know. But it passes."

"I can't even think of another man. Does that pass?"

"I'm the wrong one to ask, Brenda. After the experience with my husband I wasn't exactly wild to start another relationship."

"There must have been other men?"

Kathleen shrugged. "Remember, I was a brand-new working mother. And I threw myself into politics. I was much too busy to even consider a personal life."

"And now?"

Kathleen sipped her coffee. "That's an interesting question."

"Then there is someone?"

"I'm not sure, at least not yet. A friendship I considered casual seems to be developing into something more, maybe."

"I love romance, and this all sounds so mysterious."

"Not really. Anyway, everything is on the back burner until this Chesney case is completed."

"From the sound of it," Brenda said, "that may take weeks, maybe longer. Even judges aren't required to work nights. It might be nice to have someone to relax with after a tough day, especially since this Chesney case sounds so stressful."

"It would be nice, but I can't."

"I don't understand."

Kathleen suddenly felt embarrassed. "I don't want to mislead you—it really isn't a romance, not yet anyway. It's just something that happened, a surprise, I think, for both of us. And it has to wait until the trial is over."

"Why?"

"The man is Jerry Mitchell."

Brenda's eyes widened. *"The* Jerry Mitchell?"

Kathleen nodded.

"The attorney for Chesney?"

"That's why everything has to wait."

Brenda asked the waiter for another martini, then turned to Kathleen. "My God, Kathleen, I'm in no position to say this— especially with my own background—but do you think it was wise to get involved with Mitchell?"

"He has an excellent reputation."

Brenda nodded. "He does indeed. Still, he is this city's leading criminal defense lawyer, and you are, well ... Shouldn't you disqualify yourself if you're involved?"

Kathleen was about to tell her about the circumstances of her father's death, and the more pertinent ethical position she found herself in because of that, but decided against it. Perhaps later, when she knew Brenda better. "I did ask Quinlan to assign the case to another judge."

"Obviously, he refused."

Kathleen nodded. "He wanted my reason."

Brenda shook her head. "And if you told him, he would make sure it was in every newspaper."

"Since Mr. Mitchell and I are really no more than friends, it would not only be just embarrassing, but it would be grossly unfair to Jerry Mitchell. Besides, I just couldn't give Quinlan that satisfaction."

"You're in a tough spot, Kathleen."

Kathleen nodded. Brenda Hastings had no way of knowing the depth of her difficulty. "I know I am."

"You'll have to be very careful. For the next few weeks you'll be existing in a fishbowl. And a number of people would just love to see you embarrassed."

"It might result in something more than just mere embarrassment, Brenda. I might end up being ruined."

The waiter brought the drink. "Would you like one of these?" Brenda asked. "It might help."

Kathleen smiled and shook her head. "I have a few motions to dispose of when I get back. And I have to plan for tomorrow. I need a clear head more than anything else."

"To each her own." Brenda sipped her drink, then looked at Kathleen. "Look, you may need a friend before all this is over. If you do, I'm it. Okay?"

Kathleen smiled. "Let's hope everything goes smoothly. If not, I'll take you up on that offer." She reached across the table and patted her hand. "Which, by the way, I deeply appreciate."

—◄ ►—

Jane Whitehall's hand shook slightly as she dialed. She hadn't been so excited in years. Telephone booths seemed to have become extinct, so she had to make the call from a pay telephone in the hallway just off the restaurant's bar. She prayed she would get a good connection. This was something she couldn't risk shouting about.

Everyone on the newspaper had to go through the managing editor's secretary to get to him, something that Jane Whitehall found irritating in the best of circumstances, and outrageous now as her anxiety level skyrocketed.

"Hello, Jane. What's up?" Jack Bennett always sounded as though he were half-asleep. No matter what the provocation, the managing editor remained infuriatingly calm.

"Jack, I'm here in the hall of a saloon on DeWitt Street, so I don't want to shout. Can you hear me?"

He chuckled. "What's the matter, Jane? Can't pay your bar bill?"

She controlled herself, resisting the urge to call him an asshole. Bennett was always a bit prissy about her use of language and she didn't want to offend him, not now.

"I've just had lunch with the widow Hunt," she said, looking around to make sure no one could overhear.

"Who?"

"Regina Hunt," she snapped. "The widow of the lately departed Big Mike Hunt."

"Oh yeah. So?"

"Jack, I've got a story here so hot that it will blow the lid right off this town."

"It won't get written in a saloon, Jane. And telling me over the phone isn't practical. I'm no longer a rewrite man." He sounded disdainful.

"Asshole!" She regretted saying it as soon as the word came out. "Look, Jack, this is really big, and I need some help."

"Go on." His irritation was evident, despite his sleepy voice.

Jane composed herself before she spoke. "Mrs. Hunt claims that her husband was murdered."

"What?"

"She tells me he had a stroke and was on life-support machines. She says his daughter Kathleen came down and had them turned off. She killed him."

"You sure this woman is the widow of Mike Hunt?"

"Yeah. I know her. I met her when Big Mike retired. She's the official widow."

"Is she nuts, you think?"

"Who isn't these days? No. She sounds all right. Likes her cocktails, but otherwise she's rational. We can always check her story out."

"Right. But why do you need my help?"

"She's up here from Florida. Regina Hunt wants to take revenge on her stepdaughter, but she plans to fly right back. I told her we'd pick up her hotel and food bill if she'd stay until we developed the story."

"Jesus, Jane, you know our goddamned budget! The people who own this paper don't care about anything but the bottom line. I don't think I could justify that."

"Holy shit! Do I have to spell it out for you? Tomorrow Judge Kathleen Talbot starts a big case, the Chesney murder. Dennis Chesney is charged with turning off the life-support machines and killing Paul Martin. He's accused of doing exactly what Regina Hunt says Judge Talbot did to her own old man."

Bennett whistled softly.

"It could be the story of the century—families, murder, people in high places, everything our readers love and buy newspapers for. It's big, Jack, honest-to-God."

"Our lawyers would have to check everything. Judge or not, we could end up looking down the wrong end of this thing if our facts turn out wrong. Where is she staying?"

"Right now she's over at the Mariner, but I want to move her."

"Why? It's not the best, but it's clean—and it's cheap."

"She registered there under her own name. Anybody can locate her if they try. We want to keep this as an exclusive, Jack. If we salt her away in a nice place, under an assumed name, she's ours alone."

"Would she agree to that? I mean, giving us an exclusive?"

Jane smiled. Regina Hunt was easy. All she needed was the prospect of a little revenge and the provision of a lot of liquor. "She'll agree, Jack, I'm sure. She wants a nice big piece of her stepdaughter's ass—the bloodier the better."

Bennett paused, then spoke quietly but firmly. "If she'll agree to an exclusive, I can square putting her up at some fancy place, meals and whatever. And if what she says checks out, we can baby her for as long as the story plays." Again he paused. "But, Jane, if it doesn't check out, a lot of people around here are going to be angry with me. They don't like spending the company's money. And if that happens, I will be very angry with you. Understand?"

"Look, Jack, I've never let you down before, right?"

"So far."

"And I won't now. I'll spirit Regina Hunt away to a good suburban hotel where she'll be nice and cozy and anonymous. Then I'll check out what I can here, and I think we should send someone down south to find out what happened at the hospital where Big Mike died."

He spoke very quietly. "If what Mrs. Hunt says turns out to be true, it could ruin Kathleen Talbot."

"More than that," she snapped, "it could maybe put her pretty little ass in jail."

"We'll have to be very careful. We won't be able to do anything about the story until it's thoroughly checked out."

"All the better," she said.

"What do you mean, Jane?"

"Jack, if we were to break this tonight, she'd be able to get herself excused from the Chesney case. But that's not the point. The real core of the story has to do with a jurist sitting in judgment for something she herself did—that's the angle. By the time we know if we've got something, she'll be ass-deep in the Chesney trial and she won't be able to get out. And it's going to be a long one. God, she'll be caught like a bug on a pin. She won't be able to wiggle loose, and we can make it a front-page zinger every day, and the lead feature on Sunday. It's a fucking dream!"

There was a long silence on the other end. "Do you have something personal against Kathleen Talbot?"

"Hell, no! She's a little pretentious, but most judges are. No, I've got nothing against her, Jack. But I know a blockbuster story when I see one."

"We have to remain objective, Jane. Let's not forget that."

"I told you I have nothing against the woman!"

"This will destroy her."

Jane scowled. "So what! Fuck her, she's a big girl. If you go around pulling plugs on people, you take a risk. What applies to Chesney should apply to her."

He remained quiet again for a moment, then continued, this time in a less formal voice, "Okay, take Mrs. Hunt to the hotel. Get her statement. Record it on tape, then type up the basics and have her sign it."

"No problem."

"And keep everything to yourself."

"Look, Jack, that's fucking insulting! It's my story, I'm not about to screw it up."

"Get what you can from her. As you say, it's your story. I think you're the logical one to check things at the hospital down south."

"Goddamn you, Jack. That's a job for a drone. I'll be needed here to stay on top of things."

"Do what you have to do, then call me. If things get tight, I'll assign a team to help."

"I don't need or want a fucking team!"

"What are you worried about? You'll get your byline. But you're going to need that hospital confirmation—you get it?"

"You shithead!" She realized she was shouting, but she didn't care. "Remember this is my fucking story. I found it, I dug it up. It belongs to me."

"It will be your story, Jane, I can assure you of that." He once more sounded sleepy, almost bored. "Oh, one other thing."

"What's that?"

"Jane, I hate to ask this again, but try to do something about that foul mouth of yours."

—◀ ▶—

Jerry Mitchell had returned from the jail with the certain knowledge that Dennis Chesney would not be able to testify.

Pete Norbanski was waiting for him in his office, seated behind Mitchell's desk with his feet up. "What's up? You look like you're about to explode." Norbanski had his own office and desk, but he seemed drawn to Mitchell's larger and more elaborate quarters. He made no move to get up.

"Did you contact those doctors and alert them to stand by?" Mitchell glared down at Norbanski, who hesitated, then reluctantly surrendered the large leather chair.

"As well as I could," he replied, changing to the leather couch. "They wanted definite dates, but I told them I couldn't cut it that fine. Anyway, all of them are alerted. They know they'll probably have to take the stand sometime in the next couple of weeks, after the jury is selected and the prosecution puts in its case. They are pissed, but none of them said they couldn't make it."

"Good." Mitchell took off his suit coat, threw it carelessly over the back of the chair, then sat down.

"Are you going to plead insanity?" Norbanski asked. "I thought you had something else in mind."

Mitchell nodded. "I just came from the jail. Chesney answers only in grunts. He won't take his medicine, and he's depressed as hell. If I put him on the stand in his condition, the jury will hate him. I hoped he wouldn't slip this far. A longtime cop can be a hell of a good witness, but not this time."

"If you don't put Chesney on the stand the jury will hold it against him. I don't care what kind of instructions the judge gives at the end, they'll think Chesney's got something to hide."

"That's one reason I'm using the doctors. The jury may realize he's in no condition to be a witness.

"So you *are* going to raise the insanity defense."

Mitchell shook his head. "Can't."

"Why not?"

"Chesney isn't crazy enough. In the old days you could plead insanity and it was a toss-up, but now juries are grabbing at a compromise verdict. They're coming in with 'guilty although mentally ill.' It's the same as a straight conviction; it just makes the jury feel better about their decision."

"If you're not going to plead insanity, then why use psychiatrists?"

Mitchell leaned back, stretching out his long arms, then putting his hands behind his head. "Pete, juries are peculiar. They need excuses if they're going to find for a defendant. I'm going to claim Chesney's acts didn't constitute a crime. But if that's all I do, they'll convict. They have to feel sorry for Chesney, underneath all the legal arguments. They think they're making logical choices, but everything will depend on their gut reaction. The logic has to be there too, but you need to pitch to their sympathy or their desire for fairness."

"How are you going to use the doctors?"

"You've read the reports. They've all examined Chesney. Their craft is subjective. Every one of them says Chesney was under pressure when he shut off the machines. I'll have them talk about his state of mind, but I'll really be using them to drum up sympathy for an overworked detective trying to do his job under difficult circumstances. Since I can't put Chesney on the stand, I'll use the doctors to establish his state of mind."

"That could be dangerous."

Mitchell smiled without humor. "That's right, Pete. It's like threading a needle. If I go too far, the jury will decide he's mentally ill and convict. If I don't go far enough, they could think he's a cold-blooded monster."

"Mease won't be twiddling his thumbs while all this is going on. He could hurt you."

"That's what makes it a ball game, isn't it? He's young, but he's good." Mitchell turned and looked out the window. "You know, the trial of a lawsuit is like two very good swordsmen who come at each other with razor-sharp rapiers. There's no way you're not going to get cut. It comes down to who does the most effective slicing, and there's no way to predict that."

"You have the most experience."

Mitchell nodded slowly. "But Mease has the best case. So it will be a very even contest." He sat up. "Have you prepared the files on the prospective jurors?"

Norbanski grinned. "What else did I have to do? They're right there on your desk, everything nice and neat and clipped into that blue notebook."

Mitchell picked up the notebook. "Some lawyers believe picking the jury determines the case. After that, it's decided."

"Do you?"

"Sometimes. It depends. If the judge lets the lawyers conduct the voir dire examination, it can be. I've won many a case by cleverly framing my questions to the prospective jurors. I've tried the case right then."

"What happens tomorrow? Will Judge Talbot let you do that?"

Mitchell smiled at Norbanski's inflection. "You mean because we're friends?"

"Whatever."

"It's been discussed at a pretrial conference. She'll ask most of the questions. Mease and I can also question, but she has to approve them first. For me, that's like running on one leg. But the same thing applies to Tom Mease."

Norbanski grinned. "So the judge won't let you poison the jurors' minds ahead of time."

"You got it."

"Maybe it will make the jury selection go faster that way."

Mitchell shook his head. "I doubt it. I plan to request the privilege of questioning in certain areas. Mease will too. He'll oppose me, and I'll oppose him. We'll do more wrangling than anything else. That'll take time."

"Sounds tiresome."

Mitchell's expression was solemn. "No, not really. There's a great deal at stake here. One mistake could turn the case around for either side. Mease knows that, and so do I. The process will eat up time, but it's necessary."

"Are you ready for tomorrow?"

Mitchell picked up the notebook. "I'll review your notes on

the jurors, take a little time to think of what I'll be doing, then I'll be prepared."

"Are you going to work late?"

"No. This may be my last free night until this trial is finished. I'm going to grab a light dinner, take a walk, watch a little television, then turn in."

"I betcha Mease is scared shitless."

"No. He's a professional. He'll probably be doing the same thing."

Norbanski raised one eyebrow. "And the judge?"

Mitchell again looked out the window. "That, I don't know. Many things could be decided by this trial, not just the fate of Dennis Chesney, and it will be her first big case—she may be nervous." He returned his gaze to his young assistant. "But that's not my concern, is it? I have one thing to do, as I see it, and that's to win."

"And to make sure Mease doesn't use his blade to cut your nuts off, so to speak."

Mitchell smiled. "You're very encouraging. That vivid little picture will be my last thought tonight as I drift off to sleep."

--◄┃ ┃►--

Foley saw Sullivan at the small round window to his courtroom. That was the signal that Sullivan would meet him in his chambers.

Foley made a great show of flapping the wide sleeves of his black robe and looking at his wristwatch. "This court has some pressing business on another matter," he said quickly. "We'll take a short recess."

The clerk rapped the gavel as Foley hurried off the bench and walked through the small outer office into his chambers. Sullivan sat on his couch.

"What was that all about?" Sullivan asked. "The lawyer looked excited."

"He was. It's a divorce case and everything has been split up except a personal-injury claim."

"Oh?"

"The husband lost his leg at work, and the wife wants a piece of the action if he collects."

"It wasn't her leg."

Foley sat behind his long desk. "That's what the man's lawyer says too. But the law's against him."

"Make new law," Sullivan snapped. "Some of these women want everything, the last drop of blood. I'd throw her ass out if it was before me."

"But it isn't," Foley said quietly. "What's up?"

"Bad news. Irving Solomon is thinking about getting out of the executive-judge race."

"Bullshit."

Sullivan, his thin face a mask of soulful piety, shook his head. "No. I just talked to him myself. He's seriously considering it."

"So what? We've got commitments from Broadbent and Sawchek to appoint Steve Chilinski as prosecutor. One of them is bound to win now. We won't need Irving's commitment."

Sullivan shrugged. "Irv tells me that some of his people want to vote for someone else. He says that's one of the reasons he's thinking of dropping out."

"So?"

"According to Irv, most of his people—at least the ones who talked to him—want to vote for Kathleen Talbot."

Foley sat up straight. "We don't have a commitment from her!"

Sullivan nodded. "Exactly. If she gets in, your nephew can kiss the prosecutor's job good-bye."

"Damn," Foley said. "And we've worked so hard, too."

Sullivan smiled. "Yes. It's been fun. Broadbent thinks we're going to vote for him, and so does Sawchek."

"And Irving."

"Yes. No matter who won, if it was on the first ballot, we couldn't lose."

"Why are you putting it in the past tense?"

Sullivan's features grew somber, his usual expression. "The Talbot woman is riding a streak of luck. You know the old saying: when you're hot, you're hot."

Foley sneered. "And when you're not, you're not. Maybe

she'll fall on her ass. Lucky streaks have a way of ending, you know."

"Do you have anything in mind?"

"Not at the moment. Besides, we don't have to do a damn thing."

"Why?" Sullivan asked.

"Because tomorrow she starts the Chesney case. No matter what happens, she's going to come out smelling bad. It's one of those damn cases where everybody is going to blame everything on the judge." Foley seemed to have convinced himself. "You'll see. That broad won't be any kind of a threat."

"Suppose you're wrong? Sometimes a case like that can make a star out of the judge. Like I said, she's riding a winning streak."

"The Chesney case will ruin her."

"And if it doesn't?" Sullivan asked.

"Then we'll have to think of something, won't we?" Foley stood up. "Well, I've got to go out there and figure out who owns what part of that leg." He smoothed out his robe. "I'll see you when I'm done. If we both think about it, maybe between us we can come up with something really goddamned nasty."

"You sure she won't go for your nephew?"

Foley shook his head. "No. Steve's a good boy, but he doesn't have any experience. She says she wants whoever is selected to be picked on merit."

"Jesus. Thinking like that could ruin the American political system."

"You bet your ass." Foley assumed his stone-faced judicial expression and was the picture of forceful dignity as he stepped back out into the courtroom.

CHAPTER 24

"GENTLEMEN, IS THERE anything else?" Kathleen sat behind her desk facing Jeremiah Mitchell, Pete Norbanski,
Tom Mease, and Marty Kelly. They had been discussing the
procedure agreed upon in the pretrial conference.

Mitchell wished he could talk to Kathleen privately. Just the
sight of her caused a surprisingly painful yearning. "I can't
think of anything else," he said.

"And you, Mr. Mease?"

"I'm a bit concerned that the prospective jurors have to pass
through those rowdy demonstrators out there. That could be
intimidating. Both sides, the pro- and anti-mercy-killing groups,
got into a scuffle this morning."

"What do you suggest?" Kathleen asked.

"It might be a good idea to have them come through a side
entrance. Maybe you could give instructions to that effect?"

She looked at Jerry Mitchell, aware that his eyes had been
fixed on her. "Any objection, Mr. Mitchell?"

"No. I share Mr. Mease's concern."

Kathleen nodded. "I'll set that up and inform the panel. I
may have the jury sequestered after selection, but that's a
bridge to be crossed when we get there." She looked at them.
"Well, let's go to work, shall we?"

The lawyers got up and walked out into the courtroom. For
as long as he could remember, Marty Kelly had always associated this almost ceremonial entrance with the procession of the

bullfighters into the arena. There was no music, just interested—sometimes concerned—faces watching the lawyers, the signal that the trial was about to begin. Mitchell led the way, followed by the much shorter Polish Pete Norbanski. Mitchell moved with ease and a dignity associated with very tall men. Tom Mease, muscular and short, walked with a stalking pace, not unlike a fighter rolling on his toes and ready for battle.

There was standing room only in the courtroom. Kelly knew that most of the crowd were prospective jurors, more than a hundred people, waiting in excitement and nervous anticipation. Some desperately wanted to have a chance to sit in judgment, while others feared it. Most of the rest were media people, plus the few lucky onlookers who managed to get in for the first day of the much-heralded trial.

Dennis Chesney sat quietly at the counsel table, staring ahead at the empty chair where Mitchell would sit. He didn't seem to notice the entrance of the attorneys, or even care that he was about to be put on trial for murder.

The empty jury box, fourteen seats in two rows, awaited the first set of candidates to be called and questioned.

The crack of the gavel sounded as Kathleen entered the courtroom and was followed by the clerk's loud and nasal voice. "All rise! The circuit court, criminal division, is now in session. The Honorable Kathleen M. Talbot presiding!" The second crack of the gavel, after the judge had mounted the bench, signaled that everyone could sit down.

"*People versus Chesney*," the clerk announced in a loud voice.

Tom Mease stood up. "The people are ready."

Mitchell seemed more to uncoil than stand as he got up from the counsel table. "The defendant is ready."

Kathleen nodded and both men sat down. She looked out at the crowded courtroom. "Ladies and gentlemen," she said crisply, "you have been called here today for possible selection as jurors in a criminal case . . ."

Marty Kelly felt his pulse quicken as Kathleen's speech to the prospective jurors continued. Kelly had been a lawyer for many years, but he still found the beginning of any trial exciting. He looked up at Kathleen Talbot and wondered what she might really be feeling. Along with Dennis Chesney, this trial might also decide her fate, but she showed no emotion, her face set in a composed and dignified expression as she spoke. But Martin Kelly wondered if her pulse might be racing just a little too.

---◆ ▶---

Jane Whitehall felt a sense of frustration she had never before encountered. The administration people at the small Southern hospital, from the director down to the record clerks, were friendly and polite, but she had been informed in a charming drawl but firm language that what she wanted was confidential and not available to her eyes.

She already had access to all the public records. That had been easy enough. She had a signed release from Regina Hunt. And she had photocopies of Kathleen Talbot's appointment as guardian of both Regina and Big Mike. The death certificate was a matter of record and easily obtained. But it revealed nothing to substantiate Regina's claim about Kathleen Talbot. And Jane had no intention of leaving that gaping hole unfilled.

And her penny-pinching managing editor was becoming irritable over the delay. Regina's care and comfort was running up a solid bill, and Jane's trip was also adding to the ominous dollar count. Jane knew he wouldn't stand for much more. If she couldn't produce, he would call a halt to the entire story.

To Jane, it wasn't just the story anymore, it seemed as if her own career hung in the balance. That risk, plus the sense of being so maddeningly close, caused her a rare sense of panic.

She drove her rented car once more to the hospital, parked, and went in. Somewhere inside the small hospital was the file on Big Mike Hunt containing the information that would prove, or disprove, Regina's charges. The newspaper wouldn't print anything without that file. She didn't know what she was going to do, but she was determined to get that file one way or another.

She turned away from the administration offices and wandered through the corridors, coming finally to the emergency room.

A young blond man dressed in hospital whites stood in the reception area studying a chart.

"Can I help you," he asked in a soft Southern accent. She noticed the small button pinned to his chest: "Jesus Saves."

"I'm just looking around, thanks."

He studied her for a moment, then lowered his voice. "You're that newspaperwoman from up north, aren't you?"

"Yes."

She noticed that below the small plastic button he wore a hospital identification tag with the initials "P.A." after his name.

He looked around. They were alone. "Lady, are you trying to stop the abortions they do here?"

"Something like that."

"Good," he said, his voice just above a whisper. "They do the devil's work here. Someone has to stop it."

Her pulse quickened. "Yes, yes, abortions," she said quickly. "That and mercy killing."

He nodded solemnly. "You're interested in that Mr. Hunt, I hear, that case where they turned off the machines."

"Yes, I am."

"He was still alive, you know," he whispered.

"How awful," she whispered back. "Do you suppose I could see his file?"

He looked at her wide-eyed. "I could be fired for that!"

"Jesus would be so proud of you!"

He paused as if carefully weighing what he was about to say. "I'm against what they're doing here. Maybe I can get it for you."

"That would be wonderful!"

He put a finger to his lips to quiet her. "But I can't be seen talking with you, you understand?"

"What do you suggest?"

"Could you meet me tonight?"

"Just tell me where."

Ted Sawchek lay on his back, enjoying watching Roseann as she writhed above him, doing all the work. Her small well-formed breasts bounced wildly as she continued her frantic efforts. She was beginning to sweat.

"Oh, that's good," he moaned, "really good. Keep going, honey. Don't stop!"

She collapsed atop him finally, exhausted after bringing him to climax.

Sawchek studied her, a pretty little thing, trying desperately like the others to spring the marriage trap. He was enjoying them all. Not only the sex, but the cloying attention he was receiving as he lay on his "sickbed" in his bachelor apartment.

"Will you be all right?" she asked. "I really have to go now."

"I'll manage," he said with just the right tone of bravery.

He watched her get dressed, savoring it almost as much as when she stripped. But he was relieved when she finally left.

Aiming the TV remote control, he turned on the late news. As he had expected, the Chesney trial was getting major attention even without anything happening. The jury selection was progressing, according to the local anchorman, and the station had yet another interview with a doctor about the implications of life-support systems, a series the channel was using to satisfy the unusual public interest in the case.

Sawchek chuckled. He had dodged that bullet. Kathleen Talbot had good legs, but no one, pretty or not, could run fast enough to keep out of trouble before that trial was over. The operation had been a small price to pay for escape.

The knee operation had been easy, the resulting pain minimal, and the stiffness was to be expected. The hospital stay hadn't been necessary, medically, but it had done the job politically. And, pleading a long recovery, Sawchek was enjoying playing the invalid. He had been given instructions for exercising the knee, and he halfheartedly followed the program. He used a cane more for show than necessity.

His female visitors supplied everything he needed—food, liquor, and sympathy. None of them expected him to leave his "sickbed" to take them out, so their ministrations cost him nothing.

It was safe enough to go back to work now, but he was waiting until Talbot actually swore in the jury. Then there was no way she could get out of it. And he was enjoying life too much anyway to be penned up in a courtroom for a while. He stayed politically active by telephone, keeping in contact with key people.

Sawchek again used the remote to check for other entertainment, but found nothing to his liking. He decided to have a drink, and call it a night.

He sat up and swung his legs over the side of the bed. The pain shot through him as he tried to stand, making him fall back on the bed. He looked at his right knee. The joint was swollen and the skin stretched; the new scar seemed even larger. Tentatively he touched the knee and found it hot and tender even to the lightest pressure. The swelling had happened so suddenly.

He tried to stand again, but found it too painful to persist. He fell back on the bed, rolled to the other side, and reached for the telephone.

He dialed his doctor, Chuck Lindell, but got his answering service. A bored voice informed him that if it was an emergency he should go to the hospital.

Sawchek stared at his swollen knee. "I can't go to the hospital," he snarled into the phone, "because I can't walk. In case you missed it, I'm a circuit judge. Now, you get hold of Dr. Lindell, and you tell him that if he doesn't get his ass over here right away, I'll take him and his goddamned insurance company for every cent they have. You got that?"

The voice, still bored but now coldly hostile, said Dr. Lindell was unavailable, and if he couldn't get to the hospital, he should contact the emergency medical service.

The knee was now throbbing hotly. "Look, whoever the hell you are, I'll not only sue Lindell, but if you don't get this message to him, I'll sue you!" Sawchek slammed down the telephone.

He glared at the swollen knee. It hurt. Suddenly his pride in escaping the Chesney case vanished.

"Jesus," he murmured, "I could lose the fuckin' leg!"

Jane Whitehall waited at the appointed meeting place. It was a small county park, just up a narrow road in a clearing, with a scarred picnic table set up next to a small, muddy stream.

She was alone. The moon overhead provided the only light, intermittently obscured by passing clouds. Out in the country, night seemed so much darker, and so ominously quiet.

She was beginning to feel uneasy and wondered if it might all be some kind of elaborate and dangerous ploy. A lone woman, parked in a darkened car in a place so completely isolated that even screams would never be heard.

She had turned off her engine, and the residual heat made it uncomfortable to sit in the car, especially on a warm, humid night. She rolled down the windows to try to get some air, but had to roll them up again to escape the swarms of hungry mosquitoes. Her clothing stuck to her sweaty body.

Jane's pulse quickened when she saw the car approaching, its headlights illuminating the narrow dirt trail into the small park. She stuck her cigarette between her teeth and quickly started the car's engine.

The approaching vehicle blinked its lights, then pulled up nearby.

Thoughts of the murders and rapes she had covered raced through her mind. If there was more than one man in that car, she planned to gun the engine and escape before they had a chance to get her.

The other car's interior light blinked on as the driver opened the door. It was the blond young man, still dressed in his hospital whites. He slammed his car door shut, walked to her passenger side, and quietly tapped on the window. She rolled it down partway.

"I'm here," he said in a strained voice.

Jane knew she was taking a risk, but she reached over and unlocked the door. She quickly snuffed out the cigarette and pulled down her skirt.

The young man got in and sat next to her. He extended his hand. "It's probably better if you forget my name."

His hand was sweaty. "No problem," she replied.

His voice was just above a whisper, as though they might be overheard. "I've got what you wanted." He was carrying a large envelope in his right hand. "The file on Michael Hunt . . . and the file on his wife."

238 ◇ WILLIAM J. COUGHLIN

She nodded. "Good." She found herself also speaking in a near-whisper.

"Ma'am, I don't want you to get the wrong idea about folks in these parts. Most of us are God-fearing Christians."

"I'm sure you are," she said.

"This is a Christian community, and we're proud of it," he continued. "And most of the people who work with me at the hospital are good, religious people."

"You're a doctor?"

He smiled, his face visible by moonlight. "No. I'm what they call a physician's assistant. I work under the direction of a doctor."

"Oh?"

"Anyway, we do have some doctors and a few members of the hospital's staff who don't keep to the commands of God."

He was nice-looking, even in the near-darkness. "Tell me about them." She was no longer afraid.

"Some take drugs," he said, his voice still subdued. "It's a disgrace. Even one of the surgeons. He doesn't realize anyone knows, but—"

"He could kill someone."

The man nodded slowly. "Yes. We keep an eye on him, let me tell you. But he's clever. Anyway, he's good at his job. But if he ever makes a mistake, he'll regret it. You know what I mean?"

She nodded. All fanatics were alike.

"Now, some of the other doctors get the idea they can take human life. Several of them perform abortions. Oh, they give it a different name, but it's the same procedure. They think they're foolin' people, but they aren't."

"And people like Michael Hunt?" she prompted, hoping to get him onto the subject.

"It was deliberate killing, plain and simple. I didn't know Mr. Hunt. I work in orthopedics, but I read the file. That doctor of his took God's laws into his own hands. That wasn't mercy, it was murder. And that's not the first time, either."

"Happens a lot?"

"They say what they do is legal. But there's a higher authority than our foolish state legislature."

"May I see Mr. Hunt's file?"

He nodded. "I made photocopies when no one was looking. That was sneaky, I admit, but done in a good cause. I did the same thing with his wife's file. She has a drinking problem."

He handed the envelope to her. "I'm trusting you," he said. "Please protect me. No one must know I'm your source. Jobs are pretty scarce down here."

She clasped the envelope, then smiled. "Don't worry. As far as I'm concerned, I never even saw you."

"I hope you can use this to help stamp out this damnable form of murder."

"You can bet on it."

"I don't bet," he said as he opened the door. "We hold that to be a sin." He paused, looking at her, the overhead light shining on both of them. "I'll pray for you, lady. I know you're doing the Lord's work."

"Thank you."

He hurried back to his car. She waited until he drove away, then flipped on the map light and quickly scanned the contents of the envelope. The doctor's name was Grapentine. There was a signed release setting forth Kathleen Talbot's permission to turn off the machines. There was a neatly typed detailed report of death. The rest was a jumble of treatment notes and lab reports.

Everything seemed to be just as Regina Hunt had said.

Jane replaced everything in the envelope. She started the engine and turned on the lights, then drove carefully up the little road until she reached the paved highway.

Her heart was pounding at a furious rate.

It would be a national story. She would go over everything at the motel, try to get some sleep, and catch the first plane out in the morning.

She was trembling with excitement. . . . With some breaks, it might even be worth a Pulitzer.

CHAPTER 25

KATHLEEN LOOKED OUT at the crowded courtroom as the clerk administered the oath to the jury, swearing them in, the act that constituted the official start of the trial. From now on there was no going back, no adjournments. Lawyers, jurors, and judge were all locked together until the end.

She waited until the courtroom settled down, then looked over at Thomas Mease. "You may begin," she said.

Mease got up. It was a clear, bright morning and sunlight streamed in through the high court windows. Mease walked to a position directly in front of the jury.

"Ladies and gentlemen, as you have been told, this is a charge of first-degree murder. The prosecution will show that the defendant"—Mease turned and pointed at Dennis Chesney—"did willfully kill and murder Paul Martin. We will show . . ."

Kathleen listened with half an ear as Mease continued with his opening statement. The lawyers could state to the jury the facts they expected to prove, but they couldn't argue their position. That would come later. But many lawyers—good and bad—often tried to step over the line and bolster the facts with argument. She had to be prepared if Jerry Mitchell objected. But Mease was being workmanlike and careful, so her complete attention wasn't demanded.

Jerry Mitchell sat quietly, his long legs stretched before him and crossed at the ankles; his posture suggested complete confidence and relaxation. They had seen each other every day during the jury selection, each so carefully formal with the other, but that contact seemed to make their personal separation even more acute, at least for her. Kathleen wondered if

Jerry felt the same way. It was much more difficult than she had imagined it would be.

Dennis Chesney, who had become so thin, continued to act as though the proceedings had no connection with him. He was quiet, seldom spoke, even to Mitchell, and seemed to pay no attention to what was happening in the courtroom.

Marty Kelly, looking like a little dandy, sat at the counsel table, his face reflecting almost a parental pride as Tom Mease continued his polished presentation.

Young Pete Norbanski sat behind Mitchell. Each day his outfits were more bizarre, at least in color and texture. But Jerry had told her Norbanski was developing into a first-class criminal lawyer, and she noticed that he was alert and quick to counsel Mitchell. Both teams, prosecution and defense, seemed in an odd fashion to be evenly matched.

A number of uniformed policemen were present to help maintain order in the courtroom. There had been a few minor outbursts earlier, but nothing really serious. Crowds of pickets representing differing views continued to pace in front of the Hall of Justice, and a few scuffles erupted at first. Now everything seemed calm. Kathleen wondered if, like before a storm, that calm might be misleading. She had received a number of threats, both in writing and by telephone.

She glanced again at Jerry Mitchell. Michael had been asking about the tall lawyer. She wondered which of them missed him more. Mitchell had become very important in the life of her son. Jerry Mitchell looked up and caught her eye. His expression didn't change, but they were both caught up in a startled and silent communication. Both then looked away.

The media people were out in full force. Every time a television cameraman appeared, the people parading outside the courthouse took on a new vigor. The policemen assigned to the halls ensured that order prevailed when the crews there began to film.

Kathleen noticed Jane Whitehall sitting in the press section. Whitehall had sent her an "urgent" note requesting a meeting. Interviews had become a problem, and Kathleen had decided not to give any more until the trial was over. The balance between judicial ethics and the public's right to know was a delicate thing; but Kathleen felt it was at least questionable, if not unethical, for a judge to become so involved in the day-to-day commentary concerning the trial. Still, Whitehall was a member of the local press, and perhaps she could see her for a few minutes and explain her reasons for not giving interviews.

Whitehall seemed oddly agitated, shifting in her seat, her eyes constantly on Kathleen. It was behavior far removed from the newspaperwoman's usual relaxed, almost bored public attitude. Kathleen decided she would see her either at the break for lunch or at the end of the day.

Mease's voice was intruding into her consciousness. "But Dennis Chesney wasn't satisfied with that," he said, his voice rising. "No. When he went to Paul Martin's bedside, he was no longer a policeman, he was a cold-blooded killer!"

"Objection!" Mitchell rose quickly to his feet. He looked at Mease, paused, and then slowly glanced up at Kathleen. "I have been very patient, if the court please, but Mr. Mease has gone from an opening statement to a closing argument without giving the rest of us a chance to hear any testimony. Now, I came here expecting to participate in a trial, but Mr. Mease has apparently skipped right by that part of the proceedings."

Before Kathleen could reply, Mease snapped: "Most of us wait until we get our turn, Mr. Mitchell." He glared at his opponent.

Kathleen used the gavel, cracking it once. "That's quite enough, gentlemen," she said quietly but firmly. "Mr. Mease, the objection is sustained, your remarks were argumentative both in content and in delivery." She looked at Mitchell. "It will be sufficient, Mr. Mitchell, for the rest of this trial, if you merely make your objection without appending a short speech to the jury. Fairness cuts both ways."

Mitchell smiled slightly and nodded. "Fairness is all any of us can ask," he said as he sat down.

Mease glowered at him, then began again to address the jury. This time his voice was sharp but without the previous dramatic inflection. "We will show that Paul Martin was alive when Dennis Chesney walked into his room, that he . . ."

Kathleen listened, satisfied that Tom Mease was once more on track. She glanced around the courtroom.

244 ◇ WILLIAM J. COUGHLIN

Jane Whitehall looked as if she were about to jump right out of her seat.

━◄ ►━

". . . and we will show that Dennis Chesney . . ." Tom Mease's voice crackled in the quiet, expectant atmosphere of the court-room as he continued his opening remarks to the jury.

Jane Whitehall felt as if she were going to explode. The documents she had brought back from the South were now in the hands of the newspaper's lawyers to determine if anything was subject to libel. In addition, her managing editor had ordered her to confront Judge Kathleen Talbot with Regina's allegations. He insisted that it was only fair and that the judge's reaction might provide an additional legal way to present the story. He also told Jane to have Regina Hunt available to talk to the lawyers.

It was the story of her career, but a cruel fate seemed to mock Jane. She had tried to reach Regina, only to find that the woman hadn't returned to her hotel room. Although she was missing, her clothes were still there. Jane had no way of knowing whether Regina was on her way back to Florida or had just passed out. If her boss found out that the widow Hunt was an unreliable lush, Jane knew she might have to kiss the whole story good-bye.

She listened as Tom Mease continued to make a snapping opening statement. He was young, and he knew what he was doing. But in the midst of her own torment, she was too preoccupied to even think about him sexually.

Judge Talbot wasn't giving interviews, so the court clerk said, but he had agreed to give the judge her message. So far Jane hadn't received any reply. She looked up at Kathleen Talbot on the bench. The realization that the woman in the black robe—so regal and so cool—might hold the key to Jane's future only served to make the reporter more nervous.

Jane could handle the tension no longer. She got up and tiptoed out of the courtroom. She nodded to the television men in the hallway and quickly lit a cigarette, inhaling deeply, hoping to control her rising worry.

The elevators were jammed, so she headed for the marble staircase. As she walked she began to calm down. Problems were nothing new to her. There were ways to solve anything. In the lobby she dialed the hotel. As she feared, nothing more had been heard from Regina. Then she phoned her managing editor.

"Did you talk to the judge?" Jack Bennett asked.

"Not yet," she said, forcing herself to sound calm. "The trial's begun. I'll catch her at lunch or when they break for the day." She made it sound as though it were a certainty. "What do the lawyers say about the hospital records?"

The newspaper retained a prestigious law firm, and one of the principal partners was a national libel-law expert. Although the firm had a reputation for being conservative, their legal opinions usually provided suggestions as to how something might be used if they considered it to be otherwise libelous. There was more than one way to skin a cat, and the lawyers seemed to know them all.

"The records are terrific," Bennett said without any enthusiasm, "but not the way you got them."

"I didn't steal them."

"No, but your source did, and that's the problem."

"What problem?" she demanded.

"You can't name the source, right?"

She felt dizzy. "You know I can't, Jack. I told you how I got them." She had told him every detail, proud of her ingenuity.

"Yeah. Well, without something more, we can't rely on those records all by themselves."

"You have Regina Hunt's statement."

"Jane, are you sure about that woman? The records indicate she was in the drunk tank down there."

She steeled herself to keep control. "Jack, her husband was dying, and in a strange place. She was without family, without friends. She drank a great deal, too much, obviously. But think of the circumstances. And remember who put her into that drunk tank. Kathleen Talbot. Anyway, the bare facts of what she says are supported in detail by those hospital documents."

"I'd like to talk to her myself."

Jane felt a chill pass through her. "Don't you trust my judgment?"

"Of course I do, Jane. This might be the story of the century, as you say, but we have to be damned careful of the libel laws, too."

"Kathleen Talbot's a public official, for Chris's sake!"

"Not down south, she wasn't. Not when she made the decision about her father. She might not even be considered legally a public figure, given everything. The only redeeming factor is the Chesney case. Without that, we wouldn't even consider the story, and, obviously, it wouldn't even be news."

"But the Chesney case does exist!" she shouted. "And it is news. Jesus, is everyone over there nuts? If anyone else picks this up, we lose it."

She was answered only by a long pause. "Look, don't let your enthusiasm color your judgment," he said quietly. "The lawyers tell me there are two ways, maybe three, that would protect our ass from being sued."

"And they are?"

"When you talk to Judge Talbot, she may make a statement that would take the matter out of the right of privacy and put the whole thing into the public spotlight. A lot would depend on what she said."

"What's the other way?"

Bennett coughed slightly. "If either the defense or the prosecution asked her to excuse herself and declare a mistrial on the basis of what she did—and its relationship to the subject of the trial—then that act would open the floodgates. Then she would be a public official, under the law, and we'd be protected."

"I don't understand."

"Look, Jane. If one of the lawyers makes everything public as part of a public criminal trial, we can print anything we damn well please. It's as simple as that."

"What's the third way?"

"If Regina Hunt brought some kind of lawsuit against Kathleen Talbot, we could run the story—our state law permits that."

She lit another cigarette. "Jack, while we're fucking around with the fine points of the law, some other writer, less intimidated by lawyers, is liable to grab this thing and run with it."

"All life is a risk," he said.

"This is my goddamned story!"

He chuckled, but without humor. "It is, Jane. And whether it sees the light of day pretty much depends on what you do."

"You mean about the judge?"

"Yes. Also, perhaps it might be wise to talk to the lawyers—separately, of course. If they raise the issue at open trial, we can run the story."

She threw the cigarette halfway across the lobby. "Jesus, talk about ethics! You don't mind cheating and stealing just so long as we don't get sued!"

"Jane . . ." His voice, still quiet, now turned icy. "My ethics have very little to do with the matter. As you say, this is your story. What happens is primarily up to you."

She almost broke the public telephone as she hung up. Several people turned to look at her.

If she didn't come up with the right approach, everything she had worked for would be lost. Her dreams of a column, of a journalistic prize, all would be gone.

Her hands were shaking as she extracted yet another cigarette from her purse. As she lit it, she forced herself to think calmly.

Now it was more than just a story, it was her career.

There had to be a way to force the story into print, and she was determined to find it, no matter what the cost.

—◄ ►—

Regina Hunt lay naked on the rumpled bed. She sipped the Bloody Mary he had prepared, her second of the morning, and began to feel much better. She could hear him puttering about in the tiny kitchen of his studio apartment. The aroma of frying bacon stimulated hunger.

"Can I help?" she called.

"Nope. Besides, never interfere with a professional." She smiled. God, he was handsome, and what a magnificent body! He had an appetite for sexual pleasure and adventure that she had never known—very experienced for one so young. They had gotten pretty drunk and tried some things she had sworn she would never do.

Regina stirred her drink with her finger, then licked the red liquid off. They had gone through a river of vodka since she had met him. It was only two nights ago, yet it seemed as if she had known him forever.

He walked in, as naked as she was, holding a steaming plate of eggs, hash browns, toast, and a mound of bacon. He put the plate on the bed between them and sat down. "You want coffee?"

"Later. This looks wonderful."

"Hey, it's what I do for a living. I *should* be good at it." He had told her he was working as a short-order cook until he could get back into the restaurant business. He was quite young, not yet thirty, to have owned and operated a large restaurant. He said he had sold the business and had been cheated by lawyers and accountants.

She liked his smooth, long muscles. He bore tattoos on both biceps and on one thigh, which had put her off at first, but now she thought they were cute.

"I really should let that newspaperwoman know where I am," she said.

He munched on a piece of toast and smiled. "Hey, I thought that was my job. I'm your business manager now, right?"

She nodded as she helped herself to the eggs.

He grinned. "Boy, Regina, they're getting a million dollars' worth of shit from you and all you get is a free hotel room. You really do need a manager. We'll let the newspaper broad stew in her own juice for a while, then maybe later today I'll call."

"Walter, do you really think they'd pay me money?"

He nodded slowly. "Well, maybe now they won't. You gave them everything they needed, but we can still try. If we score, we can use the money toward that new restaurant in Florida."

"That'd be nice." She had told him of the money Big Mike had left her. It wasn't sufficient to live really comfortably, just enough to get by. But Walter had some wonderful ideas about running a restaurant. She was convinced that together—with her money and his expertise—they would end up rich.

He nibbled at a strip of bacon. "You sure all this won't get you in trouble? The stuff about your stepdaughter, I mean. Those judges got a lot of power, and the fuckers can get real mean."

"She'll be lucky if they don't put her in jail."

He slowly shook his head. "I don't know. If we can't get any dough out of the newspaper, it might be just as well for the two of us to get the hell out of here and go on down to Florida."

"You mean, just give up?"

He reached across and stroked her stomach. "Naw, nothing like that. We just operate from your place in Florida, that's all. That bitch judge will get what's coming to her, you've already seen to that. But down there we'll be safe. Those legal cats don't screw around."

"You sound like you know."

He smiled and picked up the half-empty gallon of vodka from the floor and liberally laced her drink. "I had a couple of run-ins with those people, nothing serious."

"Like what?" She sipped the drink.

He laughed. "I ain't no murderer, if that's what you're thinking. Naw, I got busted for a fight once—not my fault. And one time they arrested me for smoking a little weed. Chickenshit stuff. But we don't need no trouble, so if we can't score, we'll hit the road and get rich among the oranges." He playfully caressed her thigh. "Do you like that?" he whispered as his hand moved slowly up her leg.

—◄ ►—

Marty Kelly was beaming as he walked into the Learned Hand. He waved at some lawyers and moved quickly toward the bar. "I think I'll have a light lunch today. What's good?"

Herman, the day bartender, shrugged. "Just sandwiches, you know that. And they're always the same."

"While I consider your vast menu, I believe I'll have a small libation. A double whiskey, straight up, if you please, Herman."

"How's the trial coming along?" Herman asked as he placed the drink before Kelly.

"Delightful." Kelly bolted down the drink and nodded to

signal a refill. "At long last, we are under way. Thomas Mease, demon prosecutor, finished his opening statement just before lunch break. Damn good, too, I might add. The lad has a wonderful future before him."

"I still don't know why you guys are crucifying Denny Chesney." Herman scowled. "Hell, he's a good guy, and what he did sure doesn't sound like murder to me."

Kelly shrugged. "Herman, I'm glad you aren't on the jury. But I agree, Chesney is a very nice man."

"Then why rack his ass?"

"I imagine Jeremiah Mitchell will express the same sentiment this afternoon when he makes his opening statement, although his language may lack some of your fiery imagery."

"He's making an opening statement right after the prosecutor? I'm no lawyer, but isn't that unusual? I thought they always did that after the prosecutor put in all his testimony."

Kelly raised the refilled glass in salute. "It seems you've acquired a fair amount of knowledge about our mysterious ways. And, I might add, this is a much better place to learn the law than some dreary old law school, Herman."

"Hey, that's all I hear all day, lawyers talking about trials. Some of it has to rub off."

Kelly sipped his drink. "You're right about the opening statement. Usually a defense lawyer waits until just before he puts in his case. It's a tactical decision. You want to make sure the jury has your position fresh in mind. But this time, Mitchell has opted to open right after Mease, which is his right."

"Why?"

"Mease did a good job. Mitchell doesn't want the jury to mull over that too long without hearing the other side. This is not going to be a short trial. I'd do the same thing if I were defending Chesney. Just like the rest of us, jurors are human, and Mitchell wants to quickly balance the impression Mease has made."

"What do you think will happen?"

Kelly sighed. "I'll take another, Herman, and you better have them dish up a ham sandwich from the kitchen. I'll need something to balance this liquor."

"C'mon, Marty, don't duck. What's going to happen to Chesney?"

"I think they'll convict, but it's a tricky case."

Herman shook his head. "Jesus, poor Denny Chesney."

Kelly smiled slowly. "Of course, you never know what a jury may do. And in this one, especially."

"Why?"

"Have you seen the lunatics demonstrating in front of the courthouse?"

Herman nodded. "I go by there in the morning. I see the signs. The cops have each group marching in separate circles. I've heard a bit of name-calling back and forth."

"The whole thing is kind of amusing. In one circle you have the antiabortionists, the right-wing Christians, every spectrum of the right-to-life attitude." He chuckled. "Then, like a mirror, you have the other collection. The pro-suicide folks, the dignified-death people, the pro-abortionists, and the militant women's groups. If it wasn't for the cops out there with them, they'd go for each other like opposing armies. That might be fun to watch."

"What do they expect to gain?"

"The demonstrators? Probably nothing. Usually they come out only if the television people look like they might be interested. But this time nobody goes home because they suspect the other side might get some kind of advantage. Apparently they'll all be around until the trial is over, marching, chanting, and happily singing. Of course, the nice autumn weather helps. If it was cold and snowy, most of them would take their convictions to a more pleasant place."

"I saw some priests the other morning, marching with the antisuicide folks."

"Ah, Herman, the clergy is well represented on both sides, so I'm told. The Catholics and fundamentalists march with one side, while some Anglicans and Unitarians troop along with the others. If trouble breaks out and someone is killed, they'll have immediate spiritual assistance, no matter what their beliefs."

Herman poured Kelly another drink. "How's Chesney taking all this?"

Kelly sipped the whiskey. "Not well. He seems to be ignoring the whole proceeding. If Mitchell puts him on the stand, Mease will cut him to ribbons, unless it's all a trick."

"Trick?"

Kelly shrugged. "It's possible. Chesney could be faking a depressive illness. He was a good cop and a skilled witness. If we are lulled into a false sense of security, he might take the stand and turn things around."

"Think he will?"

"No. Chesney doesn't look good. I think it's genuine."

"Won't the jury tend to think he's guilty if he doesn't testify?"

Kelly smiled. "We hope so. He has a right not to testify, but jurors don't give a damn about that. If he doesn't take the stand, he'll lose a lot of points, no matter what the judge may tell the jury."

"How's Big Mike's little girl working out? Does she know what she's doing?"

"Be respectful. She was my former employer. As a matter of fact, she's doing very well. You wouldn't think she was new to the job if you didn't know."

"Any word on who will finally end up with the prosecutor's job?"

"No change that I know of, Herman. It's still tied up in the logjam over who will become executive judge. The black robes won't name a new prosecutor until then, and there's no sign of anyone lining up enough votes to win."

"Judge Talbot is a candidate for executive judge, according to the papers."

"She is, but right now she's got her hands full. Presiding over Chesney's trial is like having a tiger by the tail—you don't dare concentrate on anything else."

"I still think it's shitty what you're doing to Denny Chesney."

"You think him not guilty, then?"

"I do."

"Then we're honor-bound to do everything to win."

Herman frowned. "What do you mean?"

"It's an old prosecutors' saying—there is no pride in convicting a guilty man." Kelly laughed. "It's only when you nail an innocent man that you know you're skilled at your craft."

"That stinks, Kelly."

"It does, but there's some truth in it too."

Jane Whitehall returned to the courtroom, her frustration having boiled into anger. She had tried again to reach Regina Hunt, without success, but she had heard from her managing editor.

"Do you know anyone named Walter Vegas?" Jack Bennett had demanded in that calm, icy way of his.

"No," she had replied.

"Well, he called me. He said he's Regina Hunt's business manager and she won't cooperate further unless the paper comes up with fifty thousand dollars." Bennett's fury had been barely concealed. "I called the hotel and canceled its star guest. And you have until tomorrow morning to come up with a way to legitimize that little story of yours, or you can forget it."

Jane had taken a short walk around the Hall of Justice to calm down. The demonstrators were still marching around the front entrance, but most seemed tired, their enthusiasm worn down after a long day. By the time she had completed the circuit, she felt sufficiently in control to return to the courtroom.

Jerry Mitchell was nearing the end of his opening statement. Both he and Mease clashed several times, but the defense lawyer was working his usual magic. Jane glared up at Kathleen Talbot. Her presence on the bench seemed to her like a lingering personal taunt.

Mitchell, his deep voice rumbling with conviction, assured the jury that no crime would be shown and that they would be convinced of his client's complete innocence by the end of the trial. A smattering of applause was quickly silenced by Kathleen Talbot's gavel.

"The hour is late," Judge Talbot said. "We'll start with the first witness tomorrow morning."

Both lawyers nodded their silent agreement.

The court clerk rapped his gavel as Judge Talbot left the bench. As the clerk completed his little litany about court being recessed, Jane rushed up to him.

"Will she see me?" she demanded.

"Christ, take it easy," the clerk snapped. "I told her. As soon as I wrap things up here, I'll check."

"Check now. It's important!"

His eyes narrowed. "It's always important with you newspaper people. I have a job to do too." His tone bristled with annoyance. "Keep your underwear on." He began to make furious notes in the court file.

Jane wanted to slap him, but she turned, looking for either of the two lawyers. Mitchell was talking intently to his young assistant and his client. But Tom Mease was standing by himself as the jury trooped off to their room.

She hurried over to Mease. "Can I see you?"

He smiled. "Sure, Jane. What's up?"

"I have something to show you."

He studied her for a moment, as if trying to determine what she was up to; then he spoke quietly. "How about over by the windows. No one's there."

The courtroom atmosphere seemed strangely relaxed. The media people who hadn't left were talking and smoking. The policemen looked relieved: the day-long tension was finally over.

"Here." She pulled copies of the hospital reports from her purse and handed them to him.

He leafed through them. "What's this?"

"The records of Big Mike Hunt's death."

"So?"

She forced herself to reply calmly. "They show that Kathleen Talbot, his court-appointed guardian at the time, had her father's life-sustaining machines turned off."

"I don't understand . . ."

"Look, goddammit, the judge hearing this case committed the same crime Chesney's accused of. My paper wants to know what you're going to do about it."

The relaxation was gone from his expression. "Jesus, that's a hell of a thing to charge, Jane."

"It's all there in those papers."

He read them, this time more carefully. "Where did you get these?"

"Does it matter?"

He nodded. "It could. I can't give you an answer now. I'll have to check into this."

"When?"

"When what?"

"When can you give me an answer?"

Mease sighed. "I'll have to check this all out, and I'll have to consult with my bosses. Maybe tomorrow, maybe the day after."

"I have to know tonight."

He shook his head. "That's impossible."

Her anger was being replaced by a sense of cool cunning. He was just another source. He could be tricked like anyone else. "You'll look like an asshole in the paper, you know that?"

Tom Mease stared at her. "That's a risk I'll just have to take. I'll let you know when I can."

She restrained herself from any other comment. Jerry Mitchell was moving toward the back of the courtroom.

"Hey, Mitchell," she called. "I want to talk to you."

He stopped and turned.

She knew Mease was watching her as she hurried through the empty spectator rows to confront Mitchell. If Mease was worried, he might change his mind.

"Jane, I take it you know Pete Norbanski?" Mitchell introduced his companion.

She nodded at the young lawyer. "Take a look at these," she said, thrusting another set of the hospital documents into Mitchell's large hand.

He took the papers but didn't look at them. "What's this all about, Jane?"

The words spilled out in a torrent as she told him of Regina's accusation and the documentation that supported her charges. She tried to contain her excitement.

He listened politely. "Even if what you say is true, what do you want?"

"You should move to disqualify the judge," Jane snapped. "She's still here, so is Mease. You could do it now."

He chuckled mirthlessly. "This is something I'll have to look into, Jane. As you know, it's not my habit to go off half-cocked. This is going to be a long trial; no one is leaving town. I'll study the whole matter and let you know what I'm going to do—if anything."

"If anything?" She pretended outrage. "Goddammit, that woman's done exactly what your client is accused of. She's unfit to sit on this case. You have a duty to your client." She felt she had to do something to make him react. She purposely spit out the words. "Maybe all the rumors that you've been sleeping with her are true."

Mitchell's placid expression didn't change. Only Pete Norbanski's face betrayed sudden anxiety.

"Jane, my dear," Mitchell said softly, "I realize you're trying to goad me into some kind of action, but don't be crude. You have much more class than that."

She tried a different tactic. "Jerry, I'm just trying to protect you. When this all comes out, you'll look very bad unless you do something first. It's your reputation I'm trying to—"

He laughed. "Nice try, Janey, but no soap."

"Mrs. Whitehall!" The clerk's voice echoed in the almost empty courtroom. "Judge Talbot will see you now."

CHAPTER 26

KATHLEEN FELT UNUSUALLY tired. Although they had not reached the actual testimony, the selection of the jury and the preliminary skirmishing during the opening statements had been tense. Both lawyers were skilled, both ready to pounce on any weakness shown by the other. She had had no opportunity to relax, no chance to coast mentally. Such a constant state of being alert was taking its toll.

As she hung up her robe, she felt a stab of loneliness. She wished she could talk to Jerry Mitchell. Just the relief of chatting with him about the events of the day, trivial or important, would have renewed her spirit. She desperately missed the closeness, even though she could see and hear him every day.

Kathleen told the clerk to bring in Jane Whitehall. She didn't really feel like talking to any media people, but it would take only a few minutes to explain. That, and the signing of a few orders, would free her for the rest of the evening. She planned to take Michael for a walk, then out for dinner at the new restaurant that catered to children. Michael didn't like restaurants, but he loved clowns and ice cream, and the new place offered an abundance of both.

Jane Whitehall came in and closed the door without asking permission. Kathleen concealed her annoyance.

"Jane, I have decided it would be best if I gave no interviews during the course of the trial. I'm bound by the state code of judicial ethics, and . . ."

Jane didn't seem to be listening. She pulled a large unsealed envelope from her purse and handed it to Kathleen. "Take a look at this," she said, standing before the desk.

"What is this?"

"Take a look."

Kathleen pulled the folded photocopies from the envelope and opened them. The first was a copy of the court record appointing her guardian of her father. At first she didn't recognize the others until she realized they were the reports of her father's treatment at the hospital. They were dated from the day and hour he had been admitted. Her father's death certificate was also attached.

Jane stared down at Kathleen. "Your stepmother says you killed your father."

Kathleen felt her heart racing. It was like a nightmare, that terrible sense of being pursued by a nameless, horrifying dread, with no hope of escape—the kind of nightmare that usually ended with waking up just as capture was about to take place. Only she was fully awake, and this was a dream that would not end.

"What is it you want?" Kathleen heard her own voice, so surprisingly calm, so icy that it sounded like that of a stranger.

Jane's eyes had narrowed into glittering slits. "I want a statement from you. Your stepmother gave us an affidavit making the charge that you ordered your father's life-support machines turned off. Those hospital records show everything she told us was absolutely true. You did exactly what Dennis Chesney did." Jane's words came out in a near-hiss, her excitement unbridled. "My editor wants to be fair. He wants you to have the opportunity to give your side of this thing before we print it."

Kathleen wondered if she were still breathing. Everything seemed frozen in time. The dream quality persisted.

"Look, I'm not saying you were wrong in what you did," Jane said, her voice less insistent but her tone cloyingly insincere. "Making judgments isn't my business. But it's obvious what happened to your father, and I want to know how that differs from what Dennis Chesney did."

Kathleen heard a distant siren, the wail of an ambulance.

Other normal sounds of city traffic came drifting up from the outside. She was suddenly aware that the leather couch had a small tear on the underside of one arm. She seemed to be keenly aware of every small, unimportant thing in the room.

Jane placed her hands on the desk and leaned closer to her. "Hey, we could be on your side, you know. This was bound to come out sooner or later. We can give you a chance to tell your side of the story now. Some of the others won't, you know that. They'll howl for your skin. We're your only chance!"

Kathleen quickly regained her sense of perspective. Something was wrong; Jane Whitehall was playing it too strong. There was only one possible explanation.

"Get out," Kathleen said quietly.

"I won't get out, not until you make a statement. Why did you do it? How did you feel? Look, dammit, you're accused of murder!"

"Get out," Kathleen repeated, "or I'll have you thrown out."

"Then it's true! You did kill your own father!" Jane's voice had risen to a shout.

Kathleen picked up the phone and touched the red button, summoning the court officer.

"Jesus, I'm the only one who can protect you," Jane snarled. "You had better make a statement now. You'll never get this chance again."

"Get out," Kathleen said, surprised at her own controlled tone.

A young policeman opened the door tentatively. "Did you want something, judge?"

"Please show Mrs. Whitehall out," Kathleen said firmly.

The policeman's eyes widened in surprise. "Okay. C'mon, Jane," he said, smiling to hide his nervousness.

"Not until she makes a statement," Jane snapped, her face shaking with manic determination.

"Please, Jane," he said, his voice an urgent whisper.

"What about it, Talbot? Did you kill your father or not?"

Jane's shout ended whatever indecision the police officer had. "Whoa," he said. "That's enough, Janey." He gripped her arm firmly and half-lifted her, pulling her toward the door.

260 ◇ WILLIAM J. COUGHLIN

"Silence won't help," Jane hissed. "No matter what you do, it's all going to come out!"

The policeman had her out of the judge's office and the door closed before she could say another word.

Kathleen sat quietly at her desk, her heart pounding, her stomach churning. She was amazed she had been able to act with a calmness she certainly didn't feel. Jane Whitehall's frantic actions indicated her newspaper had no printable story at this point, unless she gave them a statement. Even a "No comment" might have given the newspaper an opening, but she had denied them even that, although she felt no sense of triumph.

Kathleen turned her chair and stared out the big window, looking but not really seeing anything. She was only vaguely aware of the tears slowly coursing down her cheeks.

She wondered what Jerry Mitchell would think. She had never told him, or anyone, of the terrible decision required of her and the resulting action. She wondered what anyone would think of a judge who presumed to sit in judgment over another human being for actions that judge herself had committed. It wouldn't matter that what was legal in one state was prohibited in another or that the motivation was vastly different. The difference wasn't boundary lines on a map, or family ties; it went much deeper than that. And she regretted she hadn't faced the question earlier.

When Jerry found out, he would also be faced with a decision. He was a man of honor, she knew that, and he would have to do what was best for his client, no matter what the consequences.

And young Tom Mease—he too was honorable.

Kathleen shook her head. It was a nightmare. She could see no other result than personal ruin. She wondered if in some way she was being repaid for what had occurred in that hospital so far away. She wished she had been able to work out the sense of guilt that seemed so irrational, but always present, just beneath the surface of her mind.

She felt sickened at what lay ahead. She wanted to talk to Jerry, but that, especially now, was completely out of the question.

Still, she needed advice, and a friend. She turned—every movement was slow and ponderous—as if she weighed a ton. The world had suddenly been transformed into a distorted funhouse mirror.

Slowly she dialed the number.

—◄ ►—

"You sure we're doing the right thing, Walter?"

He grinned at her; he seemed to exude confidence. She liked that. He was like Big Mike, only he was younger and more gentle. Regina knew she had finally found someone who would take care of her.

"Like I told you," Walter said, handing their tickets to the flight attendant at the boarding gate, "you gotta watch out for yourself in this life. I talked to the head guy at that newspaper and I could tell right off that he was a double-crossing son-of-a-bitch. They were only using you, Regina. They got what they wanted, the penny-pinching bastards."

"But if I don't stay . . ."

"Hey, don't worry. You did what you set out to do. They'll nail the ass of your stepdaughter, you can bet on it. They got your statement—they don't need anything more from you. And unless they come up with some dough, they ain't going to get anything more."

"Walter, you're a real businessman."

He chuckled as they found their seats in the first-class section. It was the first time he had ever flown first class and he looked forward to it. "Regina, by the time we're through, we'll stand all of Florida on its ear. Forget about this two-bit shit. Soon you'll own the biggest and best restaurant Florida has ever seen."

Regina settled in. They had come directly from the airport bar, but she was ready for another drink. The airlines wouldn't serve them until they were in the air. It seemed like such a foolish rule.

"You know," she said, finding and adjusting her seat belt, "what I can't understand is why we haven't seen anything in the papers about it. You'd think they'd have run something by now."

He shrugged. "Like I told you. Some of those judges have a lot of hidden power. It's a damn good thing we're getting out of here. You never know. We got a new life ahead of us. There's no use taking unnecessary risks."

"Big Mike had power," she said, "but he could never keep anything out of the papers."

"See, you never know in this life." He patted her knee. "Safety first." He leaned back in the plush seat. First class was great. He decided he could get used to it. Maybe she had enough money to open a restaurant, maybe not. But in the meantime, he would have the chance to finally taste the finer things of life.

"Are you happy, Walter?"

He squeezed her knee. "Hey, what's not to be happy?"

Jane Whitehall stormed out of the courthouse in a frenzy fueled by her anger at Kathleen Talbot. The demonstrators had gone, leaving only the clutter of fast-food cartons and crushed cigarettes in their wake.

She wanted a drink, yet she was afraid that if she started drinking now she might not be able to stop. It had been the most frustrating day of her life.

Crossing against rush-hour traffic, she almost dared the angry drivers to hit her. She yelled back a few choice names to those who shouted at her.

But as she walked, her anger ebbed and she was struck by the irony of her situation. She had dug up the hottest story of her life, only to be thwarted by her own managing editor and his refusal to run it. She was so close, yet so far. It seemed as if her editor, Jack Bennett, and everyone else were in league with the fate that teased her so maddeningly.

The lawyers, both Mease and Mitchell, had declined decisive action. It would matter little if they later changed their minds and made formal motions for disqualification. Everyone would then have the story, and she would lose her exclusive. All her work would be for nothing.

Kathleen Talbot was no fool. As much as she now detested

the woman, Jane had to grudgingly admit that the judge had skillfully dodged the issue, giving her nothing upon which to build a story.

Jane stopped to check her purse. She thought she had made more than enough photocopies, but she had only one set left. The original copies were at the newspaper.

She walked quickly, aimlessly, trying to find a way out of her own maze. Jack Bennett had set her personal deadline for the morning, but she knew him. If she couldn't deliver the story by tonight in time for the morning edition, it would be all over.

She slowed her pace as she contemplated the gloomy prospect that Kathleen Talbot might even end up as executive judge. Antagonizing the executive judge—the most powerful local public figure—could well end the career of any political reporter.

She knew Bennett. He'd put her on the copy desk. Oh, he'd think up some hokey title, that was his style, but he'd take her out of the action. If she didn't like it, well, there was always the door; except that good newspaper jobs were dwindling, along with good newspapers. It was the first time she had considered what might happen to her if her shot at Kathleen Talbot missed. Sheer desperation made her realize she did have one final option.

She crossed the street, this time with the light, and hurried to the civil-court building. It was past working hours there, but maybe he was still around.

The halls were nearly empty as she took the elevator.

The courtroom was locked, but she knocked. The clerk, in shirt sleeves, opened the door. "Jesus, Jane, we're closed."

"I know," she said, sliding past him. "The judge still in?"

He frowned. "Court's closed."

"I didn't ask you that," she replied evenly, keeping the tension out of her voice. "Is the judge still here?"

"Maybe he's busy."

"Ask him if I can talk to him."

He relocked the door. "Oh, you newspaper people are a real pain in the ass, you know that?"

She managed what she hoped was a bright smile. "So they say."

"Hold on a minute."

She waited in the empty courtroom while the clerk went back into the judge's chambers. The electric wall clock made a faint buzzing sound in the stillness.

The clerk shuffled out, frowning. "He's says to come in, but he says it'd better be important."

Jane walked into the inner office. Tim Quinlan lay half sprawled on the couch, a newspaper across his stomach, a bottle of brandy on the floor next to him. He made no move to get up.

"Court's closed," he said, snapping the words. "What the hell do you want?"

"You look busy."

He pushed himself to a seated position. "Save that shit for your readers. I'm in deep thought about weighty judicial matters. Now, what the hell brings you up here?"

She took a seat on a straight-backed chair, crossing her legs. Those legs had conquered better men than Timothy Quinlan. "I need a statement from you."

He frowned. "I told you, the store is closed. No statements. If you want a drink, there's a glass behind you."

She nodded, turned, and held out the dingy glass. He poured several fingers of brandy into the glass.

"I'm serious," she said as she sipped the brandy. "I need a statement."

He belched. "On what?"

"It seems one of your judges has been accused of murder."

His eyes widened. "What the hell are you talking about?"

Quinlan had been drinking, but he still wasn't drunk. She fished her last set of photocopies from her purse and handed them to him.

He adjusted his bifocals and frowned at the papers, quickly turning the pages. "This is all about Mike Hunt."

"That's right."

"Big Mike's dead."

She smiled. "You got that right."

"I don't understand what . . ."

"His daughter, your judge, had his machines turned off. Big Mike's widow calls it murder."

"Regina?"

Jane nodded.

Quinlan's high, whining cackle seemed to come from somewhere deep within the depths of him. "Shit, Jane, Regina's a little bimbo with no more brains than a squirrel. Screwed good, I suppose, but Mike Hunt married her to have someone to do the laundry."

"Bimbo or not, the charges are borne out by the evidence you have before you. Everything from the hospital supports what she says."

"Ah . . ."

Jane sipped at her brandy again, determined that this time she wouldn't overreact. "Tim, the court could come out of this looking very bad."

He squinted at the copies again. "How so?"

"Kathleen Talbot is trying the Chesney murder case."

"So?"

"What's Chesney accused of?"

"Murder. He shut off the machines . . . Holy shit!"

She finished the brandy, then helped herself to some more. "Exactly. He's accused of doing what those documents show she did herself. It will all be in our morning edition," she lied. "I just thought I'd give you advance warning. You're an old friend, and it seemed like the only right thing to do."

He blinked, his expression slack with confusion. "She should have excused herself from that trial . . ."

Jane shrugged. "But she didn't."

"Oh, sweet Jesus," he said, taking the bottle from her and pouring his glass almost half-full. "This is going to hit tomorrow?"

She nodded.

"What did Judge Talbot say?"

Jane sipped at the glass. "She refused comment."

"The attorneys, the ones trying the case, know about this?"

"Yes."

"That ties it. They'll be screaming for another judge, a mistrial, the fucking works!"

"I'll need a statement from you, Tim."

"Why?"

"You're the executive judge. People will think you knew about this all along."

"What?"

Jane felt completely in control. It was a beautiful sensation. "As I said, the court itself may come out of this looking bad."

"I didn't know any of this, I swear it." He gulped down the brandy, his face beginning to glisten with beads of sweat.

"You had better take some formal action. I can still work it into tomorrow's story."

He pushed himself upright and began to pace nervously. "That goddamn woman," he muttered. "She's been nothing but trouble from day one."

"That's your official statement?" Jane taunted.

He glared down at her. "No. You want to take notes?"

"Go ahead, I'll remember."

"You can say that I'm appointing a special commission to look into the entire matter." He thought for a moment. "I'll name three judges to act as an investigative panel. They'll start at once. These are very serious charges."

"And what are they supposed to do? Whitewash?"

"No!" he snapped. "If it's murder, they can recommend a warrant. If it's a breach of ethics, they can recommend removal."

"Tim," she said quietly, "if I type that up, will you sign it? My damn editor changes everything, and I want to make sure you're quoted correctly."

"You write it and I'll sign it. You can use the clerk's typewriter."

She was going to pour more brandy, but thought better of it. It was going to be a long, busy night. "Who's going to head up this panel of yours?"

Again he paused to think; then a slow, almost evil smile spread across his thin features. "Broadbent."

"Webster Broadbent is Talbot's rival for your job. He'll crucify her."

He grinned and freshened his drink. "Isn't that a damn shame?" He was still cackling as she began to type.

Judge Timothy Quinlan signed his name with a flourish, and Jane Whitehall hurried out to the nearest telephone.

Bennett answered his own phone.

"Jack," she said in a voice so composed that she sounded almost bored, "you'll never guess what's happened."

—◀ ▶—

Mease found Marty Kelly at the fifth bar he tried. Kelly didn't have to leave bread crumbs; his trail was testified to by bartenders and waitresses.

Kelly was perched on a high bar stool, his tie askew, his mustache drooping at the corners of his mouth.

"Hey, it's the demon prosecutor himself," Kelly announced with a lopsided grin. "You better not do any serious drinking, Tom. One of us has got to try that case tomorrow." His words were slightly slurred. He was a bit ahead of his own schedule.

"There may be no case tomorrow," Mease said, taking the adjoining stool. "I've been trying to find you."

Kelly frowned. "What . . . ?"

"A beer," Mease said to the bartender, then turned again to Kelly. "Marty, I don't know what the hell to do. Just as we finished today, that damn Jane Whitehall laid some heavy shit on me. I need your advice."

Kelly slowly shook his head. "What time is it?"

Mease glanced at his watch. "Just after seven."

"I've been drinking since noon, my boy. I have many fine qualities, but temperance isn't one of them." He laughed a little too loudly. "Advice I can give—how good it might be, given my condition, is open to serious question, but go on. You've piqued my curiosity."

Mease quickly described what Jane Whitehall had told him. He showed Kelly the documents, but the older lawyer couldn't focus sufficiently to read them.

"Give it to me again, Tom. I'm having a difficult time understanding all this."

Mease sighed. Kelly was in no condition to be any real help. "Marty, the judge had her father's life-support system shut off. His physical condition was basically the same as Paul Martin's when Chesney pulled the plugs on him."

"So?"

"Jesus, she did exactly what Chesney did, and now she's hearing Chesney's case. Whitehall says it will be all over the newspapers tomorrow."

"That Janey's got a pair of nice tits, ever notice that?"

"You're not being very helpful, Marty."

Kelly nodded and smiled. "I cautioned you about my delicate condition. So what do you care what the newspapers do?"

Mease sipped at his beer. "I haven't talked to anyone about this, not even Arnie Nelson."

Kelly shrugged. "You probably should tell Nelson. He's our boss, at least for the moment."

"He's too goddamned dumb, Marty. Whatever he did, he'd fuck up everything, you know that."

"Looks bright, though," Kelly replied. "God, what a career he'd have if he didn't have to open his mouth." Kelly finished his drink and motioned for another. "You're probably right. Arnie was the one who signed the Chesney warrant in the first place, which certainly wasn't too smart."

"Whitehall says if we don't do something, we'll be smeared for inaction."

"What does she want us to do?"

Mease shook his head. "I don't know. All I can think of is a motion for a mistrial. We could ask for a new trial and a new judge."

Kelly watched the bartender fill his glass, but didn't drink. "That could be dangerous," he said quietly.

"Why?"

"If the prosecutor asks for a mistrial, after the jury has been sworn, it could result in double jeopardy if the charge is brought again. It's a nice little question of constitutional law."

"What the hell, Chesney's not sanctified by this proceeding. If the judge dropped dead, there'd be another trial."

Kelly nodded. "But that's something outside the control of the prosecuting attorney, isn't it? If we bring a motion to boot her, that is within our control. Jeopardy could attach." He shook his head. "And if that happened, given all the publicity of this trial, we would really look like jackasses."

"But if we do nothing . . ."

Kelly fondled the glass in front of him. "We can ask to discuss the issue with the judge privately."

"But the newspapers . . ."

Kelly's eyes narrowed as he looked at Mease. "This is serious business, Tom. If Whitehall is right and this hits the front page, and it certainly should, then you make a statement saying our office has the matter under advisement. Say nothing else. They'll pounce on every word, so don't you go building their story for them at this point until you know exactly what's going to happen."

"That sounds like we're ducking. We could look like wimps. After all, Marty, Kathleen Talbot was our boss. It might look as if we were protecting her."

Kelly's eyes remained on his drink, as if it were a crystal ball capable of revealing the future. "And you've been mentioned as a candidate for prosecutor. I'm sure you're a little concerned about how that looks too."

Mease swore. "Look, Marty, I didn't have a chance. I don't give a shit how I look, just so long as I don't come out painted as some complete ineffectual jerk." He paused. "And we have a duty also."

"Oh?"

"Our client is the public. We have to do what's right."

Kelly's voice was almost inaudible. "You believe that shit?"

"Yeah, I do. When it comes down to the bottom line, I do."

Kelly lifted the glass and turned as if in salute. "Well, my young friend, unfortunately, I do too. Which puts a great deal more at risk than our reputations." He downed the drink. "Now, if you could kindly help me home, I think I'm going to quit, at least for this evening. It looks as if we'll have quite a day ahead of us tomorrow. And mornings, as you know, are the times when I'm at my best." He lurched as he climbed off the stool. "Honor, duty, self-interest—God, this is turning out to be so purifying. I wonder how it will end."

Jerry Mitchell had returned to his apartment deeply troubled. One of the worst mistakes a lawyer could make, he knew, was to become personally involved in a trial. Emotions clouded objectivity, thereby making all judgment questionable. He was not personally involved in his client's cause, but he was involved with the judge, and he wondered if that wasn't even worse.

Mitchell truly enjoyed the challenge of trying a lawsuit, finding a sense of exhilaration in existing on that razor's edge. He often thought the tension of a trial was like a drug, something that seemed to accentuate sensations, to propel the mind into a sharpness not experienced otherwise. But this time everything was different.

Kathleen lived just across the park. And while he couldn't see her apartment from his windows, in his mind's eye her face was all the more visible. He wanted to call, to talk with her, one friend to another. But that was impossible—she was the problem he wanted to discuss.

He regretted ever putting himself in such a position. It was to have been an ordinary murder case, containing a unique legal question perhaps, but nothing more than that. Now it was much more.

Suddenly Mitchell's spacious apartment felt as uncomfortably confining as a jail cell, and he needed to get out.

The September night was mild, the soft autumn breeze carrying just a hint of the chill to come. He walked without any destination, grateful just to be doing something physical.

He had spent over an hour with Dennis Chesney, explaining the legal possibilities. It was Chesney's life, not his, that was at stake. It was Chesney's decision to make, but Mitchell wondered if Chesney had the emotional health to reach a rational decision. Mitchell was keenly aware of his duty as a lawyer. Chesney's welfare was paramount, beyond his own, beyond that of Kathleen Talbot, whom he now reluctantly realized he loved.

The first fallen leaves of the season danced about his feet as he continued walking.

He had explained every option to Chesney. They could demand a mistrial, ask that the judge disqualify herself, appeal if she refused. It would be a wedge, an opening to ask for a reduction of the charge in the future, perhaps even a way to work out a plea.

If the prosecutor asked for a mistrial, or if the judge, on her own motion, disqualified herself, it might be argued that jeopardy attached, and Dennis Chesney could never be retried. He would walk out of jail a free man, the prospect of a deadly prison sentence lifted forever.

All of those options meant ruin for Kathleen Talbot. But Mitchell recognized his main duty was to his client. What might happen to Kathleen couldn't enter into his assessment of the case.

He had suggested to Dennis Chesney that they wait to see if the prosecutor or the judge acted. If not, then Mitchell could bring the motion for mistrial. It was the only reasonable tactic.

But Dennis Chesney didn't want a mistrial. Freedom beckoned, and Chesney refused to grasp it.

Mitchell was torn, but he had tried to persuade Chesney that they had to take every advantage they could. Chesney's expression was somber as he insisted that such a course, even if it resulted in his freedom, would leave him branded a murderer for all time. He wanted the trial to go on; he wanted a decision, no matter what it might be.

And nothing Mitchell said could alter Chesney's decision.

Now, as he continued his stroll, Mitchell wondered if he had to honor that choice, although he wanted to for personal reasons.

Mitchell found himself standing across from Kathleen's apartment. He looked up, aching to be with her. . . .

Tomorrow Kathleen might be ripped to shreds, her reputation, her career, ruined forever. And because of circumstances, and duty, he could not help her.

The wind had picked up, and the temperature was dropping. He stood there oblivious of the weather, conscious only of the dreadful chill deep within his own soul. Tomorrow he might even be the one who would deliver the death blow.

CHAPTER 27

THE TELEPHONE SEEMED to be ringing in a dream, so Kathleen continued to sleep until she was awakened by Marie's voice.

Marie was standing at the foot of her bed. Kathleen glanced at her window; it was still dark.

"Mrs. Talbot, there's a call for you."

Kathleen snapped on the bedstand light and squinted at the clock. It was just a few minutes after six.

"Who?"

"A lady. Judge Hastings. Shall I tell her to call back?"

"No. Thank you, Marie. I'll take it in here."

She had spent most of the evening with Brenda Hastings, discussing what might happen and what she could do about it.

Kathleen picked up the telephone. "Brenda?"

"It's all in the paper, front page, plus a large feature with pictures."

"Bad?" Kathleen asked, now fully awake.

Brenda hesitated. "That bitch Jane Whitehall really did a job on you. Maybe you had better not go in today."

Kathleen sat up. "That's out of the question."

"Quinlan is quoted as setting up a panel to look into your conduct."

"What?"

"According to the paper, he's appointed a three-judge panel

273

to hold hearings on whether you should be removed from the Chesney case, and other things."

"What do you mean, other things?"

Brenda's voice was almost a whisper. "He's quoted as saying they may recommend your removal as a judge. Also, he says criminal charges may be recommended."

Kathleen felt a rising sense of anger. "Who the hell does he think he is? God?"

"This is a terrible article, Kathleen. Whitehall's done a nasty hatchet job—it sounds as though you're on your way to prison. I don't think I've ever seen anything quite as vicious." She paused for a moment. "I think you'd better retain counsel."

"Under what authority can they remove me? Only the Supreme Court can do that, as far as I know. They have superintending control by statute."

"I still wouldn't go in today, not until you've talked to a lawyer. This is one you don't want to handle yourself, Kathleen. It could be dangerous."

"Dangerous? What do you mean?"

Brenda paused, then spoke decisively. "Politically, it's obvious. Whether they can remove you or not isn't the question; they can ruin you, and it looks as if they are really going to try. Also, to be blunt, Kathleen, every nut in the city has an interest in the Chesney case; they're all on one side or the other. This story could inflame some of them. You may need protection."

Kathleen looked again out the window. Dawn was coming, its first rays making the tops of the trees more visible against the sky. She had always liked dawn, but now it seemed ominous, as if she was seeing it for the last time.

"I'll call Jim Rayburn and ask him to represent me. He's a former Supreme Court justice. That should give me some edge when things get rough."

"Kathleen, I'd call him now, before you go in. I doubt if things can get much rougher. And I'd ask for a police escort."

Kathleen wanted to hang up, go back to bed, and, like a child, pull the covers over her head in the hope that it would all eventually go away, but she was overruled by reality. "I'll call Rayburn, then I'll go to court. If I think I need any protection, I'll make arrangements."

"Would you like me to go with you?" Brenda asked.

"I appreciate that, I really do, but I don't think it's necessary."

"Okay, whatever you think. But I'm available, and I've had a little experience at being an outcast. If you need me, just holler."

"Thanks."

Marie, who seemed to sense something was very wrong, brought her a cup of steaming coffee, then left her alone.

As Kathleen sipped the coffee, she considered the alternatives. Even a resignation wouldn't help. She couldn't quit in the middle of a trial, and even if she could, it wouldn't stop the publicity and it would probably convince everyone she was guilty of everything being charged.

There was no other course open; she would have to fight. But she feared the conflict and its possible consequences. There was no guarantee that even the Supreme Court would be in her corner if things got bad.

There were no guarantees of any kind.

She slipped into her robe and started for her study. She had Jim Rayburn's home number there in her book. It was a beginning.

Marie was standing in the hallway, tears rolling down her cheeks. She held something behind her.

"What is it, Marie? What do you have there?"

Marie's mouth jerked with emotion as she handed the morning paper to Kathleen. "It's . . . it's awful," she stammered.

Kathleen took the paper. Her picture was on page one, along with the old campaign picture of her father. The headline was one word: MURDER?

"For God's sake, Mrs. Talbot, don't let Michael see that . . . that thing."

Michael was too young to read, but someone might tell him what the pictures meant.

She took the paper and hurried into the den, found the number, and dialed.

Rayburn answered on the second ring. "Yes."

"Jim, this is Kathleen Talbot. I need some help."

"I just opened the morning paper," he said evenly.

"Can I talk to you?"

"I presume about representing you?"

"Yes."

There was a very long pause. "Judge Talbot," he said at last, "let me give that some thought. I'll get back to you."

Kathleen replaced the receiver. Things were even worse than she had imagined.

◄ ►

Ted Sawchek whispered an indecent proposal to the young nurse's aide who brought his breakfast. She giggled, blushed, then hurried from his luxurious private room.

Sawchek had allowed Chuck Lindell to put him in the hospital, although he had loudly accused Lindell of being a butcher. But the infected knee seemed to be responding to the medication, and Lindell wanted Sawchek off his feet. The hospital seemed the logical choice. The elegant private room—a new attraction offered by the hospital to offset competition—provided color television and a stereo in a setting resembling a tastefully decorated hotel suite.

The food, specially catered, was excellent, and Sawchek was enjoying himself. He had his eye on one of the nurses, a divorcée, whom he was determined to bed—if not in the hospital, then later at his own apartment. And he had full use of the telephone—an important consideration for a man trying to become the executive judge.

As usual, the morning newspaper was delivered along with the tray. Sawchek poured steaming coffee from the silver pot, then opened the paper. The tray, pot, and coffee went flying when he saw the banner headline and the pictures.

He ignored the coffee-stained sheets as he devoured every word, cursing aloud when he read that Broadbent had been appointed head of the investigative panel. That old prick Quinlan had given Broadbent an unfair advantage, and Sawchek knew he would have to move quickly.

He grabbed the call button and signaled for the nurse.

Service was always good for the favored patients in the

luxury private rooms, and the object of his lustful interest quickly walked in.

"Oh, judge, I see we've had a little accident," she said, nodding toward the tumbled tray.

"Accident, my ass. I have to get out of here. Get me my clothes, and whatever form I have to sign."

She began to pick up the tray and the spilled breakfast. "You'll have to check with Dr. Lindell," she said, still smiling. "Did something upset you?"

"I don't have to check with anybody. I'm going to sign myself out."

She sat on the edge of his bed, her hip just touching his thigh. "You can do that, of course, but why not talk with Dr. Lindell first? Your knee is coming along very nicely." She ran her hand gently over the top of his leg. "You don't want anything to happen to that," she said, "a big, handsome man like you."

"I have to get out of here," he said. "It's business."

"Dr. Lindell will be in at noon. Can't it wait until then?" Her voice was husky with promise.

"Maybe. Do you think you could spend a little time with me before he comes in?"

She cocked one eyebrow, her smile somewhat less professional. "You never know."

"Well, perhaps I could wait until after I talk to Lindell."

She stood up, her ample breasts straining against the white nylon of her uniform. She gently patted his shoulder. "Good. I'll send in another tray, and have someone change your sheets."

"But you'll come back?"

"Absolutely."

She left and walked back to the nurses' station. All the females on the floor had been targets for Sawchek during his short stay. They would enjoy hearing of his latest ploy and his expectation of a sexual interlude that would never happen. It was too bad he was leaving. Judge Sawchek had been providing most of the amusement for everyone on the floor. He was a nuisance, but they would miss the comic relief.

◄ ►

"You saw the newspaper, I take it?" Brenda Hastings asked. She had called Jesse Williams as soon as she reached court.

"Yes."

"Does the article change your opinion of Kathleen?"

Williams chuckled. "Brenda, shame on you. You should know me better than that. But it is a terrible thing to have happen to her. She hasn't come in yet, but I plan to see her when she does. It's essential that she know she has friends."

"I advised her not to come to court today, but she said she would."

"Kathleen Talbot isn't the kind to duck," he said, "which may be a wonderful character trait, but it can prove to be a disadvantage at times. How is she feeling?"

"I don't know if she is capable of feeling anything. I think she's numb from the shock. Have you ever seen such a vicious attack?"

"Not recently. Unfortunately, it's the kind of thing the public loves—people in high places, accusations of murder. It sells papers."

"Quinlan should be shot," Brenda said.

Again Williams chuckled. "For starters, yes. But he's done quite a job on Kathleen. And Broadbent will finish it off, I'm afraid. He'll milk this for everything it's worth. Webster can smell the executive-judge job. And he's determined to have it, even if it means ruining someone else. Fortunately, we have one thing on our side."

"Such as?"

"Webster Broadbent is basically a stupid man. It's the intelligent villains who cause the worst damage."

"A little child with a gun can still kill, Jesse."

"Not if you take the gun away from him first."

"What do you have in mind?" she asked.

Williams' voice lost its accustomed casual inflection. "Who is representing Kathleen?"

"She tried to get Jim Rayburn."

"Good choice," Williams said. "His being a former member of the Supreme Court won't hurt."

"But he didn't agree to do it."

His eyebrows shot up. "Oh?" He thought for a moment. "Do you think Kathleen would object if I sounded out someone else?"

"At this point she'd welcome it. I spoke to her this morning. I don't think she's slept at all. Anyway, she doesn't have a lawyer so far. Who do you have in mind?"

"Well, he might not want to do it, so let it be my little secret for a while. It just might surprise everyone. I'll talk to Kathleen in any event, then I'll let you know."

"I think all this may clinch things for Webster Broadbent, don't you? As executive judge?"

His laugh lost its softness. "No, Brenda, not while I still have breath in my body."

◄ ►

"Who's that old guy in the pool? He swims pretty good." The fat man had come in for a swim before attending the club's weekly businessmen's luncheon.

His companion, a gray-haired corporate executive, followed his gaze. "That's Marcus Kaplan."

The fat man adjusted his swimming goggles. "Come on, Kaplan's been dead for years. You might just as well have said it was Clarence Darrow."

"But that's not Darrow, and it *is* Kaplan."

"Really?"

"He lives here at the club, but he tends to avoid socializing. Looks pretty good for his age."

"Age? Jesus, if that really is Kaplan, he has to be over a hundred."

"No. Just past eighty. He retired from the law about twenty years ago and he's never in the papers anymore. I suppose everyone thinks he's long gone."

The two businessmen stood by the side of the pool and watched the swimmer as he stroked easily and steadily through the water.

"I've been a member for five years and this is the first time I've seen him."

The other man laughed. "That's because you only come in for luncheons or to use the bar. He spends most of his time in his suite on the top floor. I understand he has an enormous library there. He lives alone, although he has a butler."

"Everyone says he was great," the fat man remarked as the swimmer slowed and then glided to the pool's ladder. "It's like running into a historical figure. They say he was the best there ever was; sort of a Babe Ruth of the courtroom."

Marcus Kaplan slowly climbed to the tile deck.

"Jesus, he's big!"

A deep voice rumbled like low thunder, echoing off the tile walls and the surface of the pool. "Six-foot-five." Kaplan took up a large towel and draped it over his youthfully lean body like a toga. "I was six-foot-seven, but age seems to have shrunk me a bit."

He toweled his great mop of pure white hair. "However, I still possess a rather remarkable sense of hearing." He walked with almost stately dignity to where the two men stood. They both stared up at him. Under great bushy white brows, his slate-gray eyes were piercing. "You made me sound like a monument, and in a way, I suppose that's exactly what I am. You should have known me while I was alive." The gray eyes twinkled.

The fat man blushed. "I didn't mean . . . well, you know."

"I'm flattered to be remembered, even as a monument." Kaplan's chuckle grew into a great low roll of laughter. "Well, the water's fine, gentlemen, and it's all yours. Now, if you'll excuse me?"

"It's been an honor, Mr. Kaplan," the fat man mumbled.

He waved in reply, then climbed the steps to the shower.

As he showered off the chlorinated water, Kaplan heard himself being paged by Jimmy, the locker-room attendant: "Mr. Kaplan, there's a call for you."

Kaplan emerged and slipped into a terry-cloth robe. "I don't take calls, Jimmy. You know that."

"This is Judge Williams."

"Judges, Jimmy, are a dime a dozen."

Jimmy's friendly dark face split into a grin. He had known Kaplan too many years to be put off by the judge's mock scowl.

"Yes, sir, Mr. Kaplan, but this one's a friend of mine. I'd appreciate it if you would talk with him."

"Which Judge Williams is it? There are several."

"Jesse Williams."

Kaplan pretended annoyance. "Oh, that one."

"He's a good man," Jimmy said, accustomed to Kaplan's ways.

Kaplan walked the short distance to Jimmy's towel room and picked up the phone. "Good morning, your honor. What can I do for you?"

"I don't know if you remember me, but I—"

"The Bannerman murder case. You were the prosecutor."

"A very young prosecutor," Jesse Williams replied. "It's nice that you remember."

"Tall black man, always smiling, quietly unassuming. As I recall, your easy manner lulled opponents to sleep and then you struck like a cobra."

Williams laughed. "Cobra or not, you beat me."

Marcus Kaplan smiled. "You made it quite difficult. I've followed your career. I understand from a number of sources that you're as good a judge as you were a trial lawyer, which was very good indeed."

"I had some great teachers. You were one."

"And you, an able student. Now that we've flattered the hell out of each other, what do you want?"

"Have you read the morning paper? About Kathleen Talbot?"

"Yes."

"She's in great difficulty, Marcus."

"So it appears."

"She needs help."

"So?"

"Would you consider representing her?"

Kaplan laughed. "You know, a few minutes ago I met two gentlemen who thought I had joined the dinosaurs. I'm afraid my days of being a lawyer are over, Jesse."

"Do you remember the old saying—if you're innocent, get Banyan, but if you're guilty, get Kaplan?"

Kaplan chuckled. "Haven't heard that one in years. I suppose it was true enough in those days. Pat Banyan was a great trial man. I think it was his saintly manner. Juries wanted to believe him."

"You made juries believe you."

Kaplan shifted his position to lean against Jimmy's desk. He had done a little too much swimming and his legs felt tired. "Thank you, Jesse. I retired over twenty years ago and I haven't been in a courtroom since. You're right, young Kathleen is in deep trouble. She needs someone who is in top form."

"She asked Jim Rayburn."

Kaplan nodded. "With his connections, he should be able to do the job."

"He refused."

"Why?" Kaplan asked.

"No lawyer wants to get into this thing. There are a lot of judges involved. No practicing attorney wants to make unnecessary enemies. I doubt that she'll be able to get anyone really good."

"Jerry Mitchell is good."

This time Williams was the one to chortle. "Yes, but he's trying that murder in front of her. He couldn't take her case, it would be a conflict of interests."

"She can get someone. Her father, whom I never liked very much, had a lot of powerful friends. She'll find someone."

"I doubt it."

Kaplan straightened up. "You know how old I am, Jesse. How do you know I haven't gone dotty?"

"I don't. But you don't sound dotty. In fact, you sound just like you did when you beat the hell out of me in the Bannerman case."

"Did she ask you to call?"

"No. I haven't talked to her yet."

"So you're just acting on your own?"

Williams' voice reflected his deep concern. "Yes."

"She may not want me—hell, she might never have even heard of me."

"Like you said, Marcus, you may be a dinosaur, but you're a famous one."

"Everyone thinks I'm dead."

Williams spoke quietly. "This is one way you could show people that you aren't."

"This is ridiculous."

"Still pay yor dues?" Williams asked.

Kaplan laughed. "I'm still licensed to practice."

"At least talk to her."

Kaplan shook his head and was about to refuse.

"You may be her only hope, Marcus," Williams said. "For you, that's old shoe, but for this young woman it's a matter of life and death."

"She may not even want me."

"Marcus, can it hurt to talk to her?"

"That's all I can offer, just a chat."

"Can you come over to the Hall now?".

Kaplan glanced at the clock on the locker-room wall. "I'll be there in thirty minutes."

CHAPTER 28

A SCOUT CAR was parked near the entry port of the garage, and several uniformed police officers stood talking to the regular security guard.

Slowing to a stop as one of the policemen signaled to her, Kathleen rolled down the window.

"Good morning, your honor," the policeman said. "We have orders to escort you to your courtroom."

She parked her car, and two stern-faced policemen accompanied her to the judges' elevator and then up to her floor.

"What's the reason for all this attention?"

One of the policemen smiled. "Our boss is worried about the possible effect of the newspaper story this morning. That sort of thing can set off any number of crazies. We're along as a precaution."

The policemen left her at her chambers. Attracted by the noise from the street, Kathleen looked out the window. Below, near the front entrance to the court building, demonstrators were milling about and shouting. Their numbers appeared to have doubled from the day before. Policemen in riot helmets stood just beyond the crowd.

"Are you ready, judge?" Her clerk's tone reflected his anxiety. "Everyone's all set."

She couldn't dispel the feeling of still being in the middle of a nightmare. "I'd like to speak to Mr. Mitchell and Mr. Mease."

The clerk nodded, and a moment later the two lawyers

walked in. Both men were solemn. She wondered if she only imagined the sympathy she thought she saw in Jerry Mitchell's eyes.

"I trust you both saw the newspaper?"

"Yes," Jerry Mitchell said, sitting down on the couch. Mease remained standing.

"As you can imagine, I have been thinking of little else since this morning. Allow me to tell you the facts. The law of the state in which my father died recognizes brain death as marking the end of life. Also, in that state the decision to continue a patient on life-support machines is left to that patient, if competent and conscious, and if not, to the patient's next of kin or legal guardian. In my father's case I was both."

"Judge, I—"

"Just a moment, Mr. Mease. Let me finish. I was advised by the doctor in charge that my father had suffered a third massive stroke, a stroke that resulted in brain death. He was dead. All life functions were being performed by the machines. I flew down to the hospital, talked to the doctor, and made the decision to have the machines turned off. My father's wife, my stepmother, had been committed by the local court to the hospital for treatment of alcoholism. She was a patient at the time. I didn't consult with her because I didn't consider her competent."

She couldn't bring herself to look at Jerry Mitchell. She had often wanted to tell him about her father's death and how it had troubled her. She wondered now what he might really think of her.

"Those are the facts, gentlemen," she continued. "My actions were all quite legal. I had given thought to disqualifying myself in this matter because of the similarities, but I decided that I could in good conscience hear the matter impartially. I still think so. However, if you disagree, and if you wish to make any motions to that effect, I would propose hearing them before we proceed any further."

Mease looked away as he spoke. "To begin with, I'm deeply sorry that all this had to come out in the newspapers. But it has. I'm not sure what to do, frankly. I tried calling Arnie

Nelson, but he's ducking this apparently. He may wish me to bring a motion, but as of this minute, I have no such plans."

"Mr. Mease, I want no special consideration," she said firmly. "I was your boss, as Mrs. Whitehall mentioned in her article. But we all must conduct ourselves professionally. You owe me nothing. Your sole duty is to represent the people."

"Judge, are you going to excuse yourself?" Mease asked.

She was conscious of Mitchell's eyes. "No."

Mease nodded. "I hope you understand me. If I'm ordered to make such a motion in the future, I must."

"I understand," she said, then looked over at Jerry Mitchell. "Do you wish to make such a motion?"

"Yesterday, at the close of trial, Jane Whitehall approached me with the documents used as the basis for her article. She intimated that I should demand that you excuse yourself. I presume she did the same with you, Tom?"

Mease nodded. "She did."

Mitchell's expression was grave. "I have a duty to my client. I immediately informed Lieutenant Chesney of what the documents contained. To be frank, I told him that it was my advice to pursue such a motion."

"To disqualify me?" Kathleen asked.

He continued to look at her. "Yes," he said softly. "My primary duty is to my client. We are all lawyers here. I pointed out that if you were disqualified, under certain circumstances he might never have to be tried again. And even if he were, I felt I would then have leverage to bargain for a lesser charge."

Kathleen felt betrayed, although she knew everything he said was completely true. "And?"

"Lieutenant Chesney instructed me not to bring such a motion."

"On what basis?" she asked.

Mitchell's expression didn't change. "He said that you had been punished enough. He was adamant that I take no action to disqualify you."

"He thinks I committed a crime?" Kathleen asked.

Mitchell shook his head. "Of course not. I'm not trying to curry favor for him, but I honestly believe he feels that such a decision, especially when it concerns one's parent, is so devastating that legal considerations have no bearing. Whether that's a subtle form of transference on his part, I can't say, but that's his position."

She continued to look at Jerry Mitchell. "A position with which you don't concur, obviously."

"As you said, we have to be professional." His usually strong voice sounded strangely muted. "Whatever personal feelings I might have must be subordinated to what is best for my client."

"Perhaps you have no personal feelings, Mr. Mitchell?"

His eyes seemed suddenly sad. "It makes little difference, at this point, does it?"

She nodded. She felt tears welling in her eyes. "All right, then, if there are no motions to be made, we'll begin the testimony. Are you both ready?"

"I'm ready," Mease said. He looked at them both for a moment, then turned and left.

Jerry Mitchell stood up. "Kathleen . . ."

"Do you honestly think I should disqualify myself?"

He hesitated, then spoke very quietly. "You are the only one who can truthfully answer that."

For a moment he looked as if he were going to say something more, but then he turned and walked out of her chambers.

Kathleen blotted her eyes with a tissue, then donned her robe. The noises from the street were getting louder.

The clerk rapped the gavel as she ascended the bench. "This honorable court is now in session. The Honorable Kathleen M.— "

"Murdering whore!" A thin, intense woman was standing in the spectator seats, shaking a fist at her.

Then a man shouted: "Murderess! Get off there. You have no right!"

The court officers descended on both demonstrators and hustled them out of the courtroom.

Her clerk turned and whispered, "Do you want the cops to hold those two for contempt?"

She shook her head. "No." Then she raised her voice so that everyone in the courtroom could hear her. "Any more incidents like that will be dealt with severely."

An anxious silence descended over the packed courtroom.

"Bring in the jury," she said firmly. "Then, Mr. Mease, you may call your first witness."

The tension was almost palpable. She looked over at Jerry Mitchell, then quickly turned her eyes away. Dennis Chesney, it seemed, wasn't the only one on trial.

---◄ ►---

Webster Broadbent checked his appearance in the mirror: he was the very picture of a judge. He swept out of his chambers, through the courtroom, and into the hall. The camera crews turned on their lights, and the newspaper photographers began snapping away.

Broadbent took the seat prepared at the table and smiled into the cameras. "I have prepared a statement," he said, using his best courtroom voice.

"I have been appointed chairman of a three-judge panel set up by the executive judge to investigate certain allegations made in connection with one of our circuit judges."

A woman photographer knelt to get a better angle, accidentally exposing one thigh, but Broadbent reluctantly ignored the distraction. "Judge Jerome Foley, Judge Joseph Sadowski, and I are to look into these allegations. When our investigation is completed, we will make a report to the executive judge and recommend any action we think proper."

Broadbent became duly solemn, aware that he wore a good expression for the evening news programs. "We have met and we are recommending to the executive judge that he suspend the judge in question from all duties until we can determine the validity of the charges."

Quinlan had liked that part, saying it would teach the bitch a lesson. Broadbent continued. "We will meet with Judge Quinlan later today."

A voice came from the mass of media people clustered around the cameras. "Are you saying Judge Talbot is being suspended?"

Broadbent didn't like the tone of the question, but he concealed his resentment. "No. She is merely being relieved of judicial duties at this time—or at least that's what we recommend."

"What about the Chesney murder trial?" a reporter demanded.

Broadbent nodded slowly. "The trial will be recessed."

"But the jury's sequestered. What about that?"

Broadbent had forgotten about that. It would be a simple matter to stop the trial for a few days, but keeping the jury locked up might make them a kind of legal hostage. "Judge Quinlan will make the decision about that," he said evenly, putting that responsibility squarely on Quinlan, whom Broadbent considered a senile old fool anyway.

"What does Judge Talbot say about all this?"

Broadbent was ready for that one. "We haven't as yet talked with the judge. She will testify before us in due course."

"What about the Judicial Commission?" a voice asked.

"They have jurisdiction when judicial misconduct is alleged. We plan to determine if this is a matter for the Judicial Commission, which, as you know, is a state agency."

"Will Judge Talbot be charged with murder?"

Broadbent smiled slowly, as if embarrassed at the question. "We won't know that until we look into the validity of these charges."

"But could she be?" the voice demanded.

"As I say, that is a question yet to be determined." He looked as solemn as he could, knowing that the headlines would be juicy reading: SUSPENDED JUDGE MAY BE CHARGED WITH MURDER.

"Does the executive judge have the power to suspend another judge?"

Webster Broadbent nodded slowly. "Of course."

"Isn't she a candidate for executive judge?" another voice inquired.

Broadbent knew it was time to leave.

"I'd like to answer all your questions, but they are premature. We will meet with the executive judge later today. Then, depending on our various schedules, we should begin our inquiry tomorrow. Thank you for your attention."

He stood up, smiled once more, then sought the security of his own courtroom.

It was a good performance, he thought triumphantly. He had all but convicted her of incompetency plus murder, without once saying so. That would end any hope she might have had about keeping him from attaining his rightful place as executive judge.

Kathleen was listening to Dr. Farrell as the medical examiner began his testimony. Tom Mease was being very careful, moving ahead, but making sure that the jury fully understood Farrell's impressive qualifications.

One of her court officers approached the side of the bench and whispered to her, "Judge Quinlan's on the phone."

"Tell him I'll call him back," she replied quietly.

The officer's expression reflected his anxiety at the prospect of being caught between two judges. "He says it's urgent, and he asks that you come to the phone."

She nodded, then spoke in a normal voice. "We'll take a short recess."

She left the bench and hurried into her chambers.

"I'm in the middle of a trial," she said into the phone.

"Not anymore, you're not," Quinlan snapped.

"What do you mean?"

His voice was more raspy than usual. "You recess that Chesney case until we look into the charges made by the papers."

"I will not."

"I'm ordering you, as executive judge."

She felt her face flush with anger, and she struggled to control her feelings. "I'm not going to do it. You have no right to order me to do it."

"We'll see about that. I'm going to send over a written order to you. And in case you get any ideas, I'm going to order your courtroom closed, and the court personnel out of there. I sign their paychecks, so they'd better do it."

"Damn you! You won't get away with this."

His choking chuckle answered her. "When we're through with you, sister, you'll be on the other side of the bench." Then he hung up.

"Kathleen?"

She turned to find Jesse Williams standing at the door. The tall man next to him looked as if he had just stepped out of a Bible illustration. His craggy, hawklike face was dominated by piercing eyes, his large head capped with a mane of flowing white hair. She stared at him.

"I would like you to meet someone who I think might be able to help you," Williams said quietly.

─◄┃ ┃►─

Jane Whitehall took a cab back to the newspaper. She had a copy of Judge Quinlan's order in her purse. Tim Quinlan was a nasty old man, but he was keeping his part of their bargain by giving her an exclusive on everything he did.

The one-page order—so terse and official-looking—would be good, flashy artwork for the front page.

Quinlan had promised he would call her if Kathleen Talbot refused to obey. The old man's cackle sounded like a death rattle when he described what steps he was prepared to take.

Jane wondered if she could plant the idea with Quinlan of having Talbot carried out of the courthouse by court officers. It could be staged, and it would sell a few papers.

When she got back to her desk, she had a sheaf of telephone messages. Most of them weren't important, but Oscar Mullins, one of the reporters assigned to the police beat, had just called. She sat down and called the pressroom in police headquarters.

"I just got in, Oscar," she said. "What's up?"

"Maybe something, maybe nothing. The cops are worried about some screwy preacher who is calling for an antideath rally for tomorrow."

"So?"

"You're handling the Talbot story, right?"

"Yeah."

"Well, the rally's planned as a demonstration against her, and it's scheduled for two o'clock tomorrow afternoon in front of the Hall of Justice. He's holding a service tonight and handbills are being circulated, urging people to come out. This guy's church is in a depressed neighborhood, so I doubt he'll get many out for his rally. Those people have more to worry about than abortions and mercy killings. But I thought you should know about it. The cops are going to beef up the protection over there."

"And they don't think it'll be much?"

"Nope. They're adding only a dozen extra cops, so that has to tell you something."

Jane took down the information Oscar had gathered—the preacher's name, the location of the church, and the inflammatory charges made in the handbill. It called for "God's Army" to arise.

"Thanks, Oscar," she said. "Let me know if anything else develops."

"You got it."

Jane leaned back in her chair. The city room was as busy as usual.

She walked over to a computer and began to input the day's lead on the ballooning Kathleen Talbot story. Her fingers flew over the keys, the story writing itself. She stopped and scanned what she had written. It was good. She sent it to Jack Bennett's electronic basket, then went over to his office.

"Jack," she said, walking in without knocking, "I'd like you to take a look at the lead I've just written."

He put aside the competitor's paper he had been marking and analyzing, and hit the keys, bringing up her story on his computer screen.

"Do you have a copy of Quinlan's order?" he asked as he read the story.

"Sure."

"Give it to Harry. It might make a nice piece of artwork for the front page."

She smiled but said nothing.

Suddenly he began to work the computer.

"What are you doing?" Alarm was evident in her voice. The damn story was perfect; it didn't need editing.

"I'm taking out that crap about the religious rally."

"It's no big deal, but it gives a dimension to the story, Jack. I think it should stay in."

He had deleted that part of her article; then he turned back to her. "What the hell do you want out there, Jane? A riot? All some jackleg preacher will produce will be fifty or so people out for a little harmless shouting and singing. If we announce his rally in the paper, it'll draw like a rock concert. Putting it in this article, you could get out a couple thousand fanatics—people deeply committed on either side—all looking for blood."

"That would be a terrific story."

"Sure. Riots are great news. Only I don't want to start one, so it comes out."

"Jack, you're overreacting."

"Look, you've gotten this Talbot thing out into the open by some rather ingenious skulduggery. But don't push your luck. Maybe Kathleen Talbot can't sue us for libel, but if people are injured in a riot that they claim we may have caused, there'll be lawsuits. They might not collect, but our owners don't like to pay lawyers to defend unnecessary cases."

Jane said nothing. The prospect of a riotous mob would make the story even bigger. And the bigger the story, the bigger her own reputation. There had to be a way around Jack Bennett, but right now it would do no good arguing with him.

"Outside of that, how do you like the story?"

Bennett shrugged. "Quinlan's acting like a dictator. What's Kathleen Talbot going to do about it? Have you asked her?"

"She won't talk to me. But Quinlan told me he'd call me if she has to be thrown out. I'll grab a photographer and go over then."

He frowned. "I really don't like any of this, Jane. Reporting the news is one thing; making it happen is altogether different."

"I'm not making anything happen. Did I turn off those machines? Bullshit. I'm just doing my job, Jack—bringing things out into the open and letting the public know."

"Jane, you're walking a very dangerous tightrope. Don't kid yourself. You're pushing this thing too hard. If it goes sour, it's your head that will roll."

"It won't go sour."

"I'm speaking to you as your editor and your friend. Be careful."

She laughed. "Come on, Jack. We're in a circulation war. Who really gives a shit about what happens in Guatemala or what the import-export ratio is? People love murder cases, and when it concerns people in high places, they eat it up. That, plus the mercy-killing angle, is pure gold—and you know it."

His eyes narrowed. "We have a responsibility, Jane. It even transcends selling papers, believe it or not."

She snorted as she turned to leave. "Jesus, Jack, if all newspaper people were like you, Tammany Hall would still be running New York and Nixon would be back in the White House."

She didn't wait for his reply. She didn't want to miss Quinlan's call when it came.

CHAPTER 29

NELSON BRAGG LISTENED, trying to pick out the preacher's words from those of the voices within him.

"If you are a true Christian," the preacher continued his harangue, "then you will have to take a stand!"

He held the morning edition of the newspaper up in the air. "You saw this! Evil is abroad in the land, my dear friends. The devil takes many forms. And Satan has been known to take the form of a woman before."

Ripples of ethusiastic "Amen!" rolled through the packed assembly.

"Whether clothed in sin or a black robe, it makes no difference, the devil is intent on spreading his evil doctrine. He must be stopped. One day, as the Bible tells us, we have to stand up and be counted." He threw the newspaper to the floor and stamped on it, staring dramatically out at them. "And that time has come for you and me!"

The usual audience response was there, but he detected a definite hesitancy. They were nervous about what might be asked of them.

He walked to the center of the stage. "In the newspaper they write the word 'murder' but they put a question mark after it. My friends, there is no question mark in God's mind. That woman judge killed her own father just as sure as if she had fired a shot into his heart. If no one does anything, we will be guilty of supporting murder by our very silence. Do you want that?"

"No!"

The hesitancy was gone.

He nodded. "Oh, it's fine to come here to church and talk

against the devil and the people who do his evil bidding, but that isn't enough, not nearly enough."

He dropped his voice to make his words more effective. "Can you imagine? That poor man raised that woman, took care of her, provided for her fine education, nurtured her"—he began to raise his voice slowly—"and when he got sick, when he could no longer help himself, what did she do?" He finished with a shout: "She killed him!"

Now he had their rapt attention. "And if we just sit around and do nothing, her action will become a guide for society. Murder will become fashionable. This time God demands your action!"

Some of them looked frightened. He shook his head. "The Bible says, 'He who is not with me is against me.' We must take a stand. We must let God know we are with him, and not against him."

He waited until the amens died down.

"Tomorrow afternoon, at two o'clock, we are going to hold a rally for God and his divine word. We will meet at the Hall of Justice and we will demonstrate against that evil woman and against all who would kill and murder." He paused and stared at them. "Are you with God? Will you stand with him? Will you have the courage to show where you stand? Will you be at the Hall of Justice with me tomorrow?"

The building seemed to shake with a vibrant roar of assent.

"I will want volunteers to pass out handbills, asking people to come to our rally. I will want volunteers to drive folks who have no transportation. I will want volunteers to make signs. We will show the power of God's word tomorrow!"

He paused to take a sip of water, allowing them to vent their emotions. He had touched off a wave of shouting, singing, and dancing, his audience apparently relieved that what he asked would be easy.

If the rally went well, he would be on the television news. It might be just the springboard to bigger things. If he could become the voice of the judge's opponents, he might attract enough attention to get bigger donations and a regular television show. It was a golden opportunity, and he intended to make the most of it.

Nelson Bragg, standing at the back of the former theater, found his voices suddenly quiet. Women were killers. His own mother had wanted him dead. The woman judge was like his mother, evil and dangerous. She had to be stopped. At long last, he understood what the voices wanted, and he felt an elation at being able to do it.

He waited until after the final hymn, savoring the first peace he had known in quite some time. He knew what he had to do. It was all so simple.

A stout woman carrying a clipboard approached him.

"Will you help us pass out handbills?" she asked.

"No. I can't."

"It wouldn't take much of your time," she insisted.

Bragg shook his head. "I am called to greater work."

She smiled. "Oh, you're helping in some other way, then?"

He mumbled. "God's work."

"Bless you," she called after him as he joined the others who were leaving. They were babbling excitedly, but it was not frightening like the voices. It was more like a low and soothing murmur.

CHAPTER 30

KATHLEEN HAD HEARD about Marcus Kaplan for years. Her father used to have an endless supply of Marcus Kaplan stories, as did most older trial lawyers, and she had never had reason to doubt them. But now, her mind benumbed by all that was happening to her, Kathleen found it hard to believe that even a living legend like Marcus Kaplan could save her in her darkest hour.

Jesse Williams had returned to his own chambers. Kathleen had her court clerk recess the Chesney case until three o'clock to give her time to discuss with Kaplan what she should do about Quinlan's order and her situation in general.

Kaplan's questions were short but searching.

"When you requested that Quinlan assign the Chesney case to someone else, what did he say?"

"He accused me of sleeping with Jeremiah Mitchell. And he thought I was trying to duck a difficult case. I couldn't tell him the real reason. I didn't think I could trust him."

Kaplan smiled briefly. "Which subsequent events certainly proved." His deep voice was vastly soothing. "Didn't you think trying this case could create a conflict, if not legally, perhaps emotionally?"

"Not at the time." She paused. There was something about this man that made her want to tell him everything. "I had questions, obviously. I was compromised by circumstances, I admit, but I honestly thought I could hear it without prejudice.

Dennis Chesney is accused of acting without right, either by law or family connection. He's charged with taking matters into his own hands with no legal justification, no matter how good his motives. In my situation, I acted in a state where such action was entirely legal, and I was not only family but I was also appointed legal guardian by the court. While the act itself was similar in both cases, our positions were entirely different in the eyes of the law. Although I didn't want to, I felt I could hear the case fairly."

"Do you still believe that to be true?" His hypnotic eyes bore into hers. "Even after all this?"

Kathleen thought for a moment. "Yes."

"If I agree to represent you, Kathleen, you must follow my advice, is that understood?"

"Well, I . . ."

He slowly shook his head. "I'm afraid there can't be any conditions, Kathleen. In order to do a good job for you, I must have absolute assurance that my advice will be followed. Otherwise, I would just be a bit-part actor in our little play, and my role would prove ineffective. I'm afraid I have to be the director or nothing. It has been a lifelong rule with me."

"I have a duty as a judge. I can't hand that over to anyone."

He nodded. "No, you're quite right there, but I'm speaking of your personal conduct off the bench." Once again, his granite features broke into a short-lived smile. "Most of my old clients found I could provide a good roadmap to direct them out of their difficulties. But they had to follow my route lines."

"Mr. Kaplan, I've heard of nothing but your magical abilities since I was a child, but I doubt if even you can help me now."

"Will you follow my advice?"

The concept of having the burdens carried by someone else produced in Kathleen a giddy feeling of relief. "Yes."

He nodded. "Well, let's see if I can remember what to do, shall we?" He stood up. "May I use your phone?"

"Of course." She got up and offered him her chair.

"Do you have a court directory?"

She handed it to him.

"Whom are you going to call? Judge Quinlan?"

He studied the directory. "Quinlan? No, that would do no good."

He found the number he wanted and dialed. "I'm calling an old law clerk of mine. He wasn't particularly bright, but he was energetic. Let's see if I'm remembered. . . .

"This is Marcus Kaplan," he said into the phone. "Please ask the chief justice if he can spare me a moment."

"Chief Justice Ward?" she asked.

Kaplan nodded. "He's developed a rather sanctimonious manner, and he looks every inch the scholar, but I think underneath it all he's still the same old Charley. We'll see. . . .

"I'll wait," he said into the telephone. Then he looked at Kathleen. "I don't want you talking to anyone, except in the course of the trial. . . ."

He chuckled. "No, I'm not dead, Charles," he continued his telephone conversation. "I read your opinion in the Farwell case. You've come a long way. That was a nice piece of reasoning, and exceptionally well written."

Kaplan chuckled at the reply. "I'd hang on to that clerk if he can write that well. By the way, Charles, this is a business call. I have a client."

Kaplan listened for a moment. "Thank you, Charles. That's very kind, but 'legend' is pushing it a little too far. Now, on to business. I represent Judge Kathleen Talbot."

He paused again. "Yes, it was a disturbing news story, and the allegations are as untrue as they are nasty. It's the kind of thing, Charles, that could poison the reputation of the state judiciary, not just that of Judge Talbot. Here's the immediate problem. Judge Quinlan has ordered the Chesney case shut down and has appointed a three-judge panel to look into the allegations. Both acts suggest that wrongdoing has occurred. But—and perhaps most important—Judge Quinlan seems to have usurped the province of the Supreme Court. As I see it, Charles, your court has been given exclusive control over all lesser courts, by constitution, statute, and court rule. Judge Quinlan apparently is either unaware of this or is opening shop for himself."

Again Kaplan listened to the reply, then continued. "If necessary, Charles, I can draft a motion to that effect and have it driven up to the state capital. You people have just opened your session, so I presume all members of the court are up there."

Kathleen studied Kaplan's chiseled features as he listened. Whatever his reaction, his expression remained the same.

"Thank you, Charles. Will you convey that to Judge Quinlan, or shall I?"

Kaplan looked over at Kathleen. "Yes. She's prepared to continue with the case. I'm here in her chambers. Will you call me back after you've spoken to Quinlan?"

As she listened to the quiet authority in Kaplan's voice, a glimmer of hope began to thread through her despair.

"Will you handle the press, or shall I?" Kaplan asked.

Then he nodded. "Thank you, Charles. I'll await your call."

Kaplan hung up. "It seems the chief justice and the other members of the Supreme Court discussed the newspaper article at lunch today," he said. "They are quite aware of the implications for all judges, and they were going to discuss what they might do tomorrow morning."

Kaplan smiled. "As I hoped, sanctimonious or not, Charley is still Charley. As chief justice he is taking superintending control of the entire matter, taking it out of Judge Quinlan's hands. He is in the process of informing Quinlan now, so that order of his has no force or effect. Charley said you are to continue the trial. Tomorrow he will discuss the next step with his court."

Kathleen exhaled heavily. "What a relief."

Kaplan's white eyebrow arched. "Don't count your chickens just yet, Kathleen. Charley is holding a press conference to announce their plans. They may do the same thing as Quinlan, but at least they won't be concerned with who may be the next executive judge."

"Will I be removed?"

He stood up. "I'm a lawyer, young lady, not a fortune-teller. But if you are"—he smiled broadly—"it will be over my broken old body."

"Webster," Quinlan rasped into the telephone, "we've been ordered not to do anything more on the Talbot matter."

"What! By whom?"

Quinlan felt tired and a little drunk. He had been celebrating what had seemed a victory. "I got a call from the chief justice. The Supreme Court is taking superintending control. We are to leave Talbot alone."

"My God! I've already held a press conference."

Quinlan sighed. "That's too bad, Webster, but at least you will get a little ink out of all this."

"Ink!" Broadbent exploded. "Ink! Goddamm it, I'll come out of this looking like a fool."

"It seems none of us will look so hot," Quinlan replied.

"What the hell do you care? You're retiring anyway. This may hurt my chance to be executive judge."

"Oh, I don't think so, Webster. What the hell, as far as the public's concerned, we were just trying to do the right thing."

"Who cares about the public? The other judges will think I was trying to undercut Talbot."

Quinlan tucked the phone against his shoulder and poured himself a fresh supply of brandy. "Well, you were. So was I."

"That's what comes of listening to you!" Broadbent shouted. "This was all your damned idea in the first place."

"You didn't voice any objection that I recall."

"What about Foley and Sadowski?"

"I just called them," Quinlan said sipping the brandy. "Foley's pissed and Sadowski didn't like the idea of an investigating panel in the first place."

"You've made a fool out of me, you senile old . . . fuck!"

Quinlan laughed, the raspy sound echoing in his empty office. "Actually, that's not a hard thing to do, Webster. Hell, you've been doing it for years."

"I won't forget this, you . . . you . . ."

"Senile old fuck," Quinlan prompted. "Actually I didn't think you knew that word, Webster." He sipped some more brandy. "Oh, I said this wouldn't hurt your chances for executive judge, but I must admit that I'm wrong."

"What?"

"I think you may have lost some votes, but I know of one you've lost for sure."

"Whose?"

"Mine."

Quinlan was amused at the pause.

Then Broadbent spoke, this time in a quiet, friendly voice. "Now, Tim, don't fly off the handle. I said some rude things, I admit, but I was—"

Quinlan smiled and hung up.

He poured some more brandy. He hated to have to tell Jane Whitehall what had happened. But it was necessary.

Jane was in a state of shock, but she called the paper's man in the state capital. He confirmed what Quinlan had told her. The Supreme Court had stepped in.

It was getting late, but Jack Bennett was still in his office. She quickly brought up the story on her computer. She couldn't let it get away from her. Desperation inspired her, and she quickly altered the story to update the high court's action. She reread it, changing just a few things.

She walked into Bennett's office and calmly informed him of what had happened.

"Take a look at the story," she said. "I've rewritten it."

Bennett used the computer screen, showing no indication of how he felt about what he was reading. Then he looked up at her.

"Better have them tear out the picture of the court order."

"Why?"

"It doesn't make any sense to run it now. It's meaningless."

"But I've covered it," she protested.

"You've made it look as if the Supreme Court is going to war with the local judges. I'm not sure that's accurate. Anyway, Quinlan's order has no application anymore. You can leave it in the story, but I want it off page one."

"Jack, this doesn't change the impact of the story. It's still big."

He nodded. "Yes, so far. And the story's still on the front page, but the picture of the order is out."

She could see he wasn't enthusiastic, and unless something else happened he would start to downplay it, to disassociate the paper from what was happening.

"Whatever you say, Jack."

"Don't look so sad, Jane. You've done a great job. Like I said, our job is to report the news, not to make it."

She nodded.

He glanced at his watch. "Damn, it's late, and I have to go to that art-museum thing tonight." He punched the key that would sign him off the computer terminal and stood up. "Janey, relax." He laughed. "But if you can't do that, maybe you can get a statement from the Supreme Court about what they may have in mind. Anyway, I've got to go."

She watched him walk across the city room and speak to the city editor. He didn't trust her. He was taking out the reproduction of the court order himself.

Soon the paper would close the various desks for the night, leaving any last-minute additions for the night copy-editor on duty at the suburban printing plant. Everything was handled electronically. If she did manage to get something later, she could send it by her own portable computer to the plant.

The triumph of the morning had flown, and Jane was plunged into a valley of depression.

The story had become like a child, her child, and she was damned if she was going to let it die.

She went back to her desk and made phone calls to the state capital. As she expected, all inquiries were being referred to the chief justice. His office refused to elaborate on his terse statement taking the matter out of Quinlan's hands.

The Supreme Court might remove Kathleen Talbot, but if they did, it would happen only after a long and tedious process. Meanwhile, her story would shrink to nothing.

There was no reason to hang around the city room, so she went home.

Jane's apartment had never seemed quite so lonely. She even wished she had young Chuck back from Ohio State. Some hot steamy sex would have helped ease the crushing feeling of defeat.

She made herself a cup of coffee and flicked on the television. She used the remote to switch around the channels but found nothing interesting. Some woman with her eyes painted a ghastly purple was singing a gospel song, and she paused to watch that. Then a clergyman came on, his teeth perfectly capped and his hair fixed with enough spray to float a battleship; he began to weave a plea for donations with an inspirational message about how everyone can improve himself and his life with just a bit more effort.

He began talking about the church's computer system and how it had helped in fund-raising. Jane didn't know if he had inspired anyone else, but he had just given her an idea on how to save her dying story.

It was just after eight o'clock. She'd have to wait. Jack Bennett sometimes checked with the man on duty at the plant. The last deadline for the morning edition was eleven-thirty, and Bennett liked to go to bed early.

She drank some more coffee. She knew this was no time to get sleepy. She had things to do.

The time dragged, but finally eleven o'clock came. She watched the local news. They gave the Talbot matter only a minute. Broadbent didn't appear, nor was anyone interviewed except the station's man in the capital. The story was already dying.

Jane took out the small portable computer. It belonged to the paper and was used mainly for one purpose—to send in short pieces to the main computer at the paper's printing plant. It was a wonderful little tool, and she had grown to love it.

She hooked up the modem so that she could send directly, then dialed the number.

"Jeff," she said to the night copy-editor, "I'm going to send an update as an add for the story about the courts."

"The story on the front page?" He sounded bored.

"Yes."

"A major change?"

"No," she replied, "just a small addition."

"Go ahead."

She carefully followed the steps she had been taught and quickly reinserted the section of the article Bennett had taken out earlier. If that fiery preacher was going to hold his rally, she would help spread the "good word." If something violent happened, her story might just get new life, Supreme Court or no Supreme Court.

She typed furiously on the small keyboard. If Bennett raised hell, she'd claim a computer malfunction had caused the offending words to remain.

It was well worth the risk.

She finished up, then called the night man.

"Did you get all that?"

"Sure, Jane. It's a perfect fit. They needed something on the front page anyway. They killed some artwork and that left a hole. This'll help fill it up."

"Happy to help out."

Given the hour, Martin Kelly was strangely sober. He sat quietly on a stool at the end of the bar in the Learned Hand. Tom Mease took a seat beside him.

"Well, how did it go?"

Mease ordered a beer. "You know our renowned medical examiner. How do you think it's going?"

Kelly smiled. "Given all the interruptions of the day, has Mitchell even begun?"

"Marty, I'd sure appreciate it if you would stick around for the afternoon sessions if you can. I really need your help."

"I'll try," Kelly said quietly. "Well, how about it? Have you turned Farrell over to Mitchell?"

"I took my time putting in the direct, believe me. Farrell has never enjoyed such careful treatment. When I got through qualifying him, he sounded like a cross between the Mayo Brothers and Mother Theresa. The dumb bastard has some impressive qualifications, outward appearances to the contrary. The jury hung on every word as he testified to the autopsy."

"How did he do?"

"Oh, just great. He always does if it isn't cross-examination. He explained everything in detail. I didn't leave anything uncovered."

"And?"

Mease sipped the beer. "Well, we had a long adjournment. It looked like Judge Talbot was about to be removed by her colleagues. Then the Supreme Court stepped in, I hear, and she came out and we all went back to work."

"Maybe I *should* be there in the afternoons. It sounds exciting."

Mease nodded. "A thrill a minute. Anyway, I stalled handing Farrell over for cross-examination as long as I could. I thought if the jury could go to bed with his golden words ringing in their ears, it would help ease what was to come."

"Mitchell nailed him, I take it?"

Mease slowly shook his head. "He's in the process. I must admit I'm learning a lot. Jerry Mitchell is a master. Anyway, he sounded as if he was Farrell's proud mother; he treated him with such respect. Then he started. Slowly, at first."

"You'd think for all the times he's testified, Farrell would be more street smart."

"Yeah, but he isn't. Mitchell began to 'discover' small inaccuracies, just enough to make the jury wonder about the autopsy. Then he went back into Farrell's background."

"At least that's solid."

Mease shook his head. "You know the part in his résumé where he says he studied at Harvard?"

"Sure."

"Well, he did, but it was a short course in English history. He was only there for a couple of weeks. It was some kind of scam for doctors who wanted to go to Boston for a vacation."

"That's hardly a big deal."

"I agree. But Mitchell pretended to just accidentally stumble across it. Then Farrell claims a course in a medical school at Frankfurt. It turns out it was the same kind of deal."

"So what? Farrell's a graduate of one of the nation's best medical schools, and with honors. And he has a couple of graduate degrees too."

Mease laughed. "Mitchell has made those look as if they had been bought from some diploma mill."

Kelly signaled the bartender for another drink. "You can repair that on redirect examination."

"Do you really think so? The jury went back to their rooms tonight convinced that we tried to put some quack over on them."

"Farrell looked that bad?"

"Worse. He tried to cover up, and Mitchell skinned him alive. Mitchell hasn't even gotten to the autopsy findings yet, and our witness looks like a damned liar."

"We have other doctors," Kelly said.

"It's not going well, Marty."

Kelly nodded. "Do you think we should consider offering a lesser offense?"

Mease slowly sipped the beer, leaving a small line of foam on his upper lip. "Second degree? Mitchell would never go for that. Not now."

"Manslaughter," Kelly said.

Mease thought for a minute before replying. "It would look like we took a dive. Besides, I don't know if Talbot would even allow such a plea, not with her own history. Jesus, if this doesn't go to the jury, if she isn't ruined now, she certainly would be if she had to make the ultimate decision."

"What do you mean?"

"Marty, suppose she allowed such a plea? She'd have to sentence Chesney to either jail or probation."

"So?"

"If she sent him to jail, say for the whole fifteen years, or even a part of that, they'd say she was being a hypocrite, since she basically did the same thing herself. And if she gave him probation, the other side would yell for her hide for exactly the same reason. She couldn't win."

"What difference would letting it go to the jury make?"

Mease finished the beer. "If they convict him on the nose, she has to give him life—it's mandatory. And she's off the hook. Even if they convict him of a lesser charge, she still didn't make the decision. And if they acquit, she's escaped entirely. Her best bet is to let it go to the jury on the main charge. In fact, it's her only chance to come out of this in one piece."

Kelly accepted the fresh drink from the bartender. "We may have to offer a lesser plea anyway if things start to look really bad. We have to protect ourselves too."

Mease nodded in silent but unenthusiastic agreement.

CHAPTER 31

NELSON BRAGG SAT up on his bed. Once again he reached into the drawer next to the bed and took out the revolver. Once again he pressed the release and popped out the cylinder containing the five .22-caliber bullets. He extracted them, rolling them in his hand, feeling the smoothness of their shining metal.

With extreme care he replaced each bullet into its chamber and snapped the cylinder back into place. He pointed the revolver at the wall, being careful to keep his finger away from the trigger. The gun felt natural, as though it were a metallic extension of himself.

He carefully placed the gun back into the drawer next to the newspaper picture of Kathleen Talbot.

Bragg closed the drawer and lay down again.

It was so beautifully quiet. The voices had stopped again. Each time they began, he found he could quiet them by going through the ritual of loading and unloading the pistol.

He enjoyed the wonderful feeling of freedom and relaxation. He thought of nothing. Everything had been carefully planned.

He had just cleaned up his room. The bottles of untouched medicine had been lined up in precise rows. He wanted everything to be neat, orderly. His clothes were laid out and ready.

If he could sleep he would. His old clock had been set. Tomorrow the alarm would go off. He would shave and clean up. Then he would dress. He would have plenty of time.

He knew he wouldn't be able to eat. He was never able to eat when he was excited. So he had made no plans for breakfast. He had checked his clothes. The pistol fit perfectly into his jacket pocket. No one would ever suspect it was there.

He would straighten the bed, take the gun, and go.

Nelson Bragg felt he would never see the room again, but he wanted it to be neat and clean. Then they would see just how neat and clean he was.

That was important.

The voices began murmuring again, but not to the degree that necessitated the ritual of loading the gun.

He felt at peace. Soon it would all be over.

CHAPTER 32

THE ERRATIC CLAMOR outside the courtroom penetrated the silences that separated Mitchell's questions and Dr. Farrell's answers.

Kathleen was vaguely aware of the muffled din, as her attention drifted between Jerry Mitchell's artful cross-examination and her own thoughts. But as the morning progressed, the noise seemed to be growing louder.

Farrell had become defensive, his answers clipped and his voice suspicious.

"Doctor, during Mr. Mease's questioning, you testified you were also an author, is that correct?"

"I've written a number of articles dealing with medical subjects," Farrell replied.

"And a book—or at least you're listed as one of the coauthors—isn't that so?"

"A joint effort with a number of doctors."

Mitchell walked to the counsel table and took a thick book from his evidence case. He held it aloft. "*The Practitioner's Textbook of Medicine,* published by Wagner and Harris, the 1983 edition?"

"That looks like it," Farrell mumbled.

Mitchell walked to the court reporter. "Please mark this as a proposed defense exhibit," he said.

"I'd like to see that," Mease said, rising.

"I'm just having it marked, Mr. Mease," Mitchell responded.

"I'll be happy to show it to you as soon as your witness identifies it."

Mease was about to say something else, but thought better of it and sat down. Kathleen watched as Marty Kelly whispered into Mease's ear.

The court reporter marked the book, giving it a number, then returned it to Mitchell. The tall attorney walked to the witness box and handed the book to Farrell. "Is this your work, doctor?"

Farrell took the book as though the very act of touching it might cause pain. He opened and studied it.

"Well, is that your work?"

Farrell appeared to be even more nervous. "I only wrote chapter twelve, and that with Dr. Lippitt of Cleveland."

"But you were the coauthor of chapter twelve?"

"You might say that."

Mitchell leaned in close to his squirming witness. "It's not what *I* say, doctor. Did you write chapter twelve or not?"

Farrell colored slightly. "Yes, but with Dr. Lippitt."

"Did you edit and approve everything in that chapter?"

"Ah . . ."

"Or was it written by someone else and you let that person use your name?"

Farrell's eyes narrowed. "No! I wrote it, at least that part that Lippitt didn't write, and I edited and approved everything in that chapter."

Mitchell stepped back and smiled. "Thank you, doctor." He stepped to the counsel table and handed the book to Mease. "You wished to see this, I believe."

Mease looked up at Kathleen. "I'd like to have a few minutes to look this over."

"Do you wish a recess, Mr. Mease?" she asked.

"No, I just need a minute or two."

Kathleen nodded. Mease and Kelly huddled over the book. She caught Jerry Mitchell looking at her, but he quickly looked away. Strident voices now were wafting up from outside. It sounded as if several bullhorns were being used by the demonstrators.

She had read Jane Whitehall's article in the morning paper,

and it was less hostile than before, reflecting, she hoped, a softening of the newspaper's position toward her. Whitehall had mentioned an afternoon rally called by a local preacher. Kathleen presumed the noise would be much louder during the afternoon session. She decided to make the lunch break shorter so that the trial could get under way before the distraction of the rally.

She felt the lack of sleep. Although reassured by the almost magical protection of Marcus Kaplan, she could not relax. Her life suddenly was beyond her control, a situation she had never before experienced. And she felt so alone, despite Kaplan and the others. She looked at Jerry Mitchell, yearning to talk to him. She was haunted by what he might think of her now, but he gave no indication, acting as though they were complete strangers. Occasionally she would find Mitchell looking at her, but she wondered if that too might be imagined.

She wished she knew. She wished she could plan for her life, but her tangled situation prevented planning anything beyond the next ten minutes.

Marcus Kaplan was up in the capital talking to the Supreme Court members. If he was successful, their investigation would be quietly done, and she would be allowed to continue the trial that had to be finished and that might finish her.

"We've examined the book, your honor," Mease said. "The book seems to be a standard medical work. However, I do object to its admission, since I don't consider it relevant to the issue before the court."

Mitchell stood up and walked to the bench. He looked up at her, and for a moment their eyes were locked in something more personal than merely an exchange between lawyers.

Looking away, he spoke. "With the court's permission, I believe I can show that the proposed exhibit is most relevant."

She knew her expression hid the emotions she was experiencing. She kept her voice calm and even. "I'll overrule the objection. But you're not barred from renewing it, Mr. Mease, if Mr. Mitchell should fall short of his claim."

Mitchell looked at her, then nodded. He turned once more to the witness. "You were coauthor of chapter twelve, correct?"

"I told you I was."

"Do you disagree with any statements contained in the text?"

Farrell had become so nervous that his face was developing a slight twitch. "No. It is a standard statement on one aspect of medicine."

"Pathology?"

Farrell nodded. "Yes, as it relates to the transplant of human organs. Some organs can be transplanted easily, others not. The chapter covers some of the technical aspects."

"Do you do much organ-transplant work, doctor?"

Farrell shook his head. "Not as such. Sometimes, especially if a young person dies, I work with the surgeons."

"Oh?"

"I take specimens of tissue from the donor and the prospective recipient. I try to determine, as far as possible scientifically, if there is compatibility."

"When you speak of organs, I trust you mean organs—parts—from someone who is dead?"

Farrell laughed, then stopped abruptly. He then glared at Mitchell. "Of course."

"You never take organs from living people?"

The doctor shrugged. "Sometimes. Say if one person donates a kidney to another. The donor has two. He can spare one."

"Is that what chapter twelve is about, living donors?"

Farrell shook his head. "No. That part of the text covers only, from the viewpoint of a pathologist, the transplant of an organ from a deceased donor to a living recipient."

Mitchell idly leafed through the pages. "Doctor, would you take a look at page two-fourteen, the second paragraph from the top?"

Farrell accepted the book and read slowly, then looked up at Mitchell.

"Yes?"

"You wrote that, or helped write it?"

"I told you I did."

Mitchell's voice was quietly reassuring. "You talk about taking organs from a deceased person whose heart is still beating in that paragraph, right?"

"Objection!" Mease couldn't keep the alarm out of his voice. "This is another of Mr. Mitchell's tricks. That book is not relevant to this proceeding—"

"Overruled," Kathleen said softly.

Mitchell continued as if nothing had happened. "Do you take organs from bodies with the heart still beating, doctor?"

"I don't," Farrell said, a bit too quickly.

"Have you ever been in attendance when it was done?"

"Objection! This is nothing more than some wild fishing expedition. I don't know what—"

Kathleen's tone told Mease that he couldn't protect his witness by diversionary tactics. "Overruled, Mr. Mease. Please allow defense counsel to continue."

Mitchell's eyes had never left Dr. Farrell. "Well, were you ever in attendance when such a thing was done?"

Farrell looked about the courtroom as though imploring someone to rescue him.

"Well?"

"My memory is. . . . well, I don't . . ."

Mitchell stood close to the witness. "This is all easily checked, doctor," he said softly. "When was the last time you were in attendance when such a thing was done?"

Farrell stared down at his shoes. "About two weeks ago."

Mitchell walked back from the witness box. "Tell us about the circumstances."

"I must object, your honor." Mease had been whispering with Kelly. "Mr. Mitchell is going on some kind of wild-goose chase. There isn't the slightest connection shown between his questions and the issue before this court."

"Mr. Mitchell?" Kathleen asked.

Mitchell replied very quietly. "If I might beg the court's indulgence, I will show that what the witness is about to testify to concerns the main issue of this case, that is, whether or not a crime was in fact committed."

"I renew my objection," Mease snapped.

"That connection must be shown quickly, Mr. Mitchell, or I shall sustain Mr. Mease."

"Almost immediately," he replied. Again she sensed his eyes had met hers for an instant too long.

"Go on."

"Doctor, was the donor's heart beating when the organ was implanted in the recipient?"

"I don't know."

Mitchell's eyebrows shot up in surprise. "Were you there?"

"Yes."

"Then how is it you don't know?"

Farrell squirmed even more. "I wasn't looking. I was more interested in the surgical implant." He grew increasingly more skittish as Mitchell pointedly waited for him to go on. "You see, a young man, just twenty years old, was in a motorcycle accident. His skull was crushed, but everything else was all right, and he had signed a donor's card." The words spilled from Farrell, as if he were trying to prove his own innocence. "A little girl needed a liver. She would die in days without a new organ. There was no time to wait."

"Was the donor's heart beating when the liver was removed from his body?"

Farrell's voice was barely audible. "Yes."

"So the motorcyclist was alive?"

"Oh, no! He was dead."

"But his heart was beating."

"Only with assistance. We were using machines."

"But he was alive when the surgeon removed the liver?"

"No. Of course not. He was dead. His brain had been crushed. The machines were the only thing keeping the heart beating. We would never . . ." Farrell's eyes widened as he realized that he had walked into a trap. "Wait! It was different from this case. We had the young man's family there. They approved."

"Was he alive or dead when you people removed the liver?"

"These things—"

"Answer yes or no!"

Mease got to his feet too slowly. Farrell spoke. "No."

"Is that because he was brain dead?"

Farrell nodded.

"You have to answer aloud, doctor. Did you consider him dead because his brain had ceased to function, and could never function again?"

"Yes, but—"

"When the brain can no longer function, according to the article you and Dr. Lippitt wrote, death occurs, isn't that so?"

"Well, some cases are . . . well, different . . ." Farrell's voice fell off. He knew he couldn't retreat from the position into which Mitchell had placed him.

Mease tried to conceal his discomfort and to exude confidence as he rose to conduct redirect examination. But he had been watching the jury, and he knew Farrell was beyond repair. He and Kelly would have to rely on other doctors.

"Get the dumb bastard off the stand," Kelly whispered.

Mease was reluctant to let go, but Farrell wasn't reliable. "Nothing additional, your honor, but I'd like to reserve the right to recall Dr. Farrell."

"Any objections, Mr. Mitchell?" Kathleen asked.

Mitchell slowly shook his head. "No. The doctor has been most helpful. I welcome his return to the stand."

"We'll take a short break," Kathleen said.

—◀ ▶—

A low profile was the best tactic, Jane Whitehall decided, and the lower the better. She had to return to the newspaper to arrange for a photographer. The chief photographer would promise anything over the phone, but a face-to-face confrontation was the only thing that assured compliance. Photographers would be assigned to the criminal court anyway, but Jane wanted someone who would work at her direction. It was her story.

Trying to avoid Jack Bennett, she got to the paper late and ducked the city room, going directly to the photography department.

As she thought, the chief photographer didn't want to send anyone with her. Their argument was both colorful and loud, much to the amusement of everyone within earshot. Finally he gave in.

Jane made arrangements with Jelly Roll Gallagher to meet her at the Hall of Justice. Jelly Roll was a prize-winning photographer. The nickname came from his strange hobby of taking pictures of naked models he would hire to roll in jelly. Gallagher's obsession never ended in anything but messy, albeit colorful pictures, but it did earn him his title and noteriety.

Jane was almost out of the lobby when she heard Jack Bennett call to her.

"Can't talk now, Jack," she called breezily. "I'm on my way to the Chesney trial."

"It will keep." His icy tone was enough to stop her.

"I saw the story, Jack," she said hurriedly. "I don't know why the computer kept the stuff about the afternoon rally in. Those goddamn things eat the good stuff but leave—"

"Knock it off, Jane." Bennett's voice was crisp with anger. "I checked. I know exactly what you wrote on your home unit and when it was sent. You even checked afterward to make sure everything went in."

She abandoned any pretense of accident. "You seemed determined to kill my story."

He glared at her. "No. I didn't kill it. I should have, but I didn't. You were like a dog with a bone, Jane. There was no stopping you. But you've gone one step too far."

"There won't be any riot, if that's what's worrying you," she said, suddenly afraid. "You're overreacting. A call for a prayer meeting from some storefront clergyman is hardly likely to tear the city apart. It was just another fact that gave dimension to the story, nothing more."

Bennett's expresion became sterner still. "I warned you. In fact, I ordered you to keep that stuff out."

Jane wasn't easily intimidated, but she knew Jack Bennett and she recognized that his uncharacteristic tone and manner were dire warnings of what was to come. "I'm sorry, Jack. You're right, of course. I just got carried away, I suppose. I've worked so hard on this thing. It won't happen again."

"I told you we don't want lawsuits, even if we win. Nothing had better happen out there today."

"Nothing will happen, but even if it does, we aren't responsible. That was legitimate news."

Bennett moved his head slowly from side to side. "Jane, I should fire you now. However, I'll let fate decide. If that preacher of yours stirs up any major trouble over there this afternoon, you can count on this being your last day with the paper."

"Come on, Jack. That's not fair."

"It's not debatable, Jane."

"Fuck you, Jack. This is a Guild paper, you can't fire me for no reason."

"I helped negotiate the contract, Jane. Insubordination is just cause, for starters. Considering what you did, I can't imagine anyone in the Guild rising to your defense."

"We'll see!"

Bennett frowned. "If there's trouble over at the Hall of Justice, you're through." He turned and headed for the elevators.

She was going to call after him, but stopped. He was right. No one would defend her if he could prove what she had done. Major newspapers all over the country were shutting down, and jobs—the kind of job she knew and wanted—were hard to come by.

If a riot broke out it would regenerate the story, only she wouldn't be around to write it.

But there might be something she could do. If she came up with a stunning angle, something really extraordinary, she might be able to save herself no matter what happened.

She hurried outside and hailed a cab.

--◀ ▶--

Brenda Hastings listened to the two lawyers in her chambers. They were both young, both aggressive. One represented an insurance company, the real defendant in an accident case. The other lawyer was a lower-rung trial associate with a big, fast-action, big-volume negligence law firm. Although they were different—the insurance lawyer was black, male, thin, and balding and the defense-firm counsel was white, female, stout, and possessed a great mane of red hair—their feisty manner, combative attitude, and cleverness made them almost twins.

"I offered her more than that faker she represents should get," the insurance company lawyer growled, "but she's too stubborn or stupid to take it."

Before Brenda could say anything, the defense counsel snorted. "Listen to that! I'm beating his rear end off in front of that jury out there and all he offers is peanuts. It's outrageous."

"Fifteen thousand is not outrageous," he snapped. "Your man was hardly injured."

"He's a welder, and his left hand is premanently weak. I wouldn't even dream of anything less that thirty thousand, and even at that, your people will get off cheap. The jury may come in with a couple hundred thousand."

"And they may come in with nothing."

Brenda's clerk stuck his head in the door. "Judge Solomon is here. Can you see him?"

"Yes," she said, then turned to the lawyers. "You're close. Both of you know that a jury may do anything. Go out there and see if you can't work out a reasonable settlement. I don't want to force a settlement, but you're two reasonable people. See what you can do."

As the two lawyers left, Irving Solomon walked in.

"I'm sorry to bother you, Brenda. I know how busy you are."

"Couldn't come at a better time, Irving. This will give those two young hotshots a chance to come to an agreement. If they do, I'll be free to move the docket along. What can I do for you?"

He went over to a leather armchair and sat down. Irving Solomon looked like a casting director's idea of a judge. His graying hair had receded, leaving only a tufted crown circling the top of his head. In his sixties, Irving was short, stubby, and scholarly. His soft brown eyes, always kindly, looked out at the world from reading glasses forever perched near the end of his nose.

"This awful business about Kathleen Talbot," he said, "troubles me."

"Kathleen is a fine person, Irving."

He nodded. "Oh, I don't mean that. I know her, not well, but I do know her. It's what's happening to her that's upsetting me."

"Irving, I have to tell you, Kathleen is a friend of mine. I—"

"I know, I know," he said softly. "That's why I'm here."

"I don't understand."

"She's being purposely ruined, at least that's how it looks to me."

"Me too."

"And it's all over this foolish executive-judge scramble."

"That, plus she's a woman, Irving. This court is hardly the cutting edge of modern thought and attitude."

He chuckled. "Present company excluded, I hope?"

"Of course. But you know who I mean."

Solomon nodded. "Yes. Only this time I think it's gone much

too far. There is such a thing as elemental fairness." He pursed his lips. "Besides, all this nonsense tends to besmirch the judiciary as a whole. We have to stop that."

"I agree," she said, "but how?"

"We must hurry and select an executive judge. As soon as that's done, this foolishness will stop."

"No one has a majority, Irving, not even you."

He shrugged. "Brenda, I never wanted the damn job in the first place. I'm a judge, not some kind of super administrator. I ran because I was asked to. Some of the others ... well, weren't too well-qualified, at least in my opinion."

"Everyone loves you, Irving."

He laughed. "Sure. I'm the most popular fellow around, but not with the majority of judges. Some regard me as a bumbling old guy who can't punch the right floor on the automatic elevator."

"Irving, I'm sure—"

"As a matter of fact, they're right. I got off on the wrong floor coming here to see you. Anyway, I've thought about it. If I really don't want the job, then why am I still a candidate? The answer seems clear enough—I'm going to get out of the race."

"Do you mean it?"

"Yes. This court has been my life. Maybe I can't run elevators, but I don't want to contribute to its shame. I'm dropping out."

"In favor of anyone?"

He chuckled. "Kathleen Talbot? Oh, you'd like that, Brenda. And I'd like to do it. In fact, I'll commit my own personal vote to her, but I can't ask anyone else to do it. That's up to them. Besides, I'm afraid your friend Kathleen has been dealt a body blow. She may come out of that murder trial all right, but I'm afraid she's finished as a serious candidate for executive judge."

"But you'll still vote for her?"

"I said I would."

"Can I tell anyone that?" Brenda asked.

He shrugged. "Why not? I'm not asking anyone to follow me, but I'm not making a secret of my own choice. God help us if either Broadbent or Sawchek gets in."

"Kathleen will be honored."

326 ◇ WILLIAM J. COUGHLIN

He stood up. "Honored is something they do for saints after they're burned at the stake. Maybe it's better if she isn't so honored." He smiled. "Tell her martyrdom is best left to those who want or need it. She doesn't."

Brenda decided to call Kathleen, but first she had to dispose of her own case.

Her clerk ushered the two lawyers back into her chambers. They had walked out in snarling hostility, but now they were smiling.

"He got a bargain." The redhead laughed.

"Rape is more like it." The other lawyer grinned.

"What's the settlement figure?" Brenda asked.

"Twenty-two thousand," the redhead said.

"Your client agrees to it?" Brenda asked the woman lawyer.

"Absolutely."

"Do you have authority to settle for that amount?" she asked the man.

He grinned. "Yep."

"All right," Brenda said. "Let's go out and put it on the record." She looked at her watch. It was almost noon. She hoped she could catch Kathleen during the noon recess. They had a lot to talk about.

--◄ ►--

Irving Solomon considered himself an honorable man. He had informed Kathleen Talbot of his decision through Brenda Hastings. But there were two other candidates, and although he didn't respect either man, he felt he had to inform them of his decision. It was, he thought, only honorable.

Webster Broadbent was curt until he learned the purpose of the call, then he was all charm. But when Solomon refused to endorse him for executive judge Broadbent turned icy once more.

Solomon reached Ted Sawchek at home, where he was recovering from complications from leg surgery. Sawchek, after hearing his news, begged Solomon for his support. When that didn't work, he tried to promise things he could never deliver. Solomon politely declined. He hung up in the middle of Sawchek's threats.

He didn't like either man, and he was disgusted with their reactions, but he had done his duty.

Irving Solomon put the matter out of his mind. He too had a busy docket, and his afternoon was filled with a procession of cases, lawyers, and issues, which was exactly what he liked and wanted.

◄ ►

"Things are heating up a bit out there," Tom Mease said to Martin Kelly as the older man joined him at the counsel table.

"Not only out there," Kelly said. "Did you stop by the office this morning?"

"No. Why?"

"There's a message from the office of the esteemed Dr. Bertram Shaheen."

"He's supposed to be here this morning!"

Kelly sighed. "That's the message. He won't be able to make it."

"Marty, are you kidding me?"

"I'm afraid not," Kelly replied. "It seems that doctors have gall bladders too. About now, Dr. Shaheen is having his removed. Can't blame him, Tom. When those things go, they're extremely painful. It's emergency surgery."

"Jesus, Marty! What the hell are we going to do? Shaheen was going to establish that Martin was alive when Chesney turned off the machines. After what Farrell did to us, we need him."

Kelly sat down. Muted sounds of a bullhorn somewhere out in the street sifted through the courtroom. "I contacted that doctor Farrell recommended. Remember?"

"Dr. Franklin Armory?"

Kelly nodded. "I called Chicago and tracked him down. He'll testify."

"I'll have to ask for a day's adjournment, although with that crowd gathering out there, I don't think Judge Talbot will be delighted to grant it. We should get this thing over as quickly as possible."

Kelly smiled. "Guess where Dr. Armory is."

328 ◇ WILLIAM J. COUGHLIN

"Chicago, I presume?"

Kelly shook his head. "No. He's staying at a hotel here in the city. He's interested in the trial and tells me he'll be delighted to testify. I've sent a couple of detectives over to bring him in. I didn't want the sight of that crowd to scare him off."

Mease frowned. "I don't want to put him on the stand cold, Marty. I don't know what he might say."

"I agree. Ask permission to put on the witnesses out of turn. You've a couple of cops and clerks who are just going to fill in a few procedural holes. Mitchell shouldn't object too strenuously. While you're putting in the testimony, I can interview the good doctor and see what kind of a witness he might make."

"And if he isn't any good, then what?"

Kelly shrugged. "Then, my friend, we are up to our ass in alligators, aren't we? There aren't any other national experts available, at least none Mitchell wouldn't have for breakfast. But let's not cross any bridges until we get to them. Let's tell Mitchell what we have in mind."

CHAPTER 33

KATHLEEN'S CLERK POKED his head in the door. "Do you want to break for an early lunch, or do you want to go on with the testimony, judge?"

She could hear the rising sound as the crowd outside responded to someone's amplified shout. She wondered if adequate preparations had been made for the afternoon rally that had been called. If she felt apprehension, she worried, how must the jury feel? She would have to say something to them.

She knew it would be foolish to adjourn. It would only encourage the mob, and they would double their efforts when the trial was resumed. It was better to get it over with. The sooner she started, the quicker the trial would end.

"We had better keep going, maybe even through lunch, given what's happening out in the street." She stood up. "Tell the lawyers I'll be ready to go in a minute. Bring in the jury." Kathleen took her robe from its hanger.

"Should we have the spectators leave?" the clerk asked. "They're getting restless and half of them look nuts."

"The constitution mandates an open trial, no matter what," she said. "So we're stuck with them, nuts or not. But tell the officers to admit only as many as can find seats. I don't want any standees during this case."

He nodded. "Yes, your honor." He hurried away to carry out her orders.

Kathleen slipped into her robe, then walked to her window

and looked out. The crowd had the street blocked off, and streams of people seemed to be coming to join them from every direction. The shouting and noise were becoming more intense.

She waited, allowing everyone a chance to get settled, then walked purposefully into the courtroom.

Every seat in the spectator area was occupied.

Jerry Mitchell caught her eye for just an instant, but she looked away, directing her attention to the jury. "Ladies and gentlemen, as you know, a protest is taking place in front of this building. It's noisy, but we're perfectly safe. In our free and open society these things happen. However, you must ignore it. And I must again remind you that nothing that happens outside of this courtroom can be allowed to influence your judgment or interfere with your important duty."

She looked again at Jerry Mitchell. "Mr. Mitchell, have you finished with Dr. Farrell?"

Mitchell stood up. "I have, your honor." Sometimes his eyes seemed entirely neutral; at other times she felt he was trying to communicate on a personal level. She felt so now, and reluctantly looked away.

"Mr. Mease, do you still wish no redirect?"

Mitchell had destroyed Dr. Farrell, and nothing Tom Mease had been able to do had helped. Mease knew better than to risk trying again. He also stood up. "Nothing more, your honor."

"Call your next witness."

"I wonder if counsel might approach the bench," he said quietly.

The two attorneys walked to the side of the bench. She was acutely aware how close Mitchell was, and she tried to put it out of her mind.

"I want to call some witnesses out of turn," Mease said, keeping his voice low so the jury couldn't hear him. "The doctor we had scheduled underwent emergency surgery this morning. We believe we'll have another witness to take his place this afternoon."

"Mr. Mitchell?" she asked.

He looked directly into her eyes. "I have no objection to calling the witnesses out of turn; they're just procedural anyway. I may object to the substitution of doctors, however. I'll have to wait to take a look at this new doctor's curriculum vitae. I'll reserve my objection until that time."

"I want to move this case along," she said.

The rumble of the demonstration outside rose a bit, as if to emphasize her statement.

"We all do, your honor," Mitchell said softly.

She knew she was blushing, but no one except Jerry Mitchell could guess the reason.

"All right, gentlemen," she said loudly.

The two attorneys returned to the counsel table.

"Call your next witness, Mr. Mease," she said again, trying to ignore the noise of the ever-increasing tumult outside the courthouse.

Father Ronald Howell drove. The Episcopalian priest let his passengers out near the Hall of Justice, then discovered that all the public parking lots were jammed. He drove through the congested streets trying to find a place to park. A small truck pulled out of a space and he wheeled in, ignoring the blasting horns of impatient drivers behind him.

Father Howell locked the car. He was a man of God, but he knew an unlocked car could be a source of temptation.

He was blocks away from the Hall of Justice, so he hurried back at a quick pace. He didn't want to miss the rally. All the right-to-life people were sure to turn out. They had to be offset by thinking people who disagreed with their narrow-minded views and loutish ways.

Ronald Howell had joined the Socrates Society after the death of his wife. She had died badly, and slowly, of intractable cancer. Howell was determined that no other human should have to suffer such a ghastly fate. No one would think twice about ending the torture of an animal, but a human was denied such a quick, merciful—and Christian—release.

Howell increased his pace to a near-run. He could hear the echo of chants and the ringing amplification of a bullhorn.

The Socrates Society advocated a dignified release for terminally ill patients who wanted it. Howell considered that absolutely sensible, although he knew his bishop had some reservations. The Chesney trial was symbolic to both sides.

Father Howell, dressed in his dark gray suit and Roman collar, turned the corner and was astounded to see thousands of people milling about in front of the criminal-court building.

Hand-held signs were to be seen everywhere. Some were printed, but most were handmade, and they all expressed various points of view on every public issue connected with the question of life and death.

A man in a flashy green suit stood on the steps of the Hall of Justice speaking into a hand-held bullhorn, but his words were indistinct as they bounced and echoed off the surrounding buildings. Whatever he was saying was greeted by either cheers or jeers.

Father Howell had become a veteran of public rallies and had developed an almost professional eye. The crowd, he estimated, was at least several thousand, and growing. He could sense the tension: violence was on the lip of exploding. He saw a dozen nervous policemen standing near the top of the marble stairs of the court building. It was a totally inadequate force to control such an enormous crowd. But then, he guessed, the police were probably just as surprised as he at the turnout.

"Killers . . ." Howell heard that word distinctly as it rumbled from the speaker, although the rest of his shouted words were jumbled. ". . . legal murder . . ." The words bounced off the crowd and produced a roaring response.

Howell presumed his people would be outnumbered. The antiabortionists seemed to have a special knack for bringing people out. The womens' organizations—he considered them allies—had a network too. But they could never quite match the numbers, although they were as vocal as their opponents.

He pushed into the crowd and tried to find the members of the Socrates Society. . . .

Although it was a cool day, Nelson Bragg was sweating. He didn't know what to do. He stood near the edge of the shouting, pushing crowd, after having worked his way to a spot near the top of the courthouse steps. But he was afraid to go any farther. Policemen, their faces set and stern, stood near the doors, watching the tumult build. And even if he had the nerve to step past the policemen, there were uniformed guards just within those front doors. They manned the metal-detector devices. They would discover his gun if he tried to go through.

He hoped the voices might tell him what to do, but if they were talking, he couldn't hear.

Atop the steps the preacher continued shouting his exhortations. Bragg couldn't quite distinguish what he was saying. The growing crowd seemed to be screaming at the man's every word. Bragg waited for some sign of what he must do. . . .

Pastor Glenn Elkins of the South Woodward Baptist Church tried to listen to the man shouting into the bullhorn, but the roar of the crowd made the amplified sound even more difficult to comprehend. What he did understand, he agreed with, although he deplored the man's manner and rough speech. The speaker was some kind of storefront clergyman, and Pastor Elkins abhorred the type, but he often had to endure the association of strange people, such as Catholics and Jews, in the fight for religious liberty and the preservation of life.

Elkins had used the church's buses to transport people to the rally. It was important to show that the moral majority was no longer silent, even if it meant keeping strange bedfellows.

". . . Black-robed whore . . ." The word jarred Pastor Elkins' sensibilities, but he approved of the crowd's reaction. Television remote trucks were filming everything. He raised his "God Is Life" sign and waved it enthusiastically. The people around him, mostly people from his church, cheered him.

He enjoyed the excitement. . . .

"Jesus, look at those idiots," the criminal-court guard said to his partner as they stood near the metal detectors. Since no one was coming into the building, they had nothing to do.

"It's getting pretty rowdy," his partner replied nervously. "I've never seen a crowd gather so quickly. Do you suppose they called for reinforcements? That handful of cops out there won't be able to stop them if they try to charge in here."

The other guard nodded. The noise of the crowd reverberated against the glass doors. "Jesus, this is getting hairy. . . ."

Father Howell was still trying to shove his way through the

mass of shouting humanity jammed around the front of the Hall of Justice. He searched, peering about, trying to find his people. Then he was roughly jostled by a man waving a large sign.

"Hey," he protested, almost losing his footing. He looked at the excited face and recognized the man with the sign. He had debated Pastor Elkins on television.

Elkins stared at him for a moment, blinking, his eyes attracted to Howell's Roman collar.

"Please have the decency to let me pass," Howell shouted above the din.

"What?" Elkins obviously didn't recognize Howell.

"Let me pass!" Howell shouted, trying to shoulder between Elkins and a fat woman next to him.

"Watch it!" the woman yelped, shoving Howell back into Elkins.

Elkins took one hand off the sign and pushed Howell.

"Don't do that!" Howell said, trying to control his temper.

Elkins glared at the Roman collar. "Papist!"

"I'm Episcopalian, not Catholic, you twit!" Howell snapped, pushing back.

Elkins, thrown forward by the press of the crowd, brought the sign down. It was only a piece of printed cardboard on a thin wooden stick, but it landed just over the left temple of Father Howell.

Howell lashed out in instinctive self-defense, his fist landing ineffectively but painfully on Pastor Elkins' upper lip. . . .

"Oh, Christ," one of the policemen on the steps said. "They're starting to fight."

"Don't even think of trying to wade into that mob," another officer snapped. "They'd tear us apart. We'll have to wait for reinforcements."

The man with the bullhorn continued shouting, seemingly unaware of the skirmish that had erupted in the mass of people jammed in front of him. . . .

Father Howell felt a jolt just behind his ear, a glancing blow delivered by a woman's purse. He and Pastor Elkins were locked together like two dancers, grunting and shoving. The people around them began to take sides.

Howell had seen crowds approach the flash point of violence, but somehow it had always been avoided. Now he found himself in the eye of a human hurricane, and he was frightened. He looked into Pastor Elkins' eyes and saw the same terror.

"This is not Christian," he shouted.

"Amen!"

The two men who began as adversaries now clung to each other for protection as fighting broke out all around them. . . .

The man on the bullhorn noticed for the first time the small pockets of fighting erupting in the moving, swaying mob.

He didn't want them fighting among themselves. That wouldn't prove anything. He wanted a vigorous demonstration against the court and the justice system.

"Men and women of God!" he bellowed into the horn. "Our fight is with the legal murderers within this building. They must be shown the error of their ways!"

He turned and gestured at the glass doors. "Are you with me?" he exhorted. . . .

The policemen saw the mob begin to move.

"Arrest that asshole!" the lieutenant in charge yelled.

The policemen charged forward, taking the bullhorn away and pinning the preacher's arms behind him.

Provoked, the vanguard of the mob began to move toward the policemen. . . .

"Shit! Here it comes!" the guard inside the building yelled. "Come on, we have to help them!"

The other guards followed him out the door, joining with the policemen as they strove to shove back the advancing crowd. The noise was deafening. . . .

Nelson Bragg, accustomed to screeching voices, remained calm as the guards charged out the door. He walked quickly, but not so fast as to draw attention, and casually went in the front door. He walked through the metal detector's plastic arch placed just inside the building entrance. The little buzzer went off.

Those in the lobby who hadn't sought safety were much too interested in the raging scene taking place in front of the Hall of Justice to pay any attention to the thin man who walked across the lobby and up the stairs.

Bragg savored the relative quiet on the stairs. He had his hand on the gun in his coat pocket. Now the message was clear: he was indeed the instrument of God. . . .

Charging ranks of newly arrived police brought the crowd under control. The police then began to attempt to disperse the mob without provoking additional violence. They had contained the disturbance with only broken windows and minimal damage to nearby stores caused by gangs of young men. A car had been set afire, and television crews were busy filming it as it burned. . . .

Nelson Bragg climbed the stairs. He joined the people standing outside Judge Talbot's courtroom. He knew exactly what he had to do. . . .

-◀ ▶-

Jane Whitehall collected every scrap of information the police department had. Her photographer was already on his way back to the newspaper with pictures so vivid no editor could refuse to use them.

Jane had gotten it all. Eighteen people had been arrested during the disturbance. The charges ranged from disorderly conduct to assault with intent to kill. Two distinguished local clergymen had been booked for assault. Twenty-two people had been injured, mostly only minor cuts and bruises, although one was in danger of losing an eye.

It was going to be a wonderfully juicy story, replete with on-the-street interviews with rioters providing every nuance of opinion, all reflecting in some way on Judge Kathleen Talbot's role in the controversy. And it wasn't over; as a result of the violent demonstration, there were sure to be terrific follow-up pieces and features in the days to come.

"I'm sorry, Jane." The man she had called sounded embarrassed. "You'll have to talk to Jack Bennett."

"Fuck Bennett," she snapped. "I'm calling in an important story here."

"Just a minute."

She waited, presuming the rewrite man was preparing to take her information. Jane was calling from police headquarters, deciding to stay with the story rather than go back to the paper.

"Jane, I warned you what would happen."

She recognized Bennett's voice. His tone was ominous.

"Jack, we'll talk later. I've got everything, the works. I can come in and write it, but I think I should stay—"

"You're fired, Jane," he said coldly.

"Look, Jack, I know you're pissed. And I suppose I can't blame you, but this story is hot and I—"

"You don't work here anymore."

"Jack, we can discuss that later. I've been busy and I—"

"Jesus, don't you understand English?"

"This is my story, Jack. The least you can do is let me write it."

"You purposely disobeyed me, Jane. You caused that riot—"

"It wasn't a riot," she interjected. "It was a civil disturbance."

"Whatever." His voice seemed to grow even more disdainful. "Because of you, dozens of people got hurt. If that isn't cause for dismissal, I honest-to-God don't know what is."

"It wasn't dozens injured, Jack. Twenty-two were treated, nineteen of them are already released."

"I don't give a damn!" he exploded. "You're fired."

"Look, Bennett," she said, hiding her fear with bravado, "you need me. I've got the whole story, and there's more to come."

"I have assigned seven reporters. They'll get whatever we need by deadline. I don't need you, and I never will."

"Jack, don't be—"

"I don't want you here. We'll send over the stuff from your desk and mail you your check."

"You can't do this!"

"I just did," he said, and hung up.

CHAPTER 34

KATHLEEN'S DECISION NOT to recess the trial during the riot proved to be a wise one. It demonstrated in a dramatic way that neither she nor the authority of the court would be intimidated. It also served to remind a jittery jury that it was they, not the unruly mob, who would have the last word.

As the ruckus outside began to subside, a uniformed officer entered the courtroom and handed Kathleen a note.

She held up a hand to halt Mease's questions. "Ladies and gentlemen," she said to the jury, "I am informed by the police that everything is now under control."

She saw the sense of relief on their faces. "Despite the sounds we heard, nothing much happened. A few people suffered some cuts and bruises, nothing more. While the police wrap things up, we'll continue this case for a bit, but we'll break early today. You're hungry, I know, and this has all been something of a strain.

"Is your next witness available, Mr. Mease?" She had seen Martin Kelly escort a tall, distinguished-looking man into the courtroom. Kelly was busily whispering to Tom Mease.

Mease stood up. "We are ready," said. "The prosecution calls Dr. Franklin Armory."

The man Kelly brought in walked to the witness box. He answered the oath in a deep firm voice, then sat down.

"What is your name, please," Mease asked.

"Franklin Armory."

"You are a doctor licensed to practice medicine?"

Jerry Mitchell stood up. "I'm not making an objection at this point," he said, "but I'm curious as to what connection this doctor might have with the case. I know he's not one of our local medical examiners."

"I'm in the process of establishing his connection," Mease snapped.

"Since there is no objection," Kathleen said, "you may continue, Mr. Mease."

"What medical school were you graduated from?" Mease asked.

"Objection," Mitchell said, seeming to enjoy himself. "The question presumes an answer."

"Sustained," Kathleen said.

"Allow me to rephrase it," Mease said, glaring at Mitchell. "Were you graduated from a medical school?"

The tall doctor's expression seemed almost serenely imperial. "Harvard."

"And after Harvard, did you receive any additional training?"

"I was an intern at Croydon Hospital in Baltimore. Then I was a resident in internal medicine at St. Michael's Hospital in Los Angeles."

"Did you complete the residency?"

"Yes. After that I—"

"Objection. The answer is not responsive to the question." Mitchell smiled. "Or perhaps, more accurately, it's a bit too responsive."

Mease nodded even before Kathleen spoke. "Just answer my questions as I put them to you, doctor," he said. "After completing your residency, what, if anything, did you do?"

"I was invited to join the faculty at . . ."

Kathleen noticed the entrance of Marcus Kaplan during the testimony. Kaplan was escorted to a seat in back of the counsel table. He merely nodded, then seemed intent on watching the proceedings. Kaplan was a man who could not be ignored. He sat with the manner of a king, watching as if a spectacle was being presented for his interest alone. The jury and spectators couldn't keep their eyes off the regal visitor. His mere presence was disrupting the trial.

Mease referred to some notes, and Kathleen took the opportunity to break for the day. "Ladies and gentlemen," she said to the jury, "it's been a long and anxious day. We will adjourn now until tomorrow morning."

"If the court please," Mitchell said, "I'd like a copy of Dr. Armory's qualifications."

"That's no problem, your honor," Mease replied. "I will give Mr. Mitchell a copy of Dr. Armory's credentials."

The clerk, anxious to close the court, rapped his gavel.

Marcus Kaplan followed Kathleen into her chambers. His stern features contained a ghost of a smile. "That young prosecutor," he said in his rumbling deep voice, "is very good. Mitchell appears to be evenly matched out there."

She slipped out of her robe and sat down at her desk. "Do you miss it?"

His eyes were eerily penetrating. "Once in a while. Now is one of the times. I suppose no trial lawyer can ever walk into a courtroom and not be seduced into a desire for action. For instance, I would like a crack at that pompous doctor out there." He chuckled. "However, I determined long ago to avoid such temptations, no matter how inviting." He paused, then smiled. "But I'm not here, Kathleen, to discuss myself, a subject fascinating only to me, I've found. I have unofficial word from our friends on the Supreme Court."

"Oh?"

Kaplan's eyes were almost magnetic. "I'm informed they've made up their collective mind. After this trial they will issue a short report saying that you acted ethically in accepting this case for trial." He paused. "Some of them, frankly, think you made a mistake, but they chalk it up to judicial inexperience. The Supreme Court will wait for a few days after the verdict before making their report, for appearances' sake."

"No matter what that verdict might be?"

Kaplan nodded. "Whether the jury decides innocence or guilt isn't at issue. They are the ones who made that decision, not you. Thus, Kathleen, any reservations some of them might have as to the possibility of impropriety in your taking this case are resolved, since you will not be making the ultimate decision."

"Isn't that ducking the issue?"

Kaplan shook his head, his massive shock of white hair moving as though it had a life of its own. "No," he said, his deep voice reverberating within the small room. "You're conducting a fair, impartial trial. You aren't interfering with the jury's province. The question is theirs, not yours, and that's what counts with the Supreme Court. Actually, that's how their report will read."

"How do you know that?"

He chuckled. "I wrote it." He smiled easily. "Don't presume that I can order the court about. I do have some small influence, but not that much. It was merely more convenient for me to draft the order for their approval."

"That still won't silence the public outcry." She shook her head. "I'm afraid even you can't help me there."

"My dear young woman, I am a complete-service lawyer. Rusty perhaps, but competent. Our wonderful morning newspaper is frightened that they'll be accused of inciting a riot. I think, legally, their fear is groundless, but I did nothing to disabuse them of it. That reporter, Jane Whitehall, has been fired, I understand, because she started the whole thing from the beginning. Fear, if employed properly, is a wonderful thing. At the moment, that newspaper would like to nominate you for sainthood if it will restore their reputation for responsibility. I've just talked to the editor. He plans to do a favorable series of features on you." Kaplan smiled. "Nothing imaginative, I'm afraid. They may not make you into a modern female version of Abraham Lincoln, but I suspect you'll come out very nicely. Your brethren will be forced to consider you very favorably as a candidate for executive judge."

"That's the least of my concerns at the moment."

He nodded. "Yes. But what I am saying is nevertheless true. Sometimes adversity can be turned to great advantage."

"Mr. Kaplan, how can I thank you?"

"Gratitude is something no lawyer should ever expect, but it's always appreciated."

"Perhaps this isn't the time, but what do I owe you?"

He didn't answer at once, his eyes narrowing. "Kathleen, you can't afford me. I want no fee as such. But I did you a service, one lawyer for another. Someday I'll ask that you do the same. Good lawyers are an endangered species, my dear. One day you can be of service to some good, competent, honest attorney who needs your help. You'll know when that day comes. At that time you can repay me, service for service."

"And that's all?"

His expression was once again stern. "You may be surprised at how high a price that may turn out to be." He stood up. "Well, my dear, this has been a busy day and I still have other things to do."

She stood up and extended her hand. "Thank you."

His grip was strong. His steadfast eyes held hers. "Just remember, Kathleen, the jury out there will be deciding more than just the defendant's fate and future."

Nelson Bragg waited in the hallway outside the courtroom. He wasn't alone. Clusters of people gathered near the door that was guarded by a very large uniformed court officer. The guard's eyes seemed to issue a silent challenge to anyone who might be foolish enough to breach the peace. Bragg stayed off by himself, conscious that occasionally the guard's hard eyes fixed on him.

All the seats in the courtroom were filled, the guard had told them, and no one could be admitted unless there was room.

The voices were whispering softly, and he felt strangely comforted, as he sensed he was being guided by a power much stronger than himself.

Suddenly the courtroom doors opened and people began streaming out. They all seemed to be talking at once. A few threats were exchanged between rival factions, but the antagonism was quickly tempered by the big guard's no-nonsense presence. He then announced that the court was closed for the day and that they had to clear the building.

Bragg's sense of security vanished instantly. He could never get back into the Hall of Justice again, not with the gun. He had to find someplace where he could hide for the night. The voices were starting to shriek, and he was afraid.

Most of the people waited for the court elevators, but some

were taking the stairs. He followed them, walking down to the next floor. There was no one in that hallway. He saw the door marked Men's Room, approached it cautiously, and entered. The large, old-fashioned room was unoccupied, its worn tile floors littered with paper. Ancient wooden booths housed the smelly toilets.

He enterd one of the booths and closed the door, sat down, and kicked the crumpled newspapers away from his feet.

The voices became calmer as he sat and waited.

◄ ►

Dennis Chesney was taken back to his special quarters in the jail. After the disturbance outside the court, his escort had grown from two bored detectives to six nervous uniformed officers, some of them carrying rifles.

The guard assigned to the special quarters grinned as Chesney was turned over to him. "Jesus, Denny, it must be wonderful to be a star."

Chesney shrugged.

The guard was accustomed to his prisoner's quiet ways. Despression wasn't unknown in jails. "For a while there I thought they might be stringing you up from a lamppost. Things out on the street really got hot, I'm telling you."

Chesney walked into his small apartment. The guard lingered at the door.

"I had a hell of a time getting here," the guard continued. "Shit, every nut in town was out in front of the Hall. Hey, if they don't convict you, you're going to come out of this famous." He laughed. "You'll have to give autographs. Maybe get a little ass for your troubles. There's a lot of star-fuckers out there, Denny. Take it while you can, eh?"

Chesney merely glanced at him.

"Hey, you need anything? You got dinners in the fridge there, but maybe you'd like to send out for something. Your pals in homicide said to get you anything you want. They'll pay for it. You're losing a lot of weight and they worry."

Chesney shook his head. "I'm not hungry."

"Well, if you change your mind, let me know." The guard closed the door and locked it.

Dennis Chesney took off his suit coat and tie and carefully hung them up. He lit a cigarette and lay down on the sofa.

He stared at the ceiling, watching the smoke curl upward. He wondered if he were really so different from Paul Martin. He had no tubes in him, as Martin had had, and also, unlike Martin, he could breathe without the aid of a machine. If Paul Martin hadn't been dead, then he'd been trapped inside his wasted body with nothing for company but the anguish of his own thoughts. Perhaps, when they accidentally left one of his eyes open, Martin too had stared up at the ceiling.

As a policeman, Dennis Chesney had firmly believed that wrong should be punished. And he had seen some ironic penalties inflicted not by courts, but by fate. He wondered if he was being reduced to a state not unlike Martin's, a state of suspension with no future, no hope, a condition wherein he was tormented by his own thoughts and feelings. He wondered if in some spiritual way he was slowly taking the place of the man whose life he had stopped.

If the guard was right, and he had become infamous, acquittal meant nothing. He had no future.

But no one would terminate him—he would have to do it himself. At least he was still capable of that.

Watching the smoke, Dennis Chesney found some comfort in that thought.

◀ ▶

Mease bolted down his third drink. Martin Kelly watched him.

"This is a kind of role reversal, Thomas," Kelly said, sipping his whiskey. "I'm cold sober, and if you keep on popping those things down at this rate, you'll be drunk within the hour."

"I don't give a shit, Marty. The whole case is exploding in my goddamn face."

Kelly looked around at the other court people who had drifted into the Learned Hand. "You know, if every lawyer used that as an excuse, this place would be a gold mine."

"Look who's talking," Mease snapped.

There was a twist of irony in Kelly's laugh. "Yeah, the voice of experience."

346 ◇ William J. Coughlin

Mease sounded tired. "Mitchell's beginning to make me look like a bumbling fool."

Kelly was about to call for another round but changed his mind. "You're wrong there, Tom. You've made no mistakes. Basically, given a certain level of competence, we're all only as good as our evidence."

"These fucking doctors are killing me."

Kelly grinned. "Oh, that's a common complaint. When doctors in various areas have chosen to go on strike, the death rate is cut almost in half, did you know that?"

"Who cares?"

"Well, it isn't just you they kill, you see." Despite his good intentions of keeping Mease from drinking too fast, Kelly himself needed another whiskey, so he signaled. "Anyway, you have to work with the evidence you have. The bar association takes a dim view of manufacturing the stuff."

"Martin, do you realize that this whole thing may hang on the opinion of Dr. Franklin Armory?"

Kelly nodded. "You've talked to him. So have I. He'll testify that Paul Martin was alive, from a medical standpoint, when Chesney turned off the machines. What more do you want?"

"I wish we had more time to question him. I don't like flying into a case without knowing exactly what kind of witness I have."

Kelly shrugged. "He's in town for a meeting. He didn't know he'd be a witness, Tom. The man has appointments tonight. He sounds as if he'll be all right. He certainly knows his stuff. His curriculum vitae makes him sound like a cross between Dr. Salk and Saint Raphael."

"I don't know, Marty. There's just something about him that bothers me. He seems just a bit too sure of himself. You know what Mitchell can do with a guy like that. I just wish we had more time to check him out."

"We don't," Kelly replied. "You have to take the world as you find it."

"The case may hang on Armory's opinion alone. That fathead Farrell sank us, the bastard. If Mitchell carves this new guy up, we're in deep trouble. I just wish I had more time to work with him."

Kelly took the new drink, looked at it for a moment, then bolted it down. "Perhaps we should consider negotiating with Mitchell and offering a reduced charge."

Mease snorted. "Do you think he's nuts? The damn jury seems to be buying everything he's throwing. Plus he'll have a hell of a legal argument, too, if it turns out we can't even establish the basic fact of death. He'd laugh at us."

"Still, it might be worth a try. Manslaughter maybe?"

Mease shook his head. "Arnie Nelson wouldn't go for it. He wants me to swing in the wind on this case. I know what Arnie thinks. He's betting that I come out of this with so much egg on my face I could never compete with him for the prosecutor's job."

Kelly nodded, knowing that what Mease said was true. "Look at it this way, Tom, it's just a job. If you do the best you can with what you have, what the hell do you care what happens?"

"Pride."

"You're young, Tom. Pride, they say, is the most deadly of all sins, and I think they're right. As I recall, that's what caused the angel Lucifer to end up in hell."

Mease laughed. "Martin, I always suspected you were a failed priest."

Kelly shrugged. "No, I'm not, and I'm not about to launch into a sermon either, at least not a long one."

Mease sipped at his drink. "Sermons I can do without."

"It's the price of drinking," Kelly said softly. "No one ever spends much time in a bar without getting a sermon from some drunk or other. Sports, morals, fashion, whatever—more sermons are given in saloons than all the churches put together."

"No wonder so many join Alcoholics Anonymous."

"One of the reasons, I'm sure," Kelly replied. "Now, Thomas, look at this case from a practical point of view. You've handed yourself very well. You've tried a good case with the evidence you've had. The medical evidence so far has turned out to be a bad break, but even if we had the time to import the best of the medical profession, I doubt their opinions would vary much, and you can't help that. Our duty is to try Dennis Chesney, not to crucify him. Everything is going very fast now. You've done everything you could and you'll probably finish putting your case in tomorrow, the best one you had, and then it's all over but the shouting."

"If only Mitchell would put Chesney on," Mease grumbled. "I might have a chance then. Have you been watching him?"

Kelly nodded. "Yes, poor man. And you're right, Dennis Chesney is in no condition to testify. If Armory holds up well, Mitchell may be forced to bring in a parade of his own medical experts, but that remains to be seen. If not, he'll probably use a couple of character witnesses to show what a good man Chesney is. And then you both argue, and the case goes to the jury. Whatever they decide, you still get your paycheck, which from one practical point of view is the most important thing."

"Suppose Judge Talbot takes the case away from the jury?"

Kelly chuckled. "Never."

"Why?"

"It would be foolish, that's why. God, for a while I thought the media were going to crucify her, but that street disturbance may have turned things around for her. I think she's got a good chance to walk away from this without a scratch. They may end up calling her the Teflon Judge."

"But she *could* take it away from the jury. Mitchell has to make a motion to that effect. If he didn't, it would amount to malpractice."

"He can make a motion for a directed verdict," Kelly said, "but he might as well make a motion to have pigs fly. Kathleen Talbot is no fool."

Mease drained his drink. "She may do it, Marty."

"Why?"

"She's an honorable person. She may feel she has to."

"You're not talking about honor, Tom, you're talking about pride. Like I said, pride can destroy. Kathleen is far too smart to do anything like that."

Mease motioned to the waiter for another round.

"Thomas, I never thought I'd say a thing like this, but I think you should stop drinking."

Mease looked at him and laughed. "Why?"

"Because if you get stone-ass drunk, I'll have to try that case in the morning," Kelly said. "You take care of the trial, and I'll do the drinking. I'm good at it."

"Pride, Martin?"

Kelly nodded. "That might be one way of looking at it."

Nelson Bragg wore no watch, and he lost all sense of time. He was almost asleep when he heard the cursing and the loud music.

He climbed up on the toilet seat and squatted down so no one could see either his feet or his head. The door to his booth was bolted. A chill of fear passed through him, and he began to sweat. He carefully reached into his jacket pocket and took out the pistol. It felt slippery in his nervous hand.

Whoever it was had a radio, and it was tuned to a hard-rock station. The noise echoed off the tile walls. The radio's thumping beat seemed to rise, and now Bragg could smell the acrid aroma of marijuana smoke.

He almost screamed as his toilet door was rattled.

"Motherfucker!" A snarling curse came from the other side. "Damn thing's jammed. Fuckin' animals."

A worn broom came sweeping in from under the closed door, whisking away the litter in the stall. The door was rattled once more, then nothing more happened. But the music continued to blast.

Bragg tried to control his shaking. He was afraid he might drop the gun. His heart was beating at an enormous rate.

Clear water came sloshing in over the tile floor. Then a mop was thrust in below the closed door, moving in and out like a snake's tongue. Bragg thought he might faint. At last the mop was withdrawn. Then the radio was shut off.

The sudden silence was even more frightening. Bragg held his breath and pointed the shaking pistol at the closed door.

The smoke was replaced by the choking aroma of disinfectant. Bragg could hardly breathe. Finally the light was turned off.

He was alone in the silent dark.

He climbed down with shaking legs, sitting once again on the toilet seat. His breathing and heart rate began to return to normal. The men's room had been cleaned and he had remained undiscovered. He would be safe at least until morning.

He returned the pistol to his jacket pocket and wiped off his wet hands on the cloth of his trousers. The voices in his head murmured quietly, comfortingly.

Nelson Bragg was sure he was being protected for a good reason—the reason, he now realized, he had been placed on this earth.

"Why is the policeman out there?" Michael asked.

Kathleen couldn't determine whether the presence of a police guard outside their apartment door pleased or frightened her young son. Following the disturbance at the Hall of Justice, the police had insisted on the precaution until the Chesney trial ended.

"Don't you like policemen?"

Michael nodded. "Oh, yes. But why is he there?"

She smiled, choosing her words to reassure him. "Sometimes policemen stand outside homes of judges. It's nothing to worry about."

His eyes studied her for a moment; then he seemed to accept the explanation. "Are you staying home tonight?"

"Yes. Do you like that?"

His smile was answer enough.

"What would you like to do?" she asked. "Watch television? Or have me read to you?"

"Read, please."

" 'Tabitha the Tiger'?" It was his favorite. The little picture story book was almost worn out. Marie usually did the reading but tonight Marie had sensed that Kathleen needed to be alone with her son, so she had tactfully retreated to her own room.

She sat and read to him until he fell asleep. His little hand held her thumb tightly, then his grip loosened as he slept. Kathleen tucked him in, but didn't leave the room.

He was all she had. She had never fully realized just how alone they were. He had no living grandparents, nor any uncles or aunts. There were just the two of them. If anything happened to her, Michael would have no one. She was heavily insured, so money would not be a problem if anything happened. But he would be cast into a world of guardians, and no matter how well-intentioned, it would never be an adequate substitute for the stability of a family. She touched Michael's smooth cheek lightly with her fingertips. He was so soft and pleasantly warm—the very embodiment of the warmth and love and peace she now craved more than ever.

Kathleen gently smoothed her son's hair. If she did what was expected, she would come out of it all with honor. She wanted that very much. They could go back to leading a normal life once more—the reason she had accepted the appointment to the bench in the first place.

The Honorable Kathleen Talbot. Was she really worthy of that title? She looked out at the night and felt an almost desperate need to talk to Jerry Mitchell. More than ever before she needed his counsel, his wisdom. But it was impossible. They both had duties, distinct and even conflicting.

When she had faced the choice of turning off the machines supporting her father, she had thought then that would be the hardest decision she would ever have to make. But she had been wrong. It seemed ironic that the man she loved would be the one who might force her to an even more fateful choice. Jerry Mitchell would have no alternative. He would have to do his duty.

She wondered if, faced with the choice, she could do hers.

Tomorrow she might have to face that choice. She gently stroked her son's soft hair. Tomorrow she might find out if she was indeed honorable.

CHAPTER 35

JERRY MITCHELL AND Peter Norbanski crossed the street with the traffic light. Early-morning traffic clogged the city's streets, cars barely inching along, the drivers expressing their frustration in a cacophony of blaring horns.

The demonstrators, their numbers now much diminished, marched without enthusiasm in two separate circles in front of the Hall of Justice. The circles were kept apart by a line of bored policemen. There was no longer any shouting or chanting.

"Looks like the crackpots are beginning to wind down," Pete Norbanski said as they passed through the two circles and walked up the steps to the building's entrance.

"The right to free public expression," Mitchell said, "is one of our basic freedoms, Pete. Don't tell me you object?"

"You'd think they'd have better things to do."

Mitchell took out his bar-association credentials, as did Norbanski. They showed them to the guard and were allowed to pass without going through the metal detectors or having their briefcases searched.

"Some people feel deeply about ethical issues," Mitchell said. "Genuine concern brings them out. Others need to be against something. Demonstrating with signs and shouting helps vent feelings that otherwise might be dangerous. And there's a certain sociability in it, too. Later, they can meet and rehash their great campaigns, like veterans who have shared a battle."

They waited for the elevator in the court's lobby.

"Are you going to tell Tom Mease about Armory?"

Mitchell smiled. "Wars are not won, Pete, by telling the other side what you plan to do."

"He may want an adjournment."

Mitchell shook his head. "I doubt it. There's such a thing as overtrying a lawsuit. He'll try to cut his losses with the remaining witnesses from the hospice; then I think he'll rest his case today."

Norbanski looked worried. "If he does rest, do you still plan to move for a directed verdict?"

Mitchell nodded. "I have to. In order to preserve the legal issue, the motion has to be made. If the jury should convict, I have to have a basis for appeal, and the motion protects that."

"Do you really think they would?"

"What?"

"Convict."

Mitchell looked down at his shorter associate. "There are no guarantees, Pete. No one can be absolutely sure with a jury. Anyway, I have a duty to protect Dennis Chesney's legal rights no matter which way I think things might go. I told Dr. Deppen to be ready to testify. We'll start off with him as our first witness."

"But suppose she grants your motion?"

Mitchell's expression showed his concern. "She won't. It's too risky. If she did, the dogs would be right at her throat again. She's too smart for that. Anyway, I think the jury will acquit and I think she does too. There's no percentage in doing anything foolish."

"Still, she might."

Mitchell didn't answer. He was torn. It was his absolute duty to defend Dennis Chesney, to do everything legally possible to obtain justice. Yet, he hoped Kathleen wouldn't grant his motion. If she did, it could possibly destroy her.

Regina woke from a troubled sleep. She sensed something was wrong, but wondered if her apprehension wasn't merely a spillover from a disquieting nightmare. She listened as the air conditioner labored against the moist Florida heat.

She reached out for Walter and was surprised to find he wasn't in bed. Regina rolled over and squinted at the clock. It was just past eight. Like herself, Walter seldom stirred before noon. She sat up and listened, but heard no sound in the house.

She lay back for a moment and wondered where he might be. She got up, pulled on a robe, and padded out to the kitchen. The light over the stove was on, but that was the only sign of life.

"Walter?" she called, her voice echoing in the empty house. She went into the study. Big Mike's favorite photographs still decorated the walls. She had intended to remove the pictures, assuming that they might cause Walter some discomfort.

"Walter?"

Regina walked back to the kitchen. She was hung-over, as usual, and her head throbbed painfully. The vodka bottle was nearly empty, but she poured a healthy jot into a glass, filled it with tomato juice, then stirred it with her finger, licking off the residue of tomato juice.

"Walter?"

They had cashed in some of the bonds Big Mike had left her. The money was to be used as a deposit if the restaurant deal looked promising. Today a broker was going to show them a property he described as "hot," but that wasn't scheduled until the afternoon.

She felt somewhat better after quickly downing the drink. Regina wondered if Walter might have gone out for a quick breakfast. He had done that once before since they had come to Florida. He told her he sometimes had trouble sleeping.

Regina returned to the bedroom. She decided to hang up the robe. Walter's clothes were gone from the closet. He didn't have many things, but what he had was gone.

"Walter?"

Regina went to the dresser. The money they had planned to use as a deposit was gone too. Then she checked her jewelry box. The huge diamond ring Big Mike had given her, the one

Walter had objected to her wearing, was also gone, as were her several sets of diamond earrings.

Regina sat on the side of the bed. A tear formed and spilled down her cheek. "Walter." This time she just whispered his name. She knew he was gone for good.

She felt as lonely as she had the night Big Mike suffered the stroke. Nothing ever worked out for her, not Big Mike, nor the revenge on his daughter, nor Walter. Nothing ever worked out.

She went back to the kitchen and finished what was left of the vodka.

--◀ ▶--

Nelson Bragg wasn't sure that he had slept, or even how much time had elapsed. His legs felt cramped, and he stood up in the darkness, remaining in the safety of his stall.

He was standing when the maintenance man opened the door and switched on the lights. The sudden burst of light terrorized and confused him. He stood stock-still; then he heard the door of the men's room close. There was no sound.

He carefully slid back the bolt on the stall's door and peeked out. He was alone.

His reflection in the mirrors stared back at him with a face he almost failed to recognize. Bragg splashed some water on his haggard features and smoothed his hair. He had a light beard, so being unshaven wasn't so noticeable.

Once more he checked the gun in his pocket. Reassured by the touch of its hard metal, he now stepped out in the hall and looked up at the clock. It was later than he had thought, almost time for court to begin. He wanted to be among the first at the courtroom door. Today he had to be admitted, had to get a seat.

He wanted coffee and something to eat, but he didn't risk going to the lobby. He had more important things to do. The voices murmured with great sense of purpose. He walked up the stairway to the entrance to Judge Talbot's courtroom.

A different guard stood at the door, his eyes just as icy and inquiring as those of the man he had replaced. Bragg entered with the other observers and found a seat.

He knew he was trembling. But this time it wasn't out of fear; it was from excitement.

Jane Whitehall stared at the paper's morning edition. She would have covered the story much differently, and much better. There was no punch, no feeling; and worse, the paper treated Judge Kathleen Talbot as if she were a majority stockholder. Someone had really scared hell out of Jack Bennett.

She finished her third cup of coffee before making the long-distance call. The paper had contacted her months ago, but she had rebuffed them. Now she wished she hadn't been quite so insulting.

The Canadian weekly had been bought up by a group of Americans looking for a vehicle for their right-wing views. *The National Comet*'s name had been changed to *Satellite Eye*, but it was still a collection of titillating, trashy, and questionable stories. The only change was on the editorial page, now slanted to reflect the interests of its new owners. The tabloid's headquarters had been moved from Toronto to New York. They had wanted her to come to work for them then. But she had been caustic in her refusal. It would be demeaning to work for a scandal sheet. But right now it was better than not working at all.

She was put through to the managing editor.

"This is Jane Whitehall," she said, keeping her tone bright and cheery. "Do you remember me?"

"Yeah, and I remember what you said about us, too."

"It's my sense of humor," she answered. "Sometimes people mistake it for something else. It's just a matter of getting used to me."

He laughed. "Sure, Janey, and it never snows in Alaska, too."

"Well, I hope you didn't—"

"Hey, don't ruin things by apologizing," he said easily. "I like you just the way you are. In fact, despite what you said, I was going to call you."

"You were?"

"Yeah. I've been reading your articles about your local woman judge. Good shit, Janey. You've got the kind of talent we're interested in. It's about time you considered getting out of the Midwest and doing something on a national scale. How about it, kid? You want to work for us?"

She fought to keep the surprise out of her voice. "That would depend on a lot of things."

"Like what?"

"Oh, money; that's always important. Also, my assignment and what I could expect to be doing."

He chuckled. "Yeah, you're ready for a change, Janey. Otherwise you wouldn't have called. Look, why don't you hop a plane this afternoon and come in to New York? We'll put you up at a good hotel and pay all expenses. I'll take you to dinner, and we can iron out the details. Okay?"

She wanted to appear to hesitate. "Well, I'm pretty busy . . ."

"Hey, Janey, we need your talent. Besides, you'll love it here. Everybody's a bastard. Call me when you get in."

The phone buzzed. He had hung up without waiting for her reply. She slammed down the receiver in anger.

She was fuming. Dinner, he said, but she knew the type; he'd expect sex for dessert. She began to calm down. If the offer was right, it wouldn't be the first time she had climbed between the sheets for a job.

And she would be a national reporter. The assignments might be about two-headed children and sex crimes, but it would be writing, and she knew she did that very well.

It would show Jack Bennett what he could do with his precious journalistic ethics. Jane Whitehall was too big, too good for the drab Midwest. She was tired of the Bennetts, the Kathleen Talbots, the restrictions against creative reporting, as she liked to call it.

She was ready for New York. Jane called an airline and made reservations.

-◀ ▶-

Kathleen began the trial precisely on time. Demonstrators

still marched at the entrance of the Hall of Justice, but they were few in number and their enthusiasm had diminished.

Tom Mease quickly and expertly conducted the direct examination of the distinguished-looking witness, Dr. Franklin Armory. Mease questioned the doctor without any interruption by Jerry Mitchell, despite damaging testimony as to the cause of death. Mitchell made no objection inasmuch as the doctor stated that it was Dennis Chesney's act in turning off the machines that was the unquestioned cause of death.

Mease waited for Mitchell's objections on several occasions and appeared surprised when none was made. Mitchell merely looked on as though he were nothing more than a casual spectator.

Mease completed his direct examination. He walked over to the counsel table and whispered into Marty Kelly's ear, "Did I forget anything?"

Kelly shook his head. "No," he whispered back. "You did a good job. The jury seems impressed. Armory's a good witness. He's repaired the damage Farrell did to the case."

Mease straightened and looked at Mitchell. "You may take the witness."

Jerry Mitchell looked as though he was reluctant to leave his chair, but he managed. He walked to a point directly in front of the jury. He smiled at Dr. Armory, who smiled back, albeit frostily.

"I've spent much of the night reading some of the articles you've written, especially recent ones, doctor," Mitchell said. "I found them fascinating."

Dr. Armory nodded with imperial dignity. "Thank you."

"Doctor, what is your definition of death?"

Armory's slightly condescending expression did not change as he answered immediately, "It is that moment when the soul escapes from the body."

"Is that your personal definition, or does that come from some scientific body of knowledge?" Mitchell's manner was friendly.

"It comes from the ultimate scientific body of knowledge."

"And that is?"

Armory looked pleased to answer, "The Bible."

Mitchell glanced back at Mease, noting the alarm on the young prosecutor's face. "Tell me, doctor, where in the Bible do you find that medical definition?"

Armory drew himself up and answered in a firm voice, "Jeremiah, for one. Jeremiah called death the harvestman. He is, of course, the man for whom you were named, Mr. Mitchell." Armory chuckled and looked over at the jury to see if they appreciated his small joke.

"They tell me, doctor, that I was named for my uncle."

"Objection!" Mease's voice failed to hide his panic. "Who or how Mr. Mitchell was named is irrelevant."

"Sustained," Kathleen said.

Mitchell nodded, as if agreeing. "Now, doctor, although you weren't present, Dr. Farrell testified he participated in several organ transplants. Have you ever been in attendance at any similar procedures?"

"No."

Mitchell smiled. "Have you ever recommended any of your patients for transplants?"

"I have not," Armory answered quickly.

"Forget about transplants from deceased donors, doctor. Have you ever recommended, say, the transplant of a kidney from one living patient to another?"

"No." The doctor's voice began to take on even more confidence.

"Have you ever treated anyone who had kidney trouble?"

"Of course. I'm an internist."

"Any patient of yours ever have irreversible kidney failure?"

Armory nodded. "It has happened."

"And you didn't recommend a kidney transplant?"

"No."

Mitchell walked a few steps closer to the jury. "Kidney transplants have been around for a while, haven't they?"

"They have been done."

Mitchell's voice was now barely audible. "Successfully? I mean that both the donor and the recipient lived?"

"So I am informed."

"Then why don't you recommend such a procedure?"

"Scientific reasons," the doctor snapped.

"Scientific?"

"The kidneys are the seat of man's emotions," the doctor said firmly. "Such transplants are forbidden."

"Who says that, doctor?"

"The Bible."

"Oh?"

Dr. Armory glared at Mitchell. "It's right there in black and white in Isaiah!"

Mitchell looked at the jury. "You are, as you testified, a professor of medicine?"

Armory nodded. "I am."

"Do you teach a regular class?"

"Objection!" Mease rushed forward, trying to keep his face from showing his surprise and dismay. "Dr. Armory's qualifications are without question. We have shown—"

"Overruled," Kathleen said. "He's your expert. Mr. Mitchell has a right to examine his qualifications."

Mitchell waited until Mease had returned to his seat.

"I asked, doctor, if you teach a regular class."

"No."

"Is Dr. Maguire the dean of your medical school?" Mitchell asked.

"He is."

"I talked to Dr. Maguire by telephone last night—"

"Objection!" Mease seemed glad to have a legitimate complaint. "If Mr. Mitchell plans to testify, I want him sworn."

"Sustained," Kathleen said. "If you wish to call witnesses, Mr. Mitchell, you have that right. But you can't testify for them."

Mitchell bowed slightly. "I appreciate that," he said, restraining a smile of amusement. He turned once again to the witness. "Now, Dr. Armory, you're not an active professor at all, are you?"

"I am a professor emeritus."

"Retired?"

"Emeritus," he repeated. "I am not retired. I can be called on to serve, if needed."

"Do you engage in the active practice of medicine now?"

"No."

"You haven't taught or practiced since October 19, 1981, pursuant to an agreement with your school and your state's board of medical examiners, isn't that true?"

Armory frowned. "That was my decision. I lecture on medical ethics now. Chiefly at seminars and for a number of church groups around the country."

"Were you hospitalized when you made that decision?"

"Objection, that doesn't bear on his qualifications." Mease's tone indicated he recognized defeat.

"I'll take the answer," Kathleen said.

"Were you in Mercywood Hospital when you made that decision, doctor?"

"That had nothing to do with it."

"What kind of a hospital is Mercywood?" Mitchell asked.

Mease stood up, then changed his mind and remained silent.

"It is a place for people who become overtired," the doctor said with firmness.

"And how long where you in Mercywood?"

"Several months," Armory replied easily.

Mitchell's manner was gentle. "Have you ever been in that hospital since that time?"

"Twice," the doctor replied.

"Doctor, you said death occurs when the soul escapes from the body, is that correct?"

"Yes." Armory's manner had never changed once, nor his tone of absolute certainty.

"And how do you determine that the soul has flown?"

"Man can't."

"Who, then?"

"God, of course." The doctor smiled. "Remember, Mr. Mitchell, God can raise anyone from the dead. He alone makes the determination."

"How do we know when God has made that determination?"

"Life stops."

Mitchell's voice was soft, almost encouraging. "And does that mean the brain has ceased to function?"

Armory shrugged. "I suppose it's as good a test as any. But God makes the final determination."

Mitchell walked to the counsel table and looked down at Mease. "Your witness," he said quietly.

Mease slowly shook his head as he whispered to Kelly, "I knew this guy was too good to be true. I should never have relied on Farrell. I should have made a few phone calls."

"Armory looked good on paper," Kelly said softly. "You can't win them all, Tom."

Mease got to his feet, forcing a smile as if to show that Dr. Armory had been a wonderful witness. "No questions, your honor."

-◄ ►-

Nelson Bragg had never known such agitation. He sat wedged between two stout, well-dressed women who were so intent on the trial that they never noticed his trembling. He kept his hands clasped tightly between his legs. He tried to listen to the testimony, but his voices kept interfering with his concentration as they rasped louder and with increasing fury.

The weight of the pistol in his jacket pocket seemed to be getting heavier as each minute passed. He was conscious of the scrutinizing eyes of the courtroom officers, who he thought were looking at him with special interest.

Nelson Bragg struggled to control himself. The voices were demanding action, but he couldn't force himself to move, not yet, not until the moment was right. But he would have to do something soon. Time was running out.

-◄ ►-

Tom Mease was a good workman. Despite Jerry Mitchell's destruction of his medical experts, he continued on with a show of confidence and enthusiasm. Mitchell had no questions of Paul Martin's widow, who glared at Dennis Chesney as Mease led her through the identification chain of evidence.

The nurse's aide who had attended Martin identified Chesney and placed him in the room with Martin.

The Oriental doctor, who spoke softly, testified to his conversation with Chesney. The doctor told of the events when he was called back into the room after Chesney had shut off the machines.

"And the last person you saw with Paul Martin when he was alive was Dennis Chesney?" Mease asked.

"Mr. Martin wasn't alive," the doctor said quietly.

"Pardon me?"

The doctor sat with a certain stillness, his small hands folded on his lap. "Mr. Martin wasn't alive, not in a medical sense."

"You mean after the machines were turned off?"

"Objection," Mitchell said quietly. "The question is leading, and I think it important that the doctor do the testifying."

"Sustained," Kathleen said.

"When you returned to the room after leaving Dennis Chesney, you said you found the machines turned off. Was Mr. Martin dead at that time?"

"Yes."

Mease paused, then turned to Jerry Mitchell. "You may take the witness."

Mitchell stood and spoke quickly. "Doctor, before the machines were turned off, was Mr. Martin dead?"

"In my opinion, he was."

"Objection!" Mease said, rising. "This witness has been called to testify to what happened, not as an expert."

Mitchell turned to the judge. "I think I can cure that, with the court's permission. The doctor has rather impressive qualifications. I should wish to qualify him as an expert."

"My objection stands," Mease snapped frantically. Mitchell was about to use his own witness against him, always a powerfully persuasive tactic that never failed to impress a jury. Mease looked up at Kathleen. "If he wants to use him as an expert, let him call the doctor as his witness after I've put in my case."

Kathleen spoke firmly. "The objection can be cured, Mr. Mitchell, if you qualify him. If you can establish him legally as an expert, I will take the answer."

Mitchell bowed slightly. "Thank you." He glanced at Mease for a moment, as if offering silent sympathy, then turned to the witness. "Now, doctor, where did you go to medical school? . . ."

Mease listened in concealed discomfort as Mitchell expertly

turned the doctor, Mease's last witness, against him. At last, and mercifully, Mitchell finished. He turned to Mease. "You may take the witness."

Mease shook his head. Anything more could only make it worse. "No questions," he said.

Mease turned to Martin Kelly. "Well?" he whispered.

Kelly shrugged. "That's it, Tom. When you're out of witnesses, you're out of trial, to paraphrase a popular beer commercial."

Mease nodded. He slowly stood up. He knew the jurors were watching him, so he walked up to the bench with a show of confidence.

He looked up at Kathleen. "Your honor, the people rest."

She turned to Mitchell, who had also approached the bench. "Mr. Mitchell, are you ready to proceed?"

"I am, your honor." His voice was friendly but firm. "However, before I do, I respectfully request that the jury be excused so I can present a legal argument."

She nodded. "The jury will be excused." The moment she had dreaded so had finally come.

CHAPTER 36

JERRY MITCHELL WALKED to the lectern in front of the bench. He never used notes, relying on his excellent memory. He believed that pausing to refer to notes was distracting and tended to disrupt the focused attention he worked to obtain.

He waited patiently until the jury had departed and the courtroom settled down. He looked up at Kathleen. Her face was devoid of any visible emotion. He knew his own expression was equally formal. He wondered if she were experiencing the same tumult of emotions that assaulted him.

"Your honor," he began, "I move that the court direct a verdict of not guilty in this case. Two things must be decided in each and every criminal case—the facts, and the law. The jury decides the facts. The judge decides the law. It is our position that no question of fact exists in this case."

He sensed Mease stirring at the counsel table, but no objection was made. "We admit, for the purposes of this motion, every allegation of fact made by the prosecution. Lieutenant Dennis Chesney, the officer in charge of the Paul Martin case, turned off the so-called support machines at the place and on the date alleged."

Mitchell leaned easily against the lectern. "And we admit that he had no permission from the Martin family or from the attending doctors to turn off those machines. Dennis Chesney may have committed an offense, and he may have committed a

367

civil wrong, but what he did was not murder, because Paul Martin was already dead."

"Objection." Mease stood and spoke from his place at the counsel table. "I'm reluctant to interrupt counsel for the defense, but what he states is patently wrong. I—"

"Sit down, Mr. Mease," Kathleen said quietly. "You'll get your chance. Go on, Mr. Mitchell."

Mitchell nodded. The newspapermen were busy taking notes at the press table. "As I said, Paul Martin was already dead when Dennis Chesney turned off those machines. I don't say, your honor, that what he did was right. I don't say what he did wasn't perhaps a crime, but it wasn't murder, as charged, and it wasn't any crime included in the charge of murder. In order to be charged with murder, it must be shown that the defendant took the life of another. Dennis Chesney didn't do that. There was no life remaining to be taken."

"Mr. Martin was breathing," Kathleen said quietly. "Do you admit that?"

Mitchell looked directly at her. "No."

"The medical people in attendance said he was breathing. That is the testimony, uncontradicted, at least so far, Mr. Mitchell."

"Your honor, if I may disagree, that is not the testimony as I understand it. The machines were doing the breathing, not Paul Martin. True, his chest went up and down, and an exchange of air took place in his lungs, but it was being done by artificial means. He was not breathing on his own." Mitchell knew he had to carefully word what he was about to say or it could be used against him. "The proof of that, unfortunately, is what brings us all here today. When the machines were turned off, the breathing stopped."

"Isn't that when death took place?" Her voice sounded strained.

He looked at her for a moment, wondering if he was seeing distress in those lovely eyes. "If the court please, death took place when the brain ceased to function. Brain death, as defined by a number of federal and state courts, occurs when the brain ceases to function, and that is determined by the absence of recorded brain waves. That, as we have heard, was the condition of Paul Martin prior to the machines being turned off. Paul Martin was legally dead when Dennis Chesney shut off the machines."

"That is a question of fact, isn't it?" Her tone was so soft, her words were hardly above a whisper.

"Not in this case," he said, puzzling at her reaction. "Every medical expert the prosecution has presented, even Dr. Armory, has—"

"Objection," Mease snapped. "This is a motion, not argument. He shouldn't characterize what a witness says."

Mitchell turned and smiled at his young opponent. "Are you saying, Mr. Mease, that Dr. Armory's medical positions weren't just a little . . . well . . . bizarre?"

"That will do." Kathleen's words were spoken almost mechanically. "Objection overruled. Continue, please, Mr. Mitchell."

He stared at her. The color had drained from her cheeks. He decided to finish quickly.

"Your honor, every doctor, including Dr. Armory, said the medical test for death is brain death. Dr. Armory, who relies on the Bible, said it was as good a test as any other."

She spoke, again in a voice so low he could hardly hear her. "That may be the medical test, Mr. Mitchell, but the court must be concerned with the legal test."

She was looking past him. He paused and turned slightly, then realized she was looking at Dennis Chesney. Chesney, as usual, sat quietly, expressionless, his eyes fixed on the floor.

Mitchell studied Kathleen. She showed no emotion, but he thought her eyes looked moist. "Our state legislature has not acted in the matter," he continued. "There is no statue fixing a test for death in this state. And in this state no court has had to address that question directly."

Kathleen looked back to Mitchell. "Then it is a question of fact, to be determined by the jury."

"I'm afraid not," he replied. "It's a legal question, and it must be decided by the court. While our state courts haven't spoken on the matter, other state decisions are helpful. In California—"

"Are you referring to the Randazzo case?"

"Yes. And others." He recited the case citations from memory.

"I've read most of those decisions, Mr. Mitchell." Her eyes again shifted to Chesney.

"All of them have said, to one degree or another, that when the brain ceases to function, death occurs. As you know, many courts have so held—even when the body is still capable of breathing without assistance. If the brain is dead, your honor, the person is dead."

She leaned back in her chair. She looked as if she were about to speak, then changed her mind.

"The charge here is murder," Mitchell said. "But I urge your honor to find as a matter of law that Paul Martin was dead, brain dead, when the machines were turned off, and thus Dennis Chesney did not cause the death of Paul Martin and therefore cannot be guilty of murder, in any degree." Mitchell looked at her, realizing perhaps he was the only person in the courtroom who sensed the level of her distress. He had said what he had to say; there was no purpose in causing her any more agony. "I respectfully request that your honor direct a verdict of not guilty. Thank you."

She didn't look at him. She seemed distracted. "Mr. Mease, do you wish to respond?"

Ted Sawchek sat in his chambers. He was still on sick leave from the court, but he had come in to try to improve his chances for the executive-judge job.

If only Kathleen Talbot could be persuaded to give up and throw her support to him, the prize, and all that went with it, would belong to him.

He was so close.

Sawchek stood up and grabbed his cane. The leg was still stiff and sore and seemed to be getting worse rather than better.

He was determined to persuade Kathleen Talbot to support him, no matter what he had to promise her. She had to realize, he reasoned, that if the Chesney case went sour, she would have no chance at all. If he could show her just how risky her position was, she might come over to his side. It was worth the try.

But he knew he would have to talk to her in person. A telephone call wouldn't do it.

The judges' private elevator was down at the other side of the building. He decided to go through his empty courtroom and take a public elevator. It would save walking on his painful leg.

He knew she would probably politely tell him to go to hell, but he was determined to make the effort. All life was risk.

Kathleen knew what Tom Mease would say, so she listened only with half an ear, her thoughts returning to the terrible decision she had had to make concerning her own father. It was almost as if she herself were on trial.

And, in a way, perhaps she was, she thought. She had been the prosecuting attorney when Dennis Chesney had been charged with murder. Arnie Nelson had acted foolishly, and she regretted that she hadn't reversed what he had done. Hers had been a political decision, which, she remembered, had seemed so correct at the time. Now both she and Dennis Chesney seemed doomed by her initial failure to act.

"Chesney isn't a foolish man . . ." She heard Mease's crisp words. "He's a senior detective. He knew exactly what he was doing, and he knew he had no right to do it."

Mease, unlike the cool and reserved Jerry Mitchell, spoke with passion and vigor, as if he were addressing a jury. "This is not a question of law, as Mr. Mitchell so glibly puts it," he continued. "The question of life and death is for the jury to decide. Whether Paul Martin was alive or dead when the machines were turned off is, I repeat, a question of fact. And if the jury decides he was alive, then Chesney committed murder."

It would be easy, she knew, to agree with Mease. There was no law in the state, no prior decisions in point; it was uncharted territory. No one would question her motives if she turned the question over to the jury.

But they would if she took it away from the jury.

"Mr. Mitchell would have the court believe that life is some legal technicality, like a liquor license, given and taken for the sake of convenience." Tom Mease was warming to his own thoughts, making an emotional argument, but Jerry Mitchell gave no sign that he intended to interrupt him.

"Life is precious," Mease said, hissing the words dramatically. "It isn't to be snuffed out by some overzealous policeman who takes the law he was sworn to uphold into his own hands, and becomes judge, executioneer, and . . . God!"

Mease paused, as if waiting for Mitchell's objection or a remonstrance from the bench. He seemed surprised when none came. He continued in a quieter voice. "This is a murder case. The guilt or innocence of Dennis Chesney is a matter for the jury, and only the jury. Paul Martin was alive and breathing when he was killed by the intentional act of Dennis Chesney."

Mease paused, glancing for a moment at the press table, gratified at the activity of the reporters as they took notes. "I ask that the motion be denied. Thank you."

Suddenly the courtroom was completely silent. All eyes were fixed on Kathleen Talbot.

Dennis Chesney seemed to be the only person in the courtroom who wasn't staring at Kathleen.

She looked at Chesney, suddenly realizing that she was deciding the question of innocence or guilt for both of them.

Honor—it was such an overused term, so often spoken without thought of its real implication and meaning. The test of honor, in the abstract, was so easy, but in reality it was frightening, demanding both sacrifice and courage.

The faces in the crowded courtroom reminded her of an exquisitely detailed painting, every feature on every face vividly etched in her consciousness. The lawyers, the officers, the spectators, everything, seemed fixed forever, as if time itself had somehow stopped.

She swallowed, then forced herself to speak loudly and firmly.

"The motion for a directed verdict of not guilty is granted."

There was a momentary pause, then the courtroom erupted. She heard shouts, noises, and the repetitive cracking of her clerk's gavel.

"Court's adjourned," she said, rising to walk from the bench and hoping to escape the newspeople who were rushing forward.

A sound, like a sharp echo of the clerk's gavel, came from the back of the courtroom. Kathleen saw people diving away from a scrawny man who stood in the spectator rows pointing something at her.

He was shouting. It sounded like "whore" but she couldn't be sure, then she heard the peculiar snapping sound again and felt a burning sensation in her left side.

The odd little man turned and dashed for the courtroom door, people frantically scrambling out of his way.

Suddenly Jerry Mitchell rushed to her. Gently but quickly, he pushed her down beneath the judge's bench and covered her with his big body, his face a mask of terrified concern.

The burning in her side was becoming painful and she touched it to discover a peculiar wetness.

Nelson Bragg burst out of the courtroom door. He had never known such fear. The voices were screaming in a rising crescendo beyond anything he had ever known.

The big guard stationed at the door was chasing him. He could hear the guard right behind him as he tried to reach the stairway. The gun slid from his slippery hand but he didn't care.

Judge Sawchek, using a cane, stepped out of the elevator right into Bragg's path, just as the huge guard came up behind Bragg. Bragg was thrown into Sawchek when the guard tackled him, and all three men went skidding down the marble hall.

Other officers grabbed Bragg, who was crying and babbling incoherently.

Ted Sawchek thought his cane had been broken; he had distinctly heard the snap. The cane looked all right, but when he tried to get up, pain shot through both legs.

"Lie still, judge," one of the guards said, his voice shaking with excitement. "I think your ankle's broken."

"What the hell's happening?" Sawchek demanded.

"Get a doctor and a wagon," the guard snapped to another policeman. Then he looked down at Sawchek. "You're okay, except for the ankle," he said.

Sawchek grimaced, raising his head to take a look. "Oh shit!" he snarled. "It's my good leg!"

-◀ ▶-

Kathleen looked up at the faces. Jerry Mitchell and a court officer were cutting her robe with a pair of scissors. Mitchell's big hands were bloody.

"Lie still, Kathleen," he said, "and let's see what's happened."

She heard him tear the fabric of her blouse and felt embarrassed that people were looking at her. The pain was insistent now, a sharp ache. Each breath made it worse.

Mitchell gently pulled the bloody fabric away until he found the bullet hole in Kathleen's left side just below her breast.

Jerry reached up and stroked her face and hair. "You've been shot," he said gently. "But it's not bad at all, just a minor flesh wound."

Jerry smiled at her, trying to be reassuring, but silently praying that the emergency medical crew would arrive quickly.

CHAPTER 37

JERRY MITCHELL HAD ignored the press waiting in the hall-way outside the surgical lounge. Two steely-eyed uniformed policemen were at the door keeping control of the situation. The lounge, furnished like a cheerful hotel lobby, was for the use of family and friends of patients undergoing surgery. The small chapel room at the side of the lounge served as an ominous reminder of the fragility of life.

Mitchell used the lounge telephone to call Marie.

Her voice was strained when she answered.

"Marie, don't be alarmed, but Judge Talbot's been shot."

"I know," she replied. "The fools put it on television as a bulletin. Michael saw it. He's frightened. How is she?"

"I don't know," Mitchell answered honestly. "She was shot once, in the chest. She's in surgery right now. I'll talk to the doctors as soon as she's out."

"Please call me," Marie said, barely controlling her voice. "I tried telephoning the hospital, but they couldn't tell me anything except that she was critical."

"All gunshot victims are automatically listed as critical," he said, to provide her with a reassurance he himself didn't feel. "May I talk to Michael?"

"It would help," Marie said.

"Hello." The little voice reflected the boy's concern and confusion.

"Do you know who this is?"

375

"The giant," Michael said.

"Yes, Michael, the giant. I'm at the hospital. Your mother's been hurt slightly, but it's nothing to worry about," Mitchell said easily. "The doctors are bandaging her up now. She'll be fine."

"Can I see her?" Michael, although only four, was testing the truth of Mitchell's statement.

"I suppose so," Mitchell answered, impressed at the boy's quick intelligence.

"When?"

"Maybe tonight, maybe tomorrow," Mitchell said as if he really meant it. "It depends on the rules here, and your mother may be coming home tomorrow. So we'll see, okay?"

"Will you take me to see her?"

"Sure. As soon as I can. If not tonight, maybe tomorrow. I'll stop by there tonight, okay?"

"Okay." For the first time, Michael's voice became less tense.

Marie came back on the telephone. She too sounded calmer. "I'll call you as soon as I know anything," Mitchell said.

He hung up just as Brenda Hastings and Jesse Williams were arriving. They hurried over to him.

"Any word?" Brenda asked.

"Not yet," Mitchell replied.

Williams looked down at Mitchell's suit jacket. The bloodstains had dried. "Were you hurt?"

Mitchell shook his head. "No. Just Kathleen."

"What does it look like to you?" Judge Hastings asked.

"I don't know. She was shot once, in the side, about here." He indicated a point on his left chest. "It will depend on the path of the bullet, I suppose. She was conscious when they took her to the ambulance."

"The police have the man who did it," Williams said. "But no one knows why. Someone said he's crazy."

"How long has she been in surgery?" Brenda asked.

Mitchell looked at his watch. "Not long, as far as I know. I would guess less than an hour now. The surgeon will come in when he's done."

"That's quite a collection out there," Williams said, nodding toward the closed lounge door. "They have remote television trucks in the street, and crews assigned here and in the emergency room."

"It isn't every day a judge is shot, thank God," Brenda said. "And it's a result of all that damn controversy." She looked at Mitchell. "I understand Kathleen tossed the Chesney case out, just before it happened."

Mitchell nodded. "That apparently triggered off the gunman."

"What's happened to Dennis Chesney?" Williams asked.

Mitchell was grateful to think of something else. "My young associate is taking him to a hospital. I made the arrangements in case there was a favorable jury verdict. Chesney is seriously depressed. He needs treatment."

"Will he agree to it?" Williams asked.

"He wasn't wild about it when I first talked to him, but I made it a condition of my defending him. He's an honorable man; he'll stick to his word. All this has been a devastating shock for a dedicated policeman, but I think he'll respond to therapy. At least I hope so."

Their attention was drawn to rising sounds from the press as the lounge door was opened by one of the officers. Judge Jerome Foley stomped in, his bulldog face as dour as ever.

He nodded to the other two judges, then spoke to Mitchell. "How is she?"

"She's in surgery. We don't know."

Foley eased his squat bulk into an overstuffed leather chair. "What are you looking at?" he snapped at Brenda Hastings.

She blushed. "This is the first time I've ever seen you without Sullivan."

His laugh, a rare occurrence, startled them all. "This should shatter all the rumors we hear about an invisible cord tying us together. He's in court, working. I came here to . . . well . . . to show solidarity with Kathleen Talbot." His face once again resumed its normal hostile expression. "We, some of us, haven't treated her very well. Especially Quinlan, that old . . ." He nodded toward Brenda to indicate he would forgo the word he had in mind. "Sullivan feels that way too."

"We should dispose of the question of who will be executive judge," Jesse Williams said. "That would be one step in the right direction."

"The sooner the better," Foley snapped.

They were interrupted by a tall doctor clad in green cotton operating togs. A surgical mask had been pulled down and lay at his neck.

"The Talbot family?"

"Judge Talbot has only a four-year-old son," Mitchell said. "We are friends."

The doctor's smile was formal. Mitchell felt a rising sense of fear.

"She was shot in the left chest with a small-caliber bullet," he said. "The slug was mashed, but it looks like a twenty-two. We get pretty expert at guessing the size of bullets, we see enough of them here."

"How is she?" Mitchell demanded.

"Lucky, that's how she is," the doctor responded.

"Getting shot's not so lucky," Foley growled.

The doctor nodded, startled by Foley's fierceness. "Yes, I suppose it's not. But the ammunition must have been old. It didn't have much kick to it, apparently. The bullet penetrated the skin, hit a rib, traveled a few inches, and stopped. There was absolutely no organ damage. She'll be sore for a while, but that's it." He looked at Foley. "That's the lucky part, you see. We get people in here who have been shot and the bullets tear back and forth, bouncing off bones like little pinballs. That's the usual situation. But not here, thank God."

"May I see her?" Mitchell asked.

"Well, we didn't know what we had when we put her under, so we anesthetized her for major chest surgery. She'll be out for a couple of hours, then she'll be pretty groggy after that. She's being transferred to the recovery room. You can see her, but it won't be for quite a while."

"If I bring her little boy in tonight, will he be allowed to see her?"

"Four years old? I think not. The hospital has rules—"

"He heard it on TV—the news about his mother getting shot," Mitchell said.

"Yes, I heard she's a judge. They asked me to talk to the newsmen—if that's all right with you?"

"Fine," Mitchell said, "but what about her son."

The doctor sighed. "The nurses will raise hell, but rules were meant to be broken. Bring him in just before the end of visiting hours. I'll leave instructions."

"Thanks."

"Any other questions?"

"How long will she be in the hospital?" Brenda asked.

"A day, maybe two. She's in good shape, but we'd like to make absolutely sure." He smiled, again formally. "Well, I suppose I should talk to the newspaper people now. Excuse me."

Brenda dabbed at her eyes with a handkerchief. "Thank God," she said.

Jerry Mitchell already had.

-◀ ▶-

The detective looked down at Nelson Bragg. "Sleeping like a baby," he said to the ward attendant.

"He's got enough Thorazine in him to knock down an elephant. The guy was a babbling basket case when they brought him in—crazy as hell."

The detective nodded. "You got that right. He's on probation now, and he has a long history as a mental patient."

"Is that judge he shot going to die?"

The detective shrugged. "I don't know, I haven't heart."

"You'll never get a conviction on this whackball. Take my professional word, this guy is as nuts as they come."

"We'll see. Right now he's charged with assault with intent to murder, and half a dozen other felonies." The detective sighed. "In the old days, these loonies would get out on an insanity plea and be salted away in the bin for the rest of their lives; but now you guys let 'em out as soon as they stop shouting and wetting themselves."

The attendant laughed. "Don't blame me, I only work here. It's the doctors, and they have to follow the law."

"I suppose."

"What will happen with this guy?"

"Well, given all the circumstances—you can't go around plugging public officials and expect to get away with it—they'll charge him, then maybe let him plead to a lesser crime with a plea of guilty but insane."

"What happens then?"

The detective's laugh was caustic. "He ends up howling in the prison's psycho ward instead of a hospital."

"What's the advantage of that?

"He won't get out. He'll have to serve the full term."

"And if he's tried?"

"Juries are getting pretty wise. With his history and record, they'd probably come out with the same verdict, guilty but insane." He turned to the attendant. "Give me a call when Bragg comes out of the happy juice. I have to talk to him."

"Won't do much good," the attendant said. "Before we hit him with the medication, he was busy talking with someone else."

"Who was he talking to?"

"His mother, as far as we could tell. He's sure pissed off at her."

—◄ ►—

They often dined at the Bavarian Gardens. Max Schroeder, the owner, personally escorted them to a good table.

Judge Jerome Foley scowled at the menu. "You'd think they'd vary this once in a while. Jesus, it's always the same."

"What do you care?" Judge Michael Sullivan asked. "You always order the knockwurst anyway."

"Maybe I wouldn't if I had more of a choice."

They gave their orders to a waiter, who quickly returned with two vodka gimlets.

"What do you think will happen tonight?" Sullivan asked. "I think this emergency meeting of the judges is risky." Sullivan's long, saintly face was a mask of piety as he daintily sipped his drink.

"It was my idea," Foley growled.

"That doesn't make it any less chancy. Anything might happen."

"Something should. I agree with Jesse Williams—we have to do something. A jerk like Quinlan shouldn't run the court, even on a temporary basis. Everybody's a little nervous after Kathleen Talbot got shot today, and I sense an urge to get this executive-judge business over."

"Maybe we should have waited until she could come to a meeting. It seems unfair to call it on the day she got popped."

"The timing is perfect. Everyone's willing, finally, to do a little cooperating. Besides, Jesse is going to see her at the hospital tonight before the meeting. Maybe even get a written vote from her."

"Our rules don't permit proxies," Sullivan said.

"Nobody's ever been shot before, either. I doubt if anyone will seriously object."

"They will if they think she might vote for herself."

Foley tore a roll in half and buttered it. "Let's be practical. She would have had a chance if she hadn't taken the Chesney case away from the jury. But she did. If she hadn't been shot, there'd be a petition to remove her from the bench by now. Even with a wounded martyr's status, there'll still be questions. She'll know enough to keep a low profile."

"What do you hear about Sawchek?"

Foley snorted. "He got what he deserved. He was going to try another hustle on Kathleen Talbot, that's what I hear. He shouldn't have been down on her floor anyway. He just couldn't get out of the way fast enough."

"How bad is he hurt?"

Foley finished his drink and signaled for another. "My son-in-law, the radiologist, got a look at the films. He's a resident at the hospital there."

"I know."

"He says Sawchek's left ankle is badly broken. They put him in a cast, but he still may need surgery eventually—something about putting a pin in the joint." Foley chewed the roll. "That right knee of his is already screwed up from surgery, some kind of fancy infection. My son-in-law says Sawchek'll be able to walk okay, but stiff-legged. It'll look like he shit in his pants."

Sullivan smiled. "Blind ambition, that's his problem."

"Did he telephone you?"

"Who?"

"Sawchek." Foley laughed. "The son-of-a-bitch's cast hadn't dried before he was on the phone to me, asking for my sympathy and my vote for him as executive judge."

"What did you say?"

Foley took the fresh drink from the waiter. "I struck the usual bargain."

"Sawchek doesn't have a chance."

Foley shrugged. "Aw, you never know, Michael. He's pretending he's the one who stopped the gunman. If the newspapers belive him, he may end up as some kind of hero."

"Will you vote for him?"

"Of course not."

Sullivan sighed. "Well, this is all getting rather sticky. If Kathleen Talbot is out of the running, that leaves Webster Broadbent, and I don't trust him."

Foley chuckled. "No one does. Besides, Webster's gone half-nuts. Tim Quinlan didn't intend to do it, but he set things up so Broadbent came out looking like an ass when they tried to remove Kathleen Talbot from the Chesney case. Some of Broadbent's key supporters have dropped away. He's still got a chance, but he's fading fast at the finish, and he knows it."

"So, who's going to get it? Maybe you or me?"

Foley's laugh was sharp and loud. "You and I aren't the most loved and trusted jurists on this bench, or haven't you noticed?"

"It's wide open. Anyone could win," Sullivan said primly.

"True enough," Foley replied, "but I think the majority will want someone who inspires confidence, someone who isn't primarily a politician."

"What about your plan to put your nephew in as prosecuting attorney, or have you given up on that?" Sullivan asked.

"I never give up, you know that. The kid may be bright enough, but he could use a little seasoning. I'll still give it a shot, though."

The waiter set steaming plates in front of them.

Foley cut a piece off the knockwurst, wrapped some sauerkraut around it, and chewed. "This is good, and it kills the aroma of the booze. I don't want the brethren running around saying I'm a drunk."

As he nodded agreement, Sullivan's face contained an expression of deep spirituality. "Sauerkraut will conceal everything from whiskey to beer." His long face grew almost mystical as he surveyed his plain meal. "But it causes me to fart, and while the other judges might be able to stand that, I couldn't."

"We must always preserve the dignity of the bench," Foley said as he chewed.

"At all times," Sullivan agreed, looking longingly at the sauerkraut. "But we had better hurry. We don't want to be late. I'm dying to find out who'll win."

"Broadbent, I want a word with you!" Broadbent, who was maintaining a brave smile, but with a great deal of difficulty, turned and saw Ted Sawchek awkwardly coming forward in a wheelchair.

Most judges had left immediately after the meeting. The few who were speaking to Broadbent hurried away when they saw Sawchek coming. They wanted no part of what could possibly turn out to be a messy confrontation.

"How are you, Ted?" Broadbent managed to keep the smile fixed. "I was surprised to see you here. I thought you'd still be in the hospital."

"Damn you, Broadbent, if you had thrown your votes to me I could have won."

"I had more votes than you," Broadbent snapped, the smile fading. "If anyone should have thrown their votes to another, you should have, and to me."

"I have charisma," Sawchek said, his voice shaking with anger. "You're just Morton Penn and the unions' messenger boy. I'm a leader, everyone knows that. I could have gotten more votes, but you had all you could ever expect."

"I have no time to argue with you," Broadbent said.

"You fucked me up, and I won't forget it."

"Sawchek, how in the world can you possibly figure that?"

Sawchek, his legs in protective casting, forgot and almost fell out of the wheelchair as he tried to get up. He slammed his back against the chair in frustration. "I had the best chance of anyone. I would have taken care of you. You would have gotten anything you wanted if you'd supported me. Now look what we got!"

"I get along fine with Jesse Williams," Broadbent said. "He'll be a wonderful executive judge."

"Hey, he thinks you're a bigoted asshole. But what the hell, you are. He'll put the screws to you, Broadbent. And Morton Penn will drop you like a hot potato. Those labor guys like a winner the same as everyone else. You're a loser, Broadbent, let's face it."

"Jesse Williams is approaching retirement. In a few years he will be history. When that happens, I'll be elected, you'll see."

Sawchek grinned. "The fuck you will. Williams will cut your political nuts off before that happens."

"And what about you?" Broadbent snapped. "Do you really think you have a chance?"

"Sure."

Broadbent didn't even try to hide his surprise. "You do?"

"I'm a fucking hero, that's why. I'm the guy who caught the guy who shot up Talbot's courtroom. When Williams retires I'll remind everyone of my courage. Everybody likes a crippled hero."

"You are a crook," Broadbent hissed. "You'll limp right into prison one of these days. Williams won't protect you, or your pals."

This time Sawchek sneered. "You miserable faggot. I'd have that job now if it weren't for you."

Broadbent looked down the empty hallway. Everyone had gone. He smiled. "Allow me to assist you," he said, moving behind Sawchek's wheelchair.

"I can do it myself, you asshole."

"We all like to help a crippled hero now and then," Broadbent said, seizing the hand grips at the back of the wheelchair.

"I said . . . Whoa!"

Broadbent pushed down, lifting Sawchek's legs, and kept tipping the chair until the back of it hit the floor.

"Hey!"

Broadbent stood up, walked around the tipped chair, and smiled down at Sawchek, who was on his back, wriggling like a bug, his legs in casts sticking up in the air like two sticks.

"You fucking scumbag!" Sawchek screamed. "You had better pick me up!"

Broadbent stepped into an empty elevator, turned, and smiled at the struggling Sawchek. "Have a nice evening," he called pleasantly as the elevator doors were closing.

Sullivan and Foley saw the end of the incident as they were coming out of the meeting room.

"Like two spoiled little boys in the playground," Sullivan said quietly with disdain.

"Jerks," Foley replied.

"Should we help him?"

Foley shook his head. "You know how it is with heroes, they have their pride—we'd just embarrass him. Somebody will find him—eventually." Foley's fierce expression softened into a smile. "There's no reason to become involved. Let's just slip out the back elevators."

"Discretion?" Sullivan asked.

"Wisdom," Foley replied.

Martin Kelly was slightly behind schedule: not in amount of drinks consumed, but in the number of saloons usually visited. The Learned Hand got all his business today. He was waiting for Tom Mease, who had promised to meet him there but who hadn't shown. Unusual behavior for Mease, who was usually annoyingly punctual.

Kelly motioned for another whiskey, deciding to have one more and then, if Mease failed to show, to move on.

The shockwaves of the Chesney case were still causing talk. It was the main source of the day's barroom gossip, and Kelly, as a witness to the event, had enjoyed telling about it at first—but as the hours wore on, he became bored talking about it. Chesney was free, although he understood Jerry Mitchell had sent him to a hospital. Kelly had always liked Dennis Chesney, even if he had participated in trying to put the homicide detective away for life. It was all part of the job. Other people made the decisions, Kelly liked to say. He was merely a soldier who did what he was told. Lawyers were often called hired guns, and Kelly's gun was for rent.

Tom Mease finally walked into the Learned Hand, appearing a little strained. He seemed much too serious, almost preoccupied as he sat down next to Kelly.

"Ah, I was just about to give up on you, Tom. Drinking is serious business and requires determination and dedication if it is to be done properly."

"The judges had their meeting," Mease said, taking a seat at the bar. His voice sounded unusually strained.

"So what? They've been meeting every week since Harry Johnson went to that great courtroom in the sky. They meet, disagree on a successor, then fix a date to meet and disagree again."

"Not this time," Mease said. "They have elected a new executive judge."

Kelly's alcoholic happiness was blown away like smoke in a fresh wind. "Who?"

Mease asked the bartender for a beer. "Well, it wasn't Broadbent or Sawchek."

"And not Kathleen Talbot, I'll wager—not after what happened this morning."

Mease nodded. "They picked Judge Williams."

"Jesse Williams?"

Mease nodded.

"Jesus, that's great. Jesse used to be on the prosecutor's staff. He knows our problems. Of course, he's getting old and won't be on the bench for very long."

"It was a compromise, I understand."

Kelly was still puzzled by Mease's subdued manner. "You're pretty well-informed," he said.

"They picked a new prosecutor too."

Kelly was instantly sober. "God, not Arnie Nelson, I hope?"

"No."

"Maybe that's bad. At least I could bamboozle Arnie. Was it labor's guy?"

"No."

"Holy shit! Not Foley's nephew! He's a nice kid, but still wet behind the ears."

Mease shook his head.

"You seem to be shocked, Tom. I presume the new boss is less than attractive?"

"Depends."

Kelly exploded. "Jesus Henry Christ! Don't leave me hanging, young man! Who the hell did they pick?"

Mease seemed to study the beer. "Me."

Kelly chuckled. "Oh, sure. Come on, Tom, who'd they pick?"

"Me. Is that so improbable?"

Kelly studied Mease's serious face. "Yes—no offense. The

only backing you had was Kathleen Talbot's. Wounded or not, after the Chesney decision I doubt if she'd have much influence with the other judges. They are a bunch of rather hard-eyed realists, and political animals. They'd want to see how the chips fell before they did anything for her. And they'd be looking for someone to suit their own advantage."

"Unless they compromised because no one could muster enough votes for their own choice."

Kelly finished his drink. "Tom, are you having a joke at my expense?"

Mease shook his head. "No. Judge Williams proposed me—on the recommendation of Judge Talbot, I'm told. There were four ballots. I won on the fourth, but by only one vote. Not exactly a landslide, but it counts."

"My God, you *are* serious!"

"It just happened. I had to wait around to find out."

"I imagine Arnie Nelson will be taking it hard."

Mease shrugged. "I haven't thought about it. Frankly, I'm having a hard time getting used to the idea myself. Judge Williams said he wants to swear me in this Friday."

"You'll do a good job, Tom. Congratulations." Kelly raised his glass in salute.

Mease tried to smile, but failed.

"Worried?" Kelly asked.

Mease nodded. "Sure. It's a big job, Marty. The responsibility is enormous. I'm scared, to tell the truth."

Kelly nodded. "That's natural. You didn't expect it and you haven't even thought about what you would do if you got it." He laughed. "But I'm older, Tom, and you'll see, in a week or two you'll be ordering people about like it was the only thing you ever did in your life."

"I doubt it."

"Are you going to fire Arnie?" Kelly finished his drink and nodded to the bartender for a refill.

Mease looked surprised.

"Firing people is part of the job, Tom, like it or not. Don't worry about Arnie, some law firm will hire him as a greeter. He looks like God's idea of a lawyer, even if he can't find the library. He'll do all right." Kelly's voice dropped slightly. "And you may wish to let some others go too."

"Like who?"

"Me."

"My God, Marty, why would I do a thing like that?"

Kelly's solemn tone matched his expression. "I'm a drunk. As a friend and fellow lawyer you may have viewed me as amusing, but now you're the boss. You'll be looking at me from an entirely different viewpoint." He sipped at the freshened drink. "Over a long life I've had similar discussions with other employers. It happens."

"Martin, I . . ."

Kelly smiled. "Tom, I am what I am, to quote St. Paul and Popeye. You know me, I'm good until noon, that's all. I've done all the expected things, dried out, been dried out, gone to the meetings, everything, but this is my choice. I don't wish to change even if I could."

Mease began to smile. "Are you telling me to fire you?"

Kelly shook his head. "No. I suppose I'm trying to say that I'd understand if you do."

Mease got up, finished his beer, then placed the glass on the bar. "Well, I've got to go. This is all so new. Somehow I've got to figure out what I'm going to do."

Kelly held out his hand. "You're a good man, Tom. This is just the beginning for you."

Mease's grip was firm. "Or the end. We'll see." He began to walk away, then stopped and turned. "Oh, Martin, there is one change."

"Oh?"

"I understand we have you until noon, and that's no problem. You're still head of the homicide section."

"Thanks, Tom."

"Only, from now on, get in a bit earlier in the morning."

Mease was gone before Kelly could reply. He wondered if his new boss was joking or not.

Kelly bolted down the whiskey. "Innkeeper," he called loudly to the bartender, "another libation. I think I'm celebrating, but I'm not sure. However, it's better to be safe than sorry, isn't it? Better make it a double."

CHAPTER 38

KATHLEEN GOT OUT of the hospital bed cautiously. Even small movements caused pain in her left side. But, she discovered, if she moved slowly and carefully, she could keep the discomfort down to a minimun. She threw the newspaper out of the way. The front page was devoted almost entirely to the shooting, with pictures of her empty courtroom, old file photographs of herself, and even a picture of the man who shot her being restrained by police.

The paper carried interviews from jurors, spectators, demonstrators, and lawyers. A chronological history of the Chesney case was given a box of its own on page one.

But it was the editorial page that told Kathleen the direction from which the wind would blow. A cleverly worded opinion raised questions about her ethics, not only as to her fitness to preside over the subject matter of the Chesney case, but also it hinted at impropriety in her relationship with Jeremiah Mitchell because of his role as defense attorney.

For the moment, because she had been wounded, she would enjoy a brief period of protection. But then the attacks would start in earnest. It was the kind of thing that sold papers and earned awards.

She had been unable to even touch her dinner after reading the newspaper. Kathleen gingerly dressed in the clothes Marie had sent over. Marie wisely had selected loose-fitting garments.

After dressing, Kathleen sat on the bed to rest, surprised at how easily she tired. She remembered vaguely the previous night's visit by her son and Jerry Mitchell, so dreamlike because of the effect of the anesthetic. But her sleep during the night had been disturbed by pain.

The homicide detectives paid her a routine visit in the morning, taking a brief statement. She had napped for short periods during the rest of the day, sleeping through, she had been told, Jerry Mitchell's afternoon visit.

Her doctor, who had stopped by in the morning briefly, stepped into her room.

"Well, look at you!" He was grinning. "Damn, I must be one hell of a surgeon. You look ready to take on the world."

"I've decided to leave," she said. "This is no place to get a decent's night sleep."

He laughed. "I can't argue that. But I think you should stay with us for another night, at least."

"Why?"

He shrugged. "You don't have to, put it's always smart to hedge your bets. You're doing fine, judge, but I'd like to hang onto you for another day, just to make sure."

"You said there was no major damage."

He nodded. "Right."

"So why can't I leave?"

"You can, if you really want to. I'll sign the discharge papers. I'll give you a prescription for pain medication. You're going to be sore as hell for a while. And you'll have a small scar when everything mends. Not very noticeable, even in a bikini. All that bruising around the wound is from bleeding. It will turn a beautiful shade of purple, then fade."

"My bottom hurts."

He laughed. "That's because we gave you a bit of Demerol in your south end last night. That will work out in a few days." He sighed. "If you leave, just watch out for an increase in pain, or difficulty in breathing. I don't expect either, but if the symptoms change or increase, call me immediately."

"Anything else?"

"I'd take it easy for a while, if I were you. The wound wasn't bad, but you still need some time to heal. I don't want you pulling those few beautiful stitches I put in before I'm ready to take them out. Take a short vacation, if you can. Lie on a beach somewhere."

"That's it?"

He nodded and held out his hand. "Judge, keep my card. I'm good at everything from hernias to gallbladders. Gunshot wounds are only a hobby."

She waited until he left, then gathered her few possessions in the purse Marie had sent. She checked her money to make sure she had enough for cab fare.

It took almost an hour for the paperwork to be done. Then a nurse came in, put her in a wheelchair, and took her to the hospital entrance. The nurse snipped off her plastic identification bracelet and wished her well.

She eased herself slowly into a waiting cab. "The Hall of Justice," she said to the driver. She knew the court had just closed for the day. "The side entrance on Randolph."

Kathleen looked out at the city during the short ride. It was cloudy and becoming dark, the days growing shorter as autumn approached. The few trees along the street were already beginning to change color. The melancholy combination of day's end and the tangible evidence of dying summer fitted a mood suited to what she had to do.

The cabdriver pulled up at the court's side entrance. "The place is closed, lady," he said as she paid him.

"I can get in. There's a guard on this side door at night."

"Be careful," the driver said as she slowly got out. "They had a shooting there yesterday. No place is safe anymore."

The night guard, surprised at seeing her, insisted on escorting her up to her courtroom. He left her alone after snapping on the lights. The only other people in the building were the cleaning crews who were beginning to work their way through the otherwise silent old court building.

Kathleen, tired, sat for a moment in the clerk's chair and surveyed the courtroom. The quiet, almost eerily peaceful scene—the empty tables, the empty spectator rows and vacant jury box—contrasted with her recollection of the chaos of the

Chesney trial. It was all over, she thought, in more ways than one.

Almost reluctantly Kathleen went into her chambers. She sat for a moment, then began going through the drawers of her desk. She had been a judge for only a few months and was surprised by how much clutter she had accumulated. She found the invalid order from Judge Quinlan, informing her she had been removed as a trial judge. Quinlan's order had had a short life, lasting only until Marcus Kaplan persuaded the Supreme Court to intervene. She was about to toss it away but then decided to keep it as a souvenir, like an old dance card or a Playbill, a token of a significant event in the past. Tim Quinlan, too, she had been told, was a thing of the past, resigning after being ousted as executive judge, his brief time in power over forever. She couldn't muster any pity for him, or for any of the others who had been so eager to ruin her in order to advance themselves.

She found an empty box in the clerk's adjoining office, then returned to her own office and began to pack what she wanted to keep, discarding the rest.

The street below was quiet. The evening's traffic was beginning to ebb. The shouts and tumultuous noise of the demonstrators were now only echoes of the past.

Kathleen was surprised to see her robe hanging in its accustomed place. It was torn beyond repair and matted darkly with blood. Whoever had hung it up hadn't wanted to take the responsibility of throwing it away without permission. The robe was like a dark and silent ghost, a symbol of a duty she was about to abandon. A judicial robe was just a piece of cloth designed to show that the wearer possessed specially entrusted powers. Such robes, she knew, had been red originally, but changed by the British to black as a sign of mourning when their Queen Anne died, and never changed back except by a very few English courts. Americans had adopted that symbol of judicial office, in black, as they had adopted the English Common Law. The purpose and history of the robe made little difference to Kathleen now. Her torn and useless garment looked like an accusing specter. It would be tossed out with the other useless mementos. The box was already full with the few things she wished to keep. She would have it sent later.

She decided to take one last look at her courtroom. She hadn't expected to feel such a sense of loss and of place.

"Good evening, Kathleen. How are you feeling?"

She jumped at the sound of the deep voice. "You startled me! How did you get in here?"

Jerry Mitchell sat at the counsel table in the chair he had occupied all through the trial. He smiled. "The night guard let me in."

"No one is supposed to—"

"You forget," he interjected, "this courthouse is really my home. I told the guard you were expecting me."

"I would like to be alone."

"I went to the hospital and found you had checked out." His voice rumbled in the empty courtroom. "I guessed that you might come here."

"Please go, Jerry."

He made no effort to stand. "What are you up to?"

"Please . . ."

"Packing? Are you thinking of quitting, by any chance?"

"It's none of your business, but I am going to resign."

Mitchell nodded slowly. "I talked to my old hero, Marcus Kaplan, today. He's representing you before the Supreme Court as a volunteer. He's of the opinion they will hold a few hearings about the Chesney matter for looks, let a little time go by, and then declare the whole thing a tempest in a teapot. Marcus, as you know, is seldom in error."

She felt exhausted. "I appreciate his efforts, but they're wasted. When I resign, that ends the matter. The Supreme Court will have nothing to decide." She leaned against the side of the bench.

He started to get up, but she shook her head and walked up the two steps to her own chair on the bench. "There's really nothing more to discuss."

"Kathleen," he said gently, "I won't take much of your time. There's one more case you have to hear. It's short but fascinating." He stood up and announced in a surprisingly formal tone,

"*The People versus Talbot*," startling her as his words echoed around the empty courtroom.

"This is nonsense."

"Bear with me for a few moments, Kathleen. This is important to both of us."

"Look, Jerry, I—"

"What are you going to do, witness?" he asked, his voice suddenly professional and formal. "Practice law? Here?" He slowly shook his head. "No, not if you've been run off the bench in disgrace. No firm will want you. And your former brethren, with a few exceptions, will turn their backs on you. And if you take your wonderful little son and run off, what then? Start over? People do, of course, but usually because they have to. You don't."

"Don't you read the newspapers?" She found herself responding in her own courtroom voice, addressing him in the manner she had used throughout the trial. "They are about to make me out to be a cross between Typhoid Mary and the Spider Woman. If I stay, they'll come after me like a pack of wolves. You mentioned my son. I don't want him growing up and reading those kinds of stories about his mother. I don't wish to expose him to that."

"That's exactly what you'll do if you run away. Then there'll be nothing to stop them. They'll have the last word and it will become the official version. One day, even if you go to Tahiti, Michael will somehow stumble over their little version of history, no matter how hard you try to shield him. What will he think then?"

"There is no alternative," she said quietly.

Jerry Mitchell, as he had so often during the trial, walked to the front of the bench and looked up at her. "If you run, you're ruined. If you fight, you'll win."

"And if I'm not up to making the fight?"

His eyes were gentle. "You are. The only one you're afraid of is yourself. I believe you've convicted yourself without benefit of trial. That's not very fair, your honor, no matter how you slice it."

"Jerry . . ."

"Kathleen, you've confused your own actions with those of Dennis Chesney. I began to see that as we tried the case."

"You think I let him go because of what I did?"

He shook his head. "I don't, but you may think so, and that isn't fair. You did the right thing under the law, both in your father's case and Chesney's. You need to get rid of the guilt that haunts you."

"Guilt?"

Mitchell's eyes were fixed on hers. "You think you killed your father."

"I ordered the machines shut off."

He again shook his head. "He was dead, Kathleen. That's what the Chesney trial was all about. I proved beyond all reasonable doubt that Paul Martin was dead when the machines were stopped, and by the way, I proved that your father was too. I hoped you knew that."

"But . . ."

"You couldn't let Chesney risk a jury verdict, your sense of honor wouldn't allow it. He was innocent. You are too, Kathleen." He paused for a moment. "On that basis, I ask that you also acquit yourself."

She was aware that tears were beginning to silently spill down her cheeks, but she was unable to stop.

"You can make this fight, Kathleen. Not just for your own sake, but also for Michael's. And you won't be alone. You have the great Marcus Kaplan on your side, and Jesse Williams is the new executive judge and your true friend."

"And you?"

"That depends on whether I win this case or not."

"Oh?"

"Of course, I have a difficult client, but I want to win this case more than any other I've ever tried."

"Do you really want me to stay on the bench and fight this thing out?"

He nodded. "That's the verdict I'm asking."

She brushed away the tears. "You win another case, Mr. Mitchell." She started to get up, but the movement caused a twinge of pain.

He quickly moved to her side.

She grinned at him. "You're not going to knock me down again, are you?"

He gently stroked her hair as he kissed her. "Not until you're healed."

Kathleen held his hand against her face. "The doctor thinks I should find a quiet beach for a while. Want to come?"

"In this state?"

She laughed. "It's getting chilly. I'd prefer the Caribbean."

"I was afraid of that. We'll have to get married. I don't want to be crossing state lines with a single woman."

"The Mann Act's not enforced anymore."

"That's my condition, take it or leave it."

She kissed his hand. "Just like a lawyer," she whispered. "You force a hard bargain, but all right."

He kissed her softly. "I love you, Kathleen, I've known it for a long time."

"I love you too." She kissed him with passion, causing some discomfort in her side, but Kathleen Talbot was far too happy to care.

William J. Coughlin
The Twelve Apostles £2.95

No law firm stands higher or more proud than Nelson & Clark – so awesome, so influential, so prestigious that its senior partners have come to be known as *The Twelve Apostles*..

Now, with the death of a partner, the fight to fill his chair has become a battle royal – between a beautiful woman, and the man who loves her.

Christina Giles – the kind of woman men never forget. But driven into the arms of a tyrannical tycoon, she finds herself the pawn in a corporate takeover – and stands to sacrifice everything.

Dan Spencer – the firm's number one trial lawyer. He knows love and the law don't mix, but he's out to win both Christina and that Apostle's seat.

From walnut-panelled offices to glittering restaurants, from London to New York to Dublin, *The Twelve Apostles* is an epic confrontation between lawyer and client, corporation and corporation, man and woman . . .

Her Father's Daughter £2.95

When Hunter Van Horn is killed in an air crash, everyone assumes that both control of his mighty but ailing empire and his seat on the Vault – the secretive group of New York power brokers – will pass to his feckless son, Junior. But Hunter chose as his true heir the daughter from whom he'd been estranged for years . . .

Victoria Van Horn, beautiful and rich in her own right, she cannot resist the challenge, even when she discovers that her father's enemies are now set on destroying her . . .

Cecilia, Junior's scheming wife who will do anything to improve her wealth and social position . . .

Chilton Vance, Hunter's trusted right-hand man who ruthlessly sets Victoria up to further his own ambition . . .

Barry Lytle, the smooth-talking congressman who uses Victoria in his quest for a Senate seat . . .

Lucas Shaw, the youngest member of the Vault, whom Victoria hires to build her waterfront development and who shows her there is more to life than wheeling and dealing . . .

Sweeping from glittering Manhattan to the sleazy Hudson river waterfront and the hustle and bustle of Hong Kong, this is a spellbinding story of power and passion at the top.

John le Carré
Smiley's People £3.99

His new number one international bestseller – the ultimate espionage novel.

'A Russian woman in Paris; a murder on Hampstead Heath; an asylum in Switzerland; a brothel in Hamburg – the story moves effortlessly around the European chessboard'
MELVYN BRAGG, EVENING STANDARD

'Abounds in breathstopping scenes . . . an enormously skilled and satisfying work' NEWSWEEK

'A work of art' LISTENER

Walter Tevis
The Queen's Gambit £2.50

Plain, round-faced and a natural loser, Beth Harmon's life in the orphanage was pretty unbearable, until an old man introduced her to a world where the mind can teach itself to conquer and to win. That world was the grid of the chessboard.

Beth's astonishing talent for chess catapults her to the top of the US rankings by the time she's eighteen. But the cost of her crown is isolation and despair. Abandoned by her lovers, almost destroyed by drugs and alcohol, she finds herself in Moscow facing the greatest players in the world. Suddenly Beth discovers that chess is no longer about winning and losing. It's become a matter of life, or death . . .

'More exciting than any thriller I've seen lately; more than that, beautifully written'
MARTIN CRUZ SMITH, AUTHOR OF GORKY PARK

'Don't pick this up at 10.30pm if you want a night's sleep'
THE SCOTSMAN

Christopher Hudson
Colombo Heat £2.95

When Guy Tancred arrives in Ceylon in the winter of 1941, to oversee his company's vital rubber production, he expects all the tedium of a backwater. Little does he anticipate that soon he will be drawn in to secret intelligence operations as the war against Japan gains momentum. And he has no idea that his planter brother, Harry, has forsaken the crumbling colonial lifestyle for Buddhism. Least of all does he expect to fall in love with Jill, Harry's beautiful but restless wife.

His path is crossed by others: the spoilt, pretty daughter of one of Colombo's most influential families; the Sinhalese boy driven through frustration to revolutionary politics; the Governor himself, who sees the old order changing and feels there is no place for him in the new.

And all the while, in places far away, the grand strategies are plotted which will converge in Colombo on Easter Sunday 1942 – and leave nothing looking quite the same again.

'Riveting . . . it's a novel which is crammed with messages, it's a novel to get one's teeth into, it's a novel which is living history' JOHN BRAINE, LONDON STANDARD

Martin Cruz Smith
Gorky Park £3.99

'Superb . . . from the opening pages where three frozen and mutilated corpses have just been discovered in the snow of Moscow's Gorky Park to the grand finale' NEW YORK TIMES

'Brilliantly worked, marvellously written . . . a genuinely frightening, genuinely original vision' SUNDAY TIMES

'Straight to the top of the international thriller class' GUARDIAN

'Chief Investigator Renko – vulnerable, decent, brave and smart – takes his place alongside the best creations of le Carré' NEW YORK TIMES BOOK REVIEW

All Pan books are available at your local bookshop or newsagent, or can be ordered direct from the publisher. Indicate the number of copies required and fill in the form below.

Send to: **CS Department, Pan Books Ltd., P.O. Box 40,
            Basingstoke, Hants.   RG21 2YT.**

or phone: 0256 469551 (Ansaphone), quoting title, author
            and Credit Card number.

Please enclose a remittance* to the value of the cover price plus: 60p for the first book plus 30p per copy for each additional book ordered to a maximum charge of £2.40 to cover postage and packing.

*Payment may be made in sterling by UK personal cheque, postal order, sterling draft or international money order, made payable to Pan Books Ltd.

Alternatively by Barclaycard/Access:

Card No.

Signature:

Applicable only in the UK and Republic of Ireland.

While every effort is made to keep prices low, it is sometimes necessary to increase prices at short notice. Pan Books reserve the right to show on covers and charge new retail prices which may differ from those advertised in the text or elsewhere.

NAME AND ADDRESS IN BLOCK LETTERS PLEASE:

....

Name ————————————————————————

Address ————————————————————————

————————————————————————

————————————————————————

————————————————————————

3/87